Sanctuary's Price
Red Rock Pass, Book 3

He's only been surviving. Her magic can show him how to live.

After a decade under a corrupt alpha's thumb, Dylan Gennaro is still reeling from the changes in his life: a new home, a new alpha, a pack at war. Even normal things like an ending relationship. Still, when he's asked to work with an outcast witch, he agrees without hesitation. Maybe by protecting her, he'll rediscover his own inner strength. If, indeed, it exists.

Sasha Wallace lost her mentor in a vicious attack that left her scarred in spirit as well as body. While she's grateful for the refuge offered by the Red Rock alpha, it's tough living with the pack's suspicion. Even though—or maybe because—she's willing to use her powers to help them fight their war. Except for Dylan. When she's finally free to find a new home, he'll be the only one she regrets leaving behind.

Their attraction is a balm to their wounded hearts, until their journey for knowledge brings them face to face with a terrifying vampire. Neither has the strength for this fight—but if they can let go of their pasts and trust each other, they might just be able to do it. Together.

Warning: Contains dangerous magical binding spells, a flannel-wearing vampire lumberjack, paranormal road-trip hijinks and a quietly brilliant werewolf willing to defy his society and his past to protect the witch he loves.

Sanctuary Unbound
Red Rock Pass, Book 4

They've been hiding from the past. Now it's time to fight for their future.

New England is ideal for vampire Adam Dubois. His cozy home in the Great North Woods reminds him of a happier time when werewolves and witches were stuff of legends, and he was a simple lumberjack.

Hiding from past failures has worked for over eighty years, but a life debt owed to the Red Rock alpha has forced him to leave his retreat—and come face to face with a woman who challenges and tempts him on every level.

Hiding secrets is a lonely business, and Cindy Shepherd is lonely with a capital L. Red Rock isn't exactly crawling with available men, but her interest in the mystery-shrouded new vampire in town seems mutual. After all, it's only sex—there's no danger he'll dig deep enough to unleash the demons of her past.

Casual flirtation turns deadly serious when Adam discovers that the vampire plaguing Red Rock is using his mistakes as a road map. When it comes to his life, he knows Cindy has his back. But in order to secure the future, they both must trust each other with more—even if it means sacrificing themselves to save everything they hold dear.

Warning: This book contains epic werewolf battles, mystical vampire blood bonds, unexpected sex on the kitchen floor and a dangerous attraction between a secret-burdened werewolf and a vampire lumberjack.

Look for these titles by *Moira Rogers*

Now Available:

Red Rock Pass Series
Cry Sanctuary
Sanctuary Lost
Sanctuary's Price
Sanctuary Unbound

Southern Arcana Series
Crux
Crossroads
Deadlock

Building Sanctuary Series
A Safe Harbor
Undertow

Bloodhounds Series
Wilder's Mate

And the Beast Series
Sabine

Print Book Collection
Sanctuary
Sanctuary Redeemed

Sanctuary Redeemed

Moira Rogers

Samhain Publishing, Ltd.
577 Mulberry Street, Suite 1520
Macon, GA 31201
www.samhainpublishing.com

Sanctuary Redeemed
Print ISBN: 978-1-60928-026-0
Sanctuary's Price Copyright © 2011 by Moira Rogers
Sanctuary Unbound Copyright © 2011 by Moira Rogers

Editing by Anne Scott
Cover by Tuesday Dube

This book is a work of fiction. The names, characters, places, and incidents are products of the writer's imagination or have been used fictitiously and are not to be construed as real. Any resemblance to persons, living or dead, actual events, locale or organizations is entirely coincidental.

All Rights Are Reserved. No part of this book may be used or reproduced in any manner whatsoever without written permission, except in the case of brief quotations embodied in critical articles and reviews.

Sanctuary's Price, ISBN 978-1-60504-682-2
First Samhain Publishing, Ltd. electronic publication: October 2009
Sanctuary Unbound ISBN 978-1-60928-046-8
First Samhain Publishing, Ltd. electronic publication: June 2010
First Samhain Publishing, Ltd. print publication: May 2011

Contents

Sanctuary's Price
~9~

Sanctuary Unbound
~149~

Sanctuary's Price

Dedication

This is for Anne, who has always been Dylan's biggest fan. We'd also like to extend special thanks to Donna Locklin and Cynthia Lin for helping us with some names.

Chapter One

By the time he managed to set fire to the damp wood in the dusty old fireplace, Dylan had resorted to giving himself half-hearted pep talks. "Could be worse. You could be dead. Could be back in Helena. Could be stuck listening to Bobby bitch about how they fucked up the *Battlestar Galactica* finale."

The soggy wood in the fireplace smoked at him in agreement. The stench would have been bad enough to a human nose, but for a werewolf...

Dylan sighed and pushed himself to his feet. The rain that afternoon had drenched the stack of firewood out back, but he hadn't thought to bring any of it inside before this evening. Not when the house was still so far from livable.

He'd had ample opportunity over the last month to make it so, but he'd gotten comfortable in Cindy's house. Even when things hadn't been entirely blissful, he'd had the luxury of a roof over his head and the knowledge there was plenty of time to renovate the rundown little house. Plenty of time to make it his.

He eyed the bedroll he'd begged from Brynn—the bag belonged to Joe, and was high quality, at least—and squared his shoulders. The house had four walls and a roof that mostly didn't leak. The plumbing worked sometimes and it wasn't so cold he'd freeze to death hunkered down in the sleeping bag.

Far from livable...but he'd make do. He always did.

With a feeble fire lit, Dylan turned his attention back to the scarred wooden table. The renovation plans he'd been working on had been shoved haphazardly to one side, leaving space for the sack Brynn had pushed on him along with the sleeping bag. Upending it on the table revealed two boxes of toaster pastries, a box of crackers, three cans of soda and a bag of licorice.

The sight made his chest ache even as he smiled. Just snack food, and probably the first things Brynn had put her hands on when she'd realized he had no intention of staying long enough to face any questions Joe might have about Dylan's sudden change in residence. But Dylan had known Brynn for years, maybe even knew her better than her older sister did. Licorice and strawberry pastries—Brynn's nervous comfort food. Something she clung to when life was overwhelming.

And badass warrior alpha wolf Joe Mitchell had obviously been doing his best to make sure she had anything she needed, no matter how silly those things were. It was sweet.

It sucked.

Guilt stabbed at him, and he snatched up the box of crackers and tore open the cardboard top. Brynn had gone through hell, and she had Joe. Her sister Abby had gone through hell, and she had Keith.

Dylan had a smoking fireplace and a toilet that didn't flush consistently.

It really, *really* sucked.

The soft knock carried easily through the dead quiet of the house, but the door opened immediately. Gavin, Red Rock's alpha wolf, stuck his head through the door. "Busy, Dylan?"

Even if he had been, he couldn't have sent the man away. "No, come on in. I was just..." He held up the box. "Having a snack."

Gavin arched one graying eyebrow as he walked in. "I went to Cindy's. She said you were over here, roughing it. Reliving your Boy Scout days?"

Dylan fought a wince. No word of Cindy being upset, no indication she'd said anything more damning. In a way, it was almost worse. Things hadn't been great with Cindy, but she'd been important. It would be nice to think he'd been important too.

Quit your bitching, whiner. It had been the motto in his apartment, words repeated in a wry voice by werewolves too low in the pack to be anything but punching bags for unbalanced alphas. He repeated the words silently now and felt that same wry amusement. It could always be worse.

Gavin still watched him expectantly, so he forced a smile.

"Figured I might as well get to work on this house, if I want to fix it up any time this decade."

The alpha hummed and jerked his head toward the hearth. "Mind if I sit? I need to ask a favor."

Dylan eyed the dirty hearth and felt a twinge of self-consciousness. "Sure. Want a soda?"

"No, thanks. Sammie's expecting me back soon." Gavin sat down slowly, braced his hands on his knees and took a deep breath. "It's about the witch, Sasha."

For one terrible second, Dylan thought Cindy *had* complained to Gavin. But their fight over Sasha had been days ago. Besides, Gavin looked too worried for this to be something so petty. "Is she okay?"

"She's fine, as far as I know. Mostly, anyway." He ran a hand through his already-messy hair. "Trying to help. Trying to stay busy."

Sometimes when he closed his eyes he saw Sasha, eyes blank with fear and the pale skin of her neck bearing ugly bruises in the shape of Alan Matthews' fingers. The instincts that had gotten him into so much trouble with Cindy stirred, tingeing his words with a concern he couldn't hide. "Brynn said she's been leaving your house a little. Going to sit with Abby and Keith sometimes?"

Gavin hesitated. "Taking care of chores while Abby takes care of Keith. It's hard for Abby to let people near him."

Dylan had heard as much from Cindy, whose visits to Keith's bedside left her tense and exhausted. "That's good though. I mean, that Sasha's been getting out at all, after everything that happened to her."

"Indeed." Gavin rose and paced a few steps. "It's a lot to ask, this favor. Sasha's learning our ways, but the death of her mentor has left her without a teacher. Most of the wolves here who could teach her can't get within ten feet without making her cringe. But you..." Faded blue eyes focused on Dylan's face. "Sasha trusts you."

It was wrong to feel that thrill at Gavin's words, to feel so proud of having someone look at him and see safety, a protector. But after a decade of being everyone's joke in Helena, Sasha's blind trust was intoxicating.

Which was exactly what Cindy had accused him of being when they'd fought over Sasha. Intoxicated. Drunk on male ego and the thrill of someone needing him. Words hurled in anger that she probably hadn't meant, but they still stung.

Gavin's eyes saw too damn much, so Dylan turned away. "I'll do anything I can to help, but I'm not exactly an expert on our ways. You of all people know that."

"I do know that. But you're picking it up fast, Dylan. It might be good for Sasha, in a way, if she felt you two were taking the journey together."

"Maybe." Noncommittal, and pointless. He'd do it. If it had been any other person, he would have done it because he owed Gavin everything. But it was Sasha, scared, trembling Sasha, and just the thought of her turning that trusting gaze on him stirred something instinctive inside him.

He heard Gavin stand. "I'll understand if you can't do it, you know. If it's going to cause problems for you."

"I don't think Cindy's inviting me back." It was supposed to be a casual statement, maybe even a joke, and he was surprised by the raw pain in his voice.

The heavy weight of Gavin's hand landed on his shoulder. "I'm sorry to hear that. I wish I had something to say that would make it easier, but... All I can tell you is that you'll make it through this, just like everything else."

Dylan closed his eyes and soaked in the comfort Gavin offered, the strength of an alpha who protected his pack, who sheltered them with his strength and compassion. In Helena there had been no comfort in the pack. Survival, maybe. Camaraderie from shared suffering and shared secrets. But nothing like the complicated but reassuring dance of protection and obedience that he'd found in Red Rock.

It made the idea of him being the one to teach Sasha even more absurd. "What things does she need to learn? Because if it's the social shit, I can't do it. I'm still lost."

"No, we'll take care of that." Gavin tapped his fingers absently against the edge of the table. "We have a room in the apartment above the bar, a library of sorts with records and history volumes. Werewolf lore, essentially. Some magical histories too, though not many."

It felt like meddling. "Did Abby tell you?"

Gavin cocked his head. "Tell me what?"

The confusion seemed honest, and it brought with it a rush of longing. God, he'd missed books. Studying. The dusty-smelling manuscripts in the stacks at the college library, ancient stories of history and legend that he'd pored through on Friday nights...

Ten years ago. When he'd been twenty-one and human, and his reputation had been that of an up-and-coming scholar of history instead of a passable carpenter.

Dylan clenched his fingers around the box of crackers, and the thin cardboard buckled under his grip. "I used to like to study things. History, mostly. But it wasn't really considered a viable contribution to the pack."

It took Gavin a moment to answer. "Well, it is here. If you can handle the lore, you'll be doing more than your share already. Twice that if you and Sasha can manage to determine how our legends and hers dovetail."

"Sure." It would be better than sitting out here by himself all day long, but the house wasn't going to fix itself while he spent his days reading through old history books. He glanced around the pathetic little living room. "Might need to hold off a few days, though, at least until this place is livable."

"Why don't you just stay in the apartment? Rain should last through the week, anyway."

"Are you—"

The walkie-talkie on Gavin's belt crackled to life, and his wife's voice spilled out. "Gavin, you need to come back here now. Bring Dylan. Cindy's already on her way. Justine just showed up and she's in bad, bad shape."

Gavin snatched up the radio as he turned toward the door. "On our way. What happened, Sammie?"

"Damned if I know, baby. She's babbling and I hope to hell she's wrong, because she's talking about vampires."

Dylan stumbled. "Vampires?"

"Damn it." Gavin shoved the radio back onto his belt and caught Dylan's arm. "Thought there weren't any left around these parts. Come on. We have to hurry."

"Shit." He found his footing and moved to keep up with Gavin. "Justine—does she mean our Justine? The one who lives in Helena?"

The alpha's jaw hardened. "Yeah."

She'd always been an anomaly in the Helena pack, a woman who stood outside the harsh realities that dominated the lives of most of the pack's females. In his ten years in the pack, Dylan had seen one man lay a finger on Justine. That finger—and the arm attached to it—had ended up torn from the man's body. Their late and unlamented pack leader had always favored the swift and brutal method of teaching lessons to his pack.

And I emptied a clip into his head a few weeks ago. Dylan could live all of the hundred and twenty years attributed to Gavin and not accomplish anything else as satisfying as killing Alan Matthews.

Except doing so had obviously revoked whatever protection kept Justine safe within the Helena pack. Dylan refused to feel guilty as he followed at Gavin's heels—not to the alpha's house, as he might have expected, but instead to the large bar that seemed to serve as Red Rock's unofficial meeting spot.

A crowd had gathered outside the building, but the way cleared as Gavin stomped toward them. "Where are they?"

A man Dylan vaguely recognized flashed them a worried look. "Sam and Joe took her into the back office."

Which explained why Joe hadn't been home while Brynn had been busy loading Dylan down with snack foods and camping supplies. Gavin started forward, but Dylan hesitated, unsure what part he was supposed to play in a meeting of some of the strongest wolves in the pack.

Gavin made it two steps into the bar before turning. "*Now*, Dylan."

The office door hit the wall, and Gavin growled. "A binding ceremony?" he demanded. "Sammie, have you lost your mind?"

The bulk of Joe's body blocked Justine from sight but, from the worried look on the man's face, Dylan surmised the situation was bad. He eased into the office and closed the door just as Samantha's temper evidenced itself in a wave of power terrifying enough to make him cringe.

Gavin's wife was every inch as tall as Dylan and looked forty of her reputed seventy years. Before coming to Red Rock, Dylan had never met an alpha female; their life expectancy tended to be short in Helena, a fact that had spurred his desperation to get Abby out of town.

It was hard to imagine anyone threatening Samantha. She turned to glare at her husband, her eyes dark as she slammed a white pillar candle down on the desk. "She's going to die if someone doesn't do something fast, and I'm not watching that happen."

Gavin spun and caught Dylan's gaze. "Go to our house and get Sasha. Hurry."

Dylan reached for the doorknob, but froze when Sam's voice lashed through the air. "Wait. She's been through enough."

Caught between conflicting instincts, Dylan turned a pleading look on Joe, asking silently who he was supposed to obey.

Before Joe could speak, Gavin's roar cut through the quiet, along with a lash of power that left Dylan fighting the urge to back into a corner. "Goddamnit, *go!*"

Gavin was more than capable of handling his wife. Dylan wrenched open the door and ran.

The knock at the door was light and even, but Sasha still nearly dropped her bowl of popcorn. Gavin and Sam were both gone, and all she had to do was go to the door and tell their visitor. *They're not here. I'm—*

I'm alone.

Her hands shook as she set down the bowl and walked to the front door. Glancing through the window, she caught a glimpse of dark clothing and short red hair.

Dylan. She relaxed and opened the door. "Gavin and Sam aren't here."

The tension around his eyes brought back her nervousness. "I know. Gavin sent me. I think he needs your help."

Her heart in her throat, Sasha reached for the borrowed jacket hanging on the rack by the door. "What's wrong?"

"A woman from the Helena pack showed up looking for help. Samantha said—" Dylan broke off and rubbed his hand over the back of his neck. "Well, shit. I don't know what's going on, except Sam's talking about vampires and Gavin's...upset."

Sasha swore as she pushed past him. "She was attacked by a vampire?"

Dylan dragged the door shut before hurrying to catch up with her. "So you're saying there *are* vampires? Because I was living a Dracula-free existence until about ten minutes ago."

17

"There aren't many." Most of the ones she'd met would never have risked a fight with a wolf. It was little better than suicide. If this one had won... Her hands shook. "You said the woman was alive?"

"Yeah. Sam said she was in bad shape, and it looked like she was getting stuff ready to try a binding ceremony."

Sharing energy through a bond with another wolf might buy the woman some time, but the sickness that came with a vampire's bite would affect the other wolf as well. "It's not the safest plan."

Dylan shifted closer to her until his arm brushed hers with every step, and too late she noticed a man watching them from the shadow of a nearby building. His gaze felt unfriendly, but he looked away when Dylan fixed a pointed glare on him.

After a tense moment, the man dropped back, disappearing around the building. Dylan kept walking as if nothing had happened. "Tell me about the vampires. What happens to someone who gets bitten?"

"My mentor said a vampire's bite can kill a wolf slowly, like a poison."

He seemed to mull that over as they passed two more houses and slipped into the alley between the motel and the general store. "Is it a physical thing? Like actual poison? Or something magical?"

She wished she knew. "I'm not sure. It could be either. I've never seen—"

Her breath cut off as they came out of the alley to face a gathered crowd. Sasha fixed her gaze on the bar's door and tried to ignore the wolves' chilly stares. They didn't trust her, but it wasn't personal.

It didn't make it easier. The crowd's distrust evidenced itself in prickly power that flowed from the strongest ones. Dylan's hand came up to rest against her lower back, and his power was steady and unwavering.

He kept her moving forward as he prompted her to continue talking. "You've never actually seen a vampire? Or just never seen someone who's been bitten?"

It took her a moment to speak through the fear closing her throat. "I've met vampires, and I've seen bitten humans. Just not wolves."

Maritza's voice echoed in her head as they pushed through

the door and made their way to the back hall of the bar. *A vampire can feed on a werewolf's magic, but the beast will usually fight it. It makes them feverish, sick. They often die.*

A throbbing wall of tense magic spilled out of the office, and Sasha stumbled. "I can't—" She swallowed her own words and gripped Dylan's hand.

"It's okay." Dylan rubbed his thumb over her fingers in a soothing gesture before tugging a little on her hand. "It's just Gavin and Sam being pissy at each other."

"Okay." *You can do this, Sasha.* "Okay."

An anguished moan met them in the doorway. Joe Mitchell stood at the end of Gavin's desk, restraining a pretty, petite blonde lying on the desk.

Sasha had expected blood and rent flesh, some sign of a struggle or fight. Instead, dozens of rows of small puncture wounds marked the insides of the woman's arms. Her stomach turned, and she pressed the back of her hand to her mouth. Had the woman let herself be bitten? "What's going on?"

Samantha turned, and the friendly, encouraging look Sasha had come to expect from the older woman was gone. Fury stood plainly in her face, and her entire body was rigid. "They've had her since the day after Matthews died. Five weeks. Justine's been my contact inside the Helena pack for more than a decade, and someone wanted to find out just how much she knew about us."

In spite of her fear, Sasha stepped forward and touched the raised welts on Justine's arm. The bites were infected and hot. "What could a group of vampires want to know so badly?"

"Not a group. One vampire." Sam returned her gaze to Justine, and power twisted dizzily around the room as the alpha reached down and cupped Justine's cheek with a whispered word. The power soothed the woman momentarily, and her struggles reduced to soft whimpers. "She's been in and out of consciousness. I can't keep her calm," Sam whispered. "This is the fourth time I've had to quiet her. I want you to bind her to me so it isn't so difficult."

If Sam hadn't spent the last few weeks telling her over and over to trust herself, Sasha would have stayed put. Instead, she moved to the end of the desk and laid her hands over Justine's chest. "Step back."

Joe let go of the woman's shoulders, but Sam barely edged

out of the way. Sasha waited until Sam let go before bending her head and calling forth the magic that slept inside her.

The calming spell was simple, one of the first an apprentice could master during her training, and she whispered the words confidently now. She felt it begin, the swathe of comforting, quieting magic that would grow and envelop Justine.

The spell complete, Sasha straightened and shook her head. "You can't bind yourself to this woman. She's dying."

Sam's jaw tightened. "I can give her more time. Maybe enough time for someone to find a way to save her."

Sasha glanced at Gavin. "It's dangerous. If the bond isn't broken before—"

"I'll do it," Gavin interrupted. "I'm stronger."

"Barely!" Sam took a deep breath and moderated her tone. "You may be a little stronger, but you're the alpha and we're at war. You're not expendable."

"Damn it, Sammie, neither are you!"

The woman on the desk didn't react to the surge of power in the room, but the other wolves did. Sasha caught Dylan's gaze, and she could feel his tension clear across the room. "Isn't there someone else?"

It was clear from his expression that he didn't know. "Keith's not completely healed yet, and Cindy—" His tiny hesitation made her remember the doctor was his lover. He wouldn't want to put her in danger. He cleared his throat. "She's busy trying to keep Abby sane since she won't bind herself to anyone else. And Joe's got his hands full with Brynn."

"It doesn't matter," Sam said, her quiet voice cutting through their conversation. She spoke to Sasha, but her gaze stayed locked on her husband. "Gavin knows there's no one else, but he doesn't deal well with me putting myself in harm's way. So I'll compromise. One week. If we can't find a way in one week, I'll let her go."

Justine might have a week left, if she could draw on Sam's strength, but it could take months of research to find some esoteric spell or therapy to help her.

Still, Sam was willing to risk it. Sasha closed her eyes. "This will hurt." With those words, she drew Sam's energy toward and into herself, shuddering when the full force of it hit her.

It was intoxicating, this magic, but it felt foreign in her

body, and it wasn't hers to keep. She murmured the incantation and laid her hands on Justine's head.

The pain must have been intense, but Sam did nothing more than grunt softly as the bond settled into place. The scrape of boots on the floor and a muffled curse were the only sign something more had happened. Sasha opened her eyes in time to see Gavin catch Sam as she listed forward, deep lines of pain etched on her face.

Dylan appeared at Sasha's shoulder, so close she could feel the slightest hint of his aura even though he wasn't quite touching her. "Are you all right?"

She fought the urge to lean into his strength. "I'm fine. But I need to get to work." She needed to get upstairs to the library, to the collection of records and histories Gavin had been telling her about the last few weeks. "Can I do anything else, Gavin?"

He waved her away, one arm still holding his wife. "Joe and I will take care of Sammie and Justine. Dylan, can you?"

It didn't seem to be a full question, but Dylan answered it nonetheless. "Yes. Of course. Should I stay here tonight?"

The alpha was already headed for the door as Joe gathered Justine in his arms. "If you'll bring Sasha home when she's finished."

"Of course," he repeated. His hand fell away and he hurried to open the door before Gavin reached it.

Sam stopped walking and turned to meet Sasha's gaze. "Are you okay here with Dylan?" Her voice sounded hoarse and exhausted, but she ignored Gavin's impatience. "We can have the books brought to the house if it will be easier."

Sasha gave her a reassuring smile. "Dylan and I will be fine. Don't worry so much. Just go rest."

"Okay. And Sasha... I won't blame you if you can't save her. But I would have blamed myself if I hadn't given you a chance to try."

The pained promise made the hair on the back of Sasha's neck lift. "I'll try like hell, Sam. I swear."

Gavin nodded once, his normally light eyes dark with worry, and hurried out. Joe followed close behind him, though he spared a gently encouraging look for Sasha.

When she and Dylan were alone, she rubbed her hands over the thick fabric covering her arms. She began to shiver, a delayed reaction to the loss of the energy she'd expended. "How are you at speed-reading, Dylan?" she tried to joke.

"Actually, I'm good at it." He reached down and tugged his navy blue sweatshirt over his head, revealing a plain white T-shirt and a leather shoulder holster. "Put this on until I can see about warming it up upstairs."

"No, you should keep it. It's not—" Her teeth chattered. "It won't help. It's the magic. It drains me, and I just have to rest."

Dylan held out the sweatshirt. "I may not be as obnoxiously overbearing as Joe or Keith, but I'm not going to be able to concentrate with you shivering and looking miserable. So humor me while we find you some food and build up a fire. Please."

Sasha bit her tongue and pulled the warm fleece over her head. "I'm not hungry, but thanks for the shirt."

"I don't think the kitchen upstairs is stocked," he said as if he hadn't heard her. "But I know where Olivia hides the cookies down here. And I haven't had anything but crackers since lunch." He grinned at her, crooked and a little mischievous. "Come on. Ransack the pantry with me."

"Okay, but..." She glanced at the desk and the pile of items that had obviously been swept quickly off of it and onto the floor. "After that, you're helping me with research."

"Until you pass out," he promised. "Hell, until we *both* pass out."

Sasha followed him out into the darkened bar. She knew from her time in Red Rock that it wouldn't normally close down, even after an injured refugee showed up looking for sanctuary. "Did Olivia go home?"

"Guess so. People were starting to leave when I went to get you. Anything that freaks Sam out is scary enough to terrify the shit out of the rest of us, I guess." He smiled again, this time in obvious encouragement. "Except you. But you know more about this stuff than we do."

"I'm scared." The second she said the words, she wanted to take them back. Weakness was embarrassing under the best of circumstances. With wolves, it had almost cost Sasha her life.

Dylan just shrugged one shoulder and pushed open the door that led to the bar's kitchen. "Smart people usually are. We know how bad things can get."

"But we can't stop those bad things from happening."

"Not yet." He moved past the large stainless-steel

refrigerator and reached up to open a cupboard high above the industrial sink. "But we keep trying. There's a lot to be said for that, you know, Sasha. It's easy to keep trying when you're Keith or Abby and don't have any other choice. The rest of us have to work at it."

"So I keep telling myself." A stool stood in the corner, and Sasha pulled it closer to the counter and watched him. "You don't scare me." It shouldn't have been surprising; the energy radiating from Dylan was gentle, constant. It rarely flared, and he'd always been careful not to upset or alarm her. "You don't scare me at all."

"Good." He pulled a battered tin from the top shelf and pried off the lid to reveal a stack of chocolate-chip cookies. "I'm not all that scary anyway."

Sasha touched the raised pink lines traversing her cheek. "I guess not."

He glanced up at her, his gaze focusing on the scars instead of her eyes. The edge of the cookie tin bent under his fingers, but his voice stayed steady. "Hey. I'm here, and I'm armed. No one's going to hurt you, okay?"

It had been weeks since the last attack on Red Rock...and the night Alan Matthews had threatened her. The bruises had faded, and she'd managed to stop flinching so damn much. But what stayed with her, hazy but unmistakable, was a snapshot of memory: Dylan, walking through the streets with her cradled in his arms.

Now, his distress made her chest ache. "That's not what I meant." It hadn't even occurred to her to worry that Dylan couldn't protect her if something happened.

"We're not all monsters." Dylan sounded like he might be trying to convince himself more than her. He set the cookie tin on the counter in front of her in obvious, silent command before turning to the refrigerator. "Tell me more about vampires. I still can't believe they actually exist."

She took a cookie because he expected it. "There's not much to tell, really. They're as different as wolves, or people, for that matter. I've met some vampires who were perfectly civil, and others who were feral. They mostly just drink blood and live a long time."

Dylan disappeared behind the fridge door and she heard him shifting things around on shelves. "That's nuts. Man, I told

Abby there weren't any vampires. I guess that teaches me not to act like I get this shit even after ten years."

He looked to be in his midtwenties, about her age. If he'd only been a wolf for a decade, he probably wasn't much older than that. "I got the idea from Gavin that the Helena pack wasn't focused on educating new wolves."

A snort answered that question. "Depends on your definition of 'educate', I guess. Guys like me, we're around for tithes and cannon fodder. The only thing my pack tried to teach me was my place in life as everyone's punching bag."

The ache in her chest deepened. "I'm sorry, Dylan."

He finally resurfaced from the depths of the refrigerator with enough cold cuts to make a dozen sandwiches. He shrugged as he kicked the door shut. "Could have been worse. I could have been Abby or Brynn. Or Justine."

Just because others had suffered didn't mean he hadn't. "Maritza—my mentor—said we'd have to work with the wolves to make sure people like Alan Matthews were taken out of power. The alpha who had her killed disagreed."

Dylan dumped the food on the counter and studied her face. "Do you want to talk about it? You don't have to, but I don't mind listening."

She wondered what he would say if she *did* open up, if she told him how she'd watched Maritza die, how the wolves had told her she was next. If he knew how many scars she carried under her clothes.

She bit her lip. "Another time, maybe, with beer and pretzels. We have work to do tonight."

"That we do." He leveled a look on her that was every bit as stern as Sam at her worst. "And you're going to eat before we do it, because I know how hungry expending power makes me. You're just going to have to humor me."

There was something almost pleading beneath his stubborn expression, and Sasha caved. "I like corned beef and Swiss cheese."

Relief flashed in his eyes. "Get ready for the best sandwich you've ever had."

When Dylan lifted Sasha, she stirred and looked up at him,

her dark blue eyes unfocused. "What is it?"

"Shh." He'd tried to ease her out of the chair without waking her, but now he swung her up into his arms. "You need some rest."

She didn't argue. "I can walk."

He didn't doubt it, but it felt nice having her snuggled against his chest. Not necessarily in a physical way, though a certain male appreciation was inevitable, but nice on a deeper instinctive level. Taking care of Brynn had felt right in the same way.

He shifted her closer as he started toward the apartment's small bedroom. "I can put you down if you really want, but you promised to humor me. Consider it a lesson in soothing werewolf instincts."

"Okay." Sasha rested her head on his shoulder. "Did you find anything?"

His chest felt tight, and that stabbing guilt returned, along with Cindy's angry words. He shoved them away and tried to concentrate on her question, and not on how good it felt to simply hold another person. "Not much more of use. I've put aside a few books that look hopeful but aren't in English. I think one might be Gaelic. Another is definitely Latin, and my Latin was never very good."

One small hand curled around the back of his neck. "Mine is decent. Does Gavin read Gaelic?"

"We'll have to ask him." Her hair smelled like the shampoo Sam used, but Sam always smelled like wolf and the woods and Gavin underneath it. Sasha smelled like old books and a little bit like Dylan himself, thanks to the sweatshirt she'd spent the evening in. The scent stirred something a lot deeper than friendly companionship. *Shit. Rein it in. Rein it the fuck in.*

"Mmm, tomorrow." Her breath tickled his neck. "Thank you for being here, Dylan."

He was so beyond screwed. "No problem, honey. Listen, I'm going to tuck you into bed, and I'll be out on the couch if you need anything, okay?"

"Okay." She laughed softly. "You're always carrying me places."

"Uh-huh. I'm your very own knight in shining armor."

He lowered her to the bed, and she gazed up at him with gentle eyes that held no humor or mockery. "All you need is a

25

gallant white horse."

Dylan covered another of those painful twinges in his chest with a teasing smile. "Werewolves and horses don't get along so well."

"Guess you're stuck carrying me, then." She sat up and brushed her coppery hair back from her face as she kicked off her shoes. "Good night."

"Night, Sasha." She seemed awake enough to get herself under the covers, but he knew he'd be checking back to make sure. Just like he'd watched her all evening for signs of hunger or fatigue. Like how he'd looked forward to finding some scrap of interesting lore in the books he'd been reading, just for the chance to watch her eyes light up.

So very, very screwed.

He backed out of the bedroom and pulled the door shut behind him. A quiet cough drew his attention, and he turned to find Gavin leaning against the open doorway. "Sammie was worried, so I told her I'd check on you two."

He was over thirty, and too damn old to blush because he'd gotten caught tiptoeing out of a woman's bedroom. "Sasha's exhausted. And I'm sleeping out here, on the couch." *Yeah, that doesn't sound defensive at all.*

Gavin just shrugged one shoulder. "Where else would you sleep?"

Dylan tried to figure out if Gavin was teasing him, but the alpha's face was inscrutable. "Better than the floor," he said finally, opting for a cautious route. "I was going to find a walkie-talkie in the office and let you and Sam know."

"Mmm. Want me to take her home, or will you be fine with her here?"

"She's pretty wiped out, but Sam would probably feel better if she was back at your place." He wouldn't even take it personally. Sam couldn't help herself any more than Keith and Abby and Joe could when it came to Brynn. Stronger wolves trusted no one but themselves when it came to the people in their care. They sure the hell didn't trust people like him.

But Gavin shook his head. "Sammie will be glad to know you're here with Sasha. You'll take care of her."

Gavin's confidence was a reminder that he wasn't just another midpack wolf. He was the town's newest folk hero, the subordinate wolf who had defied his corrupt alpha not once but twice, the second time with a bullet between the eyes. And if he'd done it even a year earlier, so many lives could have been spared. Compliments on his supposed courage grated on Dylan's nerves when the truth was far more chilling—anyone could be brave when he had nothing to lose.

Except now you have something to lose. It took everything in him not to glance back over his shoulder at the door. "I'll take care of her."

"I know." The alpha's answer came easily, but he didn't leave. "How did it go tonight?"

"You've got a lot of books in there." And no discernible system of organization. "I was actually thinking about seeing if Brynn felt up to helping us sort them into some kind of system. She used to be great at those things. But I was worried..."

"That she still needs time to adjust. I understand." Gavin's gaze sharpened. "How did Sasha fare?"

"With the research?"

"With you."

Dylan stiffened. "I'm not that inappropriate, Gavin."

The alpha's voice was mild. "I didn't think for a second you were. But I wondered how far Sasha's trust extended." He walked in and crossed the small living room with slow steps. "Do you know what happened to her?"

His eyes flickered to the bedroom door, and he couldn't stop the image of the way her fingers had brushed the scars on her cheek. Abby and Brynn had both been attacked, but werewolves rarely bore scars from anything short of magical weapons. Hell, his own body was proof enough of that.

But Sasha... For the first time Dylan wondered what other scars she might have, scars that wouldn't be so obvious. "I know that she was attacked, and her teacher died. And that Alan roughed her up the night I killed him."

"Magic is useful. Matthews would have kept her." Gavin cleared his throat. "It's what the other alpha planned to do, I think. He killed Maritza because she was too strong to control. Sasha, on the other hand, has power and training, but not too much of either."

Dylan's hands clenched. He knew all too well what came next. Women who were useful had been Alan's favorite prey. Turn them, break them, use them. He'd seen it dozens of times. "Keith got there in time, though." *Please let him have gotten there in time.*

"Keith said they had orders to hurt but not bite her." For a few seconds, he seemed far away. Then his eyes cleared. "Yeah, he got there in time. So she came here with some scratches...and more terror than I've seen in a while."

"She trusts me," Dylan whispered. "I don't know why, but she trusts me."

Gavin leaned on the back of the worn sofa with a pensive, almost worried expression. "I understand needing to be needed, Dylan, maybe more than most. But if it's not Sasha who makes you feel these things—if it could be someone, anyone, else—" The alpha scrubbed his hands over his face. "Do you see what I'm asking?"

"I'm not—" He stopped himself before he ended up snapping at the alpha. "Have you talked to Cindy, or am I just obviously a man with an ego problem?"

"Neither. But I've been around a lot of years." He sighed and shook his head. "Never mind. I guess I got it wrong. Not the first time, and it won't be the last."

It was an out, and somehow it made Dylan feel less cornered. He exhaled and moderated his tone enough to sound casual, or at least less defensive. "Are you asking if I can tell the difference between instincts and interest?"

"You're smart. You can tell the difference. What I'm asking you for is another favor."

Dylan tried not to tense. "Okay."

"I'm asking you to be sure before—" He cut off and cocked his head. Dylan heard it a moment later, the soft sound of the box springs shifting and then bare feet on the hardwood floor.

He'd already taken a step toward the door before he realized he'd moved. He jerked to a halt and refused to look at Gavin as he lifted his voice enough to carry through the door. "You okay, Sasha?"

The door swung open. "I heard voices." Her gaze slipped past him to land on Gavin, and her eyes widened as her heart began to thump faster. "Is it Sam? Justine?"

"Justine's better. Resting." Gavin's voice was low and even. "Sammie was worried you'd be pushing yourself too hard tonight. I told her I'd check on you."

She stepped forward and stopped beside Dylan, her arm barely brushing his. "We're tired, but fine."

The hard, too-fast beat of her heart stirred an instinctive need to touch her. Soothe her. He swallowed hard and indulged himself under the guise of smoothing a tangled strand of her hair. "You should still be resting, though."

"I thought something might be wrong." Her fingers grazed his.

Gavin's pause was almost imperceptible. "I'd better get back. Do you want to stay here, Sasha, or come home with me?"

Her eyes met Dylan's. "I should go so you won't have to sleep on the couch."

He bit back the urge to protest only because he knew in his heart she'd be safer in the alpha's house than in the apartment with him. "The couch is probably more comfortable than where I planned on sleeping tonight. If you ever need to stay here, don't worry about me."

"You never know with late-night research sessions." She hesitated and pulled his sweatshirt over her head. "I left my jacket downstairs. It'll be warm enough. Thanks, Dylan."

The heavy cotton carried their combined scents, and Dylan struggled not to let his wolf's sudden interest show. "Any time, Sasha."

Gavin watched him as she walked out and headed down the stairs. "Will we see you at the house tomorrow, Dylan?"

Dylan was too smart to think it was a question. "What time should I be there?"

"Lunch. Olivia will cook." The alpha stepped out but paused with his hand on the doorknob. "Have a good night, son."

Not even the fond endearment could completely ease the tension that filled Dylan as he closed the door. It took a few moments to identify the feeling as the wolf's unease. He'd learned the hard way over the past decade to squash any instincts that rose inside him, doubly so when they pertained to women. In Helena feelings like that had been a quick way to put a woman's life at risk.

But you're not in Helena anymore. His fingers clenched around the sweatshirt as he fought the urge to pull it over his head, just to appease the wolf with Sasha's scent tangled up with his.

He definitely wasn't in Helena anymore.

Chapter Two

Sasha's vision blurred, and her hand trembled on Justine's. She tried to hold the cleansing spell just a little longer, but the magic slipped through her fingers, dissolving into nothing. "Any change?"

"No." Dylan's voice sounded apologetic, and almost as tired as she felt. "I thought for a second maybe..."

"Damn it." Frustration gnawed at her. "Damn it all, anyway." It was the third cleansing they'd tried in as many days, each one more aggressive than the last.

And each one a spectacular failure.

"I don't understand." Sasha rubbed the back of her hand across her forehead. "It should be helping, at least a little."

"Hey." Dylan circled the bed and touched her shoulder, his fingers tightening for just a moment in a supportive squeeze. "We're going to figure it out, Sasha. We are."

The contact felt good, and her muscles tensed before she could command them not to. "Right. So we need to get back to work." Her jacket lay on a chair beside the bed, and she snatched it up. "I'm going to the library."

"Sasha. You need to stop for a few hours."

Four days of what felt like wasted effort made her begrudge stopping, even to eat or sleep. "You do what you need to do." It would give her a few hours free of the distraction Dylan had begun to pose. "I just want to check a few things."

He shook his head. "If you're going to the apartment, I'm going with you."

"No, Dylan. I need—" She needed time alone. Time to get her head straight and stop thinking about him, and to find a way to save Justine and Sam. "I need a drink."

"Okay." He offered her his hand along with a hint of a smile. "Let's go to the bar. Brynn told me that she's going to try to get out of the house tonight. She could use a familiar face, I bet."

The bar had been packed when they'd left the upstairs apartment. Most of the people in it, wolf or human, only stared at her, whether in curiosity or hostility. The stares reminded her that she didn't belong in Red Rock, that she was an outsider.

The more time she spent with Dylan, the more she needed that reminder.

It didn't help that he treated her with an offhand, casual fondness that could so easily be mistaken for something more. Sometimes the stares that followed them were more assessing than hostile, the suspicions so blatant Sasha could almost hear the thoughts.

He seemed oblivious, though. "Gavin?"

"Not tonight. I can't." Sasha couldn't bear to see his face when she told him she'd failed yet again. "I'll talk to him tomorrow. Please, Dylan."

Dylan released her. "Can you wait for me downstairs? I'll let him know we're going to have another late research night. Otherwise Sam will worry."

She was still a little weak from the magic, so she made her way down the stairs carefully. The main floor of the house seemed quiet without Sam crashing around in the kitchen or yelling for Gavin to take out the trash. Sasha shivered inside her jacket and tried to stay still as she waited for Dylan, but her nerves were raw. She felt on edge, almost twitchy.

It seemed like an eternity before she heard the whisper of his sneakers on the stairs behind her. "You ready?"

"Are you sure you want to go?" The words hurt, but she forced them out anyway. "Spending time with me can't be helping your social life much."

The corner of his mouth ticked up. "If you had decided to stay here for the night, I probably would have gone and worked on my house alone in the dark. Not much of a swinging social life."

"I guess I'm keeping you from your renovations too."

"That's not—" Dylan's friendly expression vanished. "Are you sick of me? If you're sick of me, say it, Sasha. I won't be upset."

It was so far from the truth that she laughed. "No. But people around here don't like me very much, especially after what happened the night the Helena pack invaded." She'd saved Keith's life, she knew that much. Still, half the people in town were terrified of her, of her magic, and the other half only seemed disgusted. "That's what I meant."

"Well, screw them. Come and hang out with us. Brynn could use someone around who's not being polite to her because they're scared shitless of Joe." Dylan pulled open the door. "She probably knows how you're feeling, you know."

Most of the pack wouldn't trust a wolf of the full moon, no matter the circumstances. "Yes, she probably does." Sasha avoided his gaze. "Can we talk about things that don't matter? I don't want to think about the ones that do, at least for a while."

"Sure. We can talk about anything you want." He tugged her out the front door and into the cool night air. "I don't know if you've seen much of Brynn since the attack, but if you haven't, be prepared. She's still not very human sometimes."

"Her change was hard, but she's tough." Sasha stared up at the stars and let Dylan pull her along toward the street. "How long have you known them? Brynn and Abby?"

"A few years. God, almost seven now. One of my roommates worked with Abby. Brynn was still a kid when I met them, and Abby was working insane hours trying to take care of both of them, even though she wasn't that old herself. Abby's always been the one you want looking out for you." The ironic self-deprecation was back in his voice, hidden under a layer of forced casualness.

"And you." She wanted to kick herself when she heard how shy and besotted she sounded. "I mean, you took care of her too. You brought her here."

Dylan looked a little uncomfortable. "Yeah. I did. But it wasn't as heroic as everyone makes out, you know. I took a risk, but there wasn't anything else I could do."

"I don't think it was heroic. Not like you're obviously defining the word, at any rate."

"Is the definition of heroism really that subjective?"

"I don't think it was particularly noble of you," she clarified. "You were ready to sacrifice yourself because the alternative—watching Abby go through what Matthews had planned for her—would have been worse. It's not necessarily heroic. It's what you do for the people you love."

"Yeah." His fingers tightened around hers. "And having people act like you're some incredible person just because you did what you had to... It actually sucks a little bit."

She wanted to squeeze back, to let him know she was there for him. Then she remembered Cindy and pulled away. "I understand."

"I guess you do." She felt the weight of Dylan's gaze as he studied her. "What you did for Keith and Abby was incredible, you know. And what you did for Brynn too. Since you got here, all you've done is save people."

"Have I?" Keith was still bedridden, Dylan himself said Brynn was barely human. "Maybe."

Dylan moved fast. He got in front of her somehow and turned to catch her arms before she could bump in to him. He leaned down until his face was only inches from hers, and his eyes glinted in the moonlight. "Yes, Sasha. You have."

How was she supposed to keep her distance when he looked at her like that? Her heart began to pound, and she was grateful for the thick jacket that hid the goose bumps his touch elicited. "It's not helping Justine and Sam much at the moment, though, is it?"

"You're doing the best you can. That's all you can ask of yourself." The words were firm, almost harsh, but the tingle of power around him didn't seem angry or upset. If anything, his annoyance seemed to be directed at himself.

Sasha wanted to soothe him, to stroke her fingers over his cheek and draw him close. Instead, she changed the subject. "You promised me a drink."

He let go of her. "Yeah, I did. Come on."

The bar wasn't crowded, but it felt like a hundred eyes turned to fix on them as they crossed the threshold. Silence fell as everyone stopped talking at once, leaving only the faint strains of Led Zeppelin spilling out of the jukebox.

Brynn rose from her chair near the bar, angry challenge rolling off her in waves even Sasha could feel. "Hey, Sasha. Dylan."

Dylan's hand fell to the small of Sasha's back in an old-fashioned and protective gesture. "Let's go sit with Joe and Brynn."

Joe favored them both with a broad smile. "Knocking off early tonight?"

Sasha peeled off her jacket and bit back the defensive explanation that sprang to her lips. "We tried another cleansing, but it's not working."

His expression faded into one of sympathy. "Hey, Gavin was smart to stick the two biggest brains in town on this. You'll get it done."

Sitting so close to Brynn was uncomfortable. She glared at the people occupying the surrounding tables until everyone had turned away, only relaxing into her chair when Joe tapped her arm.

He whispered something to her, and she hissed a curse. "Don't try to placate me. They're being rude and I'm not going to pretend they're not."

"I don't care what they think, Brynn, or what they say." It was a lie, but only a small one, and Sasha offered it gladly.

Brynn's gray eyes narrowed. Sasha knew lying had been pointless, but the other woman didn't call her on it. "Well, at least with us sitting together they won't know who to stare at. They're not sure if they should worry about you giving them magical warts or me flipping my shit and killing one of them by mistake."

Considering the looks Sasha had been getting since she'd healed Keith, at least half the town would be hard-pressed to choose between those two fates. "Maybe we should glare back and make them think we'll team up to do both."

"Joe's a spoilsport. He doesn't want me getting into fights."

Joe finished his beer and shrugged. "Call me crazy, but I prefer my girlfriend in one piece."

"What do you want to drink, Sasha?" Dylan sounded like he was struggling not to laugh.

"Beer, please." Her fingers brushed Brynn's hand. "How's Abby doing? I haven't been by to see her yet this week."

Brynn tensed, and the prickly, frightening power spilled outward once more. She seemed oblivious of the way her magic flared, though Joe stroked her arm again. "It's hard for her. Keith's doing better though. He's up and about now, and crabby as hell that Abby won't quit hovering."

"That's good." Sasha hadn't meant to upset her, but she also didn't want to walk on eggshells and make her feel like a freak. "I know she's been worried."

"Yeah. Ab's good at worrying..." Brynn's narrowed gaze fixed on a table near the bar. "Make them shut up, Joe, or I will."

"Brynn, *stop*." He cast the people at the table a glare as well but wrapped his fingers around Brynn's. "It's not going to help."

"He's right," Sasha whispered. She didn't know what they were saying, but she could guess. They didn't trust her anyway, and she'd been spending so much time with Dylan, one of their new heroes...

Joe hissed in a breath, and Sasha saw the lines of blood where Brynn's nails had pierced his skin. "Brynn, baby—"

It was hard to recognize the calm, easygoing person Brynn had been in the woman who sat across the table now. Something feral stirred in her eyes, and the hair rose on the back of Sasha's neck as power spiraled upward.

Brynn shook off Joe's hand, snatched up his empty bottle and threw it across the room with alarming strength. The sound of shattering glass was nearly eclipsed by an enraged, pained growl. Brynn snarled in return and moved so fast Sasha barely had a chance to jerk back before the woman went over the table.

Joe lunged after Brynn as the man she'd hit jumped up, and Sasha slipped out of her chair and to the floor. She could cast something that would stop the fight, but they might turn on her for using her magic against them.

Strong hands closed around her shoulders, and she thrashed a little before recognizing it was Dylan who held her. "I'm okay."

"Shh." A table crashed behind them, and Dylan wrapped an arm around her waist and half-dragged her into the corner. "We need to stay out of it. Joe's the only one who can calm Brynn down."

She could see Joe over Dylan's shoulder, slipping one big arm around Brynn to hold her back from the man she'd attacked. His face was impassive, but she knew it wouldn't stay that way if anyone touched Brynn.

Brynn's head whipped to the side and she snarled, but it wasn't the same as when Keith and Abby clashed. Abby's quiet demeanor held a frighteningly strong woman who backed down to no one. Brynn's feral strength rode close to the surface, but when Joe held her head to his and whispered something, the fight melted out of her.

Joe sent Brynn's opponent skittering back with one hard look, and Dylan turned to Sasha. "I'm sorry," he told her. "I should have known..."

"Known what?" She couldn't stop shaking.

He looked back to her and rubbed her shoulder. "Brynn is trying to find her place in the pack. It means she's making every little thing into a challenge, because her wolf is so much closer to the surface than anyone else's."

"Oh." The stairs and the path to the backroom were blocked by people who'd backed away from the fight, but they could probably make it to the front door. "Can we go upstairs? I think it would be best."

"Yeah." Dylan rose and pulled her up with him. "Come on, stay behind me. I just want to catch Joe's attention."

The sheer press of angry energy in the room made it hard to move, but Sasha made herself stand. She stuck close to Dylan, her fists clenched in the back of his shirt, and tried to ignore the accusatory looks. As far as they were concerned, the strife was all her fault.

"Joe." Dylan's quiet, firm voice cut through the angry muttering. "Are you taking her home, or do you want to come upstairs with us?"

He didn't hesitate. "We'll catch you next time, Dylan. You need anything, you let me know."

Sasha caught a glimpse of Brynn over Dylan's shoulder. Joe had one arm still locked around her body and was backing toward the door, his expression challenging anyone to say a word.

No one did.

"Follow them outside," Dylan said quietly, his gaze still fixed on the room. "I'll be out in a moment."

"But I—"

"Please."

Sasha let go of him and crossed the room. The occupants of the bar stepped back, cutting a wide swathe of space around her, and she'd never felt more alone in her life.

Sasha rubbed her gritty, burning eyes and reached for another book. "Did you turn up anything in that diary from the Sacramento pack?"

"A lead..." His voice trailed off as he turned a page and squinted at the tiny, faded writing. "A vampire from Germany who joined forces with an alpha female in Austria in the 1600s."

"Joined forces?" She stretched, her muscles screaming in protest. They'd both spent far too much of the last week hunched over the desk in the tiny library, researching and bouncing ideas off one another long into each night. "Like they worked together, or something more intimate?"

"Sounds like both, actually." He frowned as his gaze tracked her movements. "You should take a break. You've been sitting here too long."

Sasha had tried to get him to stop and eat when his stomach had started to growl earlier, but he'd had none of it. The only time he would agree was if she told him she was hungry, even if she wasn't. *Like now.* "I could use a breather, actually. I'm starving."

Just like that, Dylan set the book aside and rose to his feet. "Olivia said she'd leave something warming in the crock pot up here. We can eat without going downstairs."

"Good." She still hadn't grown accustomed to the stares, which ranged from curious to hostile, and now they all stared at her and Dylan. They were wondering if he spent so much time with her because he had to...or because he wanted to.

They moved around the apartment's tiny kitchen, not speaking as they served their woefully late lunch. Sasha was careful to avoid touching him; the tension and weariness that rolled off him in waves already made her want to thread her fingers through his hair and comfort him. She had tried to fight the instinctive awareness that cued her into his moods, and contact would only intensify it.

She ladled the thick stew into bowls and uncovered the basket of dinner rolls on the counter. "Want to eat in here or sit in the dining room?"

He nodded to the tiny two-person table nestled against the wall. "We can eat in here, if you want."

"Sure." They settled into their chairs, and Sasha gathered her courage. "Are you sleeping here tonight?"

"Yeah. The house isn't really ready, and Olivia says she

doesn't mind. She doesn't need the place, not since she finally moved in with Sully."

"No, I mean..." The question had come out all wrong. She studied Dylan's bent head and struggled to figure out a way to rephrase it. "Why aren't you staying at Cindy's anymore?"

His shoulders tensed, and his usually placid power flared enough to betray his unease. Dylan didn't look up from his stew, just kept stirring it absently as he stared into the bowl. "I'm not really invited."

She'd run into Cindy at Justine's bedside a few times over the last week. Sasha had attributed the tension to Cindy's perceptiveness, to her somehow knowing about Sasha's developing fascination with her boyfriend.

But this was more than awkwardness. "It's—it's not because of me, is it?" The question was revealing and terrifying, but Dylan would have had to be blind not to notice her growing awareness of him. "I can explain the situation to her, tell her you're doing Gavin a favor."

"No, Sasha." He finally raised his head, but it was impossible to read his expression even though the look in his eyes was gentle. "It's not your fault. Sometimes things don't work out. It doesn't have to be anyone's fault."

"I know that. But I wouldn't have blamed her for not being happy about this." She shrugged to hide her pain. "Most of the people here don't want me around."

Dylan dropped his spoon into the bowl and caught her hand. "Hey." His thumb smoothed across the backs of her fingers. "Even good people can be scared into acting like idiots sometimes."

She managed not to jerk away from his touch, but she couldn't hide the way her pulse sped. "I know that too. But you don't need me complicating things for you."

"Seems life's pretty complicated as it is." He released her, but the warmth from his fingers lingered. "Think about how many things can go wrong in a normal relationship, then add the wolves. *Then* add the fact that most of us came from screwed-up packs. Maybe the people here have forgotten how good they have it with Gavin as their alpha."

And if you factored in being human... Sasha shook herself. She wasn't involved with anyone, and she wasn't going to be, so she changed the subject. "Tell me about the legend you found in the diary. About the vampire and the alpha."

"It was in Austria, in 1680 or so." Dylan settled into his chair and picked up one of the rolls Sasha had set on the table. "Wolves were pretty patriarchal in that region and time period, and I got the feeling from reading between the lines that life sucked for the women. Maybe as bad as it is in some of the cities now, only with nowhere to run to get away from it."

"So how did this woman gain and maintain power?"

He polished off the roll and shook his head. "That's the part I'm still trying to translate. My German's not bad but this account is heavy on the dialect. From the context, it seems like somehow her vampire lover was able to feed on the power from the pack and then give it to her. She was strong to begin with, but he gave her enough to subdue even the strongest wolves."

"There's a ritual some vampires use to—" Her spoon clattered to the table as she remembered the rows of bites on Justine's arms. "Jesus, I didn't even think of it."

"What?"

"Not torture." Her hands shook, and she clenched them into fists. "Harvest."

Dylan's eyes widened. "Do you think it was literal? That the vampire didn't just feed on the pack's power, he fed on the wolves and...what?"

"They need the blood anyway, and the ritual helps them focus the energy transfer. Maritza said it was like a bond, only unilateral. There's no give and take." She pushed back her bowl and stood. Fear made her clumsy, and she knocked over her chair. "We have to get over there."

"Wait, Sasha, I don't—" His face paled and he shoved away from the table and caught her before she could stumble. "You think the vampire is still draining power from Justine."

If only it were that simple. "Not only Justine." She dragged in a deep, ragged breath. "Sam. Dylan, that much energy—"

"Shit." He dragged her through the kitchen, snagging his coat on the way. "Here, put this on, and we'll go down the backstairs."

"Dylan." She could easily dissolve the bond between Justine and Sam, but breaking the vampire's bond with Justine would be harder, perhaps even unsafe. "It's not going to be easy, and I need to know if you can be there, or if you need to stay away."

39

His fingers froze on the door handle. "Not easy as in dangerous?"

"A lot of what I do involves having to—to *feel* the magic. How it works from the inside out. So I pull it into me first." His face blanched, but she kept talking. "I know I can take the blood bond from Justine. What I don't know is if I can break it."

"No. *Hell* no." His knuckles had gone white, and she thought she might find the shape of his hand imprinted on the doorknob when he let go. "Sam and Gavin won't let you do it either, Sasha. They're not going to let you kill yourself, so if you can't find a way to do it safely, don't even bring it up."

Irrational anger seized her. "I wasn't asking for your permission, and I can't just let her die."

"And I can't just let you die!" The words came out low and hoarse, and Dylan clenched his eyes shut a moment later. He dragged in an uneven breath and exhaled on a curse. "The Gaelic spell. The one Gavin helped us translate. You can use that, on me."

"No." She took a step back. "No, it's the same damn thing. It may as well be a bond, Dylan. It's too—" *Intimate.* "It's too much for you. For both of us."

He took the words the wrong way, and she saw the pain in his eyes. "I may not be Joe or Keith, but I'm not an invalid. There's enough power in me to help keep you safe."

"Stop it. It's not about that." If she cast the spell, they'd be inside each other, with no place or way to hide anything. Sasha hadn't been able to conceal her physical reactions from him during the time they'd spent together, but she wasn't ready for him to see beyond that. Still, there was no other way. He was right; Gavin would never let her risk herself so completely.

"All right," she whispered. "I need the book."

He watched her for a few heartbeats, as if he didn't quite trust her not to bolt if he left her alone. Something flashed in his eyes, but it was gone before he let go of the doorknob. "Put on the coat." This time it sounded like a request instead of an order. "I'll grab the book."

"I'll wait." She donned the jacket and clenched her fists so hard her nails bit into her palms. What effect the vampire's blood bond would have on either of them was a terrifying unknown, and the thought of dragging Dylan into a situation she couldn't quantify, much less control, scared the hell out of her.

But it was clear he wouldn't let her do it alone. He reappeared less than a minute later with the book in hand and a serious look on his face. When he reached for the slightly dented doorknob, he glanced at her. "I'm sorry I yelled at you, Sasha. I know you just want to help. And that's why I worry."

Sasha moved without thinking. She wrapped a hand around the back of his neck and hauled his mouth to hers. He had to understand the desperate need inside her before she opened herself to him, so she parted her lips and sought his tongue.

The priceless volume hit the floor with a thud. Dylan caught her around the waist and spun her until her back hit the door. He kissed her with the same intensity that had transfixed her over the past week, with complete focus and a level of expertise that made her heart pound. A groan worked its way up from deep in his chest, low and a little needy, and the skilled play of his tongue against hers melted into something less refined.

He wanted her, and not with a placid human desire either. The man might be the one pressing her into the door, his warm chest a solid weight under her hand, but the wolf's power stirred as he groaned again, tickling her skin as that dark, primal magic focused all of its attention on her.

Her desperation broke, giving way to heavy, liquid desire, and she pulled her mouth from his with a shaky moan. Her lips tingled, her body throbbed and every cell of her being protested the broken contact. "I'm sorry."

Dylan rested his forehead against the door for several endless heartbeats, his breath coming only in harsh pants. Then he shuddered and bent to scoop up the book. "You might be sorry." He opened the door and hustled her out onto the landing. "If you think I was an overprotective ass before, you may want to kill me by sunset."

It played into her greatest fear a little too well—that his attraction to her was one of sheer instinct, borne of a need to shelter and protect. That he looked at her and saw not a woman, but a broken needy shell. "I'm not fragile, Dylan."

"I know." He pulled the door shut and nodded to the stairs. "We'll talk about it later, when everyone's safe."

She wanted to argue, but there wasn't time, so she

clambered down the steep staircase and hurried out into the street.

Gavin nearly looked his age when he pulled open the door and leaned against it heavily. "What is it, Sasha?"

She panted, her side burning. "I think we found a way."

He glanced at Dylan even as he moved to allow them inside. "How?"

"She thinks it's a blood bond." Dylan barely seemed winded. "She thinks the vampire's still connected to Justine and now, wherever he is, he's feeding on Justine's magic *and* Sam's."

"Shit." Though the muttered curse was harsh, Gavin looked relieved. "We have to break the bond."

"Sam's will be easy enough." Sasha shrugged out of her jacket and took the book from Dylan. "I'll have to take the vampire's magic from Justine. Dylan will—will help me."

Gavin's eyes fell to the volume in her hands. Recognition flared in his eyes, and he pinned Dylan with an intense look. "Are you sure about this?"

Dylan spoke bluntly. "She trusts me, and I trust her. There isn't anyone else, and I'm sure the hell not letting her do it on her own."

"It's the only way, Gavin." Sasha headed up the stairs without waiting for the alpha to speak.

She found Sam in the alphas' bedroom, curled in the center of the large bed with her knees drawn up to her chest and her face alarmingly pale. She hardly seemed conscious, but dark eyes fluttered open as soon as Sasha stepped over the threshold. "Sasha."

Sam's cheek was cold, and Sasha made a soothing noise. "Dylan and I came to help. Where's Justine?"

"Second guest room. Across the hall from yours..." Her voice faded, then came back sounding even weaker. "Taking more than I thought. I can't hold on much longer."

"You don't need to," Sasha told her. Gavin appeared in the doorway, and she motioned for him to come closer. "I'm about to release Sam's bond to Justine. She'll need you here. Stay with her."

Dylan stood in the hall, and Sasha slipped her hand into his. "I'll be careful," she murmured as they walked to the room where Justine lay.

The woman didn't stir. Her skin had gone past pale to take on a grayish hue, and Sasha shuddered when she touched her. She was cold, still. Almost lifeless. *Please don't let us be too late.*

It took a moment to draw Sam's energy out of the woman. It didn't feel as if Justine fought, but the resistance was there, brittle and greedy. When the bond finally gave, Sasha jerked and sought Dylan's eyes. "He knows I'm here. He feels me."

Dylan slid both hands onto her shoulders and squeezed. "I'm here. What's the easiest way for you to work through me? Do we need to be touching?"

"I don't know. I think so." She wanted to sink against him. Instead, she motioned him to a chair in the corner. "Sit. I'll need a minute to look over the incantation."

She opened the book as Dylan lifted the chair and set it down closer to the bed. "You can sit in the chair and I'll kneel in front of you."

"No, you need to—" She stuck the book under her arm and moved him to stand in front of her. "Stand here, and we can keep the chair in case we need it, okay?"

He didn't argue, but the incantation had already drawn her attention. She studied it carefully. When Gavin had translated the spell for them over dinner, it had been a mere curiosity. But now that she had to merge the words with her own magic and take control of Dylan, her hands shook.

Sasha didn't speak as she began to weave the spell, just laid a hand on the side of his neck and called to the magic sleeping inside her. It unfurled and reached out, calling for an echo inside Dylan.

Warmth came first, a trickle of power tinged with desire and curiosity, and she realized she'd touched the animal inside him. A soft grunt escaped Dylan, and when his eyes opened they were an eerie gold. "Sasha." Just one word, just her name, but it came out rough and a little wild, all the things Dylan never was.

She hesitated, and a heavy, expectant silence fell in the room. The spell allowed for distance; she could stay this way, inside him but separate, with one final wall between them. His power would be harder to command, but she could do it.

Their gazes locked, and the words whispered out of her. Magic swelled, and Sasha felt enveloped, open. Alive. Their hearts pounded in unison, and her fears suddenly seemed far away and unreal.

Dylan's fingers skimmed her arms as he lowered himself to his knees with effortless grace. His hands slipped to her hips, and he held her in place as he dropped his forehead to rest on her stomach. "Alan was right. You're more powerful than any of us."

She steeled herself against his disbelief and the scorn he leveled at himself for thinking he could protect her. "Dylan, I need you right now. Can you help me?"

He shifted his fingers to her waist and inhaled, and she felt the satisfaction that filled him as he rubbed his cheek over her shirt. One hand tightened, and the fabric bunched and lifted enough for his wrist to brush her skin.

Electricity shot through her. Sasha moaned, only too aware of his motivations. The same instinctive drive pulsed in her, reflected by the spell. She wanted to drop to the floor with him, to roll over and bare her belly. Submit and then explore, lips and hands and teeth, until she knew a hundred ways to make him come.

Dylan growled softly and edged her shirt higher. His warm breath hit her stomach, followed by the scalding heat of his tongue.

Her knees almost buckled. Sasha reached for Dylan, and only the sudden remembrance of the sick woman behind them stopped her. She cupped his face instead, urging him to look up and meet her eyes. "Dylan, we have to help Justine. *Now.*"

For several tense moments, nothing happened. Then he shivered, and the fierce intelligence she'd seen over the past week gathered slowly in his eyes. "Sit." His voice was hoarse, almost a growl. "In case you get dizzy."

"No, I have to be close. I'll be fine."

Dylan expressed his disapproval with another quiet noise and turned, tugging her lightly with him until she faced the bed. He knelt behind her, his forehead pressed to her back. "Take what you need," he whispered. "I'm strong enough for this."

Of course he was. Someone weak could never have done the things Dylan had done, taken the same chances. "Just hold on."

Sasha closed her hand around Justine's and touched her face. Almost instantaneously, a wave of dizzying rage hit her. They'd angered the vampire by taking Sam away, but he was curious too. He wanted to know—

"Who are you?"

One bracing breath, and Sasha isolated the rage and inquisitiveness. It coalesced, and Dylan tensed as she reached out and took it. Justine howled in pain as the bond stretched thin between them and snapped, shattering through Sasha and Dylan.

"I know you."

Dylan's body went tense, his fingers clenching on her hips. "It feels—" A rasping groan and he shuddered. "The magic feels like Helena's beta. Alan's second-in-command."

The magic lashed through her again, and this time it wasn't directed at her. It was directed at Dylan, and it felt hungry.

"No," she whispered, steeling herself to deflect the dark tendrils that reached for the man behind her. "You can't have him. He's mine."

Separately, either of them would have been vulnerable, but the vampire couldn't take them both. Still, it was all Sasha could do to hold his hunger at bay. His fascination drove him harder, made him clamp tight around her.

"Then I'll take you, little witch."

Dylan's fingers clenched on her waist, and his growl of challenge shook through her body, drowning her in a wash of possessive magic. It wasn't as strong as Gavin's or as overwhelming as Keith's, but Dylan's power felt steady and warm, a slow-burning fire that enfolded her in its protective grasp.

With Dylan's magic fueling hers, it was almost easy to twist free. She pulled back and brought Dylan with her, dragging them both from the grasping clutches of the vampire's spell.

An angry shriek followed her, along with a vicious promise. "I know you now. I know him. I'll drink his power and use it to bind you."

"No, you won't." It took every last bit of the energy inside them both, but Sasha isolated the spell and crushed it. The pain was blinding, driving her to her knees, and she clung to the edge of the bedspread, exhausted. Her chest heaved and she still couldn't breathe, but inside was silence. She and Dylan were free.

Chapter Three

Dylan woke with a pounding headache in a bed that smelled like Sasha.

He didn't want to open his eyes at first, and not just because sudden movements might send the pain in his skull spiraling from pounding to splitting. The soft pillow under his cheek carried an intoxicating scent, one he was all too quickly becoming addicted to.

Of course, he had to open his eyes, because Sasha wasn't the only woman he smelled in the room. He squinted blearily at the chair next to the bed, and Abby's features slowly came into focus. "Hey." His voice sounded rough and hoarse, though he couldn't remember why.

She set aside her magazine. "Welcome back. How are you feeling?"

"Where's Sasha?" The words came out before he could stop them, but the driving need to know overrode everything, even his headache. "Is she okay?"

Abby's concerned expression melted into mild surprise. "Sasha's fine. She and Cindy are across the hall in Justine's room."

Oh shit. Dylan tried to force himself upright, but his entire body felt like he'd been run over by a particularly large truck. He sagged back to the bed and rubbed his forehead. "God. How long have I been unconscious?"

"A few hours. Sasha's pretty spry, though, and Gavin seems to think it's because she sucked up most of your energy with that spell." She leaned forward and helped him sit. "That sounds dangerous, by the way."

"Less dangerous than her trying to do it on her own," he

muttered. The world swam a little as he swung his legs over the edge of the bed, but the headache was already fading, replaced by gnawing hunger. "Don't give me shit about it, Abby. We all owe her."

Abby steadied him. "I know we owe her, Dylan, maybe better than most. She saved my sister and my mate. Don't think I take that lightly."

"I just..." He closed his eyes and took a steadying breath. The instinct to talk to his friend was overridden by the knowledge that Abby was a woman with too many burdens already. His problems seemed pathetic in comparison. He executed a graceless change of subject and hoped she'd drop it. "How's Keith? Is he home by himself?"

"He said my hovering was getting on his nerves, and then he ran me out." She arched an eyebrow, the concern back on her face. "What were you going to say?"

He didn't want to tell her, but it was *Abby*. Brynn had been his little sister and even occasionally his partner-in-crime, but Abby had been the rock who'd kept him sane when his life seemed like nothing but a never-ending string of quiet wounds. "I'm worried about her. Sasha, I mean."

She studied him in silence. "Because of the magic, or because of the way she's being treated here?"

"Because I know what it's like to have something to prove." Dylan braced his elbows on his knees and rubbed his face again. "Shit, Abby. I've been fucking up everything I touch."

"Hey." She scooted her chair closer to the bed and touched his arm. "Why would you say that? Dylan, you saved my life, and Brynn's too. You're the only person I owe as much as Sasha, so stop it."

That gnawing guilt returned, magnified a hundredfold. "Your life wouldn't have needed saving if I'd kept you out of my shit, and neither would Brynn's. This damn town wouldn't be going to war and Sasha wouldn't be alone and hurt—" He bit off the words as another stab of hunger arced through him, this time strong enough to make the wolf rumble uncomfortably inside him. "Shit, I've got to eat. I'm starving."

"Let's go downstairs. Gavin's tending Sam. We can talk while you eat."

He made it to his feet and to the doorway without toppling over, which would have been more than his tender ego could take at this point. It felt cowardly to creep past the door to the guest bedroom where Justine lay, but with his head swimming and his body protesting, the last thing he could handle was facing Cindy *and* Sasha.

It was easy to see how Abby must have been annoying Keith, because she hovered all the way down to the kitchen, and made Dylan sit as she heaped a plate with food and heated it in the microwave.

Even an attempt to find himself something to drink was foiled, and he watched with a mixture of amusement and annoyance as she filled a glass with lemonade for him and set it on the table. "I'm starting to see Keith's point, Abby. I'm not an invalid."

"Shut up and let me do this." She placed his plate in front of him and sat across the table, her chin on her hands. "I'm pathetic, I know, but I can't help it."

The words brought back a memory of the first time he'd gone to Abby's apartment for dinner. Almost two years into their friendship, and it had been the warm, steady caring in her eyes that had finally overcome his determination to keep everyone at arm's length. He'd spent the hour before he arrived wandering in circles around Helena in an attempt to bore anyone who might be following him, knowing that leading any of his packmates to her house would put the Adler sisters in danger.

Abby and Brynn had been his secret, the one spot of brightness in his dull life. Over the years he'd even managed to fool himself into thinking they'd be safe from the horrors of his existence.

You selfish fucking bastard.

Abby had always been perceptive, and now was no exception. "Stop beating yourself up," she suggested, twirling the salt shaker between her palms, "and tell me what's going on between you and Sasha."

Dylan bought time with a hearty bite of food. He washed it down with the rest of the lemonade and met his friend's eyes. He still couldn't think of anything to say, so he told her the truth. "I don't have a fucking clue, Abby."

"Fair enough. Think Sasha does?"

He had only the haziest memory of her skin under his fingers and her magic curled around him, warm and curious and laced with nervous but honest desire. "I don't know."

"I see." Abby tapped her fingernails rhythmically on the table. "I made the mashed potatoes the way you like them. So much garlic Joe said he could smell them from his place."

Dylan knew Abby well enough to know the respite from her questions was temporary. So he took it with good grace, complimented her on the mashed potatoes and tried to pretend he had something in his head besides thoughts of a quiet, terrified witch.

He did a shitty job, but at least Abby was nice enough to let it be. *For now.*

She began to talk about nonsense things, probably just to fill the silence. The sound of soft footsteps on the stairs quieted her, and Abby looked up as Cindy came into the kitchen. "How's Justine?"

Cindy glanced at Dylan and began to unroll her shirtsleeves. "She's already getting stronger. I gave her more antibiotics for the infection, and she should be able to shake it now."

Dylan let out a breath he couldn't remember holding and relaxed. "Good. That's good. What about Sam?"

"Better." Cindy dragged out a chair and sank into it. "What about you, Dylan?"

He pointed to the empty plate in front of him. "I just needed some food, I guess. I'm fine."

She frowned. "You should eat more. You should also never pull another stunt like that one this afternoon. You could have *died.*"

Dylan stiffened at the no-nonsense command, one she probably expected him to obey without argument. And with good reason—he'd been obeying most of her offhand orders in the time he'd been in Red Rock, and had the sneaking suspicion that things would have gone a lot better between them if he'd fought a little more.

But the fight he was about to start was one he didn't need witnesses for. He glanced at Abby, hoping she'd read the silent plea in his eyes.

She was already rising from the table. "I've got to get home to check on Keith. Cindy, we'll see you tomorrow. Dylan...stop by, okay? When you get a chance."

"Of course. Tell Keith I feel his pain."

"Uh-huh."

Cindy watched Abby go, her shoulders tense. "Something you couldn't say in front of her?"

He hated seeing that wariness in her even more than he'd hated her anger. "This isn't really the time, but it's never the right time. And we both have things to say to each other."

Some of her tension melted into an obvious regret. "I'm sorry. I said some really shitty things to you the other day. Things you didn't deserve."

It would have felt a lot better to hear if he hadn't been starting to realize she'd been right. Dylan rubbed a hand over his face and fought a weary sigh. "There might have been some truth in it, Cindy. More than I wanted to hear."

She smiled a little, though her eyes grew bright with tears. "I didn't say I was wrong, just that I shouldn't have treated you so badly."

He groaned and closed his eyes, not sure he'd be able to take it if she cried. "You were right, but you were also lying. Things were going to hell before Sasha."

In true Cindy fashion, she admitted it readily. "Without a doubt. I think…I wanted both of us to be something we're not."

"Yeah." Her words should have hurt more. He'd expected them to, had been braced for the pain of being judged insufficient yet again, but the relief of having the truth between them outweighed everything else. He opened his eyes and hoped his answering smile didn't look bitter. "I'm not Joe or Keith. Hero isn't my default setting."

"Now that's a load of crap." Cindy stood and hesitated before leaning over to kiss his cheek. "She's really nice, Dylan. I'd feel a smidge better if she was heinous, or at least difficult, but…she's sweet."

Fear knotted in his stomach. "And you and I both know that sweet doesn't belong in our world."

She didn't argue or offer him platitudes. "Just promise me you'll be careful."

"How about I start by promising to eat? Baby steps, and all."

"Right." Cindy pulled a hand through her hair. "Gavin wants to see you. He said something about a trip to Maine."

Dylan took both of the plates Abby had set in front of him to the sink. "What's in Maine?"

"Damned if I know." She pulled a soda from the refrigerator. "But he mentioned Sasha too."

Gavin could have mentioned Sasha for any number of reasons that didn't involve sending her halfway across the country, which meant Dylan's immediate, irrational protective anger was out of place. He tilted his head and tried to remember everything he'd ever heard Gavin and Sam say about Maine. "Isn't there a town there? One of the sanctuaries? Except I'm almost certain no one from there showed up at the summit last month. Idaho, Alaska...Alabama, maybe? No Maine."

Cindy chewed her lower lip. "I'm not sure. I only caught a little of the conversation, and I wasn't really trying to listen."

"I guess there's only one way to find out." He pushed off the counter and grinned at her. "You should go rescue Keith. Abby's going to drive him out a window in about fifteen minutes."

"I hope not. I'm getting tired of patching him up."

The tension of the past weeks had eased enough that he felt comfortable squeezing her hand. "Thanks, Cindy."

"You're welcome." She stood on her toes to kiss his cheek. "Our grand affair might be over, but I still care about you. Don't forget that."

"Same goes to you." He smoothed her hair back and forced himself to acknowledge he was killing time to avoid the moment he'd have to go upstairs and face the same sort of kindly rejection from Sasha. "I suppose Gavin will come down here and drag my ass upstairs if I don't go under my own power, huh?"

Her expression gentled, and she kissed him again. "I think you'll be fine, Dylan. I'll see you later."

Soft footsteps on the stairs meant his time was up. He straightened and stepped back, fighting the sudden tension that filled him when he realized the tread was too light to be Gavin's. "Bye, Cindy."

She made it out the back door just as Sasha appeared in the archway between the kitchen and the hall. "Hi." Bare feet peeked out from under the hem of her jeans as she fidgeted. "Gavin wants to talk to us. He said to wait for him down here."

His body stirred at the sight of her, giving lie to all his stupid rationalizations about why Cindy's rejection hadn't hurt more. He cleared his throat and turned to the fridge. "I was going to get something to drink. You want anything?"

"I thought I'd make some coffee." Sasha hesitated with her hand on the pantry door. "When Gavin's done with us, maybe we can talk."

The words killed his lust rather handily. "Sure."

She glanced at the empty doorway, as if judging the time they might have alone. "I owe you an apology, Dylan. A huge one."

"Don't." It came out forcefully enough to startle her, and he gritted his teeth and moderated his tone. "I've already had two lectures on how dangerous the spell was, but you didn't hurt me."

Sasha gripped the coffee can so hard her fingers turned white. "Not that. Justine and Sam needed help, and we had no other options. I meant..." She turned away, and the can hit the counter with a metallic thud. "I shouldn't have grabbed you the way I did back at the apartment."

He was behind her without realizing he'd moved, driven to find some way to ease her distress. His hand shook a little as he touched her shoulder, just a light, careful brush of his fingers. "It's okay. And I'm sorry I snapped at you."

She tensed under his hand, and her heart raced. "I told myself I was kissing you so you would know that I wanted you. So you wouldn't be surprised when I cast the spell."

"Secrets are hard to keep around werewolves." He let his hand rest on her upper arm and swiped his thumb lightly over her shoulder. "But you probably learned more about me than I did about you. It's all a little fuzzy."

"I want to do it again." She finally turned to face him, her gaze focused on his mouth. "I know it's a bad idea, and I want to kiss you anyway."

It was wrong to be thinking about kissing her in Gavin's kitchen with the faint scent of Cindy's shampoo still on his fingers. It was wrong, and he was wrong, and it didn't stop him from lifting his hand to touch her cheek. Her skin was warm and soft, and it was all too easy to remember how her lips had felt under his for the brief moment he'd given in and kissed her. Hungry, needy. Maybe a little unsure and a lot nervous, but those he could fix. Those he could—

His mouth was only inches from hers when someone cleared his throat. Loudly.

Dylan jerked back and silently cursed himself for being so fixated that he hadn't heard Gavin's footsteps. With Cindy there'd been no such problem; as intense as their conversation had been, he hadn't been oblivious to the world around him.

Gavin sat at the table as Sasha grabbed the carafe from the coffee maker and rinsed it in the sink, her cheeks flaming. The alpha pulled a pack of cigarettes from his pocket and stuck one in his mouth, though he didn't light it. "There's a vampire in Helena, a strong one, and we need to find out how to deal with that."

At least I'm not getting a lecture. Even though he'd probably end up with one eventually, Dylan wasn't going to question a temporary reprieve. He slid into the seat across from Gavin and turned his mind firmly away from Sasha and all thoughts of kissing her. "We found something in one of those books. About how a vampire and werewolf can work together. It would explain how Alan's second got enough power to hold the pack. He was a lot weaker than Alan."

"An old friend of mine could help, but I haven't been able to get in touch with him." Gavin tossed the cigarette on the table. "Adam isn't much for modern methods of communication, but he's too set in his ways to have moved. I need someone to go to Maine and—"

"I'll go." Sasha turned on the coffee maker and slung a dishtowel over her shoulder. "It might be better for everyone if I got out of town for a while."

All of the pain that had been suspiciously absent during Cindy's rejection hit Dylan in the gut. With interest. It made his next words too blunt and too raw. "That's bullshit."

"No, it isn't." She met his gaze steadily. "But I can't go alone, Dylan. Can you come with me?"

Pain changed to pleasure with a speed that made him dizzy. He jerked his gaze back to Gavin and tried not to let it show in his voice. "Is there a catch?"

Gavin nodded once. "Adam lives near Bedagi Creek. It's one of the sanctuaries, Irene and Lawrence's place. They couldn't make it to the summit, so I'm sending Joe and Brynn out to give them the short version."

The thought of Brynn trying to challenge her way through a pack that didn't live in terror of Joe's ire was enough to make Dylan queasy. "Is Brynn ready for that? I don't know if you heard, but she started a damn bar fight the other night."

Gavin looked ill, as well. "She's different from everyone else, just like—" He broke off and swore.

"Just like me. I know." Sasha looked pale, and Dylan had to avert his eyes to keep from coming to his feet and snatching her up in a comforting hug.

"I'm sorry, Sasha." The alpha rose and paced across the kitchen. "You haven't earned this, but you have to understand what some of the wolves here have been through..."

"I do understand," she said quickly. "When should I be ready to leave?"

"When should *we* be ready to leave?" Dylan corrected without looking at Sasha. If he saw the pain in her eyes that he thought he heard in her voice... *You have got to get a grip, man. Get a fucking grip.*

"Tomorrow." Gavin's face was creased with worry. "Brynn can't fly, so the four of you will have to drive."

It was one more bump in the road, one more task he had to complete before he could get his quiet life. So Dylan nodded. "Sasha and I can go over to the library and see if there are any books that might be good to bring. Or maybe not...is your friend a Lorekeeper?"

"No." The coffee wasn't finished brewing, but Gavin took a mug from the drain rack and filled it. "He's a vampire."

Chapter Four

Sasha folded one last shirt and tucked it into the open bag on the bed. She'd planned on going back to Gavin's to gather her clothes, but she hadn't realized just how many of her meager belongings had made their way to the small apartment over the bar. Everything she needed was there, and she didn't want to think too much about what that really meant.

A deep, bracing breath gave her the courage to wander down the hall to the small library, where Dylan had been methodically sorting through texts and journals they might need for the trip. She leaned against the doorframe and allowed herself a few moments to watch the smooth flex of muscle under his T-shirt as he moved stacks of books into boxes. "I've finished packing. Need some help?"

He glanced up with a ready smile. "Can you remember which book we found that history of the Devil's Half-Acre in? It was about vampires in New England, I think, but I can't remember where it was."

She closed her eyes and tried to recall. "It had a green cover with gold print, and the bottom part of the spine was torn."

"Green cover, gold print... Green cov—aha!" When she opened her eyes he was holding up a book. "This one?"

"That one." Her legs were shaking, so she eased a box out of the way and sat on the corner of the desk. "I never got the chance to tell you why kissing you is a bad idea."

Dylan froze with the book still held aloft, and a brittle wariness filled his eyes. "I don't think kissing me is ever a bad idea, but I could be biased."

Her stomach twisted at his expression. She wanted to change the subject, run, or maybe even kiss him anyway, but she needed to be honest with him. "I'm not staying in Red Rock, Dylan. As soon as I'm square with everyone, I'll be leaving."

"Square with everyone?" He set the book on the table and watched her. "Jesus Christ, Sasha. Do you think you owe someone in this town something?"

"Yes." She rubbed her arms to dispel her goose bumps. "Gavin and Sam. Keith. A-and you."

Pain flashed in his eyes. "You saved Brynn and Keith. We owe *you*."

"I'm not explaining this very well." Nerves always made her clumsy, even in her speech. "It's the old tradition, the one Maritza was teaching me. Keith saved my life, and I did the same for him. That's the way it goes. But if my debts are left open, if they're not repaid, like with you..." She struggled for words that would make him understand. "It doesn't matter if you expect it, or even if you want it. Until we're even, my life is yours."

"Why do you think you owe me, Sasha?" The words were compassionate. "Because of the spell? I did that to help Gavin and Sam as much as to keep you safe. It's nothing."

She blinked at him, confused. "You killed Alan Matthews. You kept him from dragging me back to Helena, from—from doing the things he said he was going to do to me. And I know you didn't do it *for me*, but that doesn't matter."

Dylan moved around the table, every movement so careful he had to be trying not to startle her. He lifted his hands and cupped her cheeks. "You do not owe anyone for saving you from Alan Matthews. You were supposed to be safe here. You were supposed to be protected. He came here to hurt us, and you suffered for it. We owe you."

His words relieved her of her debt, but Sasha had a hard time concentrating on them. His hands were warm on her skin, and he was so close... She laid her palm on his chest, and her own body responded to the strong, fast beating of his heart. "Dylan."

"Shh." His thumb swept over her lips. "Don't go to Maine to pay off a debt. It could be dangerous, and you don't need more danger. You deserve to be safe for a while."

She couldn't breathe, and her body throbbed. "Are you going?"

"If that's what Gavin needs me to do." His mouth was so

close she could feel his breath. "He's my alpha now."

"Then quit trying to talk me out of it. I'm going too." Sasha pulled him closer, her hands shaking. She didn't mean to speak, but the words tumbled out anyway. "I can't stop thinking about you."

"Funny, I was thinking the same thing today." His thumb drifted down to her chin, and he tilted her head back. "Can I kiss you? Even if it's a bad idea?"

How could it ever be a bad idea? All she could remember was how it felt during the spell, being so intimately entwined with him. So she stared at his mouth and answered with a soft, pleading noise. "I want you inside me again."

Dylan groaned and pressed his forehead to hers. "Jesus Christ, Sasha." His fingers crept around the back of her head and sank into her hair, and then his mouth was on hers, slow but hot.

Sensation streaked through her, instant and undeniable. She tilted her head and arched against his chest, trying to deepen the kiss, and he responded with a low moan and a teasing swipe of his tongue along her lower lip.

One arm slid around her, and he picked her up. When he sank to the sofa, she wound up on his lap, her knees digging into the cushions on either side of him. The position made it easier to take control of the kiss, and she did, coaxing his lips apart to seek his tongue with hers.

She felt his fingers on her neck, and a soft growl rumbled up from his chest as his other hand settled at her lower back. He kissed her for several long moments before easing back to nip at her lower lip. "Kissing me isn't so bad, is it?"

"I never said it was bad." She bared her throat and rocked down against his hips as the hot pleasure inside her gathered into a gnawing hunger. "It's really good."

"Don't sound surprised." A tiny tug at the back of her neck and she felt his breath feathering over her chin. He dropped a kiss to her jaw, then another just under it. "I'm pretty damn good at kissing."

Sasha shuddered, her entire body tight and aching. "I'm not surprised. I'm turned on." She lifted her head and captured his mouth, this time in a demanding, almost rough kiss.

He met her aggression with a low noise and easy skill, but too soon he softened the kiss. His fingers crept under the edge of her shirt as his lips slid back to her chin, and this time farther to her throat. The wet warmth of his tongue tickled over her pulse. "I know you're turned on. I can hear your heart."

Longing shot through her, and she clutched his head to keep his mouth close to her skin. "I can feel yours." It pounded under her hand, even harder than before, and Sasha wiggled, trying to ease the empty ache inside her.

"Fuck." His fingers tightened on her hip at the same moment his teeth closed on the side of her neck. He released her after a moment and rested his forehead on her shoulder with a low moan. "Okay, the wiggling is going to kill me."

Not moving was killing *her*, but she stilled and feathered a trail of kisses over his cheek to his neck. "I'll stop if you promise to keep kissing me."

Warm lips brushed her temple as his hand swept higher under her shirt. His fingers rubbed lazy figure eights over her back, and he chuckled. "I'm going to keep kissing you until you tell me I can't."

Cool air on the bare skin of her lower back broke the sensual haze, and she tensed. He had no idea that the flesh under her clothes was as scarred as her face, but he'd find out soon enough if he kept tracing his hands over her.

"No." Sasha jerked her shirt down and scrambled off his lap. Again, she couldn't breathe, this time from rising panic instead of passion. It would be unmistakable, the rage and pity in his eyes, and she couldn't bear to see it.

He froze with his hands out at his sides. "What's wrong?"

"Nothing." The lie was automatic. Sasha wrapped her arms around her midsection and backed away. "I need to go."

"I'm sorry. Don't go. I'll call someone to come walk you home."

"I don't—" It wasn't fair to let him think he'd done something wrong when the problem was hers. "It's not you, Dylan."

"The attack?"

Of course he'd have already thought of it. Her cheeks burned, and she tugged her shirt over her head before she could think better of it.

Dylan's gaze drifted from her face to her shoulders and then her torso. She watched his eyes move as he studied the scars on her body.

He didn't say a word. Instead he slid from the couch to his knees and turned his back on her as he removed his own shirt.

He had scars too, raised ridges of flesh across his left shoulder and down his back. Sasha moved before she realized it, sinking to her knees behind him. She shivered and brushed her fingertips across one prominent line. "What did they do?"

"Most things don't leave scars." His voice was no more than a hoarse whisper. "But if they want you to remember, they use magical weapons. Like the one Keith got stabbed with."

His skin was hot under her hands, and against her chest when she slipped her arms around him. "You hurt so much." She could barely speak past the lump of pain in her throat. "I want to make it stop."

He covered her hands with his. "Now you know how I feel. I don't want you to hurt."

"My scars are all on the outside." She kissed the spot between his ear and his jaw. "But you can't see most of yours, can you?"

"I don't know. They may not be visible, but seems like a lot of people see them." He turned his head just enough for her forehead to rest against his cheek. "Cindy's not angry with you, you know. She'll never admit it, but she's glad. Now she doesn't have to figure out how to get rid of me."

It was unthinkable, that any woman would want to be rid of him. "I'm worried about you, not Cindy."

"I'll be fine. I always am."

The words were practiced and hollow. "You'll survive, because you always do. But are you really fine?"

He exhaled softly. "Honestly, they've meant the same thing for a long time."

Pain twisted in her again, and tears burned her eyes as she hugged him more tightly. "I'm sorry."

"It's all right, Sasha." He turned enough to put his back to the couch and held out his arms. "Can I hold you for a few minutes?"

She hurried into his lap and buried her face in his neck, unable to silence her relieved moan. "I need this." To be comforted, protected. Safe.

He smoothed his fingers through her hair as his other arm cradled her against him. "Me too. In Helena, I couldn't get close to people without putting them in danger. I've missed it."

She realized with a start that, though her arousal had subsided, she still wanted to stay close to him, even if it meant he thought of her as weak and fragile. "I didn't mean to upset you before."

"When?"

Sasha groaned and closed her eyes. "If I've upset you so many times you don't know what I'm talking about, I need to apologize more."

His fingers slid through her hair as he chuckled. "You haven't really upset me at all."

"At Gavin's house. You thought I offered to go because I wanted to get away."

"Oh." Another slow pass of his hand, but this time it settled on her shoulder. "I wouldn't blame you. Life hasn't been easy for you here. You deserve better. I wish I could make it better."

You have. She bit back the words and concentrated on the warm weight of his hand on her skin. "There has to be a place for me. Just haven't found it yet."

"Shh." Dylan's fingers settled under her chin and he tilted her head up. His thumb swiped over her cheek, and it was only then that she realized she was crying. "When we get back from Maine, I'll help you look."

Mortification trumped her desire to stay in his arms. She crawled out of his lap and reached for her shirt. "If we're leaving so soon, I have a few more things to do."

Dylan rose to his knees and gathered up his own shirt. "And I have to go over to Joe's place. Do you want me to wait and walk you back to Gavin's?"

She'd rather have her breakdown in private. "No, I'll be okay. Later."

But Dylan frowned. "There are a few more things in the library to pack up. Do you think you could do that? Gavin can probably stop by on his way back from Joe's."

"I can handle it, Dylan." The lump in her throat grew. "Please stop."

"Sorry." He tugged the shirt over his head and ran his fingers through his disheveled hair in an attempt to smooth it. Every line of his body was tense as he started for the door. "I'll see you tomorrow then. If you need— Have a good night."

Even her bruised pride couldn't stop her words. "Thank you for everything. It means a lot."

He glanced back at her, his hand on the doorknob. The look that crept into his eyes was that of a lover, warm and full of promise with just a hint of challenge. "It's my pleasure."

Sasha was shaking when the door closed behind him. She'd been so sure his attraction to her was one of instinct, of the pleasure derived from taking care of someone who needed him. But if he felt more for her than protectiveness...

She touched her lips. There was time. No need to rush into anything when they could both take it slow and figure out exactly was developing between them.

No need to rush at all.

Joe rubbed his chin. "You know I love you, Gavin, but this assignment of ours? It's bullshit."

"It's not bullshit," Gavin snapped. "You need to check out the situation in Bedagi Creek, and Dylan and Sasha need to find Adam Dubois."

"So we're going to road trip? It'll take two weeks, and that's assuming we drive there and straight back."

In Helena, being trapped in a room with two strong, annoyed alphas would have ended with bruises at best, and broken bones on a normal day. Dylan stared into the mug of black coffee Joe had poured for him and cleared his throat. "I know it's at least partly about getting Sasha out of town."

"And the rest of it's about getting Brynn out of town." Gavin ignored Joe's snarl and refilled his own mug. "If it were just about the constant challenges, I could handle it. But people associate her with Sasha's magic now, and they're scared. Scared enough to cause problems."

"You could slap them down," Joe argued. "You're still the fucking *alpha*."

"I know who I am!" With the roar came a sharp lash of energy strong enough to force the air from Dylan's chest, and Joe backed away. "I'm responsible for everyone in this town. *Everyone*. I cannot afford to drive people out of sanctuary because I can't be bothered to show them how stupid their prejudices are."

Joe spoke in a strained whisper. "Isn't that what you're doing to Brynn? To Sasha? Driving them out of this sanctuary?"

It took every scrap of willpower Dylan had to lift his gaze to Joe's. "Not forever. If we go, we give Gavin a chance to settle things without someone ending up hurt. And Brynn may be tough enough to handle being in a town where people fear her, but it's killing Sasha. She's better off leaving for a while."

The righteous anger in Joe's eyes faded a bit. "She wants to go?"

At least Dylan could answer the question honestly. "Yes. And I want to go with her. I may as well have challenged everyone in that bar a few nights ago when I told them to back down. No one pushed it, but..." But eventually the status he'd gained by rescuing Abby and killing Matthews would fade. He'd be a mid-level wolf, a newcomer to the pack, challenging stronger wolves. Over a witch.

A witch who would add every fight, every word, every goddamn scrap of kindness to some mental balance sheet as a debt she owed him.

Joe ran a rough hand through his dark hair and sighed. "If we leave first thing in the morning, I can push it hard and make Laramie, maybe even Cheyenne before we stop."

Gavin lit a cigarette. "I don't know how long you'll have to stay, so get out there as quick as you can and take care of business. When you're done, we can decide whether you should hurry home."

Dylan glanced from Joe to Gavin. "I know part of what's got Brynn so riled is that she's protective of Sasha. Maybe if Sasha and I go on our own it would be enough. We can make contact with your friend, and Joe would be here in case there's more trouble."

"I have to go." Joe's mug thumped down on the counter.

Gavin's jaw tightened. "The alphas from Bedagi Creek didn't come to the summit. I told you that much. But when I called Irene looking for Adam, there was something wrong."

Dylan felt tension arc through him. "How wrong?"

"She didn't say anything overt, but it felt like she was asking for help."

His fingers tightened around the coffee mug until he was afraid it would shatter. It was too easy to picture bringing Sasha to Helena, to imagine what would happen to her when one of the corrupt dominant wolves decided Dylan had stepped out of line and needed to be punished—

The mug shattered.

Neither man seemed surprised by his reaction. Joe retrieved a kitchen towel and began to gather the broken stoneware. Gavin crushed out his cigarette in the ashtray on the table and leveled a serious look on Dylan. "Not like that, son. If I thought it was dangerous, I wouldn't let her near the place."

Dylan wiped his hands on the towel Joe offered him without taking his gaze from Gavin. "Sasha needs to stay out of werewolf politics. Even the not-so-dangerous kind."

"Which is why you two will be looking for Adam, not trying to figure out what's wrong with the pack there." The alpha propped his elbows on the table and leaned forward. "I stopped by the apartment on the way here, Dylan, and I told her all this. She still wants to go."

"Then I'll go with her." Dylan looked at Joe. "What about Brynn? What does she think?"

Joe tossed the broken shards of the mug in the trash. "She could use some time away, but she won't admit it. That's tantamount to abandoning Abby, and you know the Adler sisters."

"Brynn's never been good at telling Abby to mind her own business. Abby smothers her and Brynn gets pissed and snaps, then she feels bad and lets Abby smother her more to make up for it. They've been doing it for years."

"Sounds about right." Joe handed Dylan a fresh mug of coffee. "Can you and Sasha be ready by morning?"

"Yeah. We packed up the most useful books. I can read in the car if I need to."

"Around five, then. We'll get breakfast on the road."

Dylan nodded his acknowledgment before taking a sip of coffee. It was still black and too strong, but he drank it anyway. He needed it for what he had to do next. "Gavin, do you mind walking back to the bar with me?"

"Sure." Gavin rose and clasped Joe's hand in a firm shake. "Have a good trip. Check in from time to time."

"We will."

Dylan nodded at Joe. "See you bright and early."

"Early," Joe corrected with a grin. "Probably not bright yet."

Outside on the porch, Dylan sucked in a deep breath of

cool night air. "How was Sasha when you were there? Did she seem okay?"

Gavin ran his hand over the railing as he stepped off the porch. "Well enough. She was busy packing."

"Gavin..." Dylan curled his hand around the balcony and closed his eyes. "Hell, I don't know how to say this. I don't even know what I want to say. I just know I'm fucking terrified."

"What do your instincts tell you?"

After the last ten years, he'd learned one lesson so many times it had superseded instinct. Maybe it had *become* instinct. "That anyone I care about is in danger."

"No one wants to use Sasha to hurt you, and no one wants to hurt her because of you. But you know that." Gavin's eyes held a haunted look. "The question is, would it matter? If being with her meant endangering her, what then? Not what would you do, but...could you stop? Could you walk away, satisfied that you were protecting her and let that be it? Or would you still want her?"

He tried to imagine it. To imagine that sending Sasha to Maine alone would be the only way to keep her safe, and that he'd have to stay in Red Rock without her. He thought of the way her eyes lit up when she wrestled some new fact out of a dusty book, her good-natured smile and the way she'd felt under his hands and mouth.

He imagined never seeing her again, and it hurt. His chest felt tight and he shook his head slowly. "I'd still want her."

"Then you have to trust in that." The alpha laid a hand on Dylan's shoulder. "I've seen you look at her. You could replace her, fill that instinctive need to take care of someone, but I don't think it'd be the same."

Trusting his instincts would have gotten him killed in Helena. *And you're spending too much time worrying about what would have happened in Helena.* Escaping his past wouldn't do a damn bit of good if he kept living in it.

He squared his shoulders and opened his eyes to meet Gavin's gaze. "Thank you."

The alpha nodded. "If you're still worried, talk to Sasha. Figure it out together."

Another slippery slope. Sasha knew there were scars on his heart, but she'd never understand how many and how deep. Some of them would heal, but not all of them. He only had to look at the shadows in Cindy's eyes seven years after her rescue to know how long those wounds could take to heal. More terrifying was the pain that tightened Sam's eyes sometimes, even though she'd escaped from Helena long before Dylan had been born.

And they were strong wolves. Alphas with the will to fight and the stubbornness to overcome any obstacle. If they couldn't fight free of the past...

Gavin still watched him, so he tried to make a joke. "I haven't dated in a decade. I'm a little out of practice."

The older man's expression remained somber. "You could talk to Samantha," he suggested finally. "I may run a sanctuary here but, in a way, I'm at a disadvantage with a lot of you. The horrors of my life have been straightforward."

The horrors of Dylan's life had been anything but, which was the problem. "My life sucked, Gavin, but it's an insult to people like Cindy and Sam to pretend I had it all that bad."

"Having your own pain doesn't lessen anyone else's. That's the worst part of what the alphas like Matthews do." He stepped back and surveyed the forest beyond Joe's front yard. "It's insidious, Dylan. How they try to make you think it's not so bad, and they could make it so much worse if they wanted."

"They could have. They did, sometimes, just to remind us. Because otherwise we'd run off to places like this, and they'd lose their easy income and grunt labor."

"It's a perversion." Gavin bit out the words. "Being alpha is about doing what's best for your pack, not for yourself."

"It is here." Dylan stepped off the stairs and stood next to Gavin. "That's why I'll go to Maine. That's why I'll help you fight however I can. This is the way it should be."

"Yes." He started down the drive, beckoning for Dylan to follow. "Maritza intended to settle here, you know. Sasha's mentor. She felt that the prejudices and bad blood could be overcome."

Sasha didn't agree, and Dylan couldn't even blame her. Not after the past month. "What do you think?"

"I hope so. I think they have to be, if any of us are going to survive."

He had to believe in Gavin. He had to believe in the alpha's ability to realize his hopes, to bring change and understanding to his pack, because Gavin wasn't just an alpha. He was

Dylan's alpha, the first one he'd had who made him feel safer with his presence. The first one whose trust and respect he wanted. Gavin was the steady strength that had been missing all those years in Helena, the one who could make it possible for Dylan to live a life without terror and misery.

Red Rock was the first home Dylan had found in a decade...and Sasha wanted to leave it. For good.

Chapter Five

Sasha wiggled the key in the handle and almost stumbled when the door yielded suddenly. "I thought motels used plastic key cards these days."

"Guess it depends on how old they are." Brynn followed her into the room, both of their bags under one arm and a sack of snack food from the gas station clutched in the other hand. "This place doesn't look all that classy."

It really didn't, though at least it looked clean. The sparse room held two queen beds with wildly patterned bedspreads, a television and a battered desk. "It's not the Ritz, but I'm too tired to care, even if I would normally."

"Mmm." Brynn dropped both bags just inside the door as her gaze jumped around the room. She moved to the small closet and peeked inside, then wandered to the bathroom and pushed open the door. "The whole place reeks of bleach."

She could smell only the faintest trace, but Sasha nodded. "You want the bed by the bathroom or the door?" She didn't know if it mattered, but the careful way Brynn surveyed the room told her it might.

Brynn's gaze drifted toward the wall that separated their room from the one Dylan and Joe occupied. "I'll take the one by the door."

Quick escape or first in line to defend against an intruder? "I'm too tired to eat, but I could use a shower. Did you want one first?"

"You go ahead. I'm starving."

"Okay, thanks."

Sasha took her time. Even with the rigors of travel, she already felt lighter just being away from Red Rock. Free. Out here, the worst she'd had to endure was the way people stared at her face, and most people averted their gazes quickly, not wanting to be caught gaping.

Of course, she could never tell Gavin or Sam that. They'd taken her in, and they'd tried so hard to make her feel at home, but she didn't expect them to defend or protect her at the expense of their own. That wasn't the way of things, and she understood that.

She'd come closest to telling Dylan. He alone knew that she planned to leave permanently as soon as she could and, ironically, he was the only thing that made her want to stay.

The towels were scratchy. She bypassed them completely and wrapped up in her robe, depending on the thin cotton to dry her. Her hair would take a while, but she could brush it dry if need be.

"Brynn, do you—?" When she stepped out of the bathroom, it wasn't Brynn but Dylan sitting on the bed by the door. "Oh. Sorry, I didn't realize you'd come in."

His gaze swept up her body to her face, and she could have sworn he blushed before he jerked his attention back to the open book in front of him. "Sorry. Brynn's...antsy. Their bond works better with proximity, so she's over with Joe in the other room. I'm pretty sure neither of us want to disturb them before breakfast."

"Oh." Sasha turned to the dresser and reached for her hairbrush, but the sight of herself in the mirror stopped her cold. Her skin was flushed from the hot water, and her wet hair had soaked her robe until the cotton covering her breasts was transparent and clinging to her nipples. "Damn it."

He cleared his throat. "Need me to go outside for a bit? I might run down to the vending machine, since Brynn has all the snacks."

"No. No, it's okay. I just need..." She snatched her bag from the bed she'd claimed and clutched it to her chest. "I'll be right back."

It was hard to dress in the steamy bathroom, especially with her skin still damp, but Sasha managed to wiggle into her nightclothes. When she returned to the room, Dylan still sat on the bed, staring intently at his book. "What are you reading?"

"That book about the history of vampires in Maine. I had no idea it was the epicenter of vampire activity. Seems a little surreal." He glanced up at her and grinned. "I keep picturing vampires in snow pants and parkas trying to chip the ice off their truck windows."

She stretched out on her stomach across the end of her bed. "I wouldn't know. Most of the vampires I met in Europe tended to hibernate all winter. But they were older. Frail, I think."

Dylan nodded. "If you read between the lines in these books, it seems like most of them get that way. Every time anyone talks about a vampire getting a lot of power, it pretty much ends up with a discussion of how a bunch of people got together and killed him."

"Or tried, anyway. Maritza had this one friend who'd been run out of every county in Ireland."

"A vampire friend?" One of his eyebrows shot up. "Are vampires friendly with wizards and witches?"

"No." Fond memories of the no-nonsense woman who'd taken her in as a young teen washed over her. "But Maritza was never one for rules. She befriended Keith, after all."

Dylan closed the book with a great deal of care and set it on the mattress before turning to look at her. "Tell me about her."

"She was my grandmother's best friend." Sasha shut her eyes and immediately called up the image of leathery, blue-veined hands sorting herbs and tracing out runes. "My grandmother died when I was ten, and my parents the next year. Car accident." She rolled to her back and stared at the ceiling as she continued. "The court placed me with my other grandmother. My dad's mom. She spent two years thinking I was crazy or maybe possessed. Maritza was in Italy, but when she found out what had happened... She came and got me."

The corner of the bed sank slightly and Dylan's hand slid over hers. "And she taught you magic?"

"Along with my mother and Gram." She clutched his hand. "But they weren't very practiced, and there were a lot of things I didn't know when Maritza took me to Europe."

"I haven't met many witches, but you seem pretty strong to me." He rubbed his thumb over the backs of her fingers in a soft caress that sent a shiver through her. "I can feel you. Your energy, or power, or whatever it is. Like another werewolf."

"Yeah." She rolled to her side. He was warmth, a flame, and she was drawn inexorably to him. "It's the same sort of magic, just working in different ways."

"Show me how it works. Show me something magical." His voice had turned decidedly husky.

"Magical? You mean like this?" She watched him as she whispered for darkness and then light. The room dimmed, the lamps flickering and dying. When the room lit again, it was from tiny pinpoints of light that shimmered to life between them and floated up and around the bed.

Dylan stretched out beside her, his hand still curled around hers. The flickering lights cast most of his face in gently changing shadows, but she could see the slow grin that curved his lips.

It was still there when he rolled to face her and lifted a hand to cup her cheek. "Can I kiss you?"

"No." She leaned over him, her heart thumping painfully, and covered his hand with hers. "Because I'm going to kiss you."

His breath tickled her cheek as he laughed. "A perfectly acceptable alterna—"

She cut him off with an open-mouthed kiss. It was too hard, too aggressive, and Sasha didn't give a damn. He'd spent the last week tormenting her with his proximity, his smiles and the heat of his body.

A groan escaped him a moment before his hand slid around her waist. He dragged her tight against his body, so tight there was no question that he was already aroused. His other hand came up to tangle in her wet hair as he parted his lips under hers.

She felt the lights above them explode and drift down in remnants of magic. "I need you." The words were hungry and muffled, spoken into his mouth. "Dylan."

"Shh." His tongue swiped along her lower lip and he nipped lightly at it before rolling them over. She ended up on her back with Dylan over her, his weight braced on his hands. He kissed her gently at first, and then harder as his hips settled over hers.

She tried to remember the last time she'd had sex. It had to have been Spain, the wizard in Madrid she always called when she passed through. The memory slipped through her fingers, hazy and finally driven to obsolescence by Dylan's tongue slicking over hers. It had been another life, a different woman from the one arching her hips off the bed now.

Dylan lifted his head and nuzzled her cheek. His breath skated over her skin, and he lowered his lips to her ear. "Do you have any idea how badly I want to touch you?" A rock of his hips, and he groaned softly. "I've dreamt about it."

Her entire body tightened in anticipation, and Sasha slipped her hands under the hem of his T-shirt. "What did you dream? Tell me."

He scraped his teeth over her ear. "I touched you." He shifted his weight and got one hand to her waist and under her shirt. His mouth left a hot trail of kisses as he traced a path to where her pulse fluttered underneath her skin. She felt the wet warmth of his tongue just before his groan vibrated over her skin. "Tasted you."

It was positively poetic next to the sweaty, feverish dreams she'd been having. "Mine pretty much revolved around fucking you until neither one of us could move."

His fingers tightened around her waist, and he closed his teeth on her throat with a low growl.

She half expected to freeze up, for the bite to bring memories of her imprisonment crashing in on her. But it brought only pleasure, the kind that exploded through her in a shower of hot sparks and put her earlier light show to shame. "Yes..."

He licked the spot before moving down her body, dropping a kiss to her collarbone and another to the hollow at the base of her throat. "Tell me," he murmured against her skin as his lips traced the upper curve of her breast left bare by the thin white tank top. "What were you dreaming about that made you moan in your sleep?"

Sasha was beyond embarrassment, and his words drew only a throaty laugh of amusement. "You heard me, then. I wondered." His tongue flicked over her skin, and she gasped. "You. Always you, naked beside me. Or—or behind me."

"Over you, under you..." He caught the neckline of her shirt between his teeth and dragged it down with another playful growl.

The strap of her tank top slid down her arm as he bared her breast, and she dug her nails into his lower back. "Inside me."

He froze with his lips poised above her nipple and closed his eyes as a groan escaped him, this one dismayed instead of aroused. "Fuck. I don't have condoms."

Neither did she. The only place to get them in Red Rock was from Cindy's clinic, and Sasha would have gladly suffered celibacy rather than ask Dylan's ex. "Does it matter? Aren't there bases?" Her own voice sounded desperate, yearning. "Let's run around some bases."

"Oh yeah. As many as we can hit." He flashed her a hot look, his dark brown eyes looking nearly black in the dim light, and he reached for the hem of her shorts. "And tomorrow I'll buy condoms."

"Tomorrow." Her shorts and panties hit the floor, and she held her breath when he drew her legs apart. Then he stroked his hand down the center of her body, and she forgot to breathe altogether.

He didn't waste time. His mouth landed on the inside of her knee, and she felt the soft scrape of his teeth as he growled softly. The next kiss landed on her inner thigh, and his tongue swept over her skin as he pushed her shirt up high enough to bare her breasts.

When he spoke, his voice held an edge she'd never heard before. "How do you feel about running second and third bases together?"

"Wait, together—" Her heart skipped a beat, and she shoved up on her elbows. "You mean you covering them simultaneously, or both of us...?"

Dylan's hoarse laugh was strained. He laid a hand on the center of her chest and urged her back to the bed. "Uh-uh. I'm the only one up to bat at the moment, sweetheart." He cupped her breast as his breath tickled her inner thigh. "Just...close your eyes."

It was an order, and Sasha shivered as she complied. A moment later Dylan's mouth landed on her, his tongue tracing and teasing over her aching flesh. The pleasure was sharp and sweet, and she choked out a moan as her eyes snapped open. "Oh, God."

He just made a low noise of approval and caught her nipple between his fingers. Sasha grabbed his shoulders, and he responded by flicking his tongue over her clit, bringing her hips off the bed.

It took her a second to realize that the needy cries echoing through the dark room were hers. *Of course they are,* she thought fuzzily. Only she and Dylan were there, and Dylan couldn't scream with his mouth on her, his tongue stroking her faster with every passing heartbeat.

One hand held her hips still as he caressed her, his touch determined, relentless, as if he could sense every twist of need inside her and give her exactly what she needed. He sped up and slowed down, drawing her toward the brink and then holding her off, until she was shaking uncontrollably.

Orgasm seized her suddenly, almost violently, and Sasha chanted Dylan's name as pleasure swelled through her. Each wave was stronger than the last, and he barely gave her the chance to catch her breath before he eased two fingers inside her and started all over again.

"Dylan!" Her voice had gone hoarse, and she clenched both hands in his hair and tugged. "God, right—right there..."

He hummed his approval and centered his touch on the perfect spot. Ecstasy no longer coursed through her in waves but burned like fire, constant and consuming. Sasha screamed, vaguely aware of the solid strength of his shoulders beneath her hands and his skin yielding under her fingernails. *Dylan.*

The touches slowed as he eased her through the last shaking tremors. She felt his lips on her thigh as he whispered her name and rubbed her hip.

Sasha tried to sit up and reach for him, but her arms wouldn't hold her. She collapsed to the bed with an apologetic moan. "You broke me. It's my turn, but you broke me."

"Shh." He slipped one arm under her legs and the other under her back to lift her easily. Within moments, Dylan had her snuggled under the blankets, and he stripped off his shirt and joined her. His chest was solid and warm against her back, and his breath tickled as he nuzzled the sensitive skin behind her ear. "Tomorrow is your turn. Tomorrow you can do whatever you want to me. Right now, we sleep."

She turned her face to his and kissed him gently. "You're calling the game on account of exhaustion?"

"Mmm. I want you rested up before the rematch."

Having him wrapped around her, his heart beating in time with hers, was painfully intimate. Every moment of the last week had been leading to this, to the soft afterglow of pleasure slowly giving way to the contentment of having Dylan beside her.

Neither of them had been sleeping well, and Sasha barely had the strength to speak. "You're not going to stop being so damn wonderful until I'm in love with you, are you?"

He was silent for several heartbeats. Then his thumb swept over her hand and he kissed the top of her head. "You deserve wonderful."

Then I deserve you. "Good night."

"Good night, Sasha."

Dylan pulled open the back door on the SUV and hesitated as he surveyed the impressive array of weaponry and weapon-related accoutrements. "Is any of this going to blow up while I'm looking for the tape?"

Joe answered from beneath the hood. "Yes, Gennaro. I absolutely drive around with combustible shit jostling around in the back of my Blazer."

"Why do you drive around with this stuff in the back of your Blazer period? I thought Gavin said this wasn't that dangerous."

Joe peeked around the edge of the SUV. "I'm sorry, what's the question?"

"You're a scary fucker, Joe." Dylan pulled open one of the bags and dug through it until he found a roll of electrical tape. He held it out so Joe could see it. "This what you wanted?"

"Yeah. If I can wrap this hose, it'll get us to the next town, and I can replace it."

Dylan handed him the tape. "Where's that?"

"Kearney, I think. It's only a couple miles down the road." Joe tested the hose and hissed. Then he shook his hand and began to guide the tape around the fat black hose. "Even if they don't have a parts store, there'll be a gas station or general store that sells what I need."

"Gotcha." Dylan glanced through the windshield and found Brynn still passed out in the backseat, probably sleeping off the sedative Cindy had provided. "Do we need to find someplace for Brynn to change tonight? I could check the map."

"I took care of it." Joe tore the tape and cleared his throat. "You and Sasha will be all right at the motel alone, right?"

Dylan felt like a boy who had been caught doing something

naughty, which was completely unfair considering the sorts of noises he'd been blocking out the night before. The fact that Sasha had drifted to peaceful, oblivious sleep while he'd fought to ignore Joe and Brynn's two encore performances just made it worse.

He cast Joe a slightly annoyed look. "Maybe we should just get rooms on opposite sides of the damn motel."

"That's probably not a bad idea."

"You got that?"

"This?" Joe jiggled the hose and shrugged. "Yeah, I think it'll hold."

Dylan nodded and strode back to knock on Sasha's window. "Joe's almost got the hose fixed, but we're going to have to stop in the next town."

She glanced at Brynn, still sleeping beside her. "Will we need to stay there tonight?"

"Probably not. Joe found a place to stay tonight where he and Brynn can..." *Run until they collapse and fuck until they pass out.* "Burn off some energy."

"So it's an easy fix? The truck?"

"I guess." Dylan ran his thumb along the top of the door and tried to think of a way to phrase his next request that wouldn't earn him any more significant looks from Joe. "If there's a grocery store or something in town, you and Brynn could pick up some food and stuff." *And stuff. Congratulations, Dylan, you're now seventeen again.*

She met his gaze, her awareness almost palpable. "I can handle it."

"Good." No need to tell her they'd be alone in the motel. The last thing he wanted her considering was how easily Joe and Brynn had heard every moan she'd uttered the night before. "Do you need any cash? Gavin gave me some."

"No." She laughed softly. "I've actually missed being able to use my checking account."

It was a reminder of how tiny his own bank account had been. Sam hadn't given him details on how she'd managed to secure the money, but the paltry sum had barely filled an envelope, even measured out in twenties. A second envelope in his bag held five times as much in crisp fifty-dollar bills, a small fortune Sam had handed over like spare change.

Sasha touched his hand. "Are you okay?"

"I'm fine." He turned his hand over and closed his fingers around hers. "The last few years have been hard on my manly pride, but I'm getting over it."

"Uh-huh." She lowered her voice to a whisper. "If last night didn't fix your manly pride and then some, I don't know what will."

Even if Brynn was asleep, Joe was ten feet away at most and plenty close enough to hear even the softest whisper. Reminding her of that would embarrass her... *But not as much as if you don't.* He jerked his head in Joe's direction and grinned. "Let's talk about it later when wolves with superhearing aren't pretending they can't hear us."

A deep blush spread over her cheeks, and she grimaced. "Sorry."

Dylan rubbed his thumb over the backs of her fingers and resisted the temptation to say something really explicit just to annoy Joe. "It takes some getting used to."

She smiled weakly. "I keep forgetting."

"It's okay." He leaned down, and used years of practice at pitching his voice out of the range of werewolf ears to whisper a promise in her ear. "Tonight no one will be listening."

Her pulse sped, and her breathing hitched. "I'll keep that in mind."

Brynn stirred with a sleepy murmur. Dylan straightened. "Why don't you see if you can wake her up while I check with Joe. We should be moving soon."

The hood slammed down and Joe appeared, wiping his hands on a rag. "We'd better get going if we're going to make up lost time."

Dylan caught the tape Joe tossed to him and whistled as he walked to the back of the SUV. There were only a few more hours of driving before he and Sasha got a room to themselves and the privacy to make good use of it. It was all too easy to conjure up the memory of her skin flushing under his mouth, and of the way she sounded when he made her come.

In the ten lonely years since his change, he'd spent a lot of his nights in bars. He'd never gone home alone unless he'd wanted to, but the women he chose were the ones who only wanted a night of impersonal sex. Women who wanted him gone the next morning, who wouldn't tempt him with a second date that might become a third, that might become something serious enough to attract the attention of the pack.

His hands shook as he shoved the electrical tape back into one of the battered duffel bags. Sex with Sasha wouldn't be impersonal. It wouldn't be shallow and meaningless. It would be magical, figuratively and maybe literally, and a big step down a road that would very likely end in heartache.

She'd warned him of as much. She'd told him flat out, so there would be no misunderstandings. The only place he wanted to live was the one place she wanted to leave.

And all he could think of was touching her.

Dylan slammed the back door of the SUV shut with enough force to make it rattle. *Gennaro, you are royally fucked.*

Sasha shivered in the brightly lit aisle and wished she'd worn a heavier shirt. "Should we pick up some lunch while we're here, Brynn?"

Brynn started and dragged her attention from the front of the store. "Huh? Lunch, yeah. Lunch is good. And snacks."

"Are you okay?" She'd been acting strange since they'd walked in. "What's wrong?"

"I don't know." Brynn shook herself and looked at the shelves around them. "Let's get our stuff and get out. This place gives me the creeps."

They had a good twenty minutes before Joe and Dylan finished fixing the truck, but being so far away from Joe must have been taking a toll on Brynn. "I have to grab something. Do you want to meet me in the deli?"

"No." She snatched a bag of candy from the shelf. "I'll come with you. I don't think we should split up. Something's off here."

Which meant Sasha had to buy condoms in front of one of Dylan's oldest friends. "I need some shampoo and some other things."

"Fine." A bag of licorice joined the chocolate in Brynn's basket, and she jerked her head toward the back of the store. "Let's go this way."

The midday crowd was thin, and Sasha added things to the basket she carried as they walked. She turned down the aisle containing personal care items and stopped in front of the condoms and pregnancy tests.

Brynn's gaze fell on the pregnancy tests, and the jagged edges of magic inside her flared. Her shoulders stiffened as she stalked past them and studied the small assortment of condoms. "Guess asking Cindy for condoms would have been awkward for Dylan."

"'Awkward' doesn't begin to cover it." Though it applied handily to the situation now. Sasha reached for a small box. "You've known him a long time."

"Yeah. Dylan's a good guy." Brynn reached out and plucked a shiny purple box of condoms from the rack and dropped it into Sasha's basket. "He also saved me from the embarrassing task of having to ask my big sister to take me shopping for condoms."

"Oh." Sasha eyed the box in the basket and turned her gaze to Brynn. "I like him a lot."

The tight look in Brynn's eyes softened a little. "Good. Dylan deserves to have someone to like him a lot."

Guilt made her babble. "I told him. I mean, I tried, but I don't know if he understood, really."

Brynn patted Sasha awkwardly on the shoulder. "I'm thinking he understood enough. He seemed a lot happier this morning."

The words hit her like a blow, and Sasha gripped the plastic handle more tightly. "I'm not staying in Red Rock."

"Oh." Brynn studied her for so long Sasha had to will herself not to take a step back. Then she tilted her head to the side. "You told him that?"

"I tried, but I think he got distracted by some of the other things I said."

One eyebrow went up. "Must have been pretty distracting stuff."

She couldn't tell if Brynn was joking or not. "We were talking about how much I owe everyone in town. Like Keith and Gavin and—and Dylan."

"And presumably he told you that's the stupidest thing he's ever heard?"

A hysterical giggle welled up in her throat. "Yeah, we covered that part."

"Speaking as one of the two people who would be dead

without you...yeah. It's pretty fucking stupid."

Getting into the specifics of tradition with Brynn in the family-planning section of a small-town grocery was a feat beyond her at the moment. "Point taken."

"Doesn't mean it's okay to hurt Dylan." Brynn's gaze drifted back to the front of the store. "Do you feel anything weird about this place?"

Sasha closed her eyes and concentrated. For a moment, something flickered at the edge of her consciousness, at once familiar and strange. "Maybe. It's almost like... I don't know." *Like being in Red Rock.* She shivered.

In seconds the power in Brynn went from nervous to tense, flaring so erratically that it drowned out whatever that flicker had been. Brynn caught Sasha's arm with a soft, distressed noise and tugged her toward the front of the store. "Let's pay and get out of here. We need to be with Joe and Dylan."

In spite of her haste, Brynn dragged her to the last open register, at the far end of the store. The bored-looking woman rang their purchases quickly, and Sasha glanced around, watching for anything out of the ordinary.

It wasn't until they headed for the exit, bags in hand, that the same odd thrill of energy tickled through Sasha. She looked over and found the cashier in the first lane watching them with fear in her eyes.

Brynn's gaze followed hers, and she stiffened. Her nostrils flared, and her hand tightened almost painfully around Sasha's arm. The cashier dropped her gaze and hunched her shoulders in a clear show of submission, and something in Brynn's tense stance eased.

They walked out into the midmorning sun, and Sasha pulled her arm carefully free of Brynn's grasp. "Do you think she has a pack here?"

"I don't know." Brynn's voice sounded a little lost. "But she was so scared. Why was she so scared of *me*?"

Sasha thought of the raw, jagged power that burst from Brynn when she was scared or upset. "It might not be you. She might not be used to other wolves."

"I should have known she was there. But I couldn't smell anything but cleanser and food and too many humans, not for sure..." Brynn shivered. "But I knew I didn't belong there. I don't belong here at all. This is someone else's territory."

"We're not staying. Just passing through, so there's no reason for anyone to get upset."

"I know." But Brynn sounded unsure. She shivered again and reached for Sasha's hand. "I have a bad feeling. We need to...we need to go. I need to find Joe."

They'd parked the truck in the lot of an auto-parts chain store a few blocks away. Sasha gripped her friend's hand and tried to look reassuring. "It's okay. Come on. We'll hurry."

They made it to the end of the street before Brynn froze. Her head whipped to the side and both of her bags hit the sidewalk. "Dylan. Dylan's..." A growl rumbled up from somewhere in her chest, and she shot off down the side street without another word.

"What?" Panic washed over her in a cold wave, and she followed Brynn at a run. "What's going—"

Then she heard it, the dull sounds of fists hitting flesh and pained grunts and growls. She rounded the corner of the building and stumbled when she saw three men in a circle around Dylan.

Dylan looked a little worse for the wear, but he wasn't the only one. As Sasha watched he ducked another punch that was almost too fast to see and sent the attacker barreling into one of his companions. The third grazed Dylan's shoulder with his fist a second before Brynn let out an enraged snarl and jumped on his back.

"No—" Dylan's gaze snapped to Brynn and then past her to land on Sasha. He met her eyes, and grim determination disappeared in a rush of concern that sent his power surging toward her.

Oh God, run.

The thought echoed through her head, but it wasn't hers. One of the men punched Dylan in the back, and a sudden flash of pain startled Sasha. Feeling what he felt meant at least part of the spell she'd done in Red Rock was still active.

She and Dylan were still linked.

A second man grabbed Dylan's shirt and drew back his fist. Sasha closed her eyes against the sight, clenched her fists and let the gathering magic inside her explode.

She *felt* when it suffused Dylan. A low snarl rumbled out of his chest, and Sasha opened her eyes just in time to see Dylan slide out of the path of the punch, moving fast even for a werewolf. His hand closed on his attacker's arm and he pivoted and jerked back hard enough to send the man stumbling into the wall behind them.

Brynn hit the wall a second later with a pained grunt. The man who had shoved her there glanced around and, obviously judging him to be the greater threat, advanced on Dylan.

It gave Brynn time to gasp in a breath. "Dylan, there's another one—grocery store—"

The man advancing on Dylan spun and rushed Brynn. Dylan lunged and grabbed the back of his shirt, and Sasha could feel his confusion trembling through the magic stretched out between them.

"Stop," she urged quietly. "The one in the store is a woman, and she was scared to see us. That's all they are, all of them. Scared."

Dylan swept the man's feet out from under him and dropped him to the ground. "Stay," he commanded, his voice low.

The man snarled, and one of the remaining men took off at a run in the direction of the grocery store. Brynn lunged away from the wall as if to follow, but froze when Dylan snapped her name. "Brynn. Back down." His voice carried the power Sasha had given him, and Brynn froze.

The only strange werewolf left standing watched Dylan with brittle fear. "You came into our territory. You were going after Michael's mate."

"No. I wasn't." Dylan held out his hand to Sasha without looking at her. "We're only passing through."

Though he tried to hide the pain, it hit her when she slid her hand into his. He tensed at her gasp, and Sasha forced herself to relax and breathe. "It's dangerous to attack strangers. You don't know who you're dealing with."

Dylan pulled Sasha against his side, tucking her body to his in a gesture that silently laid claim to her. "Brynn, are you okay?"

Brynn lifted her fingers to her split lip and winced. "A little bruised. I'll heal."

"Good." Dylan looked steady and confident, but the arm around her waist shook. "Go look after your packmate before her mate shows up. He's a lot less understanding than I am."

The man waited for his companion to groan his way to his

feet. When they were both upright they backed away in wary silence until they reached the edge of the building, then broke into a run.

When they were alone in the alley, Sasha squeezed Dylan's hand. "You're hurt."

"I'll live." He pressed a hand to his side and winced. "One of them might have cracked one of my ribs before you showed up, though. They were playing for keeps."

The lump in her throat threatened to choke her. "We dropped our bags back there. I'll get them, and we can get out of here."

Brynn shook her head and stalked past them. "You stay with him, Sasha. I'll get our stuff. I need to move."

"We go together," Dylan countered, and though the words were quiet, they were still firm. He kept his hand curled around Sasha's as he squared his shoulders and followed after Brynn.

It didn't take long to retrieve their purchases. Brynn gathered up the items that had rolled out of one of the bags and picked up everything without a word, leaving Sasha to help support Dylan as they made their way back to the Blazer.

Joe looked up from the back of the SUV, frowned and stomped toward them. He didn't stop until he had Brynn's face framed in his hands and tilted up to the light. "What the fuck happened?"

Brynn's eyes drifted shut as the wild magic inside her found a focus in Joe and began to settle. Some of the harsh magical glare that had followed her since the fight faded, and Sasha looked away.

After a few moments of silence Brynn answered his question. "There's a pack here. Weak wolves. One of their women was in the grocery store and they didn't like it when Dylan headed in that direction."

Joe touched Brynn's lip and swore. "Do we need to do anything?"

"No." Sasha urged Dylan to the backseat of the truck. "We just need to go."

For a moment, she thought Joe might argue. It was clear he was fighting instincts that told him no one hurt his friends, his *mate*, and walked away. "All right."

Sasha opened the door and helped Dylan onto the seat. "I can help you."

Dylan smiled wanly. "I'm okay. Let's just get on the road. Trust me, in a day or two I'll be good as new."

He'd dealt with beatings so often he knew how long it would take to heal. The fact tore through her, leaving pain in its wake as she climbed in after him. "But if I can help, why not?"

Brynn buckled her seatbelt, and Joe started the engine before he even settled into his seat. "We'll be on the interstate in a few minutes."

Sasha touched Dylan's shoulder. "Come here."

After a few moments he gave in and inched across the seat. "Is whatever you want to do safe?"

"I wouldn't hurt you."

"Sasha." His tone was chiding.

She held out her hand. "It's safe." He didn't have to know she'd do it even if it wasn't.

He studied her for so long she wondered if he'd caught a stray thought. But then he laid his hand in hers.

She closed her eyes and concentrated. At once, his pain began to seep into the corners of her consciousness. She could draw it in, take it from him, but he'd pull away as soon as he realized what she was doing.

Instead, she focused on smoothing out the rough, jagged edges of his pain to make it more bearable. It took longer, and she knew the effect would be minimal. He would still hurt, and the knowledge made her ache, but this was all he would allow.

Finally, she opened her eyes and whispered, "Not so bad, right?"

"Thank you." He squeezed her hand with a smile, and she got the feeling he was thanking her more for her restraint than for her action. "We can pick up some first aid supplies before we check into the motel tonight, if you don't mind patching me up a little."

It was a far cry from the way Sasha had planned to spend the evening, but she didn't care. She'd be with Dylan, and she was starting to realize that was what mattered most. "I can do that."

Chapter Six

Whatever Brynn and Joe were discussing, it was probably important. It was probably vital to their mission or their survival or something of dire consequence that meant Dylan should absolutely pay attention.

And he might have been able to, if he'd sat on the other side of the table from Sasha.

He inched his leg over and rubbed his knee against hers. Her breath caught in the tiniest little gasp, barely even audible, and still it shot heat straight to his cock. His body didn't care that his ribs still ached when he moved too fast or that his back was a patchwork of bruises in the ugly shades it took humans a week to develop. He'd tasted her, felt her shudder under his hands...

The two nights spent sleeping chastely next to her while she worried over his injuries had been unpleasantly like torture.

A glass hit the table with a hollow *thud* and Dylan started. Brynn glared at him from across the table, though he couldn't tell if it was frustration or grudging amusement hiding behind her wide gray eyes. "How many hits to the head did you take, Dylan?"

If he spoke now, his voice would betray his arousal in a heartbeat. He lifted his water glass to buy time and wished he could dump it over his head. *Or onto my lap...*

Joe rubbed the side of his face. "Apparently, Adam Dubois has maintained a peaceful relationship with the Bedagi Creek pack for quite a few years now. Gavin doesn't know if Dubois is aware that something's up in town, though, because he can't reach him."

Sasha seemed to be paying rapt attention to Joe's words.

Then Dylan felt her hand sliding up his thigh.

If it slid much higher, Sasha was going to find out just how much her touch affected him. Dylan cleared his throat and tried to concentrate on Joe's words. "How does Gavin usually get in touch with the guy?"

"There's a young alpha pair that lives outside town. They're friendly with him and handle all of his business so he can be a reclusive, whittling hermit or something."

All Dylan could feel was the warmth of Sasha's fingers, taunting him even through the fabric of his jeans. He scrambled for something intelligent to say, but only one thing came to mind. "Oh."

Brynn laughed and pushed away from the table. "I'm leaving before they do it on the table. You going to stay and watch, baby, or are you coming with me?"

"Right behind you, sweetheart." Joe threw several folded bills on the table and rose. "We'll talk about it tomorrow. And remember, this place is nicer than the last few we stayed at. They probably have cameras in the elevators."

Dylan tried to summon a little righteous indignation, but he couldn't even manage that. Not when he'd been considering trying to get a hand under Sasha's shirt during the interminable ride to the third floor. "See you tomorrow, Brynn. Joe."

Sasha waved to them and laughed ruefully. "I suppose we're not very subtle."

He rubbed his thumb along her wrist. "I'm not feeling very subtle right now."

"Neither am I." Her eyes met his, and he saw his own need reflected in her beautiful eyes. "Can we go upstairs?"

Joe had probably dropped enough money to cover their bill and then some, but Dylan wrestled another few bills free of his wallet before pulling Sasha to her feet. "Yes. Upstairs."

It was only a few steps to their hotel next door, a quaint brick building with four floors of small guest rooms. Sasha stopped outside and fixed him with a stern look. "Before we get all...wrapped up in each other, are you all right?"

No power on earth could compel him to admit to any infirmity that might earn him another night relegated to the role of patient. Sasha seemed to have an almost uncanny knack for sensing when he was downplaying his own discomfort, so he didn't bother lying. Instead he bent down and let his breath dance over her ear. "If it makes you feel better I'll let you be on top."

She sucked in a shaky breath and gripped his shirt. "You fight dirty."

"Mmm." He kissed her earlobe gently before straightening and urging her through the hotel door. "Just wait."

The elevator *dinged* as soon as Sasha pushed the button, and she tugged him into the car. "Think there's really a camera?"

"The more important question..." the doors whispered shut and he caught her waist and dragged her to him, "...is if we care."

Her head fell back, and the pale softness of her throat called to him. "I only care about you."

Mine. It was a primal feeling, and an unmistakable one. The wolf didn't seem to care that Sasha wasn't of their kind. There was magic in her, power that made them both giddy, and the territorial instincts he'd never felt before he'd met her roared to life. He could sense the flutter of her pulse in her throat as he leaned down and pressed his lips to her skin.

Sasha whimpered and slipped her hands into his hair. "Are you sure it won't hurt you?"

"Sweetheart, we are rapidly reaching the point where stopping is going to be a lot less comfortable." He dragged his tongue over her pulse before teasing her with the softest scrape of teeth. "If you want to stop, tell me. But if you don't..."

"I don't want to stop," she murmured.

He barely heard the soft chime announcing the elevator had reached their floor. He glanced up just long enough to make sure no one was in the way before backing her out of the elevator. For a moment he was tempted to hoist her up and carry her to their room. *Go easy on your bruised ribs until later, you macho ass.*

Sasha laughed and reached into his front pocket. He couldn't help but groan, not when her fingers were so damn close to his aching cock. She flashed him a wicked smile when she freed their room key and held it aloft. "Let me open the door."

Dylan spun her and urged her down the hallway. "Sooner would be better, or I'm going to start sticking *my* hands in *your* clothes."

"Promises, promises." In spite of her casual words, her hands shook when she tried to unlock the door.

Dylan slid his hand down her arm to cover hers as he molded his body to her back. He fit the key into the lock with a low laugh. "Nice to know I'm having an effect."

"Like you can't tell anytime I'm near you."

He rubbed against her ass just enough to make it clear how turned on he was, then grasped the door handle. "Now you can tell too."

Sasha moaned and fumbled with the door. It swung open, and she stumbled inside. Her chest rose and fell with rapid breaths, and her face was flushed. "Shut the door." She began to unsnap her shirt as she spoke.

He reached for her before the door slammed shut. One tug undid the remaining three snaps, and Dylan dropped to his knees in front of her as he dragged her shirt down. His mouth landed on the soft skin just below the band of her bra, and he growled softly and cupped her ass. "I can smell how much you want me."

Her knees buckled, and she fell to the floor too. Her skirt fluttered up, and she dragged his hand high on her bare thigh as she kissed him, hard.

Even the nagging pain from his bruised ribs faded in the rush of pleasure that flooded him. He got one hand into her hair as he took control of the kiss. Dominance in bed had never seemed terribly important before, but he couldn't deny the instinctive thrill at the way her body melted for him. He wanted her stretched out in front of him, bare to his touch and begging for him. He wanted her so lost in sensation she couldn't think of anything but him.

He tore his mouth from hers with a groan and got a good enough grip on her hips to lift her to the bed. Then he rose to his feet and dragged at his shirt, fighting to get it over his head without ripping it.

"Let me." Sasha knelt on the bed and eased him out of the black cotton. She dusted his bare chest and shoulders with kisses and tiny teasing licks of her tongue. Dylan closed his eyes and threaded his fingers through her hair, content for the moment to let her explore.

She moaned again. This time, her breath feathered across

his skin and made him shiver. Her hands fell to his belt, and she closed her teeth on the spot where his neck met his shoulder.

Instinct roused, swift and brutal, and he struggled against the sudden need to shove her to the bed and cover her body with his. His fingers tightened in her hair of their own volition, and he jerked her head back just enough to meet her eyes. "You keep doing things like that and you might not get a chance to be on top."

Her eyes gleamed with lust, and her voice went husky. "Take me if you want. I don't care how, I just need you, Dylan."

The condoms were still in their bag on the bedside table. He released her and took a step back. "Get naked."

Sasha kicked off her shoes and reached for the clasp of her bra. It took her longer to wiggle out of her clothes than it should have because she kept her gaze on him, watching every movement closely. By the time he had kicked off his shoes and dropped his jeans, she'd just stripped off her skirt.

Dylan tossed the box of condoms on the bed next to her. "You like watching me, do you?"

She sat up, her hair spilling over her shoulders. "You're beautiful."

Not words he'd heard often. Maybe not ever. But it was impossible to doubt her sincerity when she watched him with such need, such passion.

He crawled onto the bed and coaxed her to stretch out on her side so he could curl up behind her. He dropped a kiss to her shoulder as he gathered her hair up from the back of her neck. "You're beautiful too. You're gorgeous."

"Nervous," she corrected. "It's silly. I just...want it to be good for you. The way you made it for me."

"Not much doubt of that." He let his hand drift over her hip and down to dip between her legs. "Tell me you want it. Tell me you need it."

The way she jerked into his touch spoke more loudly than her shaky words. "It's all I can think about. Making love to you."

It was hard to breathe. He got the condom on somehow and then he pushed inside her, reveling in the warmth of her body and the way she tried to muffle a startled moan as he rocked into her.

She leaned her head against his shoulder, her breathing rough. "Yes."

He pressed his open mouth to her shoulder. It would have been easy to roll her to her stomach, to sink into her body and lose himself in fast, frantic thrusts, but it wouldn't have been the same. He'd always done his best to satisfy his lovers, but he'd never craved a woman's pleasure so completely before.

He closed his teeth lightly on her skin before lifting his mouth to her ear. "Touch yourself. Show me what you like."

Sasha's hand trembled over his and dropped between her thighs. "Slow," she whispered, "and hard."

"Is that what you want?" He eased her leg up just enough that his next rocking thrust took him deeper. "Slow." Another thrust, and he couldn't keep from groaning as her body gripped his cock. "Hard."

"Like that." She tilted her hips back, grinding against him, and a shudder shook through her. "That's what I want."

He eased her over until she was half under him and he had the leverage to move just a little harder, a little deeper. Her hair tumbled over her shoulder, and the pale nape of her neck taunted him. "Tell me again." He lowered his mouth to her skin.

Sasha braced her hand on the bed. "Can't you feel it?" She arched under him with a quiet, desperate noise. "I've never needed anyone like this."

Magic trembled in the air between them, the power that made his wolf hungry for possession, for dominance. He bit the back of her neck and unleashed the tiniest bit of his supernatural strength. Not enough to hurt her, but enough that his next thrust made her writhe in pleasure.

An answering wave of energy exploded from her along with a hoarse cry. "Harder, Dylan."

He gritted his teeth against the urge to obey. "I don't want to hurt you."

"I won't let you," she promised with another shudder. "Please, Dylan. You've been inside me for so long, but not like this. Not this good."

The growl tore free of him before he could stop it as his control slipped. He eased his hand under her body and stroked her clit as he surged into her. "Come. I want to see you come."

Sasha hissed out a curse and a plea and tightened around his cock. Her soft skin brushed his as she moved in counterpoint, taking him deeper. "Yes, just—" She pushed off the bed, shifting her hips slightly, and screamed with his next thrust.

It was the best damn thing he'd ever felt, and he hadn't even come yet. She clenched around him, hot and tight, and her pleasure filled the air with magic—pure, raw power that spilled over him and made him gasp. Thoughts of pushing her further, of holding on until she'd come again and again shattered into a thousand pieces as he gave in to the magic. Gave in to *her*.

Scalding heat rushed over him and he did the only thing he could. He closed his teeth on the back of her neck again and muffled his groan as he came.

Sasha reached up and held his head to hers, panting gently while he rocked and stilled. "Are you okay?"

The words were so out of place he couldn't even process them. "What?"

"Your ribs." She wiggled and grinned. "But that's flattering."

Dylan bit her with another groan. "Quit that, or I'm going to forget my ribs and we'll be doing this a second time." *And maybe a third.*

She breathed a regretful sigh and stretched a little. "Uh-uh. I like you, and I want to keep you intact and fully functional."

"Good to know." He eased from her body before urging her onto her back. Her hair spread out over the pillow in a tangled mess, and his heart ached as he smoothed a few strands off her forehead. "You're so beautiful."

A blush spread over her chest and face, and she bit his hand gently. "That's what I want you to see when you look at me."

"I do." Her lips were soft under his thumb, and he leaned in to nuzzle her cheek. "Too bad they're already expecting us in Bedagi Creek tomorrow. I'd be tempted to find an excuse to stay in bed with you."

"But we have work to do." She rolled over and pressed her cheek to his arm. "Could we get away with feeling each other up in the backseat of the Blazer?"

Joe would murder him. "Maybe."

"Mmm." Her eyes grew bright, and she bit her lip. "Do we need to talk about this?"

The last thing he wanted to do was ruin his warm fuzzy feeling with another kindly reminder that she had no intention of staying in the one place that felt like home to him. He kissed her lower lip softly. "In the morning, when we've slept and had coffee."

Sasha shook her head. "No talking, I think. Let's just be...whatever we are."

"Happy. What I am is happy."

Her smile was shy. "So am I."

Warmth filled him, along with a pure, uncomplicated peace he hadn't felt in ten years. Even time spent with Brynn and Abby over the years had been tinged with longing, with the wish that he could enjoy their company without the worry and the guilt that some day they'd pay the price for it. He couldn't remember the last time everything inside him had been so wonderfully, perfectly content.

It was the difference between surviving and being okay. He was okay.

Now I just need to stay this way.

Chapter Seven

The first thing she noticed about Irene and Lawrence was that they were both scared, but not of her.

As Joe shook hands with the alphas of Bedagi Creek, Sasha gripped Dylan's hand and flashed him a questioning look. He gave a tiny little shake of his head, and she fixed a smile on her face.

"Welcome to Bedagi Creek." Lawrence turned his gaze on Dylan and Sasha, and there was something there that was eerily assessing. A moment later he grinned. "We haven't had a witch visit in too long. Some of the pack spells are failing. Perhaps you could assist us."

"I'd be happy to help." The man's gaze made the hair on the back of her neck stand up, and she felt compelled to add, "If I can, I mean. I'm only an apprentice."

Dylan moved closer and lifted a hand to her shoulder. "I can help too."

"Dylan and Sasha have a task that will take them out of town for a while," Joe said, "but they'll be back."

Lawrence returned his attention to Joe, but his wife's gaze stayed fixed on Sasha. She stood stiffly by her husband's side, and the frustrated fear in her eyes began to fade a little.

There was nothing menacing about the woman's expression, but Sasha shivered. Something was obviously terribly wrong.

Joe had apparently come to the same conclusion. He lowered his voice and leaned in closer to Lawrence. "Gavin wanted you to know we're at your disposal. Anything you need."

Lawrence's friendly smile faltered. "I've heard Gavin has too many competent alphas in town. Are you here to help, or to measure my windows for new curtains?"

He sounded almost jealous, but Sasha supposed that wasn't surprising. Maritza had told her that few of the sanctuaries in the country had resources as reliable and plentiful as Red Rock's. "Everyone has useful talents," she murmured.

After a tense moment, Lawrence seemed to relax. "Your witch is right. We all have our gifts, and Red Rock has more than most. Since you're willing to share yours, it's only fair we do the same. Irene has prepared lunch, if the four of you would like to join us?"

Dylan squeezed her hand lightly before speaking. "Sasha and I promised to carry a message to Adam Dubois first. Gavin hasn't heard from him in a while."

Joe tossed Dylan his keys. "Brynn and I would be glad to stay. Thank you, Lawrence."

Irene spoke up. "His place is easy to find. Take the main road out of town and turn right on to the dirt road just after the stop sign. It'll take you about fifteen minutes back into the woods, but Adam's the only one at the end of it."

Sasha hugged Brynn. "We'll be back. You and Joe be safe."

Dylan stayed silent until they were inside the Blazer and pulling out on to the main road. "That was weird. He acted like Joe was here to challenge him."

"Maybe he's been getting that a lot lately." Or maybe he really was just envious of Gavin's security and wealth.

"Maybe. Joe is a pretty scary bastard, I guess. He's so busy playing lovey dovey with Brynn, sometimes I forget how fucking terrifying he is."

"Joe's not terrifying." No one in Red Rock was, not even the ones who despised her. She looked out the window and changed the subject. "You've really never met a vampire?"

It seemed to take him a minute to catch up. "Uh, no. I mean, maybe? Shit, I could've been meeting them all my life and had no idea. How do you even tell?"

"I don't know." It was difficult to describe. "They *feel* different. Slower."

"Heartbeat, you mean? Or...do they even have a heartbeat?"

"I've never listened." Sasha's nervousness grew. The

vampires she'd met had all been old and very powerful, and she'd never encountered one without Maritza at her side. "Gavin said Dubois was a friend, right?"

"Yes." Dylan glanced at her, and he grew serious once more. "You're scared. What's wrong?"

"I'm still at a loss without Maritza." For once, the painful emotional void had taken a backseat to the practical fear of being on her own. "She was always good at talking, at negotiation. But I'm clumsy."

He reached for her hand. "You're not. You're just learning."

A thrill of awareness shot through her. Fear melted, replaced by a flare of desire only Dylan seemed capable of inciting. "I've always been awkward. I can't blame that on my interrupted education."

"You're not awkward with me."

"It's easy with you."

She could feel his pleasure at the words. "Well I'll be with you today. What do I do if Adam Dubois turns out to be an evil bloodsucking monster? Stake to the heart? Garlic? Crosses and holy water?"

Sasha laughed. "Run, most likely, or we could set him on fire. But if he really is a friend of Gavin's, that could be uncomfortable when we went home."

His fingers tightened around hers, and his chuckle warmed her like a shot of liquor. "Joe said this vampire used to be a lumberjack. Let's just hope he doesn't greet us at the door with an axe."

"If he does, we're definitely not sticking around to burn him."

"Especially since we'd have to ask him to chop down some firewood to do it with."

"Mmm. He might get suspicious."

"We're going to be okay, Sasha." Dylan kissed the backs of her fingers. "We'll get through this, and we can go home. And spend all the time we want reading dusty old books full of stories too incredible to be true."

It sounded like heaven. "Except most of them probably are true. Perhaps we should spend our time kissing instead."

He laughed again, that same wicked laugh that made her shiver. "Oh, you didn't think you were getting out of the kissing, did you?"

She rubbed her thumb over the inside of his wrist. "You might be particularly skilled, but I can't read and kiss at the same time."

The SUV swerved a little, and Dylan jerked away with a groan. "Obviously not *that* skilled. I don't think I should kiss and drive, or we're going to end up wrapped around a tree and then you'll see how terrifying Joe is."

"He'd miss his explosives more than his truck." They eased to a stop, and Sasha pointed out the window. "There's the dirt road."

Dylan turned. "Too bad you distracted me from that book on the vampires of New England. I'm dying to know why they're all up here in Maine now."

"It could be the sparse population."

"Seems counterintuitive, though. I mean, if you've got to feed on people, wouldn't you want more of them?"

Sasha snorted. "Only if you want them banding together in an angry mob when they get tired of you eating them."

"I guess. Where do you think Adam gets...food?"

"I don't know." Her stomach flip-flopped. "Some vampires have willing servants or partners who provide blood. Others survive on animals, for a time. But there are some who hunt."

"Sasha." He reached out, and this time his touch was obviously meant to soothe. "Gavin wouldn't send us out here without warning if his friend was likely to take a bite out of either of us."

"I know that. But sometimes..." It was a fear she hadn't dared voice. "Sometimes I wonder if Gavin has forgotten what it's like out here, Dylan. In the world beyond Red Rock Pass."

He didn't deny it. The SUV slowed a little, and he chanced a glance at her. "I think sometimes he does. I think a lot of the pack does."

"That's not bad, but it makes me worry about him and Sam, both."

"I know. But they've got Keith and Joe. And Abby and Brynn may not know the supernatural stuff, but Abby's tough enough to help Sam, and Brynn's seen the not-so-pretty side of the world."

Her throat ached. "And what about you?"

Dylan's smile was a little too fast to be real. "I can lure pretty witches into town. And fix up houses."

She couldn't bring herself to return the expression. "You're happy there."

"I was happier there. It wasn't saying much." His thumb brushed over her wrist. "I'm happy with you."

His words and touch suffused her with the same warmth that had grown between them since they'd made love. She wanted to take the chance, to ask him if he'd consider spending time someplace besides Red Rock, but the words died on her tongue. It wouldn't be fair of him to ask her to stay, and it wouldn't be fair of her to ask him to leave.

They were at an impasse. "I'm happy with you too, Dylan."

"Good." Dylan returned his hand to the wheel as the rows of pine trees on either side of the road grew markedly closer together. "I guess it's a good thing there's only one person out here. I don't think two cars could pass each other on this road."

They drove in silence until a final bend in the road revealed a small, old-fashioned log cabin surrounded by rose bushes. Next to it sat a beat-up old truck with enough grass growing around the wheels to make it clear it hadn't moved in a while. The windows of the cabin were covered in thick black curtains that made it impossible to see inside. "This must be it," Sasha murmured.

Dylan pulled the SUV to a careful stop twenty paces from the cabin and studied it through narrowed eyes. "No sunlight. Can vampires go out in the sunlight?"

"I guess. Some, anyway."

"Some? It's not a yes-or-no answer?"

"I don't know." Helplessness rose inside her. "I'm not an expert, not about vampires or—or anything else."

Dylan threw the vehicle into park and swore softly before reaching for her. "I'm sorry, Sasha. You don't need to be an expert. I'm just being an ass."

"No, I should know these things." Maybe she would, if she'd ever considered that Maritza wouldn't be around forever. That she'd be on her own one day. "I think it's tied to strength. The frailer they are, the less able they are to stand the sunlight. I think."

"Then maybe the curtains are a good sign for us." He leaned in to kiss her. "Are you ready?"

"Hey." She caught his mouth, this time in a longer kiss. "He's a friend of Gavin's. It's fine."

They made their way up to the door, and Dylan edged in front of her as he knocked on the scarred wood.

The door jerked open a few inches before Dylan's fist landed a third time. A face appeared, a man with rugged features and a tight expression that made him look threatening. His gaze jumped to her for several seconds, then returned to Dylan.

The man studied them in silence so long she wanted to turn and leave. Then his eyes narrowed. "You one of Francis's wolves?"

Even Sasha could tell there was a wrong answer. Dylan moved to put himself more squarely in front of her before he answered. "Don't know a Francis, so I guess no."

"Gavin Hamilton sent us." Sasha had to peer around Dylan to speak. "From Montana. He's been trying to reach you."

"That so?" The suspicion didn't leave his voice. If anything, it grew sharper. "He still hiding away in his mountain with Sabrina?"

It was either a test, or Adam Dubois wasn't quite the friend Gavin had made him out to be. She couldn't stop the ice that slid into her voice. "Sam. Her name is Samantha."

"He knows," Dylan said quietly. "He doesn't trust us. And neither does the werewolf hiding behind the door."

Surprise flashed through Adam's eyes, then he smiled wryly. "I bet people underestimate you a lot, don't they?"

Dylan stepped to the side, but rested his hand protectively on Sasha's arm. "I'm Dylan. This is Sasha. We came with one of Gavin's enforcers."

"Keith?"

"Joe."

Adam nodded and pulled open the door. "Then I guess you'd best come in."

The interior of the cabin was dark and cool. Once her eyes adjusted to the dim light, she could see that the front room was filled with beautiful wood furniture that looked handmade. Judging from the sharp and gleaming but well-used axe by the door, it very well could have been.

Their host pushed the door shut and bolted it before

holding out a hand. "Dylan and Sasha from Red Rock, meet Ethan. Of the Bedagi Creek pack."

The man against the wall was young but obviously stressed, with new lines creased around his eyes and mouth. "Friends, Adam?"

"We can hope." Adam crossed his arms across his chest, and the worn flannel shirt strained over shoulders so muscled they were intimidating. "They came from Red Rock."

"I heard," he murmured. "Gavin's place." He stepped away from the wall, out of the deeper shadows, and swayed as Sasha studied him. His eyelids drooped as if he was sleepy, and he shivered.

"Gavin was worried." Dylan's voice sounded quiet. Tense. "He had reason to be, didn't he?"

"I can do it," Ethan insisted. "Lawrence knows it too. He's too weak to protect the pack, but I can do it."

He was sick. Sasha took a step toward him and lifted the back of her hand to his cheek. Far from the warmth of fever she expected, his skin was cold, almost clammy. "They've done something to him, haven't they?"

"Poison. One of the Bangor vampires probably helped. The Bangor alpha's been buying up Lawrence's power, bit by bit."

She dropped her hand to Ethan's chest. "How long ago?"

His answer was weak, and too long in coming. "Three days."

His heart beat under her palm, faint and too slow. "I don't know of any poisons that can affect a werewolf for so long."

Adam laughed harshly. "Vampire blood."

Shock coursed through her. It was death magic, the kind she couldn't believe another wolf would have a part in. She tugged down his collar and lifted his sleeves, searching for the punctures of teeth marks. "Did they drink from him, or just slip him the blood?"

"Just the blood."

Dylan's fingers brushed over her shoulder. "I don't understand. What's going on?"

She glanced at him, unwilling to voice the words. *He's going to die.* "Like he said, poison. There are some things I can do, but not—not much."

"What if I help?"

Ethan swayed and almost tipped over. They caught him and helped him to a nearby bench. "It's not magic, Dylan. Not this time. I can do a cleansing, but it's mostly just herbal remedies and waiting."

Adam strode past them toward a small, neat kitchen and slammed a pot onto an old-fashioned stove. "Stubborn bastard won't let me take him to someone who can help."

Sasha rose and joined Adam in the kitchen, careful to keep her voice low, though she doubted Ethan could hear her. "If you know someone, you should do it anyway. I haven't completed my training."

"He won't go." Adam braced his hands on the counter and closed his eyes. "They have his mate in town. They're probably going to keep her hidden and play nice until Joe leaves, though, because Lawrence can't risk pissing off Gavin."

"If you know Gavin, you can't have any doubt that this will piss him off all by itself." Then his words registered, and Sasha felt faint. "Joe and Brynn. Irene told us where to find you. Lawrence must know that you'd tell us what he's done."

"Lawrence doesn't think I know what happened."

"Are you sure?" The tension was back in Dylan's voice as he crossed the room to stand next to them. "Haven't they come here to look for him?"

"No." Adam bared sharp, vicious fangs. "No one from the pack has the guts to come out here but Ethan and Emily. If Lawrence suddenly showed up here looking for Ethan, I'd know something was wrong. And Lawrence is scared shitless of me."

Even with the vampire's relatively easygoing manner, Sasha could understand why. "What is Lawrence doing? It can't be as simple as dirtying things up to avoid a fair challenge because he isn't ready to retire."

Dylan leaned against the counter and closed his eyes. "Things are hard. There aren't many jobs. People get hungry. Hungry werewolves are dangerous, and the alpha needs to protect his people. Then a wolf shows up in town and says maybe there's a little extra in the city this year. Maybe they can help out. It's the least they can do."

Adam swore. "How do you—"

"It's a gift the first time," Dylan continued, as if Adam hadn't spoken. "The next time they need some help. Labor in return for food. Young men who can help out for a few weeks.

Then a few months. Then they come back and this time they want the women." Dylan opened his eyes and met Sasha's gaze. "Why do you think we got jumped in that little town? This happens *all the time*. Alan took over four packs in the last decade like that. Why waste energy fighting when life is so hard for wolves in the small towns that they'll come to you eventually?"

Sasha's heart ached for the realities of Dylan's life, and for what the people of Bedagi Creek faced. "Will Ethan stop that? Is that what he meant when he said he could protect the pack?"

Dylan looked at Ethan, who had slumped over on the bench. "Maybe. Sometimes all it takes is one person strong enough to say no." The pain in his eyes made it clear that more often that person wasn't enough.

She gripped Dylan's hand and kissed his shoulder. "We can help. We'll start with Ethan."

Adam cleared his throat. Loudly. "I've been out of the world longer than I thought. When did wolves and wizards start kissing?"

"They haven't," Sasha said shortly. "I saw your roses outside. Any chance you have a decent herb garden?"

"Enough of one, if you don't need anything exotic."

"Not really." She gestured to the back door, and he nodded. "Put Ethan on the floor and get his shirt off, Dylan. I'll take a look at the garden and grab the first aid bag from the Blazer."

Dylan hesitated for several heartbeats before nodding. "Be careful."

"Simmer down, junior. No one's going to attack her in my backyard."

For a second she thought Dylan was going to growl at Adam. Then he bared his teeth in something that could have been a grin—or a challenge. "Sasha can take care of herself."

"Most witches can," Adam agreed, obviously amused. "I'd do what she told you to before she gives you an inconvenient itch."

Irritation flared in Sasha. She didn't like to see Adam teasing Dylan. "I could say the same for you, Dubois. I need boiling water for infusions, to start."

Adam laughed quietly and turned to his stove. "As the lady wishes."

The pungent scent of herbs filled the air along with Sasha's soft chants. She'd already been at it twice as long as any of the cleansings she'd done on Justine, but the effect on Ethan was barely noticeable. A little of his color had returned, but he still slipped in and out of consciousness.

She laid a hand on his forehead and spoke firmly, but Ethan only moaned and thrashed in response.

Dylan crouched next to her and kept his voice low. "What can I do? Do you need more magic? More power?"

Her answer was barely audible. "I need the last two days back." Her hands shook, and her frustration was plain. "Maybe a little more, Dylan. But just a little, I mean it."

He indulged himself with a soft touch on her cheek. "Just a little. I'm feeling pretty good right now."

The fact that she didn't argue was further testament to the seriousness of Ethan's condition. Sasha cupped the back of Dylan's head, whispered something and kissed him lightly.

Magic built between them, slow and warm, the kind that tickled along his skin and made him wish they were alone even before the connection between them flared open.

Heat. Worry. Quiet concern and soft power, and the desire he felt for her reflected back at him in equal measure. And underneath it all...

Love.

His heart pounded. "Me too."

Relief shone bright in her eyes, and she gave him a small, promising smile. "Later, when there's time..."

He ignored Adam's too-sharp gaze and kissed her again, quick and hard. "Take what you need. I'm strong enough."

"I know you are, Dylan. So am I." She turned back to Ethan's still form and resumed her chanting, louder this time, with a new, commanding note in her voice.

The man on the floor started to seize.

"Hold him." Sasha's rhythmic words didn't falter, but he heard the words anyway. *"Both of you, hold him down. Just a little longer now."*

Adam must have heard the words as well, because he appeared on Sasha's left just as Dylan leaned down to grasp

Ethan's right shoulder. He writhed under their hands as agonized screams ripped free of him. Sasha's brow creased with concentration, and sweat beaded her upper lip. "Just a little—"

A surge of energy burst from Ethan along with a tormented snarl as he rolled free of Adam's grasp, onto his side. Sasha held his head as he gagged and sputtered, finally vomiting a thick black *something* that Dylan didn't want to consider too closely.

He stopped coughing and dragged in loud, sobbing breaths that almost drowned out Sasha's whispered reassurances. "You're all right. You're going to be okay now."

Dylan reached out a hand to brace himself on a nearby chair as a wave of dizziness washed over him. "Is it done?"

"It's done." Sasha looked at Adam. "He'll need fluids. I can't imagine he's been able to keep much down these last few days."

Adam nodded and rose to his feet. "I've got some soup stock from the last time they brought me groceries. What about him?"

Dylan bristled. "I'm right here. And I'm fine."

"Fine," Sasha echoed, her face pale. "Could I get some— some water?"

That was when he realized that not all of the weakness making his hands shake was his own. Dylan closed his eyes and took a deep breath before reaching out to pull Sasha against him. "You okay?"

She pressed her face to his shoulder and nodded, though she still shivered. "A little tired, that's all."

Adam returned from the kitchen. "I'm going to put Ethan in my bed and then I'm going to go to town and check on your people. You know how to use a gun?"

Dylan nodded.

"Good." Adam leaned down and lifted Ethan's dead weight with no effort, proving that vampires were easily as strong as werewolves. "After I leave, if anyone shows up that you don't know, you might want to shoot first and ask questions if they can still talk."

Sasha stared at the black mess on the floor. "Death magic."

Dylan made a soothing noise and tucked her more firmly to his chest. "You need to rest for a little bit. We'll see if Adam has any extra blankets and you can curl up while I manage the food."

"I'll help you."

"Sasha, please."

"I need to help, Dylan." She somehow managed to sound firm and pleading, all at once. "I can't roll into a ball and hide in some blankets right now. I can't think that much. I need to do something."

It wouldn't help *his* riled-up instincts, but he doubted much would at this point, short of having Brynn and Joe in the car and headed back to Montana. "Okay. You want to make the food or babysit the sick werewolf?"

"I'll cook. I don't want Ethan to wake up and sense or see me. It might frighten him."

Talking to Ethan would give him a chance to see just how bad the situation was—and whether or not he had to think of an excuse to keep her in the vampire's cabin while he went back for Joe and Brynn. *Because Joe Mitchell might need you to rescue him.* Absurd to imagine. *Terrifying* to imagine.

He kissed the top of her head before releasing her. "Cook enough for all of us, if you can. Something tells me we're going to need our strength."

"Raid the kitchen." Adam stepped out of the bedroom and pulled the door most of the way shut. "I'm taking my truck into town. Chances are good they're going to be playing nice with your friends, but it'd be stupid not to check...and I know how to get in and out of town quietly."

"I'll get that broth ready for Ethan first." Sasha disappeared into the kitchen.

Dylan waited until Adam had reached the door before speaking, pitching his voice low enough that Sasha wouldn't hear it. "Do you think there'll be trouble?"

"No." Adam turned and surveyed him through slightly narrowed eyes. After a few moments he nodded, as if he'd answered some internal question. "I don't think there'll be trouble because Lawrence is a tired, desperate man, but he's not stupid. I've never met Joe, but if he's half as scary as Keith, Lawrence would piss himself at the thought of getting into a fight."

"Joe's scarier than Keith." Adam raised one eyebrow in a vaguely skeptical manner, and Dylan elaborated. "Keith's more dominant, but Joe's...harder. If I had to fight one of them, I'd pick Keith."

Adam picked up a shotgun from next to the door and nodded to the second one. "You know how to use that?"

"I grew up in Montana."

"Since I haven't been outside of Maine this century, I'm going to assume that means yes."

Dylan felt his lips tug up in spite of himself. "Yes."

"Good to know. I could be gone a few hours, so don't panic. But if Lawrence shows up here...shoot to kill."

Dylan squared his shoulders and tried not to be insulted by the hint of doubt in the vampire's eyes. "I can do it."

Adam didn't reply with words, just nodded shortly, unbolted the door, and left with the shotgun clasped easily in one hand.

Dylan checked on Sasha first. He found her digging through the cupboards, a saucepan already bubbling on the gas stove. "Some kind of stew or something?" she said, her inflection turning it into a question.

"Perfect. I bolted the door behind Adam, and I'm going to go sit with Ethan. Yell if you need anything."

"All right."

The bedroom was dark and quiet. Ethan lay as still as death on a large bed with a solid headboard that looked hand-carved. Even though he didn't move, his chest rose and fell evenly, and the sick sweat dotting his skin had dried.

Dylan shifted a stack of haphazardly folded shirts off of the rocking chair in the corner and dragged it closer to the bed. The intricate carvings on the arms and back of the chair looked like they'd poke painfully into anyone who dared sit, but he was too tired to stay on his feet. He eased into the chair and was pleasantly surprised by just how comfortable it was. "Fuck, I need one of these."

"They retail for two grand." Ethan opened his eyes. "I remember you from earlier."

"Dylan. From Red Rock. Gavin sent us here because your alpha's mate called him."

Ethan grimaced. "Irene. She's tried."

"What happened?" The generalities he had no problem imagining, but the details... *The devil's in the details.*

"What always happens to small towns." His dark hair

flopped over his forehead as he gingerly pushed himself up to sit against the headboard. "The mill closed, all the other jobs had dried up, and people couldn't go somewhere else to look for work."

"And someone offered help?"

"Help." Ethan snorted softly. "That's one way to put it. Lawrence accepted, at any rate. Guess he figured he was damned either way. Now he owes his allegiance to Francis, and the pack is paying the price."

Dylan closed his eyes, and the memories came all too easily. A van from a nearby town, two twenty-year-old submissive males and a handful of terrified women the same age. Living tithes, demanded in return for the illusion of autonomy. "How far has it gone? What's Francis asking for in return?"

"Food." The word was harsh, an epithet. "He needs to feed his vampire allies."

The bottom of Dylan's stomach dropped out. He curled his hands around the arms of the chair and forced in a breath. "Is that why—" *Why they took your mate?*

Ethan's face was etched in lines that belonged on a much older man. "Francis wants the stronger wolves. They're not hard to control when they're being drained half to death every night."

Dylan swallowed his own disgust and forced himself to ask the questions he knew Joe and Gavin would need the answers to. "How long has this been going on? And how many people have they taken?"

"I don't know. Months." Ethan looked away. "There were a few in the beginning. Lawrence said they left to look for temporary work, but they never came back. He had to have sent them to Bangor. I should have guessed it then..."

"Adam says he doesn't think Lawrence would challenge one of Gavin's enforcers. Do you think he's right?"

It took the man too long to answer. "If he did, it wouldn't be clean. What do you think happened to me?"

Lawrence had invited Brynn and Joe to lunch. Cold dread settled in the pit of Dylan's stomach. "I need to call Gavin. I need to tell him what's going on." *Just in case.* He didn't speak the words. He didn't have to.

"The closest phone is at mine and Emily's—" He hissed in a breath. "It's at our place. It's a twenty-minute drive."

Too far when it meant leaving Sasha alone to protect Ethan. "Adam's gone to town to see how Lawrence is dealing with Brynn and Joe."

"That bastard had better be looking for Emily too."

He could lie, but Ethan would know. "I don't know. But when Joe and Brynn get back here, we'll figure out a way to fix this."

"Sure." Ethan leaned his head against the headboard with a rough exhalation. "Where's the girl? The one from earlier?"

"Sasha's making you something to eat. She's worried that you'll be uncomfortable around her." And try as he might, Dylan couldn't keep the challenge out of his voice.

A hint of humor glinted in the man's eyes. "I only wanted to thank her."

Dylan unbent enough to smile. "She hasn't had the easiest time with werewolves."

"At this point, neither have I."

Neither had Brynn. Or Abby. *Or me.* Werewolves had been hurting each other and everyone around them for a long time, long enough for Dylan to wonder if maybe the wizards were right to fight against them.

A traitorous thought, perhaps. A pointless one, too. "Get some rest. Sasha and Adam and I will figure out what's going on, and when we do, you need to be in decent enough shape to take your town back."

He hesitated before nodding. "I hope your friends are okay."

"They will be." They had to be, because Dylan had no idea what sort of rescue mission he and Sasha could mount against an entire town. *And Adam, of course. A vampire, a werewolf and a witch...*

It sounded like the setup for a bad joke, the kind where the punch line never made anyone laugh.

Chapter Eight

Sasha jerked awake, unsure why. She sat up on the couch, barely breathing as she took stock of what her senses told her. The stew was on the stove, the rich aroma of it filling the cabin, and everything was quiet. There was nothing, no—

An enraged scream split the air outside, and Sasha's heart pounded. "Brynn."

She scrambled off the couch just as Dylan bolted from the kitchen and shot past her. He snatched up the shotgun and held up a hand. "Stay back."

"What? Dylan, wait—"

He ignored her as he jerked the curtains aside and peered out, then swore and twisted the deadbolt.

The door slammed open a second later, and Adam took one step in and pointed to Sasha. "Calming spell. Do you know it?"

"Of course I do." Fear pounded through her. "What's happened?"

Dylan was already out the door. Adam shook his head and gestured sharply. "No time. Brynn's losing it, and Emily can't keep her under control for long."

Joe. Sasha's hands shook. "Get her in here. On the floor." As he rushed off, she tried to clear her mind, to calm herself enough to marshal the reserves of energy inside her.

A snarl sounded from outside, one barely human. When Adam reappeared with Brynn twisting in his arms, he had four jagged scratches down the side of his face.

She looked feral. She thrashed in Adam's grasp and planted an elbow hard enough in his side that he grunted in pain. A tall woman followed them inside and laid a hand on Brynn's head. "Shh, honey. You're going to be—"

"Let me go." Brynn bared her teeth, and for one terrifying moment it looked like she was going to try to rip the woman's hand off with her teeth.

"*Brynn.*" The spell coalesced, washing through Sasha and outward, but she couldn't focus it enough to do more than take the slightest edge off her friend's agitation.

She stepped forward and framed Brynn's face with her hands. She heard Dylan's noise of protest, but he was too far away to stop her, even when Brynn's teeth snapped shut an inch away from Sasha's hand. "Settle down."

Brynn opened her eyes, which looked more gold than gray. Her lips curled back from her teeth. "Joe. We have to go back for Joe."

"We will, I promise. But first I need you to stop fighting me."

Adam winced as Brynn's heel caught his thigh. "Emily—"

"I'm trying." The woman's voice shook. "We must be too far from her Guide for their bond to do her any good. She wasn't this out of it back in town."

"Brynn was turned during the full moon." The spell wasn't working. Sasha could try to ramp up the power, pour more energy into another cast, but there was no guarantee that would work either. "Dylan, we have to find another way."

"Hold on." He dropped the shotgun next to the door and lunged for the first aid kit they'd dragged in from the car earlier. "Cindy sent something in case Brynn lost it. Some kind of sedative…"

"A shot." Sasha struggled to remember Cindy's instructions. "In the shoulder, right?"

"Yeah." Dylan pulled a syringe out of the case. "Step back, Sasha. Adam, can you and…"

"Emily." She flashed Sasha a tight smile before returning her attention to Brynn. "Come on, honey, just a little bit…"

Adam and Emily managed to get Brynn to the floor and hold her steady long enough for Dylan to use the injectable sedative. Her struggles slowed, became sluggish and uncoordinated as her gaze fixed on Sasha. "Joe. We…we need to…"

The vise of terror tightened around Sasha's chest again, and she turned to Adam, her fists clenched. "What happened to Joe?"

It was Emily who answered. She sat on her heels and pushed her dark, disheveled hair from her face. "The Bangor alpha and his vampire sidekick showed up right after your friends. The vampire decided she wanted Brynn, and when the alpha tried to make that happen, Joe made him dead."

Dylan's eyebrows drew together. "Why would she want Brynn?"

Adam shifted uncomfortably, and Sasha drew in a shaky breath. "Why did the vampire in Helena want Sam? I don't even know what kind of power a blood bond with Brynn would yield."

"Brynn's not as strong as Sam." Dylan stroked Brynn's forehead when she whimpered, and Sasha saw his hand shake. "She's not an alpha."

"Doesn't matter." Adam's voice sounded rough, strained. He eased away from Brynn, his gaze fixed carefully on some point past Dylan. "She's a moon wolf. She can't control the power, but vampires can take it from her. You need to get her the hell out of this state. Back to where there aren't any vampires."

Sasha gritted her teeth. "Gavin sent me and Dylan here to find you because there's a vampire helping the new alpha in Helena. We need to learn how the power transfer works so we can stop it."

"Fuck." Adam glanced at Emily. "Ethan's in my bedroom. Go check on him. It'll make him feel better."

When she was gone, the vampire closed his eyes. "Prudence is a vampire, and she might as well run Bangor. Francis has been under her thumb for three decades. They came to Bedagi Creek today to collect their tithe...and it happened pretty much like Emily said. Prudence wanted Brynn, Francis tried to take her..."

"And Joe lost his shit." Dylan's hand came to rest on Brynn's forehead. "Is he..."

"He's alive." Sasha knelt and checked Brynn's pulse. It was slow and steady. "If he was dead already, she would have been worse."

"They've got him locked up. Sedated too, I think. They pulled everyone loyal to Lawrence over to guard the house where they're keeping him. Made it easier to break Emily and your friend out."

And it was up to them to free Joe. Sasha avoided Dylan's gaze. "How powerful is this vampire?" she asked Adam.

He scrubbed his hand over the side of his face. "Honestly, I don't know. She was formidable when I knew her, but not scary enough to take over the damn city. But if she's been collecting strong wolves like Emily from nearby packs as food, she could be strong."

"We have to assume the worst, past and present." If they stood a chance of fighting Lawrence, his flunkies *and* a vampire, they'd need Ethan healthy and strong. "We can't face them right now. We have to wait, at least a day or two."

"No we don't." It was Emily, and she had Ethan braced against her. "Ethan's going to challenge Lawrence. Tonight."

It was foolish. Impossible. "You almost died a few hours ago, Ethan," Sasha argued. "You're not strong enough."

Dylan wasn't watching Emily and Ethan. He was watching Adam. "It's not a myth, is it? The vampire from Austria in the 1600s. The one who could take power from one wolf and give it to another."

"No. It's not a myth."

"And you can do it."

Adam still had his eyes closed. "Yeah. I can."

Having someone else around who knew how relocate power between wolves was the sort of thing that could make the difference between victory and defeat back in Red Rock. She was only one person, one witch with limited training and resources, but if she had help... "Is it hard for you? The transfer, I mean. What's the process?"

"A blood bond." He opened his eyes and glanced at Emily. "Take him back into my room. We'll do it there."

Emily nodded and turned them both around. When they were gone, Adam looked at Sasha. "Not all vampires can do it, but it's not difficult if you're strong enough. I drink from Emily, and I can take her power. But wolves and vampires...our magic isn't very compatible. Life and death. Some vampires are crazy enough to take a wolf's power and try to use it, but it eats us up inside eventually. Unless we give it to someone else."

Sasha stepped closer and took a deep breath. "But you don't keep the bond in place." Having the vampire feed off them for too long had almost killed Justine and Sam.

Adam shook his head. "Can't have more than one blood bond at the same time, so I break the first one after I have the power I need. Then I do it again. Only this time, I give the power."

She didn't know him well enough to ask these questions, but it didn't matter. She had to. "Can anything go wrong?"

"Plenty, in theory." Adam rose to his feet easily, but the look in his eyes was dark. "In practice? For me? Not much. I'm good at it."

"That sounds ominous."

"It should." He moved past her toward the bedroom but paused with his hand braced on the doorframe. His fingers tightened around the wood until his knuckles turned white, and he glanced over his shoulder at her. "As a general rule, I wouldn't trust anyone who's good at it. You'll live longer."

She tried not to shiver as she turned to Dylan. "What should we do about Brynn?"

He smoothed his fingers over Brynn's forehead. "Maybe you can take some of her power. The part that's hurting her."

"I'd rather ask first, but..." She covered Dylan's free hand with hers. "You've known her a long time. Would she want me to?"

Dylan nodded without hesitating. "If you could figure out a way to help her get control, I can't even tell you how much it would mean to her. It's going to kill her if she can't help save Joe."

She and Brynn weren't close, but Sasha knew his words were true. "Cindy said that sedative would last about an hour before she started to come around. If I do the spell right now, it could knock me out. Can you watch me and help?"

"Let me move Brynn." He gathered her up into his arms and rose. "If I put her on the couch, you can kneel next to it, and I can sit behind you in case anything happens."

He arranged Brynn on the cushions, and Sasha dropped to her knees beside her. She'd memorized the spell, but nerves still made her shake. "This will be different from when I cast it on you," she told Dylan. "It's not as intense, but I don't know how the drug will affect me."

Dylan lowered himself to the floor behind her and curled both hands around her shoulders. His hands were strong, warm even through her shirt, and he leaned down enough to whisper in her ear. "You can do it. I'm here."

Sasha began the incantation. It was becoming familiar, this particular rush of magic, and she barely even had to think about the words as she focused on drawing close to Brynn, on adjusting her own energy to meld with the other woman's.

It wasn't easy like it had been with Dylan. He'd been aware of what she was doing, open and ready, but Brynn struggled instinctively.

It's okay, Brynn. It's me. It's Sasha.

The thought calmed her just enough for Sasha to complete the first section of the spell, the one that would allow for transfer but only one way; giving an out-of-control wolf the ability to pull power from her would have been dangerous, maybe even suicidal.

"It's done," Sasha whispered. She felt drained, almost sluggish. "Dylan..."

Solid arms wrapped around her body and pulled her back against his chest. "The power's hurting her, and you need it. Take some of it."

It was true, but still she hesitated. Without permission... Then the decision was made for her as Brynn jerked and mumbled in her unnatural sleep, and a burst of energy barreled through Sasha, wild and untamed.

It was primal magic, the kind of frantic, edgy power that explained everything about the way Brynn looked sometimes, as if she couldn't find humanity under the layers of savagery. Dylan's breath caught behind her, and his fingers tightened on her shoulders. "I can...I can *feel* it."

Sasha hadn't had enough experience with that kind of wildness to control it. She closed her eyes and growled. "Help me deal with it, Dylan. Tell me how."

He swallowed hard. "Pull in enough power to help her, first. Pull it in and give it to me. I can handle it."

She took a shaky breath and complied, drawing energy into herself until she felt Brynn calm. The power roiled inside her almost like a living thing, looking for an outlet. Sasha shuddered and bit her lip until she tasted blood.

"Break the connection," Dylan ordered, his voice low and rasping.

It felt like forever before she could focus enough to try to sever her bond with Brynn. Her mind skittered from one thought to the next, lighting on so many but lingering on none. Finally, she ripped free with another growl, reeling from the cacophony inside her own head and body.

"Outside." She barely heard his low growl, but she didn't need to do anything. His arm locked around her body and he dragged her toward the door. Cool evening air wrapped around her as he got the door open and pulled her through it.

The door slammed shut, and then her back was against it, her hands trapped under his and pinned on either side of her head. "Look at me, Sasha."

She couldn't, not if she wanted to keep the primitive, ferocious feelings welling inside her in check. "Dylan—"

"Give me the power," he whispered. "Give it to me *now*, because you feel like a wolf to me. Like a wolf I want to claim, and if you don't stop feeling like that soon I'm going to lose control."

Her knees gave out, and only the weight of his body against hers kept her upright. She'd already known, on some level, what she must feel like to him now—like herself, but with a wolf's feral energy. And she *wanted* that wild look in his eyes, just as much as she wanted the warmth she usually found there. "I—"

He sucked in a frantic breath and tightened his fingers around her wrists. "God damn it, Sasha. If you like the way this feels, then take some of my power just before the next moon and I'll fuck you against a wall until you can't walk. But *not now*. Not like this."

The jittery need had completely eclipsed the reality of their responsibilities. "Christ." She knocked her head against the door to clear it and gathered the energy inside so she could direct it at Dylan. "I'm sorry."

"Shh." His lips brushed her jaw, then settled just above her ear. "The wolf likes you plenty, Sasha. You don't need the power for me to feel like this. I feel like this every time I touch you, it's just that I can usually control it."

"I understand." She didn't want him to feel her embarrassment and shame, so she distracted him with the burst of energy.

He groaned and dropped his head to her shoulder, but his magic welcomed the power she fed it. "That's it."

She wondered if this part of the transfer was always so intimate, or if it was only because this was Dylan. "Will you be okay?" she whispered.

Dylan rubbed his thumbs over her wrists gently as he took

another slow breath. With his body pressed to hers there was no hiding the fact that he was aroused, but his touch was soothing. After a moment he lifted his head and let her wrists go. "I'm okay. And I'm sorry."

"For what? I'm the one who almost forgot there are people depending on us."

He let out a desperate sounding laugh. "Sasha, I've been a werewolf ten years and I can barely handle this power. It makes Brynn half-crazy. Why do you think you'd be any better?"

Because she had to be. Ever since Maritza's death, she'd stepped into her mentor's place. There hadn't been time to explain that she needed another decade of training to handle everything, and it wouldn't have mattered anyway. She was better than nothing, and all the Red Rock pack had. "I'm so tired, Dylan."

He eased her away from the door and wrapped both arms around her. "We're going to get Joe. And then the four of us can go AWOL for a few days. Hole up in a hotel and sleep. Red Rock can survive without us. I know it won't fix everything..."

"We can't. We have to get back." If what Adam had said was true, the temptation Red Rock posed was too great. The vampire in Helena wouldn't rest until he had Sam and Justine back.

"I know. But now we know how to fight, right?" His hand came up to cup the back of her head, and he whispered his words against her hair. "Adam might come back with us. You won't be the only one who understands what we have to do."

But they had to get out of Maine first. "Adam will be focused on the vampire from Bangor, and Ethan will challenge Lawrence. So Joe will be counting on us tonight."

"If Brynn's feeling steady when she comes out from under the spell, she can carry a gun from the truck." Dylan's arms dropped and he stepped back, the movement full of tense energy. When he lifted his eyes to meet hers, they'd faded to gold. "With this much power in me... Tonight, I fight as a wolf."

She could feel it vibrating off him, the barely leashed strength that meant he could handle whatever resistance Lawrence's men offered. "We're still connected," she reminded him quietly. "Do you want me to break the spell before—before we go?"

He hesitated, then frowned. "What happens if someone hurts me while we're connected?"

"I'd feel it." Sasha looked away. "It wouldn't be smart to go into a fight without ending the spell's effects, I just..." *I'll miss you.*

"I know," he whispered, almost as if he'd heard the thought. His hand came up and he brushed his thumb across her cheek. "Werewolf fights get ugly, Sasha. I heal pretty fast, but I'm going to get hurt. And I don't want you to feel that."

"I've grown accustomed to it, that's all." It didn't even take a word to sever the connection between them. All she had to do was concentrate for a moment and he was gone. Abruptly alone in her own head, she trembled under his touch.

His fingers moved to her chin and he tilted her head back enough for a slow kiss. It felt like a reminder, and warmth flooded her as she wrapped her arms around his neck and kissed him back. *He cares, Sasha. Even if you can't feel it, you should remember that.*

Too soon, he lifted his head. "You should go check on Brynn. I'm going to see if they're done with the vampire mojo. And after that..."

"Then we fight," she said matter-of-factly, though fear formed an icy knot in her belly. "I'll be ready."

Chapter Nine

The air was cool enough for Dylan to see his breath as he trudged around Joe's SUV and pulled open the back door. He glanced at Ethan then jerked his head toward the neatly organized weaponry. "If Emily wants a gun or some explosives or possibly a rocket launcher, I'm pretty sure we've got just about everything here."

Ethan shook his head and unbuttoned his jacket. "That's not how Emily fights."

And Ethan probably wouldn't, either. Not that Dylan had ever seen a challenge for leadership of a pack, but guns and knives had been taboo for any other challenge in Helena. Fists, fangs and claws, those had been the weapons of choice.

Dylan fought a shudder as he unzipped one of the bags and looked for a gun for Brynn to use. "You're feeling all right, then? Whatever Adam did worked?"

"Yeah." His jaw tightened. "I shouldn't have let Emily do it, but more people are going to get hurt if I don't stop Lawrence's madness tonight."

The look in Emily's eyes had reminded Dylan of Abby when she got her mind set on something. He pulled a small handgun from the bag and checked it absently. "I would have liked to see you stop her."

The corner of Ethan's mouth kicked up. "Right. Easier said than done." He eyed the array of weapons in the back of the Blazer. "You came prepared, I guess. Is that what you do with Sasha? Arm her to the gills and hope for the best?"

Dylan choked on a laugh. "Shit, no. I wouldn't know how to use half of this. Joe's the one who gets hot and bothered over the idea of blowing stuff up. And Sasha doesn't need a gun.

She's a lot stronger witch than she lets on." *Or she knows.*

"She's human," Ethan countered. "Humans are fragile. That's not a judgment, just a fact."

Dylan waited for the rush of protective anger, but it didn't come. Instead he felt annoyance, prompted by protectiveness of a different sort. "Sasha can take care of herself. But she doesn't have to, because I'll be with her. And so will Brynn, who has been doing daily target practice with the man who owns all of this shit."

The man nodded. "You know her, not me, so it's your call. I'd just hate like hell for there to be bad blood between my pack and Gavin's because I dragged all of you into my mess."

My call. The responsibility was terrifying, even with the wild power pulsing inside him. He'd locked most of it away through sheer stubbornness, but he knew it was there, waiting for a chance to break free. To make him powerful.

Maybe some people might have found it to be a temptation. To Dylan, it felt not unlike Joe's trunk full of explosives—potentially useful, possibly inadvisable and inevitably deadly.

Dylan cleared his throat as he checked the safety on the handgun before tucking it into the back of his jeans. "You're not dragging anyone into anything. It's our trouble too. Joe's in danger, and Sasha's not any more likely to sit at home and wait for us to fix things than Emily is."

"All right, then." Without turning, Ethan spoke to Adam as the vampire strode toward them. "Is everyone ready?"

"Emily's changed," Adam replied quietly. "She's ready for you. A little unsteady, but fit enough to watch a challenge. Once you two leave, we can start around the back way."

Ethan nodded. "If this goes south... Well, you've been a good friend, Adam."

The vampire clapped Ethan on the shoulder with a wide, unexpected grin. "You and Emily are what this town needs, and they're going to come out and support you. I know they will."

Dylan could only hope Adam was right. Too much of their plan rested on Emily and Ethan causing enough of a division that Lawrence couldn't rally people to his cause. Adam and his friends seemed convinced that the town would fight back against their alpha given half a chance.

Maybe they were right. Maybe there'd been a time when the wolves in Helena had the heart to fight against Alan. Maybe

Ethan and Emily could save Bedagi Creek before it became another place where fear ruled.

And maybe Adam could give the people of Helena another chance to fight. Their first chance to win.

A hand touched his arm, and Dylan realized Ethan was gone and Adam stood next to him now. The vampire's face was sober, tense with anticipation. His eyes, though...his eyes held excitement. "You going to hold together, kid?"

"Yes." There was nothing else in the truck he needed, so he closed the door. "I always do."

"And them?" Adam tilted his head toward Sasha and Brynn, who were huddled close together at the edge of the clearing, speaking in soft whispers. The wind teased at Sasha's hair, which was pulled into a tight ponytail. Her manner was serious and intent, but not worried.

Brynn, on the other hand, looked tired. Tired and upset, but more herself than she'd been since the attack that had changed her. Dylan recognized the expression on her face from long experience, a mixture of stubborn determination and fierce concentration.

It was reassuring. The possibility that Sasha would have to fight wolves *and* Brynn had occurred to him more than once, and it hadn't been pleasant to ponder. Whatever Sasha had done, though, had obviously worked. His friend was back, and ready to reclaim her mate.

Mate. The wolf rumbled inside him at the word, pacing anxiously in anticipation of being unleashed. The power inside him might have come from Brynn, but it had gone through Sasha and tasted of witch, not wolf. The memory of how close he'd come to taking Sasha against Adam's door—how close he'd come to *claiming* her—was still uncomfortably arousing.

Adam cleared his throat. Noisily. "I was hoping for a status report, not a girl-on-girl fantasy break."

Dylan jerked his attention back to Adam. "First off, fuck you. Second, yeah. They'll be fine. Third..." He bared his teeth in a grin that was a little bit reckless challenge. "Once we get to Joe, I'd lay off talking about Brynn. Or looking at her. Or getting within fifteen feet of her."

"Duly noted." Adam jerked his head toward the front of the truck. "Ready?"

"As I'll ever be."

Sasha caught Dylan's gaze, patted Brynn's arm and walked over to him. "She's doing a lot better. Says she feels a little bit human. That's something, right?"

"It's a lot." Dylan ignored Adam and leaned down to kiss the top of Sasha's head. "You two ready? We should be in place when Emily starts making noise."

"The sooner the better," Sasha whispered. "Joe must be wondering where we are."

More likely Joe was going to kick their asses when he found out they hadn't run for the hills. *When he finds out I armed Brynn and let her walk back in there after him...* Dylan tried not to shudder. "He probably still thinks they have Brynn. It's the only reason he wouldn't be killing his way out of there, drugged or not."

"He'd be glad to know she's safe, at least." Sasha's eyes darkened. "Look, putting it off isn't making this easier. Everything you've seen me do has been something constructive, Dylan. Something to help someone. I need to do things differently tonight."

She seemed uneasy, so he nodded. "All right."

"It'll be dark, maybe even scary."

"All right."

She ground her teeth. "Damn it, Dylan. A little acknowledgement of understanding would be helpful. Having to do this, to let go of control... It scares me."

Dylan glanced at Adam, then wrapped his fingers around Sasha's arm and tugged her a few steps from the car. For all he knew the vampire's hearing was as good as his own, but the illusion of privacy was something. "If you're asking me to be scared of you, it's not going to happen. I trust you."

"Okay." She backed away a step. "I'm ready, then."

It sounded like a lie, but not because she wasn't ready to go. If anything, she sounded anxious to end the conversation, and that made him nervous. "Why are you scared? Is what you're doing dangerous?"

"Not any more dangerous than what anyone else is doing."

Not the most satisfying answer, but there wasn't time for more. Dylan reached to the small of his back and pulled the gun free. "I'm going to give this to Brynn, and then I'm going to change. It can take me a few minutes to recover, so I'm going to do it now. If there's anything you need to ask, any questions at all, now's the time."

"No, nothing." She dipped her head in a quick nod. "Good luck."

Brynn was still standing apart from the rest of them. She stared at the trees around them as if she could see straight to the town. Dylan had no doubt her gaze was fixed on Joe's location with a precision any compass would envy.

She didn't turn around, but she spoke before Dylan got within a few feet of her. "I think they drugged him again. He was coming out of it, but everything's gone quiet. I tried to reach him, to make him feel *something*, but it's too far and I don't know how."

Dylan lifted his hand to Brynn's shoulder and squeezed softly. "You'll be with him soon. And I think Joe would come out of a coma just to yell at you for walking back into that town, so he should be on his feet as soon as we get there."

He got the feeling Brynn smiled more because she thought she was supposed to than because she'd even heard his words. The feral power that had haunted her for the past few weeks might be muted, but her gray eyes were still wild. She reached out a hand without looking at him. "Gun?"

Dylan placed it in her hand. "Loaded."

"Spare ammunition?"

He hadn't thought of it. A month ago Brynn wouldn't have, either. "Maybe in the truck. I can—"

"I'll do it." She glanced at him, and a shiver claimed him when he considered, for the first time, that Brynn might have picked up more from Joe than an understanding of firearms. That hardness had always been inside Brynn, but it had been defensive strength before, nothing but dull edges.

Edges Joe had known how to hone.

Dylan nodded his acknowledgement and stepped aside to let her pass. He heard her boots crunch on the dry leaves as he turned his back and bent to jerk at the laces on his tennis shoes.

Modesty wasn't high on his priority list, even in front of a vampire who seemed to find poking at his pride to be an amusing pastime, but stripping down in the woods had its own discomforts. Dylan ignored the biting wind as he jerked off his shirt and kicked off his jeans. He gathered his clothes and left them on top of the truck, killing time because even standing naked in the cold wind was more comfortable than what came next.

He hated the change. Some wolves found it easy, but those were the strong ones, the ones whose control was perfect and who lived with the wolf close to the surface. Before Sasha, Dylan's wolf had been a quiet companion, a silent part of himself that gave him the strength to endure but demanded little in return. Even the days before the full moon were only mildly uncomfortable, mostly due to the need to find a warm woman and burn off sexual frustration.

There was nothing quiet about the wolf today. The power inside him excited his wolf like nothing else had. *Nothing except her.*

He couldn't turn to look at Sasha. With wild anticipation singing in his blood, arousal would be fast and hard. Even the thought of her stirred something dark, and Dylan forced his thoughts from sex to blood. A fight was coming, and that was new. His wolf knew how to endure, how to suffer in silence and rebel quietly.

Tonight would be different.

He crouched in the leaves and closed his eyes, preparing himself to call on the wolf. But the power teased at him instead, that wild magic that felt like Sasha, and he sucked in a breath and gave into it.

The change flowed over him like magic. Pain first, but that didn't matter in the rush of heat that followed. He felt wild, alive and alert to the world. *Awake*, as if the last ten years had been spent in shadow. Paws touched the earth and he lifted his nose to sniff the air, which smelled of gun oil and witch and the cold, eerie scent of death magic, of whatever lived inside Adam that made him smell dead even though he was still alive.

Odd allies for a wolf, but with magic pounding through him Dylan didn't care. The wind changed, brought with it the sounds of Bedagi Creek and Emily's howl of challenge, and he answered with a sharp yip of command before leaping for the woods.

Even when they broke free of the woods, the streets were deserted. Nothing stirred but the cold night breeze that had followed them, and the only signs of life were the howls that drifted to Sasha's ears from the center of town.

Dylan stalked ahead of her, growling low in his throat when the wind shifted direction.

Joe. It had to be. When Sasha loosened her grip on the magic swirling through her, she felt it, the men and women gathered to guard the prisoner. Some were angry, but most were simply scared, because the sounds of challenge that rose in the night meant the alpha they served might not last the hour.

Perhaps they could be persuaded to leave Joe, to join the formalities in the town square. Perhaps there would be no fight.

Adam lifted his hand, ignoring Dylan's soft growl. "Wait," he whispered, his voice barely rising above the sound of the wind. "Prudence is with him. I can feel her."

If he could sense her already, they had no hope of a stealthy approach. "If they've drugged Joe, what will happen to her if she tries to feed from him?"

Brynn growled. Adam ignored her, too. "It depends on how powerful she's gotten. She probably wouldn't risk it, though. I don't think I'd want to risk it, and I'm a lot stronger than she is."

"How do you know? If Francis has been feeding her alph—"

"I'm stronger." Adam's voice was hard, uncompromising. "She may have raw power, but power can't compensate for everything. You need the will to use it, and you're born with that or you're not. She wasn't."

Adam's insinuation that he had the will to do things even a power-mad vampire wouldn't do should have scared her. But Sasha was beyond fear. All she wanted now was for all of them to make it through the night and go home. "If I tell you not to get between me and Prudence, you have to trust me. Can you do that, Adam?"

Adam didn't answer right away. Dylan appeared at her side, his body pressed tight against her leg, and he bared his teeth in a low, dangerous snarl.

The vampire rolled his eyes. "Settle down, puppy. I'm not insulting your woman." Adam transferred his gaze to Sasha, his dark eyes cold. "If you tell me to move, I'll move. But you must do the same."

Dylan shook beside her, and Sasha dropped a hand to soothe him. "I'm trying to make sure no one gets hurt. Some of my spells can't be easily directed, so all I can do is...tailor them. In this case, make life hard for anyone who's supposed to be dead."

Adam nodded. His gaze drifted to Brynn, and that ice-cold look thawed a little, replaced by a disturbing hunger—disturbing because it wasn't the least bit sexual. His squeezed his eyes shut and swore quietly. "She'll do anything to get her hands on Brynn. Even with most of the power gone, she smells like...food."

"I can hear you," Brynn snapped.

"Good. Don't forget it." Adam opened his eyes and stared directly at Sasha. "If you have to choose, if I'm in the way...cast your spell. And tell Gavin I paid his goddamned life debt back."

It was almost funny, and Sasha tightened her fingers in Dylan's fur. "See? I told you the life debt was tradition."

He butted his head against her hip hard enough to make his feelings on the matter more than clear. Adam opened his mouth—

—and froze when Brynn made a choked noise, her head whipping around. Her lips formed Joe's name a second before she screamed, a furious sound that didn't sound like it could come from a human throat.

Adam lunged for her, but his fingers closed on the edge of her shirt, and she tore free and bolted between two nearby houses, headed straight toward the source of the nervous magic that filled the air.

Sasha cursed and took off after her, blood pounding in her ears. "Brynn, no!" If she went in there half out of her head, she might be able to power her way through whatever wolves stood in her way, but she wouldn't stand a chance against a hungry vampire.

Brynn was still a hundred feet from the front door when it burst open. A wolf shot out, and Dylan howled a challenge and darted past Sasha. He hit the wolf broadside, and they tumbled to the grass beside the porch. Two more wolves and a man rushed out of the house, and Brynn snatched the gun from her waistband and began firing.

They were outnumbered already, and Sasha wanted to stop, to help. Instead, she ran inside the house.

A man grabbed her and slammed her into the nearest wall in a practiced, fluid movement. Then he stopped, a look of disbelief flitting across his face as his nostrils flared. "You're not a wolf," he growled.

"No, I'm not." She closed her eyes and reached down for the dark magic she'd warned Dylan about, the part of herself she'd hoped to avoid. She wouldn't get through this fight without violence, so she let go, unleashing some of the anger and fear inside her.

The man dropped his gun and staggered back, clutching his head. Adam strode past her, grasped the man's head and twisted it with one sharp movement. Sasha heard a sharp crack, and Adam turned as his opponent slumped lifelessly to the floor. He lifted his face as his voice rose, loud enough to be heard over the angry snarls outside. "Prudence Goodman, I challenge you for blood rights to Bedagi Creek."

There was no response, just a clicking of what sounded like shoe heels on hardwood. Then a delicate-looking brunette with dark, curly hair leaned over the second-floor railing and smiled down at them. "What could *you* possibly want with them, Adam?" Her voice was light, clear and sweet. "Last I heard, you were eating deer and bunnies out in the woods."

Adam laughed, a harsh, rumbling noise with an edge of menace. "What brings you to the woods, darling? Can't get anyone to believe you're Stephen King's muse anymore?"

Prudence yawned. "That joke was only funny twenty years ago." She looked past him to where Sasha still stood against the wall. "You're new. Witch, right? Have you come for the wolf?"

She looked absolutely, utterly normal, and Sasha shivered. "I came for my friend."

Claws scrabbled on the threshold behind them. Adam spun, placing his body between Sasha and the door, but the attacking wolf only made it halfway into the room before the reddish wolf she recognized as Dylan pounced onto his back. Power spiraled out as Dylan snarled and snapped.

Prudence sucked in a laugh and clapped her hands. "Not a moon wolf, but I bet he'd taste like one. Adam, you cad, what have you been doing out in that hovel of yours?"

Before Adam could answer, Brynn screamed. Pain, not rage, and Dylan's head snapped up. He leapt toward the door but skittered to a stop a few feet away from Sasha, obviously torn between conflicting instincts.

Adam caught Sasha's gaze. "Do what you have to do," he

told her, his voice deadly serious. He spun without waiting for a response and sprinted out the door.

"Nice." Prudence's heels clicked again as she walked slowly down the stairs. "He went off to fight the wolves and left you here." Her eyes gleamed as she studied Sasha intently. "So why are you special?"

I can do this. Sasha repeated the words silently even as Dylan growled menacingly. Maritza had taught her everything she needed to know, and all she had to do was believe in herself the way—

The way Dylan believed in her. The way everyone in Red Rock believed in her, even if they were scared to death of what she could do.

She had to speak to call the spell she needed, and Prudence's steps sped with Sasha's whispered words. "What are you doing?" the vampire asked, still more curious than anything else.

The spell took hold, readying the magic inside her, and Sasha released a soft, pained breath. "You don't look so scary. I bet you get that a lot. So do I."

Dylan edged in front of Sasha with a low rumble of warning. He paced one step toward Prudence, and the wolf whimpering in the corner staggered to his feet and lunged at Sasha.

Everything happened at once. Dylan spun and barreled into the attacker with an angry snarl. The wolf tumbled back to the floor as Dylan lifted his head and let out a furious howl of challenge. Magic thundered through the room, a crash sounded from upstairs, and the wolf on the floor rolled onto his back in obvious surrender.

Cold, slim fingers closed around Sasha's shoulders and jerked her back. Prudence's soft laughter tickled the side of her neck. "You don't have to be scary to be powerful, my dear."

Sasha barely had time to breathe the words Maritza had taught her, a witch's last line of defense, before the woman's teeth sank into her skin. Sharp pain bloomed, and she thrashed instinctively, though she knew the iron strength in Prudence's hands wouldn't give.

Dylan roared his fury and shifted his weight, presumably in prelude to an attack. One of Prudence's hands shot up to close around the front of Sasha's throat in obvious threat, and Dylan froze, the look in his golden eyes wild.

The railing above the foyer splintered as a chair crashed through it and tumbled to the first floor. Dylan's claws clicked as he scrambled out of the way, and Prudence released Sasha with a laugh.

Joe appeared at the top of the stairs, disheveled, his bare chest displaying an array of cuts, welts and bites. His gaze fixed on Prudence, and his steps were steady and sure as he made his way down the staircase. "Where is she?" he demanded.

Sasha pressed a shaky hand to her neck. "Brynn's outside," she told him hoarsely. "Go."

Dylan had already gotten between her and Prudence, his body trembling with tension as he inched back, forcing Sasha to move to keep from tripping over him.

Prudence swayed. She swiped at the corner of her mouth, smearing blood across her fingers. She stared down at her hand, and those delicate, perfectly arched eyebrows came together as she frowned. "I don't..."

She staggered, groping for something to catch her balance on, and Dylan pounced. Wolf and vampire went down in a tangle of thrashing limbs and fur. Her earlier speed and grace had vanished, but she was still strong. Both arms locked around Dylan's body and squeezed until he yelped. He twisted and closed his jaws on her arm, and it was her turn to scream. She flung Dylan away, sent him skittering across the floor with his claws scratching up the hardwood.

Prudence rolled to her hands and knees and tried to stand. Her elbows gave out and her hands slid across the floor as her body collapsed. She twisted around, cold blue gaze finding Sasha. "Witch."

"Yes." This time, she didn't bother trying to make sure Adam wouldn't be hurt outside. She recalled the spell, building it again, whispering the words over and over until the magic exploded in a surge of *life*.

Light flared, and Prudence screamed. Sasha hit the floor just as she heard another cry from outside, low and masculine and filled with pain, but there wasn't time to worry about Adam. Prudence rolled onto her back, her face slack from agony, as the glow of magic intensified.

Dylan groaned, and this time it sounded human. He strode into Sasha's field of vision, naked and covered with blood and vicious-looking cuts and bite marks. Prudence tried to crawl away as he dropped to his knees next to her, but the spell had done its work.

He made it quick. Dylan's hands closed around the vampire's head and he twisted sharply, silencing her desperate noises by snapping her neck. He didn't look at Sasha as he dropped his hands to his thighs, the line of his back rigid and tense. "Is she dead?"

"I think so." There were too many mingled auras for her to be certain, inside the house and out, too much adrenaline and pain and desperation. "There are things we can do to make sure." Sasha crawled closer and touched Dylan. "Are you okay?"

Tension flared and he jerked away from her hand. "Fine." The word came out rough and gravelly. "Can you check on Brynn and Joe?"

Sasha stared at Dylan's back and the smear of blood she'd left there, then pressed her hand to the wound on her neck. "I'll take care of it."

There was no reason to be hurt by his words. The vampire might be dead, but they were still in the middle of a dangerous fight, and she tried to remind herself of that as she walked out the front door. Joe stood in the yard, his arms around Brynn and his mouth close to her ear.

Even looking at them felt like intruding, so Sasha bypassed them and stopped beside Adam. "Prudence is dead, I think."

He glanced down at her, swore and reached for her hand. "You're bleeding."

"She bit me. I'm sure she found the experience wholly unpleasant." Her knees felt wobbly, and a dull buzzing filled her ears. "I don't feel..."

She barely heard Adam's rough curse as the world went black.

Chapter Ten

One of these things is not like the others.

Dylan tried not to fidget with the coffee cup in his hands as he waited for Emily to settle herself in the seat on his right. Lawrence's wife, Irene, was already seated on his left, her strong hands clenched together so hard her knuckles were white. Her eyes were red and puffy and her expression looked carved from stone, but neither was surprising. Her husband, her mate, had died that night, died during the culmination of a chain of events she'd put into motion with a phone call.

And now she sat at the table of the man who had killed him.

Ethan looked a little worse for the wear, though he'd taken a shower and let Emily and the pack's doctor examine his injuries. Dylan had received similar attentions after he'd forced the doctor to check on Sasha. She'd fared better than most of them in the injury department, though exhaustion from expending too much magical energy had finally taken its toll.

Sasha was resting easily. Joe and Brynn—well, Dylan felt more comfortable pretending they were resting easily too, and prayed like hell they would be by the time he made his way back to the guest house. As for Dylan himself... *One of these things is most* definitely *not like the others.*

Three strong alpha wolves sat on three sides of Ethan and Emily's cozy kitchen table, and all three watched him expectantly.

Dylan cleared his throat and took a sip of his coffee. "I talked to Gavin. He's working with Sam now to rearrange some funds. You'll have enough money to feed the town through the winter."

Ethan's jaw tightened, and Dylan knew his pride was warring with his practicality. "I'll have to thank him, and let him know we'll repay him as soon as possible."

"Of course." Dylan forced himself to look at Irene. "I think Sam's going to call you tomorrow and invite you to Red Rock. In case you need a chance to get away."

She barely glanced at him. "I wouldn't want to be a bother."

"You are *not* a bother." Emily leaned forward, her eyes intense. "I know you probably can't take comfort from us. I don't blame you. But you need it. You deserve it, Irene."

"I don't—" She looked away, trembling, her lips clamped together tightly.

Ethan touched Emily's arm. "Plenty of time to figure things out, for all of us." He turned his gaze to Dylan. "Does Gavin need you, or can you stay a few days and heal up?"

"He wants us to stay here until we're all on our feet again." And until Joe could let go of Brynn for long enough to assess the town and make sure there wouldn't be trouble from Bangor.

"As long as you like." The new alpha drummed his fingers on the table. "I want to take a walk. You feel like taking a walk, Dylan?"

He felt like crawling into bed with Sasha, but the magic that still thrummed inside him brought with it the urge to do things that would probably scare her. He could still remember the pain in her voice after he'd killed the vampire, the way she'd reacted when he'd jerked away from her touch. But better pain than fear, and he couldn't imagine any other reaction to finding her lover covered with blood and aroused by the thought of celebrating victory between her thighs.

Ethan still watched him, so he shoved down the uncomfortable memories and nodded. "As long as it's not a long walk. I probably need sleep too."

"Understood." The man ran his hand over Emily's hair as he rose. "I'll be back in a few minutes."

"You'd better be." Emily caught Ethan's hand and kissed it, and for just a moment Dylan caught that same wildness in her eyes that he'd seen in Brynn and Joe's, that wildness he'd been fighting all night. They'd fought for their lives, dealt death and triumphed. Something primal inside demanded recognition of the fact that they were still alive, wanted the proof that came from hard, crazy sex that pushed limits and left the body drained and trembling.

Which was all well and good if your partner was another wolf fighting the same urge. Sasha was a human who'd been hurt by rough, out-of-control werewolves. The only thing that terrified Dylan more than the thought of bringing her to bed with that sort of wildness was the possibility that she wouldn't stop him, even if it scared her.

Outside, the night was silent. Ethan went no farther than the porch steps, and he lowered himself to them with a wince and a sheepish laugh. "Maybe I'm not up for a walk, after all. But I wanted to talk to you alone. I don't need Em kicking my ass tonight."

Dylan nodded his understanding and leaned against the railing. "Is something wrong?"

"Nah." Ethan rested his elbows on his knees. "You and Sasha. Are you settled in Red Rock?"

Easy relaxation vanished as the wolf scented a threat. "Not exactly. But I owe a lot to Gavin."

"I absolutely get that. I mean, hell, so do I now. But we could really use Sasha around here." He hesitated and looked up at Dylan. "There's a boy in town, nearly a teenager now. He's shown some magical aptitude, but he hasn't had a teacher..."

Dylan bit back an instinctive growl and forced himself to consider the words. A place where she was needed, but not feared. Someone to teach. Safety from the war. Peace. *If you really gave a damn about Sasha, you'd beg her to stay here.* "There's a war going on in Red Rock. I can't leave them to fight it alone."

"I wouldn't ask anyone to do that." Ethan's eyes darkened. "Look, I wanted to talk to you before I talked to Sasha. I'm not asking her to abandon her friends. I just thought maybe she could make her way back around sometime, that's all."

Guilt made Dylan queasy. "Half of the reason we're here is because the town is scared of her. She's miserable there. She *should* stay here."

The alpha held up both hands. "I'd have to be an idiot not to figure out you two are together, and I'm no idiot. Not trying to cause trouble, either."

"You're not." Dylan closed his eyes and leaned his head against the solid oak post. "Trouble was already there. We've got some stuff to figure out. But maybe it'll be easier to figure out if she knows she has someplace to go."

Ethan rose. "I'll hold off on asking her about it. Give you two a chance to talk."

In a way it would have been easier to let Ethan be the one to make the offer. It might have been fairer to Sasha too. Without Dylan present she wouldn't have to hide her wishes, wouldn't feel the need to soothe his ego or his bruised feelings...

Coward. It was another way of running away. He'd fled from Cindy so he wouldn't have to see the rejection in her eyes and told himself he was doing her a favor. If he wanted Sasha, he was going to have to fight for her.

He was going to have to sacrifice for her.

Dylan met Ethan's gaze. "As long as I'd be welcome."

"Hell, yeah." The other man held out his hand. "Any of you, always."

"Then I'll talk to her." Dylan shook Ethan's hand and smiled. "Better go inside before Emily comes out here to get you. I don't think I want to be in her way when that happens."

"Not if she's figured out why I wanted to speak with you."

Tension returned. "Because she doesn't want Sasha here?"

Ethan snorted. "Because if she knew I'd purposefully talked to you before Sasha, she'd call me a sexist ass and make me sleep on the couch for a week."

Normally Dylan might have agreed with Emily's thoughts on the matter, but with the moon magic still lingering inside him he wasn't sure what his reaction might have been to a wolf trying to lure Sasha to his pack. Not when he hadn't gotten to touch her, hold her...claim her.

Discomfort twisted his stomach, and he dragged in a breath that came out as a growl. "How do you *live* like this all the time?"

"Don't really think about it, I guess." Ethan shrugged. "No sense in fighting what you can't change. That's not going to help you much, though, huh?"

"Not really." Nothing would help but seeing Sasha and knowing she was safe. With practice born of a decade of repression he shoved his wolf down as he straightened. "I'll see you in the morning, Ethan."

He'd already turned toward the door. "Breakfast's at seven."

The short walk to their guest lodgings should have given

him time to get his instincts under control. In the past it had been easy, a simple matter of turning off anything inside him that wasn't directly related to survival. Not healthy, perhaps, but the only choice. A way to bend instead of breaking.

Then again, Sasha felt necessary to survival. Air, food, shelter...his mate. Melodramatic. *Terrifying.*

True.

So find a way to show her without scaring her to death. And after that, he'd cure cancer and find the solution to world peace.

Sasha had almost decided that she should stop staring at the wall and get up, get dressed, when the door opened. She tensed without meaning to, and she had to take in and release a deep breath before she could bring herself to roll over.

Dylan stood in the doorway, his entire body stiff and his eyes blazing. Remnants of power vibrated around him, made him seem like a dangerous werewolf instead of the considerate man who had seduced her so carefully.

She sat up. He looked the same as he had outside Adam's cabin, when she'd almost begged him to take her. Now, Sasha had no connection to the wildness tearing through him, only what she could see and sense. It would have been frightening, except that she trusted him with her life.

She opened her arms.

His fingers spasmed on the doorframe and he swayed toward her, then froze with a low groan. "Sasha." Her name came out hoarse, full of rough promise and need. "I don't want to hurt you."

You won't. She wanted to say it, and almost did. But she'd felt that uncontrollable need, and she was only human. If she urged him to, he'd let go. And if he hurt her, he'd never forgive himself.

So Sasha crawled out of the bed and stood beside it, her hands clenched into fists at her sides. "Tell me what to do. How to make sure you don't hurt me."

He stepped over the threshold and closed the door. A moment later he reached for the lock, fumbling with the old-fashioned hook until it rested safely in the ring attached to the wall. Every movement was slow, painfully careful. His hands shook as he curled them in his T-shirt and tugged at it. "Don't move fast," he whispered, the words muffled by the fabric as he pulled his shirt over his head.

"All right." She slipped her own shirt over her head with trembling hands. "What else?"

His gaze swept up her body, and the fire in his eyes grew more intense as he dropped his hands to his borrowed sweatpants. "Take the rest of your clothes off."

Her pajama pants hit the floor, and she slid her panties down her legs. The raw passion burning in his eyes made her skin feel tight, and she licked her lips as her breathing quickened. "Can I kiss you now?"

"Soon." He was already barefoot. The sweatpants landed near her feet and he stood in front of her, naked and hard. His gaze roved over her, slowly this time, lingering on the bruise on her hip and the marks of Prudence's fingers along her upper arms. When he reached the small bandage on the side of her neck his breath hissed out and an upset noise rumbled out of his chest.

When he moved, there was nothing human about it. He stalked around her in a wide arc, as if trying to study every inch of her for bruises or injuries. Only after he was satisfied did he step close enough that his fingers could skate along her shoulder. "You're safe now."

The words hovered somewhere between statement and question. "Safe." Sasha turned to look at Dylan, and her eyes met his. "I feel out of step. I think I got used to being in your head."

His hand smoothed down to the slender, finger-shaped bruises forming on her arm. He bent his head and pressed a soft kiss to the bandage covering the bite mark on her throat. "My head's not pretty right now. You're the only pretty thing there."

"I don't believe that." He still seemed jumpy, but she needed to touch him, so she laid her hands lightly on his shoulders. "This is who you are. Maybe not usually, not even under normal circumstances, but sometimes. And there isn't anything ugly about you, Dylan."

He trailed his fingers up her shoulder and curled them around the base of her neck. "I need you."

"I'm here. I'll give you anything." Sasha's pulse jumped, and she pressed her open mouth to his cheek and jaw. Her own words shocked her because she felt them so deeply. Completely. "Anything you need."

"Anything." When he repeated the word it sounded rough. Uncomfortable. He tilted her head and forced her to meet his gaze. "Then give me a promise. Promise that you won't give me everything I need. If you tell me to stop, I can stop. But I'm terrified you won't until it's too late."

"No." She pulled his hands away from her, her entire body numb except for one sick spot in the pit of her stomach. "No, Dylan. If there are things I can't give you, then you keep looking until you find them. It's not fair to either of us if you have to push parts of yourself down just to be with me. I won't do it."

He staggered back a step, then spun and braced both hands on the wall. The tight muscles in his bare back trembled as he sucked in a low breath. "You don't know what sort of things are inside me. Have been inside me since the fight. I want them *gone*."

Sasha's eyes burned and tears slipped down her cheeks. "I could take them away," she admitted, "but I wouldn't be doing you any favors. You could tell me, though, and maybe it would help."

"I killed." The words escaped as a hoarse rasp, and his fingernails scratched into the wood of the walls. "As a wolf. I killed. And it felt *good* to win."

"Of course it did. Winning feels good, that's universal. It doesn't mean you wanted to kill them."

"I wanted to take you. When you touched me in that house, I wanted to turn around and take you. I wanted to fuck you on the goddamned floor with a dead vampire five feet away, because I won and you were mine."

Every muscle in his body was tight with pain, and his aura was thick with fear and a loathing she knew was self-directed. "But you didn't do it."

He shuddered. "I almost did."

"But you didn't." She walked up beside him and leaned against the wall beside one of his outstretched hands. "We won, and we managed to stay alive doing it. So you wanted to celebrate that, and there's no more visceral, immediate way to do that than with sex. It doesn't mean there's something wrong with you."

He moved so fast that her hands were pinned on either side

of her head before she realized he'd gotten her back against the wall. "Are you scared of me?"

He still looked damn near feral, and she should have been. She should have been scared as hell, if only because she knew he didn't trust himself. "No. Ugliness scares me, Dylan, and I already told you. There's nothing ugly about you."

Something flared inside him, strong enough that it flickered in his aura. Confusion. Hesitation.

Hope.

He groaned and crushed his lips to hers, the kiss starting off bruising hard. His teeth scraped her bottom lip before he sucked it into his mouth.

Heat swept through her, and she tried to free her arms to wind around his neck. But he held her still, wrists firmly but gently in his grasp, as he deepened the kiss. His tongue explored her mouth, and Sasha moaned and arched her body into his.

Dylan guided her wrists up until he could trap them both under one hand. The other tickled down her arm and along her shoulder before inching low enough to cup her breast. He lifted his head just enough to whisper his next question against her lips. "Do you still want me?"

Now and forever. But words weren't enough, so she raised one leg and rubbed the inside of her thigh over his hip. She used her trapped hands for leverage and stretched up on her toes, just high enough to angle her hips to graze his cock.

His fingers tightened around her wrists and he bit her chin hard enough to sting before soothing it with his tongue. His body shifted to the side, pinning her to the wall with her legs straddling his thigh. "No."

Instinct and frustration drove her to bite him back, and she closed her teeth on his jaw.

He laughed, low and rough, and his thumb played over her nipple. "No. You want something inside you, you ask for it."

A shiver claimed her, and she rolled her hips against the hard muscles of his thigh. "Please."

"Please what?"

There were a thousand things she wanted, and the words that tumbled out surprised her. "Kiss me again."

Dylan hesitated. Hoisted her a little higher until she was

balanced on her toes and his mouth was inches from hers. Some of the wildness in his eyes faded as he brushed his lips over hers in the softest kiss before moving his mouth to her cheek. "I need things Cindy couldn't give me. Maybe things no one but you could give me."

It wasn't the most opportune time for him to be mentioning his ex-lover, but his worried expression eliminated any thought of comparisons. "Tell me. Trust me."

His hand released her wrists and dragged down her body as he dropped to his knees. Strong fingers curled around her hips as he rubbed his cheek against her belly. "I'm not like the alphas. I don't want your submission. I just want your pleasure."

"I've never had an alpha." Sasha knelt in front of him and pushed at his shoulders. He landed on the floor, and she climbed over him. "But pleasure is a really good place to start."

Dylan reached for her hips, dragging her up his body until she was straddling his chest. "I want you to show me what feels good. Tell me how to touch you. Tell me what you've always wanted."

"That's easy." She moved his hand up to her breast and hissed in a breath when his fingertips skated over her nipple. "I want you to tease me."

"Do you?" His thumb and forefinger caught her nipple and tugged at it. "Is that all you want?"

Desire spiked through her, leaving behind a throbbing tension that made her rock over him. "No. Teasing's only good if there's a payoff, like feeling you inside me."

The hand on her hip slid around to her ass. His eyes blazed as he pulled her higher, easing her so close that his breath tickled her inner thigh. He turned his head to press a kiss to her sensitive skin, and she felt his tongue on her as a groan shook through him. "You want this."

"Want what?" Sasha had to reach back and brace her hand on his stomach so she wouldn't fall over. "You?"

"Me." He bit the inside of her leg and soothed it with his tongue. "Even like this."

"Why wouldn't I want—" Her voice melted into a sharp moan as he touched her again. "God."

He didn't answer. He didn't say anything as his hands locked around her hips and held her steady, poised with his breath falling hot against her. He stayed like that for an endless moment, the air between them buzzing with tension and building anticipation.

Then he growled and swiped his tongue over her, dragging it all the way up to tease her clit.

He definitely had the teasing part down, and Sasha squeezed her eyes shut and tried not to grind down against his mouth. "What I've always wanted," she echoed in a whisper. "I'll show you, if you want. In a minute..."

The world upended. His fingers stayed locked around her hips as he rolled to his knees and launched them both toward the bed. Her back hit the mattress, and Dylan planted his hands on either side of her head. He stared down at her with wild eyes as he gasped in desperate, panting breaths. "If anything is too much, tell me," he whispered.

Her fingers drifted over his cheek and she nodded, entranced. "I promise."

Magic sang inside him, everything made of restless hunger. His mouth blazed a path down her throat, licking and biting and returning to the places that made her react.

She expected him to move quickly, to urge her thighs apart with his shoulders and resume teasing her with his tongue. Instead, he continued to explore, skimming over her breasts and shoulders and even the curve of her waist.

It went on and on. Sasha arched and panted and clenched her fingers in his hair, desperate for him to take her beyond the steady waves of pleasure coursing through her. "Dylan." Her legs tangled with his, and she pulled lightly at his hair. "More. Now."

He chuckled against her breast and stroked his fingers between her legs, teasing just inside her before coming up to circle her clit. "Come for me."

She bucked and groaned when he kept the touch light, fleeting. "Not until you tell me what you want."

Dylan lifted his head and stared at her. "I want you to come. I want you to feel so good you can't imagine anyone else touching you. I want you to be mine because I give you everything you need."

It was everything she loved about him, distilled into a few whispered words. His needs were irrevocably tied to hers, and Sasha trembled as she reached up and ran her thumb over his lower lip. "I knew all that the first time I kissed you, Dylan."

"Please..." He stroked her more firmly this time. "Come, Sasha."

Her legs shook as pleasure streaked through her, and his name left her lips in a breathless cry. She turned her head to his neck and bit him as wave after wave burst through her, and he dragged her head back and covered her mouth with his own.

He didn't stop touching her, didn't stop kissing her, not until she was coming again. His hand drifted over to her thigh, lifting her leg. He drew back and whispered her name, low and full of longing, and thrust inside her.

It coaxed another cry from her throat, and she wrapped her arms and legs around him. "Love you. I love you."

He'd been gentle with her before, but the wildness she sensed inside him was too intense for slow, soft lovemaking. He drove into her hard enough to inch her body up the bed. In the next heartbeat they moved, tumbling on the bed until he was on his back and she was above him, his fingers still digging into her hips so hard she knew she'd have bruises.

One hand raced up to tangle in her hair, and he urged her head up so he could look at her. "I claimed you," he whispered hoarsely. "Now *take me*."

Sasha's breath hitched as she stared down at him and slowly sat up. She grasped his wrists and pressed them up into the pillows. A few slow, smooth rolls of her hips gave way to a single hard grind. "Slow or fast?"

He licked his lips and arched against her. "Fast."

He may have been beneath her, pinned to the bed, but his words were commanding. Sasha bit her lip to hold back a moan and leaned forward, bracing her weight on their hands. When she moved again, it was with a hard, deep thrust, one made so much better when he ground up to meet her with perfect timing.

His gaze stayed locked on hers as he met her movements, her name falling from his lips with every rocking thrust. He watched her like he needed her, needed her pleasure and her acceptance and everything she was.

For a moment, it almost felt like being connected with him, like being in his head. "I can't imagine anyone else touching me."

"They better not." The words were a possessive rasp. "No

one. No one but me."

"Just you." Sasha could barely choke out the words through the haze of pleasure tightening around her. She let go of Dylan's wrists and rocked faster, circling her hips over his, her hands clenched around the top of the headboard.

He lifted his hands and touched her. Her hips, her breasts, her legs. One hand wrapped around her waist to guide her movements as the other dragged down her body. He splayed his fingers over her abdomen and his thumb found her clit, rubbing in rough, jerky counterpoint to her movements.

She couldn't stop the curse that hissed between her clenched teeth, and she faltered as fire streaked through her. "Jesus, Dylan—"

"I can't—" He growled as his head arched back, the strong muscles in his throat stretched taut. "Fuck. *Fuck*, you feel so good."

Sasha opened her mouth to tell him how good *he* felt, but all that came out was a tormented moan. She pushed harder, desperate to reach the pinnacle, to come for him again.

He made a desperate noise, then another, this one lower and edged with frantic pleasure. His touch grew more insistent, and Sasha threw back her head and screamed as a second orgasm took her. She couldn't breathe, could only grind down against him, trying to get as close as possible as paroxysms of bliss shook her.

Dylan's hand shot up and wrapped around the back of her neck, dragging her body to his. The world spun, and she landed on her back, his mouth pressed to her skin as he ground into her with a hoarse shout. His teeth closed on her neck, hard and possessive, and she felt the last of the wild power burst free of him in one dizzying rush of pleasure and satisfaction.

Sasha lay there, panting, stunned by the depth and intensity of what they'd shared. She threaded her fingers through Dylan's hair and trembled under him, unwilling to speak and break the sensual spell they'd woven.

Finally he eased away, not far, but enough to urge her onto her side. He curled up behind her and dragged at the disheveled blanket until it mostly covered their bodies. His movements were slow, exhausted, and his breath tickled at her neck as he sighed in quiet contentment. "You okay?"

"Better." She held his hand over her heart. "You need to

sleep. I'll be here when you wake up."

He murmured something soft and unintelligible as the tension that had ridden him so hard melted away. His breathing evened out and his arm became a heavy weight over her body, but even in sleep he stayed wrapped around her.

Sasha tried not to let lingering doubts mar the soft pleasure Dylan's touch always left glowing in her. Surely it wouldn't be so hard to know what to do or say when he felt better. Surely things would be the way they'd been before, when nothing had mattered but how they felt about each other.

It took her a long time to fall asleep.

A clatter from the bathroom woke him.

Dylan rolled over and found the spot next to him empty, though the faintest hint of warmth still lingered on the sheets. The bed smelled like Sasha and sex, and it brought back hazy memories of the previous night.

He sat up and winced as his body protested. He was sore today, and not just from the bite and claw marks that were already visibly healing. His muscles ached and his body felt drained, like the hangover from a full moon multiplied a thousandfold.

The only blessing was that he felt like himself, with no trace of the furious, feral magic that had clawed its way free last night.

He found the pair of borrowed sweatpants on the floor and pulled them on, promising himself he'd figure out where his belongings had ended up later. After he'd found Sasha, after he'd reassured himself that she hadn't slipped from the bed to hide distress...or bruises. *Please, no bruises.*

Knocking on the bathroom door took more courage than he wanted to admit. Luckily, Sasha opened it in only a few seconds, and she did so with a broad, sheepish grin. "I'm sorry. I was trying not to disturb you, but I'm a klutz."

His gaze dropped to her throat, to the bruise rising in the mark of his teeth. It wasn't a light love bite, but a rough mark. Terror churned in his stomach as he tried not to consider what else her clothing hid. "Did I—did I hurt you last night?"

"What?" Her hand shot up to touch the bruise, and she shook her head. "No. You didn't hurt me, Dylan."

Relief made his knees weak. "Or scare you?"

Her amiable smile faltered a little. "I wasn't quite sure what to do or say, but I wasn't scared. I was...worried about you."

"I don't blame you." He leaned against the side of the doorframe and let himself relax a tiny bit. "Let's not pump me full of crazy feral power again unless the end of the world is nigh. I'm not sure I like it."

Sasha laughed lightly and kissed the corner of his mouth. "Actually, I'm fairly sure you hated it. At least, that's what you said last night."

He didn't remember most of the previous night, which wasn't reassuring. He reached up and tugged at a wild strand of her hair. "Don't get me wrong, Sasha. If you like crazy sex, I'm all for crazy sex. I just...want to do it because we *want* to, not because I have to."

"No argument here." Her expression turned serious. "I think we need to talk about that. I mean, not about that, specifically. But about what happened."

The nerves returned, stronger this time. "Okay."

"Sit," she urged. She pulled a scarred chair from the corner and sank onto it. "First things first, I guess. We, uh, didn't use a condom last night. I'm on the Pill, so it's not a big deal. I've always used condoms for birth control before..."

Blood pounded in his ears, bringing with it the threat of full-on panic. Ten years as a werewolf and three years before that as a hormonal young human, and he'd never forgotten a condom. If women weren't safe in his world, children would have been the ultimate irresponsibility. He'd never been so drunk, so needy, so *anything* that he'd forgotten that one rule.

Until last night. His fingers clenched around the bedspread and he tried to process her words. "You're... You're okay?"

"Yeah." She pushed her wet hair from her face and eyed him seriously. "Not that it's a situation I want to have repeat itself. I mean, condoms protect you from more than just pregnancy. That's what I meant, it just...didn't come out right, I guess."

He knew what he had to do. Unclench his jaw and tell her she didn't have to worry, that werewolves didn't carry STDs. That it wasn't going to happen anymore because a life of paranoia wasn't easily overcome.

Except last night it had been.

She was starting to look uncomfortable, and that gave him

the self-control to pull himself back together. He relaxed his hands and cleared his throat. "Werewolves have some natural protection, so you don't have to worry about anything else. Other than pregnancy, I mean. But...I'm a fan of condoms. Huge fucking fan. And I'm sorry. I'm really sorry that I was that out of control."

"I understand, Dylan, and it's okay." She wove her fingers together and clasped her hands in her lap. "But I don't think we should have sex anymore when you're going through something like that. Not because I didn't like it, or because I was scared, but because you were."

The blunt truth deserved equal honesty in return. "I was scared because it's never happened before. It was too damn much. Power I could barely control, violence and blood and you being hurt while everything between us..." He swallowed and closed his eyes. "Things aren't sure, Sasha. Because we keep saying we'll talk about it later. I don't think we can keep waiting for later, because it makes me weaker, not knowing."

"Okay." She barely hesitated. "I want to be with you."

Dylan ruthlessly crushed a rush of triumph. "It's not fair to ask you to come back to Red Rock with me. And Ethan wants to talk to you. He wants to ask you to stay here."

"Well, I can't. They need me in Red Rock, even if some people don't want me there."

He opened his eyes and stared at her, trying to read anything in her steady gaze that might indicate she was going back for him, or out of some misplaced need to pay back a nonexistent debt. "You don't owe them anything, Sasha. You saved us here. Again. Gavin would be the first to tell you that."

"They need me," she repeated. "I want to finish what I started, Dylan. And then...I want *us* to decide what to do next. But if Red Rock is where you feel at home, I'm not letting a bunch of virtual strangers drive me away. What you want means more to me than that."

He opened his arms in a silent question.

Sasha came into his arms and perched on his lap, her lips against his cheek. "It's pretty simple. If I can be what you need, then I want that. That's all."

He tightened his arms around her, held her close to his chest and buried his face in her hair. "I can't leave Abby and Brynn in the middle of a war," he whispered. "I got them into this world. But when it's over, when everything's safe, we can find somewhere we both love. Some place that feels like home for both of us."

"Actually..." She pulled back enough to rest her forehead against his. "Would you think I was crazy if I said I sort of miss it now?"

"Not at all. Red Rock's a dream. Maybe that's not always good for them, because they don't remember what the rest of the world's like. But for all its faults, it's still sanctuary."

"Yes, it is." Her lips brushed his. "When do we go home?"

Home. The word shivered through him, brought a sense of safety and longing he'd never imagined could be associated with a place. But it wasn't just the place...it was the dream of peace and pack, and the promise of having Sasha there to share it with him. "Soon. There's one thing we have to do first."

Chapter Eleven

They found Adam behind his cabin by following the repetitive sound of an axe crashing through wood. The sky was overcast, but it was only midmorning, making it obvious that this vampire, at least, didn't find daylight painful.

Dylan nudged Sasha in the side. "Cross sunlight off our list of weapons for Helena."

"Wouldn't do that if I were you." Adam swung the axe up with one hand and embedded it three inches in the log in front of him without any apparent effort. "Most vampires don't do well in the sun." Unspoken was the casually arrogant assertion that Adam wasn't most vampires.

"We still have beheading and fire." Sasha shrugged one shoulder. "Should be a piece of cake. Well, if we had a vampire ally of our own, anyway."

Adam rubbed one hand against his opposite shoulder and surveyed them both. "Chopping wood's good for thinking. Had a lot to think about."

Sasha offered him a smile. "We thought we'd extend an official invitation to return to Montana with us. Just in case you were serious about wanting to work off that life debt."

"I am. But there are a few things to consider."

Unsurprising, especially since Dylan still didn't know what—or who—Adam ate to stay alive. "Sasha's the one who knows about vampires. I thought they were a myth until a few weeks ago."

Adam transferred his gaze to Sasha. "You know how vampire magic works?"

"I know enough to tell you the Helena vampire makes your friend Prudence look like a child, and I'd feel a lot better not facing him alone."

"I need to feed," Adam said, his voice soft and deadly enough to make Dylan shiver. "Not a lot. Not all the time. I'm strong enough that I'm not tied to constant blood, but if I'm going to be fighting my own kind, I'll need the energy."

Dylan frowned slightly. "Feeding on wolves. If you can't use their magic, how does it help you?"

"Never said I couldn't use it."

He'd said that it made vampires crazy. Of course, he'd also said some were willing to take the risk. The thought of bringing someone that dangerous to Red Rock chilled Dylan. "So you take power from wolves."

"No. Wolves give power to me." Adam nodded to Sasha. "She knows the difference."

Sasha's brow furrowed in confusion, but her eyes cleared as realization dawned. "So it works the same way as a spell, then." She turned to Dylan. "It's like the difference between when I took power from you and when I took it from Brynn. She fought me instinctively, and it changed things. Made the energy harder to control."

"Willing blood sacrifice is powerful magic." Adam met Dylan's eyes. "Are there wolves in Red Rock willing to give that gift?"

Not if you call it blood sacrifice. But it wasn't a question. Red Rock needed a strong ally, and he could bring them one. "Even if no one else is, I am."

Sasha tensed beside Dylan and gripped his hand tighter as she spoke. "We both are."

Possessive fury roared up inside him, stronger than he'd felt in ten years of living as a werewolf. His jaw tightened, but he refused to give voice to the protest growing inside him. Sasha deserved the freedom to make her own choices, to be as strong as she wanted to be. Even if it killed him.

Adam's eyes flashed with something almost like amusement. "My dear little witch, you have a lot to learn about werewolves. If you care about the one standing next to you, you might not want to offer strange men the chance to sink fangs into your throat."

Oddly, Adam's words made it easier to choke down his rage, though it didn't make his voice any calmer. "Sasha makes her own choices."

"I don't live to upset the man I love." Sasha sounded almost grumpy. "You're not getting near my throat, Adam Dubois, unless people's lives actually depend on it. But, in the end, I think he and I understand each other." She looked up, and her clear blue eyes met Dylan's. "We're tough, and we do what we have to do, right?"

"We do what we have to do," he agreed in a quiet murmur. And right now, he *had* to slide his fingers into her hair and tilt her head back...

"I'm still standing right here, you know."

Dylan didn't tear his gaze away from Sasha's mouth, which was soft and beautiful and clearly needed kissing. "So go pack your bags."

"If the two of you are going to make out the whole way back to Montana, I'm driving my own truck."

"Have fun with that."

The vampire huffed and strode past them, leaving Dylan alone with a beautiful witch whose smile summoned the one feeling he'd needed for a decade. Happiness. "Are we going to make out the whole way back to Montana?"

There was that smile. "Joe might try to lash us to the luggage rack."

"Let him try." And because Dylan had to acknowledge the very real possibility that Joe would not only try but succeed, he tightened his fingers in Sasha's hair. She was a woman who needed kissing. Kissing and touching and love, so much that it would take a lifetime to give her everything he wanted.

A lifetime sounded just about perfect.

Sanctuary Unbound

Dedication

This is for John, who heard about the vampire lumberjack and informed us we were to write it at once. Your wish is our command, sir.

We'd also like to extend special, heartfelt thanks to Ann Aguirre, who always listens and encourages us, and to Molli, who is the fastest beta reader in the contiguous United States.

Chapter One

Cindy gritted her teeth and peeled the backing from the last lead. "I'll have to see what the EKG shows, but you sure the hell *look* like you're having another heart attack."

Gavin had to move the oxygen mask and unclench his jaw to speak. "It's not as bad this time."

He was pale, sweaty and trembling, and she barely managed not to call him a liar. "Put the mask back on and keep it there." She turned on the machine and checked the signal integrity. "Sit still while I talk to Sam."

Gavin's wife hovered in the doorway, tension in her dark eyes even though she'd fixed a stern look on her face. "For God's sake, do what she says or I'm going to finish you off before your heart gets a chance."

Instead of arguing, he nodded and leaned his head against the raised headboard of the bed.

Cindy pulled the door shut behind her and watched Gavin through the window. "There's not much I can do here, Sam. It's the same as last time. I'm not a cardiologist."

"Damn it." Sam squeezed her eyes shut as she lifted her fingers to rub at her temples. "What if I gave him some of my energy? Sasha and the lot of them should be back this afternoon. Maybe if she used magic to bind us..."

"It wouldn't do anything but hurt you, Sam. Werewolves have accelerated healing, and we live a long time." *But not forever.* Gavin's problems were mundane, and the sort they rarely saw, even in a sanctuary town like Red Rock. "He's just...not a kid anymore."

"And this war is killing him." Sam exhaled sharply. "He can't keep this up, can he?"

Cindy urged Sam to the chair beside the doorway, keeping tight hold of her hand even after she sat. "There are a lot of things that don't help, things a werewolf wouldn't normally have to worry about. The smoking, for one. And yes, his stress level."

"He doesn't think Keith's ready. That's why he can't slow down." Sam's voice dropped to a hoarse whisper. "When Keith found Abby... You know how he's been. It was the first time we'd seen him *alive* in years. And Gavin thought he might be ready to take over. But when Keith got hurt..."

No one knew better than she how close he'd come to dying. "Keith is recovering faster than I'd hoped. The hard truth is that, physically, he's stronger than Gavin now."

"Then Keith needs to know that." Sam sat up, her fingers tight around Cindy's as she gathered the formidable will for which she was known. "Will Gavin be able to come back home tonight?"

"It depends on the EKG. He might need thrombolytics, or just aspirin." She felt helpless, and she hated it. Even your average small-town doctor could refer patients to a hospital if their condition called for it. All Cindy had was herself. Worse, she was all the town had. "I'll know more in a little while."

"Can I sit with him?"

"If you can ignore me while I work."

"Of course. Cindy, I know this is a lot to ask of you, but I need you to tell Keith. My husband can yell at me over it if he wants to, as long as he's alive to yell."

"This evening," she promised. Once she got Gavin stabilized, she could take the time to visit Keith. "Come on."

When they walked in, Gavin opened his eyes and pulled at his mask. "I heard every word you two said."

"Good. Now that you know how badly you've scared your poor wife, you won't give me as many problems." Cindy sat in front of the computer monitor and scrolled back through the electrocardiogram. "Definite ST elevation. How's the pain?"

"Better."

"Raging headache?"

He grimaced. "Just like last time."

"That's the nitroglycerin. If you can stand it, no morphine."

Gavin glanced at Sam and tried to smile. "I'm all right."

"And you're going to stay that way," Sam whispered, her

voice suspiciously thick. "You think you're going to do Keith any favors if you drop dead and he has to blame himself because you didn't trust him with this?"

Cindy stared at the monitor. It looked like a heart attack, but she couldn't be sure how much damage had been done without lab work. He needed angioplasty, but it was beyond her capabilities. "I can give you medications and hope they help, but what you really need is to go to a hospital."

Gavin shifted on the table and frowned at her. "You know that's not possible, Cindy. Too many questions."

"Yeah." Too many questions. "Okay. You can also lay off the smoking, fatty foods and stress. Which would you like to start with, Sam?"

"I've been trying to get the ornery bastard to quit smoking for years." Sam smoothed her fingers over Gavin's forehead, brushing back hair that now held more gray than black. "Cindy's going to tell Keith about the heart attacks, Gavin. And then the two of you are going to decide how to lift some of this burden from your shoulders. I'm not ready to live without you."

None of them were, which was part of the problem.

"So she's going to make him quit smoking, for starters."

Keith made a rude noise and leaned back against the counter. "Fuck. How long has this been going on, Cindy?"

She gripped the coffee mug. "The first one happened right before you came back. From overseas, I mean."

"Shit." All hints of humor faded from his eyes, replaced by guilt and a trace of anger. "How many?"

He wouldn't like her answer, but the time for secrets was over. Gavin didn't have the luxury anymore, and neither did the town. "He had a third today. I don't know how much heart muscle was killed because my facilities here are limited, but he's getting weaker after every one."

"Cindy, you should have fucking told me." Keith pushed off the counter and paced to the other side of the room, leashed energy filling the kitchen in an uncomfortable rush. "He should have told me. God damn it."

As if the decision had been hers to make. "He's the alpha, Keith. Beyond that, he's my patient. I can't go around telling people he's on his last legs, not without his permission."

Keith froze. "Last legs?"

"Apparently I'm doing a bad job of impressing upon you the gravity of his condition." Her chair scraped over the tile floor as she rose. "Gavin's led a hard life, and he spends every waking moment worrying about this town and the world outside of it. If he were human, the stress would have killed him by sixty. He's twice that age now, old even for a werewolf."

"And he didn't think I was ready." Keith swore and kicked a chair out of his way, sending it flying into the table so hard that it rebounded and clattered to the floor. "I am one self-absorbed ass."

"Uh-huh." They didn't have time for guilt and blame. "Was that before or after a crazy woman tried to gut you with a knife and you nearly died?"

Keith turned that hard glare on her. "Before, smartass."

He'd always been strong, and she had to fight not to shrink away from his anger. "Simmer down. I'm just saying that sometimes life gets in the way of our plans."

"Yeah." He bent and picked up the chair. "Joe's about an hour out with his caravan of road-trippers. I've got that much time to figure out how to deal with an alpha who might not be ready to step down, a witch half the town still doesn't trust, and a vampire some of them won't believe exists." His fingers clenched around the chair's back until Cindy thought the wood might snap. "Could this situation get any more fucked up?"

"Dylan will look after Sasha." Thinking about her ex-lover and his new flame should have hurt more. "Worry about Gavin and the vampire."

Keith eyed her as if he wasn't entirely sure he believed it didn't hurt more. "You okay with all of that? Dylan and Sasha, I mean. I know he was the first guy you got close to."

Cindy retrieved her mug from the table and finished her coffee. "It wasn't going to work, and that had nothing to do with Sasha." The worst part was having to own up to how recklessly she'd pursued Dylan. Maybe if she'd given it a little more time, she could have saved them both the heartache of a failed relationship.

"He was a nice guy," Keith said, his voice quiet and too gentle. "I liked the idea of you having a nice guy. After all you've been through, Cin—"

"Keith, please. I'm a grown woman, and this isn't overprotective big-brother time." She rinsed her mug in the sink. "Dylan *is* a nice guy. He's just not the one for me, that's all."

"Was that code for 'butt the hell out'?"

"I don't need to dance around your delicate feelings."

"Never have before. Life'd be boring if you started now."

The banter was comfortable, easy. "Is there anything you and Abby need? Abby, especially. I think your convalescence has been harder for her than for you."

"She'll be better when her sister's back in town. Brynn tried to fudge the details of what happened in Maine, but Dylan blew it and spilled the whole story."

Just the little Cindy had heard from Sam would have been enough to turn Abby's hair gray. "Her baby sister was out there with vampires and corrupt alphas, and you managed to keep her sane? You deserve a medal."

Keith grinned. "It helps he didn't give her the really bad details until they'd already hit New Hampshire. And Joe wasn't going to let anything happen to Brynn."

"No, he wasn't." It was a side of Joe she hadn't seen in the years she'd known him. She'd known there was more to him than the easygoing playboy most people saw, but his relationship with Brynn had brought out an intensity and devotion she barely recognized.

Keith's smile faded. "Hey. Smile for me, sweetheart. If I have to take over Gavin's place, I'm going to need all the help I can get."

She managed a small grin. "Just remember that Joe might be burly, but I'm smart. I'd make a damn good second-in-command."

"Screw second-in-command. You're the doctor. You're the boss of everyone." Keith tugged fondly at her hair. "Now do me a favor and go upstairs and tell my mate that I'm not an invalid anymore, or she's going to have her own heart attack when I tell her I'm about to move up the food chain."

"I can do that." Cindy leaned up to kiss his cheek and headed for the staircase. And all the way up, she told herself it was stupid to feel alone in a town full of people.

Adam couldn't decide what was worse—when Dylan or Sasha sat up front and peppered him with endless questions, or when their saccharine puppy love overcame their manners and they ended up cuddling in the backseat of his rental car.

Probably the questions. It had been years since he'd driven a car more than fifteen miles, long enough to admit that he wasn't very good at handling modern vehicles. They'd made it out of New England before he'd stopped trying to shift gears with the emergency brake, and it was easier to concentrate on keeping the car on the road when he wasn't fielding questions on the history of vampires in the States.

Dylan had offered to drive more than once, but Adam stubbornly refused to relinquish the wheel. With his quiet, rigidly controlled life spinning out of control, he needed this last illusion of order.

Even if he kept turning on the damn windshield wipers every time he tried to use the blinker.

The road ahead of them had narrowed until towering trees blocked out most of the light. He'd felt the wards ten miles back, layered so thickly across the pass he was amazed humans didn't notice them. Even knowing what the magic was and why it was there, he'd had to fight to follow Joe's Blazer off the main road. It had felt unpleasantly like passing through a thick tangle of sticky cobwebs, and the back of his neck still itched.

Dylan had finally detached himself from Sasha's side, which Adam supposed was indication enough they'd almost reached Red Rock. He cleared his throat to catch their attention and raised his voice. "Do you two feel the wards too? Or do I only get them because I'm a vampire?"

Sasha leaned forward over the seat. "They affect everyone to varying degrees. Do you feel all right?"

She was so damn earnest it made his teeth hurt. He'd never done well with gentle women, and sometimes Sasha reminded him of the well-bred daughters he'd done his best to avoid in the days before automatic transmissions and cars that told you when your gas tank was low. But none of those spoiled rich girls would have looked at him with wide, worried eyes and shouldered into his personal space like she had a right to be there.

Like *she* needed to help *him*.

His silence had gone on too long, and Dylan watched him in the rearview mirror. Adam shrugged one shoulder. "Fine. But that magic was made to welcome werewolves, and I'm damn near the opposite of a werewolf."

"I suppose." She offered him an encouraging smile. "Gavin will be happy to see you."

The painfully chipper little girl was mother-henning him. As if he hadn't been alive when her great-fucking-grandmother had been born. "Hope so. Like to wait at least a week between fights with werewolves."

"We all do." Sasha sat back and nestled into the cradle of Dylan's arm. "It's a bit of a luxury around here sometimes, though."

Adam eyed them in the rearview mirror again, his gaze sweeping inexorably to the claw-shaped scars that marked her pale cheek. Maybe he wasn't giving the witchling enough credit. Life in a town full of backwater werewolves couldn't be any more comfortable for her than it would be for him, but even with the proof of violence carved into her skin, she didn't turn away from it.

Still, she didn't have to be so damn *cheerful* about it.

Dylan nuzzled his nose against the girl's bright red hair, and Adam jerked his attention back to the road. Love made people blissful. Love made people stupid. The couple cuddling in the backseat had faced down a power-hungry vampire less than two weeks ago, and every indication pointed to the inevitable fact that their next confrontation would be five times as bad. Yet they still looked foolishly, joyfully happy.

For one brief minute, he considered mistaking the parking brake for the gearshift again, just to keep Romeo and Juliet from necking in the backseat. Of course, with his luck the car would spin out of control on the loosely packed gravel and they'd end up wrapped around a tree. Dylan might make it out in one piece, but witches were fragile things—and this witch obviously wasn't wearing a seatbelt, or she couldn't be half in Dylan's lap.

Adam tightened his fingers around the steering wheel, gritted his teeth, and promised himself he'd use kamikaze dives toward large trees as a last resort. Like if he saw tongues.

"That's it up ahead." Dylan's voice, quiet and unassuming.

At the same time, the Blazer in front of them made a sharp left. Adam jerked the wheel to follow, and the trees on either side disappeared, replaced with a steep hill leading down to an idyllic little village tucked into a picturesque clearing.

The sun had already dropped below the edge of the forest, but Adam had no trouble making out the small cluster of buildings that obviously made up the main bulk of Red Rock. Dirt roads wove into the trees, and lights flickered here and there through the branches like fireflies. The town showed its share of wear and tear, visible even at a distance, but it was easy to see the dream underneath. An old-fashioned, small-town sanctuary. He could have been looking at Bedagi Creek, if Bedagi Creek had been on top of a mountain instead of nestled in the Great North Woods of Maine.

A blonde in jeans and a flannel shirt watched them as they drove down the main street, one hand shading her eyes from the dwindling sunlight. Joe waved at her through the Blazer window, and she smiled broadly as she approached the SUV.

"The town's doctor," Dylan said, distracting him from the act of coasting to a stop. He had to slam his foot down on the brakes and nearly rear-ended Joe's vehicle before he managed to park the car. The blonde's gaze flickered to him and, for one moment, all he could see in her face was pure, undiluted strength, the kind that came from living through hell and getting up on the other side.

The dark hunger inside him stirred, attracted to the strength of her in the same way the young alpha female in Bedagi Creek had called to him. But he'd known Emily from childhood, leaving his hunger for power strongly tempered by an utter lack of desire. The blonde burned with magic so bright it could turn a man inside out, and had a body that might make him willing to go through the pain, if it meant getting a chance to touch her.

"Oh shit."

Adam jerked his attention to the rearview mirror and glared at Dylan. "Got a problem, puppy?"

Dylan refused to avert his gaze, which was most of the reason Adam liked the kid. Dylan didn't care if the man staring him down could break him in half, he'd do what he thought he had to and damn the consequences.

Apparently now he thought he had to be a nosy bastard.

"Cindy's not going to let you snack on her. And if Joe or Keith catches you eyeing her like you're thinking about it, they'll get Buffy on your ass."

"Excuse me?"

"They'll kill you really, really dead."

Not an inconsequential threat, but Joe and Keith were still youths, neither of them fifty years old. And Adam hadn't been thinking about blood for once. *Which might be worse.* "Mind your own damn business, Dylan."

The doctor leaned close to Joe's window for a few more moments, then nodded and began to walk toward Adam's car. When she drew closer, he could see the brittle tinge of wariness in her eyes.

Judging by the way the couple in the back separated and surged to opposite sides of the seat, little—if any—of that wariness was directed at him. Adam jerked the keys from the ignition and pushed open the door with a small sigh of relief. He tossed the keys on the front seat and glanced at Dylan. "If the car needs to go somewhere else, you take it."

"Sure thing." Dylan opened his own door and climbed out, a cautious smile on his lips. "Hey, Cindy."

"Dylan. Hi, Sasha."

"Hi."

Cindy turned to him and held out one hand. "You must be Adam. Gavin's told me a lot about you."

Touching her was asking for trouble, but he did it anyway. Her hand felt small in his, but not soft. She wasn't Sasha, with her fragile delicateness. Cindy's smooth skin hid strength, maybe even a hint of danger.

It turned him on more than a little.

"Cindy." He smiled, the wide, easy grin he used on the rare occasions he wanted a woman to smile back. "So you're the doctor Sam told me about." A small lie, since he didn't think Sam had told him more than that she *had* a doctor.

She arched an eyebrow and laughed. "The first thing Gavin told me was that you're a charming, horny bastard."

Son of a bitch. It figured the old wolf knew him well enough, even after all this time, to know the sort of temptation Cindy would present. "Gavin hasn't forgiven me for flirting with his wife in the early eighties. He holds a grudge."

"Right. He and Sam are at my place. Come on, I'll show you." She turned on one heel and walked across the street, her hips swaying with each step.

He was still watching those hips when Dylan spoke up from behind them, his voice worried. "Did something happen? Did someone get hurt?"

Cindy spared them only a quick glance over her shoulder. "Gavin's not feeling well."

It was the one thing guaranteed to drag Adam's attention away from the way Cindy's jeans hugged her ass. Her tone might have been casual, but he'd heard the minute strain, the way her voice came out a little flat. Amusement died and he caught up to Cindy in two long strides. "Then let's go."

Her house proved to be close to the center of town, a smart placement for their doctor, he supposed. It seemed like a nice enough little home, but on the inside it looked more like an office. Chairs and a couch lined the walls of the entryway, and the two rooms he could see into could best be described as clinical.

Cindy ignored them both, instead leading him down the hall, past the kitchen into a comfortably homey room where Gavin sat in a recliner, his face ashen.

He'd kept up with Gavin by phone, infrequent calls every month or two, Adam's only real contact with the world past Bedagi Creek. The last time he'd actually *seen* Gavin had been over a quarter of a century ago, when his oldest friend had arrived in Maine with a sweet-faced young woman with too many scars and too much power. Time had still been kind.

Gavin and time had had a falling out at some point in the last thirty years. His friend looked old. Rundown and worn out and half-dead. He looked up and grinned when he saw Adam. "'Bout time you showed up."

Adam had to fight to smile and keep his voice light, burying his worry deep. "Just biding my time. Figured Sam would leave you and shack up with me if I waited long enough."

"In your wildest dreams, Dubois." Gavin jerked his head to the chair beside his. "Have a seat. Never thought I'd get you out here."

Adam sank into the chair. "Never thought I'd come. But what can I say? Only you would send a moon-crazed wolf, a witch and their boyfriends out to fetch me. You got my attention."

"Sounds like the beginning of a bad joke, doesn't it?" He leaned his head back and turned his grin to the blonde. "Cindy, love. Tell Sammie I can have a beer, would you?"

"Hell no."

"You're a harsh woman, Dr. Shepherd."

"Mmm." She winked at Adam over Gavin's head. "May as well get the truth out there before your guest starts to think I'm a nice lady."

Adam stretched his legs in front of him, grateful for the chance to do so after so long trapped in a ridiculously small car. "Trust me, Dr. Shepherd. Gavin here is *hoping* I'll think you're a nice lady. Never much fancied them."

"Cindy can handle the likes of you," Gavin grumbled. "And she *is* nice, in spite of that."

"Mm-hmm." He met Cindy's gaze. "So what did the old bastard do to put himself in this state?"

"The old bastard is sitting right here."

Cindy ignored him. "Had another heart attack. It's one of the hazards of being an old bastard." Again, a thread of tension bled through her nonchalant words.

"*Another* heart attack?" Adam looked back to Gavin. "Hell, man, how many have you had?"

"Three." His friend fidgeted with the upholstery covering the arm of the recliner. "It's like the lady says. I'm not as young as I used to be."

Neither was Adam, but time had a way of passing him by in his tiny remote cabin. Before young Emily had taken a shine to him, he'd gone for months at a time without seeing anyone besides the casual bedmates who came to him to feed a man's hunger as well as a vampire's.

Footsteps sounded in the hallway, and Adam got another shock when Sam stepped through the doorway. Granted, few women well into their seventies possessed Sam's strong body and ageless complexion, but worry had left its mark on her face and fear in her eyes.

She hid it well as she swooped down to kiss his cheek. "Welcome to Red Rock, you impossible man."

Flirting with her when Gavin looked like he had one foot in the grave seemed like overkill, but he didn't know how else to handle the shock of seeing two of his oldest friends looking old. "I thought we agreed you'd leave this sorry ass and come live with me. I waited twenty years."

"Only twenty? You're too impatient." Her voice sounded strained, and Adam felt the first stirrings of panic. Nothing put that edge of fear in Sam's voice. Combined with the doctor's tension, it painted a sorry picture for Gavin—and for Red Rock.

Cindy leaned close to Sam, one comforting hand on the taller woman's shoulder. "I have to head to Keith's and check on Joe. Radio if you need anything, and I can be back here in a minute."

"Thanks, Cindy." Sam squeezed her hand, and Adam caught the look that passed between them. Samantha considered the doctor a friend, someone from whom she'd accept support, and it said more about Cindy's inner strength than anything else he'd seen.

His attraction to that strength made it so much harder to watch her leave.

It took Cindy five minutes, halfway down Main Street, to stop trembling.

You're doing it again, damn it. It was the only explanation. She was letting her hormones overrule her good sense, indulging an attraction to an unsuitable man.

The pull had been there, instant and undeniable, and she wanted to kick herself for flirting with him. He was attractive, tall and dark and rugged, but there wasn't time for that sort of thing. Not with Gavin sick and Keith taking over and a new threat in Helena.

Not just any threat—a vampire. And she'd do well to remember that Adam Dubois had come to Red Rock to teach them how to fight that threat.

"Cindy!" Dylan appeared from between two buildings. "Hey, I was just dropping the rental car off at Sam and Gavin's. You headed to Keith's?"

"Yeah, I want to make sure Joe's okay." Seeing Dylan jolted her a little. She wasn't pining over him, and she certainly didn't begrudge him his happiness, but he'd been her lover not terribly long ago. "What about you?"

"That's the plan." He sounded different, more confident. Whatever had happened in Maine had healed some of the slowly bleeding wounds he'd come to Red Rock with a few months before. She could see it in his face as he glanced at her. "What's really going on with Gavin?"

She'd told Keith because Sam had asked her to. Sam hadn't asked her to tell everyone. "The stress, mostly. I think Keith's going to be taking over a lot of things."

Dylan frowned. "If it's not my business, just say it's not my business. Don't lie."

She blew her bangs out of her face with an exasperated breath. "Okay, Dylan. It's none of your business."

"Fair enough." He stayed silent as they reached the end of the street and turned toward Keith's house, his boots crunching loudly on the gravel. It wasn't until they'd passed another two houses that he cleared his throat. "So. We brought a vampire home with us."

"I noticed." At least the deepening shadows cast by the setting sun might hide her blush. "Gavin seemed happy to see his friend."

"He's..." Another pause, and this one felt apprehensive. "Watch out for him, Cindy. He may be friendly with Gavin, but he's dangerous. The kind of dangerous you don't see coming."

"You think he's out to get me?" Even as a joke, the words felt illicit. "Should I string garlic around my neck?"

He dropped his gaze—only for a second, but long enough to acknowledge she was far above him in the pack hierarchy. "I'm just saying, power makes him hungry. Sometimes he looks at Brynn and I know he sees food."

"Yeah, well. If he tries to suck my blood, I'll punch him in the balls. How's that?" Not that she was making any promises if he wanted to put his mouth anywhere else.

"Never should have doubted."

"Uh-huh." Cindy stopped walking and shoved her hands in her pockets. "I appreciate that you're trying to look out for me, Dylan. But you can't do that anymore, not for a while. You know that, right?"

"Wasn't all that great at it before." He turned to face her and grinned. "I get it though. And I'm sorry. Don't beat me up."

"Right." She jerked her head back toward her house. "What's his story?"

Dylan shrugged and resumed walking. "Vampire. Old,

maybe older than Gavin. We found him making a living carving handmade furniture in a cabin that barely had running water and electricity."

"Should be right at home in Red Rock, then."

"Guess so. Don't think he's been out in the world in a while. You should have seen him trying to manage the rental car."

Laughing felt too much like mockery, and Cindy's amusement faded quickly. "I'm just thankful he came. Gavin could use an old friend around right now."

"Don't get me wrong, I kind of like him. Joe, on the other hand..." Dylan trailed off uncomfortably. "Those two are never gonna be friends."

If there was tension there, she needed to know. "Did something happen?"

It took Dylan a second too long to answer. "No. Adam's careful not to look at Brynn most of the time. But back in Maine he made it clear that the way she got turned is going to make her vampire bait. And not in a 'be my queen of the night' sort of way. More like, 'yum, dinner'."

If the raw power appealed to vampires, it was no wonder. Brynn was half-feral, wild with it. "I imagine Joe wouldn't be too fond of that."

"Doesn't seem like it. And I don't know if he's thought ahead, but I have. It means Brynn can't be involved in whatever goes down in Helena. She's too big a target. And unless Joe's willing to transfer her bond to someone else, it takes him out too." Dylan kicked at a rock and sighed. "No wonder Gavin feels like shit. Things are looking pretty damn dire."

"What kind of shape is Joe in now?" Joe was proud and a little pigheaded, but he also possessed a refreshing pragmatism. If he was in no shape to fight, it wouldn't be hard to convince him he'd be better off tending to Brynn.

Dylan flashed her a weary smile. "You're the doctor. I guess you'll have to tell me."

"Of course." She didn't want to keep walking toward Keith's house. She didn't want to hear the details of what had happened, see the extent of Joe's lingering injuries. She wanted to go home and climb into a hot bath.

Fingers brushed her arm, a tentative touch that only lasted a moment. "You okay, Cindy?"

Not long ago, Dylan's touch would have been more than welcome. Now, she shied away from it. "I'm exhausted. We all are."

"I just..." His voice trailed off, as if he knew there was nothing he could say. Not anymore. "Let's go. Joe's waiting for you."

Guilt made her tremble. She'd been the one to end things, and it wasn't fair to punish him for it. "I'm sorry, Dylan."

"Don't be. Things are awkward. Just means we're... Well, maybe not human. But normal."

Cindy stopped walking and rubbed her hands over her face. "Tell me one thing. Tell me you're *happy*."

"I am. Not just living. I'm happy."

The truth of the words was written on every line of his face. He wore a contentment that hadn't been there the last time she'd seen him, and she dragged in a relieved breath. "Then that means us splitting up was the right thing to do. That's enough for me."

"I'm glad." He tilted his head toward the road that led to Keith's place. "You ready to face this?"

Not in a million years, but there was no avoiding it. "I need to check on Joe, and we all need to talk."

"Yeah we do, but cheer up. We brought souvenirs."

And a vampire. She almost told Dylan she'd prefer the cheap trinkets, but the image of Adam Dubois's flashing green eyes rose in her memory, giving lie to the thought. "Let's go."

Chapter Two

It was after midnight when Cindy dragged herself home. She'd refused to allow anyone to walk her, needing the time and solitude to steel herself for the long night to come. Gavin might have been sitting up and talking that afternoon, but that level of activity would have taken its toll, left him weakened.

God only knew how his body could fail him next.

She pushed through the back door and stopped short when she caught sight of Adam at her kitchen table. "Hi."

He paused with a forkful of mashed potatoes hovering in the air. "Hello."

"Don't let me interrupt." She hung her jacket on the wall in the entryway and nodded to the plate of leftovers before him. "Verna made the meatloaf and potatoes. Best in three states."

Adam set down his fork and rose. "You hungry? I could heat some up for you too."

"No, God no. Sit." She turned to the refrigerator, using the seconds it took her to fetch a bottle of water to steady her hands. He moved with slow deliberation, a careful concert of movements that unsettled her because it was all too easy to imagine that sort of attention turned on *her*.

The chair scraped over the floor as he settled into it again. "Sorry for invading your kitchen, but Sam drifted off and I didn't have the heart to wake her."

"Don't sweat it. She needs the rest." Cindy took a gulp of her water and sat across the table from him. *May as well get it out there.* "What about you? Do you need anything?"

Amusement flashed in his eyes. "Salt and pepper?"

He was a smartass, but she'd asked for it with her vague words. She retrieved the salt and pepper shakers from the shelf above the tiled backsplash behind the stove. "You'll have to indulge me with a few silly questions. I know nothing about vampires."

"I eat. I sleep. I don't burst into flame in the sunlight." If he had fangs, his smile didn't show them. "And sometimes I drink blood."

"Mm-hmm. That's the part I'm curious about."

"Not surprised. Not many vampires stray out of New England these days."

"So you won't mind enlightening me."

His gaze dropped to the table, studying the salt shaker as he upended an unhealthy amount of salt onto his food. "What do you want to know? The how, the why, or the how much?"

"Yes." She tilted her head and smiled wryly. "I'm the pack doctor. These things matter to me."

"I'm not going to lure your pack mates into the woods for a nibble, if that's what you're worried about. I need some blood if I'm going to be walking into a fight, but Dylan's already offered."

Protectiveness shot through her. "He did, did he?"

One of Adam's eyebrows rose. "I'm sorry, do I need your permission to accept his offer?"

"I have no claim on Dylan." It would take the wolf inside her a little time to catch up with that, but it didn't change the facts. "Why him?"

"I've talked to five wolves from your pack," he murmured, holding up fingers as he counted each one off. "Dylan, Joe, Brynn, Gavin and Sam. Three of them are hurt or sick, and Dylan said Samantha got herself tangled up in a binding spell with a hungry vamp on the other end."

She found herself inexplicably taken aback by his explanation. "If it's going to potentially affect anyone's health, you come to me. It's what I do."

Adam frowned. "Come to you? To find another willing donor?"

"Of course. I could do it myself, if I needed to."

"Do what yourself? Find me a donor? Or be a donor?"

"Be a—" Her voice cracked, and she took a bracing gulp of water. "Be a donor. Hell, we could do it here in my office. Or do you...need to drink *from* someone?"

He looked like he was trying not to smile. "The blood is

mostly incidental. It's the power I need, especially if I'm going to be fighting one of my own. The power comes from the willing gift of blood or the violent taking of it. I've never had much luck with drawing blood and saving it for later."

Cindy had encountered plenty of things that were more of the realm of magic than they were of the physical. It had been one of the hardest things to reconcile as a doctor and a werewolf. "What's your usual ritual, then?"

"My usual ritual is not applicable in this situation." That amusement in his eyes had faded, replaced with something almost like self-consciousness. "Not with Dylan, in any case. I'm hoping Sasha might be able to come up with some sort of magical ritual to enhance the power of the gift, now that she has access to her books."

She'd learned to recognize evasion in her patients, and she saw it now in Adam. "How do you usually obtain the power, Adam? The blood?"

He sighed, a soft, tired sound. "From a lover, Dr. Shepherd."

It was so obvious that she felt like an idiot. "Oh."

"Yes." His mouth twitched. "Would you like me to attempt to explain the relationship between sex and magic? I'm not sure I know the details, but I could try."

"Wolves have plenty of connection between sex and magic. It's not an—an alien concept."

"I know. Most of my companions came from the local werewolf pack." He was *definitely* laughing at her. "It can be a mutually beneficial arrangement under the right circumstances."

"I see." She capped her bottle and rose. "I'll talk to Sasha, see if she manages to come up with anything. For the time being, I think you should consider me your potential donor. Just to avoid complications."

His gaze stayed fixed on her with an almost tangible weight, and there was no mistaking his sharp interest or the heat in his stare. "It will be my pleasure."

"Yes?" She had to get away from him before the throb of lust twisting through her made her do something crazy like ask him into her bed. "I suppose we'll find out."

"I suppose we will." He seemed to shake himself, and the oddly formal tone of his words vanished. "Now if it's okay with you, I'm going to eat. It was a damn long drive and I hate automatic transmissions."

"Make yourself at home." The words came out husky, almost inviting, and Cindy hoped he couldn't sense her arousal as she turned to the door. "Good night."

"Good night, Dr. Shepherd."

Adam was used to being the oldest person in a room. What he wasn't used to was how *tired* it made him feel.

He leaned back in his stout wooden chair and eyed Samantha, who sat at the opposite end of the long table, her fingers curled around the arms of a chair that carried Gavin's scent. His own chair held hints of Samantha's favored shampoo, making it clear she'd abandoned her usual spot for the symbolic place of power.

Gavin was tucked safely back in the doctor's house with Brynn standing careful watch, and her absence made it easier to deal with Joe's forbidding presence to his left. Adam didn't think Joe would ever believe that the power trapped inside Brynn as a wolf turned at the full moon wasn't enough to push Adam over the edge. Her blood was a temptation, to be sure, but self-control was a virtue Adam had been familiar with longer than Joe had been alive.

Of course, Joe could have chosen his spot to put himself between Adam and Cindy. Cindy avoided looking at him entirely, seemingly distracted by her murmured conversation with Keith, who sat flanked by her and Sam. Across from Keith was a sweet-faced brunette who radiated power. Adam had been unsurprised to discover that she was Keith's mate in addition to being Brynn's sister; Abby had an unshakable core of magic that reminded Adam of the young alpha female from Bedagi Creek.

And next to Abby... Adam hid a sigh as he caught sight of Dylan's fingers curling around Sasha's. The lovebirds were still playing footsie, and no one at the table seemed bothered by it.

No one except Cindy. An almost tangible aura of sadness hung around her, though the same expression lingered on her face when she looked at Keith and Abby, as well. She looked lonely. Isolated. Sympathy rose and, for once, Adam didn't bother to push it away.

He tried to catch her gaze, but Joe glared at him instead, a brittle warning in his eyes. Adam responded with an amused smile carefully calculated to be just the right side of challenging.

It would have been perfect too, if Sam hadn't chosen that moment to look at him. Her dark eyes flashed, annoyance and exasperation in equal measure. "For the love of God, does a man need to reach his second century before he stops acting like a boy?"

She sounded frazzled, on edge and off balance, and the unsteady flare of magic that accompanied the words made everyone at the table look uneasy. Everyone but Keith, that was, who proved his worthiness as Gavin's successor by sliding a hand over Sam's fingers and smiling. "None of us will ever stop acting like boys, Sam. You love yelling at us too much, and we like making you happy."

"That's the excuse they'll use, anyway." Abby scooted her chair closer to Sam's. "Say the word, and I'll take them all out back and smack them around a little bit."

"I'm not ruling it out." Sam shot Adam a look that clearly begged him to behave, and the weariness and worry that had etched lines around her eyes made it impossible to do anything but acknowledge her silent plea with a quiet nod. As soon as he did, she relaxed marginally. "I've asked you all here because something's going on that everyone needs to know about. Cindy's going to explain the details."

The doctor did look at him then, a fleeting glance that she quickly turned on the others seated around the table. "Gavin's sick." She seemed to anticipate the murmur that swept the room, and she waited until it quieted before continuing. "He's had three heart attacks, and each one is doing more to damage his heart. It's—" She swallowed hard. "It's not anything I can fix."

Since the news wasn't news to him, Adam watched the others. From the stoic look on Joe's face, he'd already known, and both Keith and Abby seemed more interested in supporting Sam. The only two who looked surprised were Dylan and Sasha, which meant the gathering was about something else entirely.

Sam took a deep breath and closed her eyes, and Adam tensed against the words he suddenly knew she was about to speak. "Red Rock's at war, but leading us in war is going to kill

Gavin and he knows it. If this were any other time I'd take his place, but my ego isn't so big I can't see the truth. We need a warrior."

Joe spoke. "Which means we need Keith. He's the one who was raised for this. He's the one who knows how to do it."

Silence reigned as Keith stared across the table at Abby. She stared back and finally smiled. "He's right, sweetie. You've always been the one, and I'll—I'll help you any way I can. With everything."

Keith nodded. While everyone was watching him, Adam watched Cindy. She looked tense, almost self-conscious, not to mention worried.

Sasha sighed and turned her attention to Adam. "What about the vampire in Helena?"

"Can't say much until I find out more." Adam shifted uncomfortably. "Didn't you say there was someone in town that the vampire had formed a blood bond with?"

"Justine," Abby answered, her expression grave. "When Recco took over the Helena pack, he used her to feed the vampire."

"For how long?"

"We're not sure, and she can't quite remember. Weeks."

Weeks of feeding would have left a taint even magic couldn't erase. "Can I see her? I might be able to tell something about the vampire. How strong he is, at least, or what sort of power he's using."

"It'll be fine if Sasha and I can be there," Cindy told him quietly. "She'll need us."

"Of course. When can—?"

Keith jerked to his feet, his gaze whipping toward the door. Abby sprang up after him, and Joe's chair tipped back to the floor as he rose as well. Cindy stiffened, frozen for a moment, her hands clenched around the edge of the table.

Dylan went pale just as the first hints of sound tickled the edge of Adam's hearing. Shouts, angry male voices raised in fear and pain. Keith shot toward the door, Dylan hard at his heels, and only then did the voices outside crystallize into words—someone screaming for Dylan, and help.

There was a backpack in the corner by the door, and Cindy snatched it up on her way out. Only Sam and Sasha remained, and Sam grabbed the witch's hand before she could rise. "Wait."

She was clearly talking to the girl and not to him, but it wouldn't have mattered if she hadn't been. Adam strode toward the door, unsettled by the tight knot of apprehension in his stomach.

Outside, he found chaos. Unfamiliar werewolves formed a ragged half-circle around Dylan's hunched form. Cindy skidded to a stop next to him, and Dylan moved aside enough for Adam to catch a glimpse of a bloody, torn body. Enhanced hearing did little good with so many people talking at once, but Adam caught snippets—Keith questioning one of the local wolves and Dylan whispering soothing, comforting words edged with worry.

The wind shifted and the smell hit him, thick, fresh blood and some that had been shed hours ago, and the scent of fear, underlain with a tingle of magic he recognized all too easily. A bond—a *blood* bond, weak but present, one that tied the injured man to a vampire.

Adam moved forward and knelt next to Cindy before asking the question he already knew the answer to. "He's not healing like he should, is he?"

"Hard to tell." She'd opened the bag already and was packing layer after layer of gauze pads against the boy's shoulder and mangled arm. "Major injuries can take longer."

She was lying, but the kid on the ground was barely coherent, much less in any shape to notice. He clutched at Dylan's arm, eyes wild. "More. All of us. At the pass—"

"Bobby, slow down." Anxiety made Dylan's usually calm voice sound nervous. "Who's at the pass?"

"The pack. All of us—all of us who could run from Recco. Injured and children..."

Joe swore. "I can't go. Brynn—"

"We'll round up a few others," Abby told him. "You need to stay here and keep an eye on things anyway, Joe." She touched Dylan's shoulder. "Sasha can help them set up here. They'll need her."

Dylan looked torn for a few seconds, then jerked to his feet. "I'm going with you. If they're from Helena, they'll know me. Cindy, can you tell Sasha?"

She didn't look up. "I'll take care of it. Go. When you come back, head for the bar. There's more room there than at my house."

A hand landed on Adam's shoulder, and he glanced up to find Keith there. "What about you?"

He shook his head. "This boy's got a blood bond with the vampire. If you want him to start healing, I need to break it."

"What does it take?" Cindy asked. "To form a bond like that, I mean. Can a vampire have more than one at a time?"

"Not without a witch, not if he wants to stay sane. But if he doesn't care..."

"We'll do what we can." She brushed her hair back from her forehead with the back of her wrist. "What do you need to begin?"

"Let's move him first. Where are we going?"

"Inside for now. If we manage to stabilize him, we can move him to the bar and wait for the others."

He picked up the injured wolf—Bobby, Dylan had called him—and carried him toward the house. The kid was covered in blood, and Adam couldn't stop his reaction to it, even when he tried to block out the scent. His mouth watered, his heart beat a little too fast, and every one of the six days since his last feeding felt like a weight around his neck. He didn't *need* the blood, but he still wanted it.

Then again, if he was going to be snapping another vampire's blood bonds, he wouldn't make it his usual three weeks between blood donations. At this rate he wouldn't last another three *days*.

A problem for later.

Inside, they found Sam and Sasha smoothing a clean sheet over the table. Sam gestured sharply, and Adam spoke as he eased the boy to the covered surface. "Bobby. From Helena."

"Dylan's roommate," Sasha murmured.

Cindy tore open his shirt and pressed her hands methodically over Bobby's abdomen, obviously checking for more injuries. "The arm is bad, Adam, but he might keep it if you can cut him loose from the bond."

Cut her loose. The words echoed in his mind as he dropped a hand to Bobby's head. Cindy's smooth, bland midwestern accent sounded nothing like the broad vowels and precise enunciation of a Boston debutante, but memories drifted up from decades before, a frantic female voice, begging for help. *Cut her loose. The rest of us will die if you don't.*

Adam closed his eyes and forced his attention to the present, to the boy under his hand and the magic twisted around him. "Even if I break the bond, he's going to be weak."

"We'll have to hope for the best."

"I can help," Sasha whispered. "Not much, not if there might be people coming in who are worse off, but...a little."

Bobby moved suddenly, his hand shooting out to close around Cindy's wrist. "No." His eyes were wild. "I'd rather lose my arm. Don't—don't waste power—" A rough swallow. "My girlfriend and her kid are out there. Hurt. And more, so many more—"

Cindy nodded slowly. "I understand. We're looking to save your life right now, that's all."

He relaxed and shuddered, and Adam used his distraction to slip beneath the shields all werewolves possessed, whether they realized it or not.

Bobby clearly didn't—or maybe his protections were so compromised by the vampire who'd been preying on him that they were of no use at all. Either way, it was easy to find the core of the boy's magic, a weak, timid flicker mingled with a power that resonated with Adam's own energy. Death magic, cold and sterile, and the opposite of what lived inside the werewolves.

Adam unfocused his eyes slightly, just enough to let the currents in the room overlay what was actually there. For a second, Sasha flared, bright, colorful light that pulsed warm and cool in turn. Witches and wizards were always rainbows, full of life *and* death, though Sasha had obviously embraced the blues and greens of the wild over the blood red of death.

He tried to turn his attention back to Bobby, but his gaze snagged on Cindy. All werewolf, all cool colors mixed with the golden glow of strength. Magnetic. Potent. The hunger inside him rose, tangled desire for a woman with craving for the sort of power she represented. With her blood, freely given, he'd be unstoppable.

It made her a dangerous temptation, one he'd do well to avoid.

Bobby groaned, and Adam forced himself to find that thread of vampiric magic again, this time following it back to its source. Geography meant little with the flows and currents of energy, but his otherworldly sight couldn't extend beyond the physical. Instead he traced the small thread back by feeling alone, riding it instead of severing it, in hopes of catching a glimpse of what they stood against.

He felt anger first. Frustration and a frightening determination coupled with reckless arrogance. The trickle of power flowed to its source, and Adam sucked in a breath as he sensed dozens upon dozens of other connections, all stretched thin but still feeding the bloated monster at the center of the grotesque web.

Bonds like this required complex spells to maintain balance, spells only a witch could provide. Without it, one long-term connection to a werewolf was madness. This many crossed the line into insanity—the kind of insanity that would throb in the vampire's aura and bleed into anyone sensitive to the touch of magic.

Severing the first connection would be easy, but it wouldn't go unnoticed. *Awaken the sleeping dragon.* The vampire would fight for every bond after that, and Adam would pay the price.

No choice. The boy under his hands would die if he didn't cut the link. And every bond he broke would take away a source of power, make his opponent weaker. Adam did it in an instant, snatching the bond as if attempting to bind the boy to himself, then releasing it before the attachment could cement.

He had to have imagined the roar of outrage echoing back across the intervening distance. Adam squeezed his eyes shut until his equilibrium returned, then opened them and met Sasha's gaze. "He's bound himself to dozens of wolves. Maybe a hundred."

Sasha shuddered, paled. "I didn't feel that when I broke Justine's bond. The vampire could—could be taking more every day."

"Maybe that's why they fled here," Cindy muttered tersely, already pressing a syringe to the inside of Bobby's elbow.

"Maybe," Adam agreed. "But it means he's going to follow them."

Her eyes blazed with cold fire, blue and chilling. "Then we'll be ready."

Chapter Three

He'd been going full-bore for the last two days, and Adam showed no signs of slowing. What he *did* show signs of was exhaustion.

Cindy had seen it often enough, both with her classmates and with herself. It was insidious, the kind of work that brought you to the edge of physical as well as mental collapse. There was always more to do, always more people to help. If you stopped, you were letting them down.

But there came a time when there wasn't a choice.

They'd already stopped using the bar as a makeshift hospital. Most of the people who had fled from Helena had only superficial injuries, but too many of them bore the blood bond that had made Bobby's healing so sluggish. Adam and Sasha had been working overtime to release all the refugees from those bonds.

And Adam was still at it. Three more people had shown up earlier in the day, a couple and their little girl. The little girl wasn't hurt, but her bond had proven difficult to break. Cindy had banished her nearly hysterical parents to the kitchen to calm them down and make them eat. Now they paced the foyer, waiting to be let back in to the small room where their daughter had been placed.

"Adam." Cindy stopped behind him where he stood by the bed. "You have to take a break."

He ignored her, just like he'd ignored her twice before. The little girl whimpered, and his shoulders stiffened as he made an almost soothing noise. "Hold on. Almost there."

She fought a sigh. If there was one thing the last forty-eight hours had taught her, it was that arguing with him was useless. Instead, she wet a cloth in the basin on the nightstand and laid it on the girl's forehead.

It was torture, ten times worse than Gavin's heart condition, because this was something she couldn't even *understand*, much less treat. She'd been flying blind, patching people up while they continued to suffer under her hands, and it had taken its toll on her, as well.

She was tired, edgy. Angry.

The girl sucked in a sudden breath, and Cindy knew the bond had snapped by the way her body relaxed. Adam, on the other hand, looked like hell. A grimace twisted his face, one of pain and steely determination, and he ground his teeth together so hard she heard it. He dragged in one labored breath, then a second, and magic cracked through the room as he stumbled back with a muffled curse.

He hit the wall and slumped to his knees, both hands balled into fists. His eyes were wild, more black than green, and they didn't quite focus. "Done." It was a hoarse rasp. "It's done."

It took only moments to check the girl's vitals, and Cindy kept watch on Adam as she did so. He looked like this last bond had half-killed him, and an instinct she didn't understand screamed at her to get him the hell out of the room.

"I'm going to bring her parents in," she told him quietly. "Go upstairs and wait for me. I'll be right up." He didn't react, so she knelt in front of him. "*Adam.*"

Something dangerous stirred just beneath the surface, feral and hungry. It took forever for him to meet her eyes. "You shouldn't be this close."

A reasonable person would be petrified. "Her parents can't see you like this. It'll scare the piss out of them. Go upstairs, please."

He rose, slow and deliberate, as if every movement hurt. He seemed to make a special effort not to look at the girl as he cut a wide circle around her on his way to the door.

He headed in the direction of the back stairs, and Cindy walked into the foyer. The girl's parents rushed over when they saw her, and she stepped aside to let them into the room. "She should be fine now, but call for me if anything happens."

They thanked her absently, all their attention focused on their daughter. She didn't blame them, and it was just as well, because she had to get upstairs.

She found Adam standing on the top landing, staring blankly at the wall. "Come on." She took his arm and dragged him into the bedroom, determined to make her suggestion before he keeled over—or she lost her nerve.

Locking the door behind them took only a moment. Cindy took a deep breath and pulled her turtleneck over her head. "You need to drink."

His gaze swept up her body in a tangible wave, and he moved before her shirt hit the ground. Her back slammed against the door, and he caught both of her wrists and pinned them next to her head with a snarl. "You *don't know* what you're asking."

Fear spiked, an instinctive reaction because he'd snapped, moving from calm blankness to feral intensity so quickly. She wasn't scared of him, and she wanted to do this. He needed her help, and the least she could do to repay him for his was to offer.

Offer.

She recalled his words from the first night, when her interest had been more vague curiosity and considerable attraction—*the power comes from the willing gift.* So she relaxed in his grip and let her head fall back against the wall. "I'm not asking. I'm offering."

His nostrils flared. His breath fell warm against her throat. "You don't understand. I haven't been breaking those bonds. I've been stealing them. Stealing them and letting them go, and every time I let one go it feels like slow suicide. I'm out of control."

"That's not true, though," she whispered. "Not if you've been letting them go, even when it hurts you."

"Yes, I make a charming martyr. But don't doubt that selfish self-preservation thrives inside me. Eventually I'll snap. And I'll take."

"So take me." The moment the words left her, she wanted to snatch them back. This was more than the concerned offer of someone used to caring for people. She was starting to sound desperate, and that had to mean she wanted this more than she realized.

She felt the slightest pressure, something magical instead of physical, as if he'd stroked her just under her skin. A groan ripped free of him, and he licked a hot line up the side of her neck. "You're so willing. I'm not *that* much of a martyr."

Yes, she wanted him. She trembled with it, burned. What she didn't understand was why it didn't feel like it was about sex. Instead, she wanted to feel his teeth sink into her flesh. Wanted to feed him, sate his hunger.

Give him what he needed.

She stood on her toes, straining toward him. Anything to get closer to his mouth. "Let me."

His body shook. His breath skated over the skin he'd licked, and he lowered his mouth. "Stop me if it's too much."

Cindy had never imagined that she'd practically have to beg a vampire to bite her. "I promise."

Teeth closed on her throat. His fangs were larger than normal canines and a little sharper, and she gasped when they broke through her skin. The pain was intense but brief, vanishing in a rush of warmth.

The warmth built into a hot flare of pleasure, and Cindy gasped again. Her nipples hardened as her body reacted, though the heavy anticipation swelling through her was disorienting.

He hasn't really touched me. The fuzzy thought scattered as he released her wrists and smoothed his hands down to her hips. His tongue stroked her skin, her body throbbing in time with each lick.

She was wet, ready, and instinct drove her to tear at his shirt. His bare chest was warm under her hands, rough with hair and hard—everything about him was so hard—

He lifted his head, just enough to whisper. "Let me make it good."

If it got better, she'd explode. "*Yes.*"

Another stab of pain, more fleeting than the last. When his lips closed tight on her throat this time, magic flared so brightly the world disappeared. He stroked her everywhere without moving his hands from her hips—teasing over her nipples, dragging between her legs and circling her clit.

Cindy shuddered and clamped her lips together to keep from crying out. It was too much, all at once, and she couldn't stop the flood of sensation that rocked her. She clutched Adam's shoulders for support and rode it out, waited for the peak of pleasure to subside.

It didn't.

Finally his hands moved, from her hips to her thighs, curling under them as he hoisted her higher, grinding between her legs.

She had to stop whimpering. There were patients downstairs, not to mention other people, but she couldn't tear her focus away from Adam. She was drowning, losing herself in him.

"Stop." The word came out weak, almost inaudible. "Adam, stop."

He froze, his back going rigid under her hands. He lifted his head, his breath falling in hoarse pants, but power still pulsed in the air between them. "Are you hurt?"

"No." It came out on a moan, and Cindy blinked. "You were going to make me scream."

Confusion flashed in his eyes. "Not in a bad way?"

"No, not in a bad way." She dropped her hands to his belt and tugged at the buckle, but he was too close. She pushed at him a little and dropped to her knees between him and the wall. "Definitely not in a bad way."

That got his attention. He caught her wrists and stepped back, a groan escaping him. "No. No, you deserve better than this."

Cindy had no idea how old he actually was. "You're not one of those guys who thinks a blow job is dirty or demeaning to women, are you?"

Something flared in his eyes. "I'm a man who thinks you attend to your bedmate's pleasure first if she's given you a gift as great as her blood."

"Okay, that's a new one." She pulled free of his grasp and rose, keeping her eyes averted from his. "You don't have to explain yourself to me at all. No means no."

He snarled and locked his arm around her waist, moving so quickly the world spun. Her back crashed against his chest, and he slapped a hand against the wall, not *quite* pinning her. "Don't pretend I denied you. You denied me. Denied me your pleasure, and perhaps you've been taking the wrong sort of men into your bed if you think I should be satisfied without it."

She closed her eyes and tried not to think about how good he felt pressed against her. "I didn't deny you anything."

He laughed, though it sounded more rueful than mocking. "My darling Dr. Shepherd. If I didn't get to watch your face or feel your body tighten on my fingers, if I didn't even get to enjoy the pleasure of your screams, then you denied me everything."

He was demanding. "Two-thirds of those things were physically impossible," she pointed out. "The other isn't happening. I have *patients* downstairs. The last thing they want is to hear me getting off."

"Fair enough." He brushed his lips over the side of her neck. "But I should warn you that I'm not incredibly quiet either."

The soft touch along with the admission made her want to melt against him, to beg. Anger swept through her—directed at herself, not him—and she ducked under his arm. "Do you feel stronger now?"

"Stronger than I have in months." His arms fell to his sides. "Years, maybe."

"Good." That was something, at least, especially since she seemed to be suffering few ill effects. She felt a little lightheaded, but that was easily attributable to the magic he'd worked with her body and not blood loss.

"Good," he echoed, but a faint note of wariness had intruded in the warmth of his voice. "I appreciate the gift. I'm sorry you misunderstood my intentions."

She touched her fingers lightly to her neck. The holes from his teeth had already closed, and she drew her shirt back over her head. "What intentions? You needed to feed."

"Yes, I suppose I did." He swiped his thumb over his mouth, his gaze still fixed on her throat. "You feeling all right?"

"Fine." Cindy almost winced when she heard the chilly tone of her own voice. It probably wasn't fair to extend her anger to him, even if he had been a jerk. "You said Dylan offered? To do this, I mean. Give you his blood."

"Yes." No inflection, and his eyes had gone hard. Cool.

"I'll explain the process to him." Better to let Adam think the encounter had been nothing more than an emergency and an experiment, her due diligence as the town's doctor.

One eyebrow quirked upward. "Best explain it to Sasha as well, then, because I won't be giving him that experience unless she asks nicely."

She was starting to think that playing dumb was the safest

181

way to deal with him, so she favored him with a nod and a vague smile. "Of course. I need to get back downstairs. Will you excuse me?"

Oh, he didn't like that. Frustration flashed in his eyes, but he didn't seem willing to call her on it. "Yes, Cindy."

Cindy tried to practice as much brutal self-honesty as possible, so she forced herself to admit that she was fleeing as she left her bedroom and hurried down the stairs. What had started as a pleasant encounter with intriguing sexual potential had gone south faster than she'd thought possible, and it was her own damn fault. Somehow, she'd managed to fall short of his expectations, and it had made her lash out.

Just as well. She hit the bottom landing and leaned against the wall in the small, dark hallway. The last thing she needed was to get involved with another man she barely knew only to discover he wanted things she couldn't provide.

Something more than what she was.

So keep feeling sorry for yourself, Shepherd. That's useful. Cindy pushed off the wall and headed for the kitchen. It didn't matter. Someone else could give Adam Dubois his goddamned mystical energy from now on, because she was finished feeling like a failure.

"Tell me I can go home and sleep in my own bed, Cindy."

Adam froze, one hand still lifted to knock against the open door, and acknowledged that he was in deep, deep trouble if Cindy's scent and presence clung to him so strongly that her own alpha couldn't tell the difference.

Granted, Gavin had his eyes closed as he reclined in the same battered old chair, and he looked only marginally more alive than he had on Adam's arrival. The stress of the last few days had weighed heavily on him to be sure, but not so heavily that the man shouldn't be able to sense the difference between a wolf and a vampire.

Then a frown wrinkled his friend's face, and Gavin opened one eye. "Adam."

Oh yes. He was in trouble. "Sam told you all those years of smoking would mess up your sense of smell. Guess it finally happened."

Gavin's frown didn't dissipate. "I was going by feel, not

scent. So, unless you're hiding my doctor in your pocket, you have some explaining to do."

Adam moved to sink into the battered leather chair next to Gavin's. "I don't suppose I can convince you I've got your doctor in my pocket?"

"Was it really necessary, Adam?"

"She's bossy. And I wasn't in great shape, Gavin."

"I understand." He finally turned his head to meet Adam's gaze. He wasn't angry, only quietly determined. "Now understand me. Leave her be, if you can. She hasn't had an easy time of it."

It wasn't news, but it stirred the guilt inside him just the same. "I didn't mean to touch her in the first place. She pushed until I snapped, and I sure as hell ain't proud."

Gavin sighed, something that almost sounded like relief. "Cindy does that sometimes. I thought—well, it doesn't matter."

"It does matter." Gavin of all people knew why. "It was willing. It was so damn willing I went from one foot in the grave to a scary kind of powerful, and I didn't take much. I know we've got a war brewing, but power's a dangerous thing for a vampire to have too much of."

"I'll explain to her why it can't happen again."

Adam couldn't keep from tensing. "How much do you plan to explain?"

Gavin flashed him a sharp look. "The reason it can't has nothing to do with you, and everything to do with Cindy. Your secrets are safe with me, Dubois."

"Christ, Hamilton. What in hell happened to her?"

"She was human, and a corrupt alpha thought she'd make a good pet. Turned out, she was too strong for that, so he punished her. Tried to break her." Gavin shifted in the chair with a grimace. "It's common. Too common."

It was a common danger even on the east coast. "How long?"

"Three years."

"Is that how long they had her, or how long ago it happened?"

Gavin grimaced again, and this time it almost looked like pain. "She came to Red Rock seven years ago."

Three years of torment, seven years of recovery. Guilt

wasn't just stirring anymore, but screaming. "God damn it. I'm a bastard, and you should have put me down eighty years ago."

Gavin didn't deny it. "Like you said, Cindy's bossy. She's bossy and stubborn as hell, so what you've got to do now is make sure she doesn't have her mind set on you, for God's sake. Not as a lover or as a project or *anything*."

"Project?" He didn't have to pretend to be mildly outraged. "What, should I be worried she's going to give me a makeover?"

"Not the kind you're thinking of, but yes."

Damn him for feeling intrigued. "I suppose you won't elaborate because you don't want me interested at all."

Gavin snorted inelegantly. "I'll expound at length, my friend, because telling you exactly what she'd do with the likes of you is the fastest way to turn you off her." He leaned forward. "She'd break you to ride. Turn you into a productive member of polite society."

After nearly a century of hiding in the Great North Woods, the idea was moderately horrific. "I think you're overestimating her charms, old friend. She's a beautiful girl with a delicious temper, but hermit living suits me."

"Then you won't have the slightest trouble minding my words. Stay away from her."

"Yes, sir." Adam closed his eyes and set his chair to rocking. "Keith's doing a good job. You trained him well, and that girl of his steadies him. But you should be damned to hell for giving him such a romantic streak. Watching the two of them together is sickening."

"Has it really been so long since you got softhearted over a woman, you cranky bastard?"

So long he couldn't remember her name *or* her face, just that she'd had curly golden hair halfway to her hips that he'd gotten to run his fingers through once while he stole a kiss.

And Astrid—

He shoved away the thought. His unrequited affection for Astrid hadn't grown deep enough to qualify, and he'd guarded his feelings closely after her death. "I keep my heart out of it these days. Better for everyone."

"The rest of us aren't so content with that."

"The rest of you aren't vampires. Haven't you ever considered it? We're the opposite of werewolves in almost every way. You folk are obsessed with your mates. Vampires aren't built to live in pairs. Maybe just groups or all alone."

His friend frowned. "And I think that's bullshit, but I'm too old and tired to rehash all our favorite arguments tonight. You win."

It didn't feel like winning. The victory was as hollow as the lonely place inside him, as the hunger that craved any connection it could make. Those brief seconds with Cindy under his hands, under his mouth, had been his hottest, wildest moments in decades. He'd taken to choosing his lovers from the weaker wolves in Bedagi Creek, content to draw what he needed to sustain himself without ever letting it become more. No love, no commitment...

No power. No passion, except the pleasure he gave them in return for their gift.

If he didn't stop thinking about it, Gavin would kill him.

"Do you have to go back?"

"To Maine?"

"Yes." The word came slowly, like a child's wind-up toy exhausting its last few cranks. "You could stay here."

The only thing he could give his friend now was comfort. "I'm in no hurry to get back."

"Good." Gavin's eyes drifted shut. "I'm sorry I called you out here like this. It should have been a happier visit."

"If it had been a happier visit, I wouldn't have come. It's not like you didn't try." Adam leaned forward and braced his hand on Gavin's shoulder. "Rest, old friend. I promise not to woo your doctor or your wife until you're on your feet and ready to knock me off mine." *And that's at least half-true.*

"Sam would break your face." Gavin chuckled quietly.

"My face is prettier than yours," Adam countered. "Granted, there's never been much accounting for your wife's taste. She might ugly me up if she wanted me to stick around."

"Sammie *does* want you to stick around."

"Then she's a fool and so are you." Adam squeezed Gavin's shoulder before sitting back. "You know I'll be here until you don't need me anymore. I owe you too much. You helped me save my people...and I'll help you save yours." If he spent all of his time thinking about present conflicts, he could ignore the temptation to dwell on the past, to pick at scabs that eighty years had barely healed.

"Keith."

"You want me to save Keith?"

"No, Keith's people. They're his now." He looked relieved and guilty, all at once.

As if it was that easy. "They're his to protect. But they'll always be yours too."

"Mmm." Gavin smiled. "Yes."

"Yes," Adam echoed. "I promised your sweet little witch that I'd let her ask me any question on blood bonds that struck her fancy, so I'm going to get as much sleep as possible before she grills me."

"Hmm."

Gavin didn't believe him and Adam didn't blame him. "Even if I were planning to go behind your back and woo Cindy, I'd have to wait until you weren't camped out in her damn house."

"People in this town aren't that prudish, Dubois, and that includes me. We're used to a certain lack of privacy."

Adam rose to his feet. "If I was after sex, I'd pay no mind to who might be listening in. But I prefer to deliver my apologies without an audience. Or are you going to tell me I can't do that, either?"

"On the contrary, I quite approve of you having to grovel for forgiveness."

"Fine." It took effort to keep the bite out of the word. "I *am* going back to your place, and I'll send Sam here to torment you for the rest of the night. I'll apologize on my own damn time."

Gavin leaned back in his chair. "Good. Tell my wife I said hello. And if you *do* see Cindy, tell her I want to sleep in my own damn bed tonight."

"Will do." And the sooner Gavin was out of Cindy's house... *No, Dubois. Stay away. Stay far, far away.*

He needed to repay his debt and get the hell back to his cabin and his life, even if that life seemed increasingly empty with every day that passed.

Even quiet and blessedly empty, the house hummed.

Cindy tugged on her thermal shirt and flannel pants. She'd never liked wearing pajamas, still didn't, but the chances that she'd be summoned from her bed in the middle of the night these days were high, even with her house cleared of patients and visitors. Sometimes, she couldn't afford the extra few seconds it would take her to stop and dress.

Soon you'll be sleeping in your shoes. The thought made her laugh as she tried to imagine the damage her heavy boots would do to the densely woven but delicate cotton sheets she preferred. *Or maybe not.*

The upstairs hallway was deserted for the first time in days as she walked to the bathroom. Her thoughts raced, and she used the mindless ritual of brushing her teeth to put them in order.

She owed Adam an apology, especially after spending the whole day immersed in busy work in order to avoid him. He'd nearly killed himself trying to help over the last few days, and she'd given him nothing but grief.

And blood. Cindy grimaced and rinsed her toothbrush, unsure whether one outweighed the other. Either way, she'd acted like a defensive ass, and it wasn't in her nature to let it lie and hope he got over it.

The sound of a knock drifted up the stairs, too gentle to be another emergency but too late to be a casual visit. Halfway down the stairs, she spotted Adam through the window.

At least it gave her time to brace herself, and to try to think of something to say.

She opened the door. "Come in."

He stepped across the threshold, unease clear in the tense set of his shoulders and the cool wave of power he brought with him.

It made her want to lay a hand on his shoulder and comfort him, and the realization jarred her. "Would you like some coffee?"

"Please."

He was starting to scare her a little, but she said nothing else until she'd set the coffee to brew and lowered herself to the chair opposite his at the kitchen table. "Is something wrong?"

"I'm not sure." He flattened both palms on the table, his wide, blunt fingers sliding absently over the wood, as if testing it for some quality. "I came to apologize."

"It's not necessary." The words were automatic, habit.

"That's for me to decide, not you. And I think I need to

apologize."

So he wanted to unburden his soul, make himself feel better. She couldn't fault him for it, since she'd been thinking the same thing not ten minutes ago. "All right."

But the words that came were odd. "I'm sorry I tried too hard. I acted like a stupid bastard."

"I don't understand."

"All that shit I spewed about getting you off..." His voice turned rough. "Not saying I wouldn't want to. Just...I was trying too hard. Trying not to be a barely verbal fool who'd nearly fucked you against a wall."

Just like that, he bared himself. Exposed his vulnerability. Cindy's mouth went dry, and she clasped her hands together under the table to hide their shaking. "You weren't the only one who acted like an ass. I felt rejected. It made me mean."

His lips tugged up in a smile wicked as sin. "Never did have much luck with alpha wolves. Too bad I have such a weakness for you."

An answering smile curved her own mouth. "You're helpless when faced with crude, difficult blondes?"

"Deadlier than garlic and crosses."

"Don't tease." She tried to look away from the full bow of his lower lip. "I could ask you to my bed."

"And Gavin would rise from his sickbed to drag me from it by the scruff of my neck like an untrained puppy." Adam's smile widened, enough to part his lips and show fang. "He knows I like my blondes feisty."

"So he already warned you off, then."

"Several times."

And yet here he was. "Are you that obstinate, or that fascinated?"

"Both." His hand smoothed to the edge of the table then traced along the side. "And I did owe you an apology. Gavin said you're one of the ones who didn't come to this life by choice, and I know about that."

Cindy stiffened. She didn't want to *think* about Preston, much less talk about him. "I appreciate your consideration."

He glanced up at her, his eyes narrowed. "Didn't show you much of that."

Tossing his own words back at him was ridiculously

satisfying. "I think that's for me to decide, not you." The coffeemaker beeped, and she rose to fill two mugs.

When she turned back, he nodded. "Fair enough. I didn't show you as much as I'd like."

"And you'd like to remedy that."

"Maybe. I've been a hermit for a long time though. Maybe I'm worried I'll fuck it up more."

She didn't want him to concern himself with such things. The more care he took with her, the harder it would be to remind herself that she didn't need another disastrous entanglement. She'd almost forgotten already, drawn in by the heat of his gaze and the memory of his hands in her hair.

Cindy thumped the mug to the table in front of him with more force than she intended. "We'd be better off avoiding any involvement."

"Don't necessarily disagree on that account, sweetheart. When the great adventure here is over I'm going back home." But he didn't sound any more certain than she.

It shouldn't have made a difference, but it did. "If we know what it is—and what it *isn't*," she reasoned, "then that's not really the same thing as getting involved, is it?"

"Not really." His voice had dropped, taken on a harsh edge. "Don't know as all the people who want me to stay away from you will agree, but I'm not sure I care."

As long as they laid out the rules, she didn't either. "No more blood. This is about sex, not food."

Only a brief hesitation before he nodded. "How much has Gavin told you about me? Anything?"

"No." She swallowed. "And I don't want to know. Rule number two."

"That's a little reckless, don't you think? Hopping into bed with a century-old vampire who your alpha thinks you're safer away from without asking a single question?"

"If Gavin thought for a moment that you posed a physical threat to any of us, you wouldn't be here, and you know it. You may be his oldest friend, but we're his *pack*. Any warnings to leave me alone would have been for my emotional benefit, not to ensure my safety." The coffee left a sour taste in her mouth, and Cindy pushed her mug away. "If you want to say no, just say it."

Adam shoved his chair back, his expression caught somewhere between anger and the sort of heat that left her knees weak. The sort that made her think of dark corners and raw, panting breaths blowing in her ear, the hard bite of fingers clutching her hips. "No. I don't want to say no."

"It won't hurt me if you do." She kept pushing, and the only thing she could think was that maybe she was trying to piss him off. Trying to make him run so she wouldn't have to.

He lifted a hand and touched her cheek, his fingers work-roughened but gentle. "It might hurt you if I don't. If you won't hear my sins, at least hear this. I don't have much experience separating sex from blood. Not that I'm not willing to try, but it'll be...new for me."

"I want you to look at me and see a woman, not dinner. That's all." It should have terrified her, giving him the unvarnished truth, but she didn't feel exposed, just excited. Hungry.

His hand fell away. "I don't see my lovers as food."

"A convenient pick-me-up, then." Cindy reached for him, then thought better of it. "I don't want to be that either."

His frown tugged down his lips and formed a crease between his brows. "I think I'm learning a great deal about how you view *your* lovers."

His words startled her, and her thigh hit the edge of the table as she took a step back. "I'm acting like an ass again." And her sinuses and throat burned with tears. "I accept your apology. You should go."

"I should." Adam rose, his bulk filling the small kitchen. "I'm out of touch and I've always been a jackass, but I have respect for all the women I bed, whether it's seduction by candlelight or a hard fuck over a table."

"I shouldn't have said any of it." Cindy pinched the bridge of her nose and growled softly. "Maybe Gavin warned you about me for you *own* good. Did you think of that?"

"Not for a second."

"Maybe you need to."

"I've known Gavin Hamilton a lot longer than you have, sweetheart." He caught her hand and tugged it away from her face. "The old bastard isn't the least bit concerned with the state of my heart."

She had no idea how she did it, but she willed away the

rising tears and stared up at him, acutely aware of his strength as he held her hand. "Now I'm the one trying too hard, and it shows."

He didn't say a word, just drew her against his chest and hooked an arm around her shoulders. "It's been a long week, and we're both cranky."

Cindy laughed at the assessment. "I stay cranky. I need to let go." She lifted her face to his. "Maybe even stop thinking."

Adam nodded, as if she'd answered some sort of question, then dropped back into his chair, dragging her with him. She ended up sprawled across his lap, straddling his legs with her hips close to his but not quite touching. "No feeding," he murmured as he lifted one of her hands. "But give me permission. Let me have one drop, just enough to show you."

He was hard under her, solid. "Yes."

His other arm went around her waist, anchoring her against his body as his lips brushed the tips of her fingers. He licked first, slow and languid, teasing one finger before she felt the prick of one sharp fang. A momentary discomfort, nothing more, and it vanished in a wave of heat as power spilled over her.

Her head fell back on a moan, and she accidentally ripped the worn flannel of his shirt. Her apology got tangled up in another moan, and Cindy ground her hips against his.

"Shh." A soothing sound instead of a command, and his breath tickled over her palm. Magic tightened around her as he turned her hand and pressed his mouth to the pulse inside her wrist. His tongue swept out, dragged across skin, and pleasure tugged low in her abdomen in response. "This isn't about food. It's about sex. Dirty, raw pleasure."

She could barely speak. "Dirty and raw, I can handle."

"I know." Another lick, another pulse of pleasure.

She was at a disadvantage, and she didn't care. He could have her control if he wanted it, as long as it remained in the realm of the physical.

As long as it didn't threaten her heart.

Cindy leaned down and rubbed her cheek against his temple. "What's your stance on kissing?"

"That it's a dying art and people should do it more."

"Mmm." His voice sent delicious shivers down her spine. So

did brushing her lips lightly over his. "Then you'll be happy to know I'm pretty good at it."

"Not surprised." He licked her lower lip. "Kiss me. Show me how you like it."

She almost lifted her hands to his face to hold him still for a soft, slow kiss. But her hands were shaking, and soft and slow weren't exactly what she was going for. So she growled and took his mouth, not bothering to disguise the lust she'd been fighting.

For a few moments he let her kiss him, but soon enough his hand dropped to her hip and tightened. His tongue surged between her lips, stroking with a maddening rhythm, and the magic coiled around them throbbed with every heartbeat.

Cindy tilted her head to get closer, already buzzing with the possibilities. Adam either knew just how to touch a woman, or he wanted to touch *her* badly enough for his ardor to overcome the need to learn her body.

Maybe it was both.

He pulled away, his hands still hard on her body and his breath hot against her lips. "And that was just a kiss."

"Just a kiss." It didn't seem like *just* anything, but Cindy wasn't about to contradict him. "What other dying arts do you practice?"

"The art of honorable retreat." His fingers smoothed through her hair as he brushed his mouth against her ear and dropped his voice to a dark, smooth whisper. "If you still want me tomorrow, I'll take you slow and hard and we'll fuck ourselves halfway to dead with no strings attached. But I'm not going to let you tell yourself I'm a late-night mistake."

She didn't know whether to be irritated or relieved that he'd pegged her so quickly. So ruthlessly. "Leave me wound up, and maybe I won't want you tomorrow," she told him lightly.

He didn't take it lightly. His breath hissed out and his hand dropped to the soft elastic of her flannel pants. "You want an audition?"

"I was teasing, sweetheart." She caught his wrist. "Tonight's a solo performance."

He laughed hoarsely. "For both of us. Time for you to take yourself to bed, Dr. Shepherd, because I'm taking you to bed tomorrow."

"You make some sweet promises, Mr. Dubois." Cindy

climbed off his lap and crossed the room on shaky legs to turn off the coffeemaker.

She'd talk to Sam the first chance she had, because Adam was right. Gavin had many strengths, but his judgment tended to be suspect about those he loved. He wanted so badly to believe in the basic goodness of people that he couldn't acknowledge that sometimes circumstances could align to turn the best of people into monsters.

Cindy was living proof of that.

Chapter Four

Adam spent half the night telling himself it would be okay to return to Cindy's house and take what they both so clearly wanted, and the rest of the night and a good part of the morning dreaming that he had.

No one came out of the master bedroom as he descended the stairs, and it was just as well. Sam was busy hovering over Gavin, and Adam knew better than to violate the sanctity of the man's sickroom with Cindy's scent fresh on his skin. Sam might be fond of him, but not fond enough not to tear a strip off him if he riled Gavin.

Besides, he had somewhere else to be. His hosts just didn't know it yet.

The sun hung balanced just above the trees as Adam stepped into the street. A light dusting of snow covered the ground and the air held the sharp, almost metallic smell that meant more was on the way. The sun held little warmth, but it was enough that he should have felt its pressure, as a warning if nothing else. The sun rarely bothered him unless he waited dangerously long between feedings, but he was always aware of it, of its subtle weight.

Not today. Cindy's magic still thrummed in his veins, strong enough to make him reckless.

He couldn't afford reckless. He followed his faint memory and walked down the hill, following the long road until it merged with the main thoroughfare. Plenty of people were out and about, human and wolf alike, but Adam ignored the curious and occasionally suspicious stares and made his way to the bar that seemed to serve as the town's focal point.

It didn't take a werewolf's nose to follow the fading scent

around the back and up an old set of wooden steps. Dylan might be surprised to find a vampire on his stoop, but Adam wagered Sasha wouldn't be. The girl was too smart and too well read not to have connected the dots by now.

Dylan answered the door on the third knock, and his placid expression made it clear that not only had Sasha connected the dots, she'd shared. "So. I guess you were expecting me."

"Maybe a little." Dylan pulled the door wide and gestured. "Sasha's been going through the books in the makeshift library."

They found Sasha hunched over an ancient desk, even older books scattered open around her. She looked up and said simply, "It was you. He got the idea from you."

Two sentences, and the most damning words he'd heard in a decade or more. "That seems to be the case."

Her clear gaze held only interest and a little fascination. "He's doing it wrong, then. Doesn't know how, or maybe on purpose. Whatever the case, these bonds have distinct directionality."

"Wait, wait." Dylan pulled out a chair and sat before gesturing for Adam to do the same. "I'm only caught up as far as the fact that the crazy vampire in Helena is doing what he's doing because Adam did something in Boston a hundred years ago."

So maybe Sasha *hadn't* told Dylan everything. Adam sighed and sank into his chair. "More like eighty, but yes. In the nineteen thirties, I did something reckless and dangerous, and now this vampire's trying to pull off the same trick."

"Or not," Sasha said again, her finger tracking down the text of one yellowed page. "There are inconsistencies. I just don't know whether they're purposeful or because he's flying blind. Maybe you can help me figure that part out."

"How much do you know?"

"Bits and pieces." Her voice lowered, took on a sympathetic note. "Rumors, mostly, from accounts written by the Boston alpha. That you fancied yourself strong enough to lead your own pack of wolves, and that you bound them to you by blood."

There had always been rumors, the more lascivious and deviant the better. "And that I took an alpha female and a witch as my lovers and we performed obscene sexual rituals under the full moon and corrupted a few dozen impressionable young women who worshiped us as gods and indulged our perverted whims."

Sasha sighed. "You asked what I know. I didn't say I thought it was the truth."

Dylan took up the cause with exhausting optimism. "Obviously none of it's true, but times were different back then and..." He trailed off when Adam quirked an eyebrow. "Okay, maybe some of it's true. I have no idea what sort of freaky stuff vampires get up to for fun."

"Vampires get up to all manner of...freaky stuff." Watching their eyes widen was almost worth dragging it out, but it was a waste of time they didn't have. "There's grains of truth in all of it. The witch had the idea first. She had a lover who was a werewolf—a female lover, and the pack wasn't sympathetic to her. I don't know how well it's tolerated now, but it most certainly was not then. And Joan—the alpha female—was strong, but young...an idealist who took her responsibilities seriously. The Boston alpha had grown tired of her insistence on defending the weaker members."

"So they came to you?" Sasha asked softly.

"They came to me. The witch had an idea, a crazy idea. I thought she was insane at first, because vampires who sustain bonds to werewolves for a long time... You've seen it now."

"And felt it," she reminded him. "What was different about what you did?"

"What was it you said? About directionality?"

Sasha closed the book in front of her and peered at several of the others. "One account specifically mentioned that your... Well, your *pack* could draw power from you, and from others through you."

Cut her loose, Adam—she's drawing too much power.

She'll die without *it.*

The rest of us will die if you don't.

Adam closed his eyes and ignored the voices. "Astrid—that's the witch—she used to call me the pack's reservoir. Power drifted toward me until someone needed it. And if they did...they took it."

"You pooled everyone's power, but also allowed everyone access to it." Even Sasha's obvious sympathy couldn't override her curiosity. "What happened?"

It was the last thing he wanted talk about with two wide-eyed kids. "What do the books say happened?"

She closed the book with a thump. "That the Boston alpha drove you out and reclaimed his pack."

"Pretty much. What happened doesn't really matter. It didn't fail because of the magic. I broke the bonds by choice and didn't try it again."

Sasha looked at Dylan, her gaze questioning, and he nodded as something unspoken passed between them. Then she leaned forward, her elbows on her knees. "Can you tell us how you did it?"

"Don't even think it." Adam flattened both hands on the table and stared Sasha down. "If you're asking because you think I should turn myself into some sort of power-mad vampire..."

"I'm asking because it's what Dylan and I *do*," she told him softly. "We collect the lore."

It took effort to rein himself in. Sasha might be growing into her own, but she was still a girl who didn't deserve the thrust of his temper. "When this is over, before I leave, I'll let you ask me any question you like. When this is over."

She nodded slowly. "At your discretion and convenience. I don't want to push or pry."

Dylan reached across the table to cover her hand in a gesture that looked protective and reassuring at once. "We only need to know a few things for now. There has to be a weakness in what he's doing, other than the fact he's going crazy."

"I'll think about it. Sasha, if you have any books that discuss the origins of the Guide bond, I think that's what Astrid based the spell on. It's probably what the vampire is trying to do—combine blood magic and werewolf binding magic."

"I'll look it up. Thank you, Adam."

"You're welcome. Any more questions?"

"Just one." She smiled. "Would you like to come to dinner tonight?"

Adam hated that he was almost touched. Sasha and Dylan and their puppy love were saccharine enough to make his teeth hurt, but there was something to be said for their dogged, unflagging friendliness. He even unbent enough to smile. "I made other plans tonight, but maybe another time."

Dylan studied him for a long moment, and there was nothing saccharine or friendly about it. Undoubtedly, he could smell the lingering traces of Cindy on Adam's skin. Adam met his gaze and, after another second, Dylan looked away. "We've got reading to do tonight anyway, Sasha. Keith wants us all to meet tomorrow morning to discuss some plan he and Joe cooked up."

"Like you said, then. Another time."

Sasha's words were a clear dismissal—a polite one, but clear nonetheless, and permission to flee. Last night his retreat had been honorable, but today it was self-serving. After mouthing the appropriate pleasantries, he left the two to their lovebird cuddling.

The sun hadn't risen so terribly much during his time inside, but it was strong enough that he saw no reason to dwell in it. Shoving his hands into his pockets, Adam set a brisk pace back to Gavin's house and tried to pretend he had any thoughts left beyond seeing Cindy that night.

He was too old to lie to himself.

Cindy stepped into the kitchen and dropped her bag at the end of the counter. "He's doing better than I expected."

"Thank God." Sam turned, the dishtowel clenched in her hands the only evidence of her tension. "Tell me he's going to be okay, Cindy. I need to hear it."

For now, there was one thing she could give Sam. "He seems to be out of the woods for now, and a lot less stressed out."

"And he can stay here?"

"Don't see why not, if he keeps improving."

"Thank you." Sam moved to sink onto one of the benches, her towel still clutched in her fingers. "I'm not ready to be in this world without him."

"Oh, Sam." Cindy sat beside her and wrapped an arm around her shoulders. "I know you love him like crazy. I'll do everything I can. We both will."

It was a sign of just how bad things had gotten that Sam leaned into her, letting Cindy support her for a few vulnerable seconds as the tension slowly bled from her body. "He's worrying about you and Adam. I told him there's nothing to be worried about, but I know I'm lying, so he does too."

Cindy sighed, but she might as well get it over with. "Depends on why you're both concerned, I guess."

"There's so much history, Cindy. When a man's been alive for a hundred years, he collects more than his share of baggage."

It was exactly what Adam had tried to tell her. What she didn't want to hear. "I'm not trying to fix him, Sam."

"That's not it, sweetheart." Sam lifted a hand to Cindy's cheek. "I'm worried he's going to try to fix you."

It would have been laughable if it wasn't so damned sad. "Then you'll be happy to hear he's as disinterested in my heart and soul as I am his."

"That's what they all want us to think. Helps them preserve their tender masculine egos."

"Mmm. I told him Gavin was warning him off for his own good, not mine."

Sam's hand fell away. "It's not that simple. You of all people should know it never is. Life is messy."

A lesson she'd learned early and a little too well. "Do you want me to leave him alone, Sam? Truly? Because I will. It's not that big a deal."

"You're a big girl. The boys are protective asses because it's in their nature—man *and* wolf—but you're a woman who can make her own choices. I'm just asking you to remember that choices are easier when you know all the facts."

Sooner or later, she'd have to hear the dirty details, the part of Adam's past that had left those shadows in his eyes. "Even if knowing those facts makes things messier?"

"If you think you're going to climb in bed with Adam Dubois and make a clean getaway just because you cover your ears and pretend the past doesn't exist..." Sam shook her head. "You're fooling yourself, honey. Life doesn't get less messy just because you swept the dust under the bed."

Cindy didn't have the energy to argue. "Let me fool myself, Sam. I can't afford to get emotional about someone who's leaving first chance he gets. Maybe I will, anyway, but...if I can just *not know*..."

Sam rose to her feet and moved to the polished oak cupboards, where she pulled down a cutting board. "I know. And he will leave. Red Rock is the dream Gavin and I built together, but sometimes I think he got the idea from Adam.

Adam was the first. But he failed, and this has got to be torment, living in the reminder of that."

"The first to build a sanctuary? For whom?"

"For wolves." Onions and potatoes joined the cutting board on the counter. "Eighty years ago."

But he failed. "He was protecting them from other wolves?"

"The mess out there didn't come from nowhere. It started a long time ago. Alphas getting crueler and colder bit by bit. Then the Great Depression hit, and *everyone* was desperate. But back then, in New England, werewolves weren't the only creatures around."

She shivered. "Vampires."

"Wolves and vampires stayed out of each other's way for the most part, from what I understand." The rhythmic sound of a knife against wood filled the kitchen, an oddly mundane counterpoint to the discussion at hand. "But if you were a wolf scared for your life, or trapped in a bad situation...well, Adam was unusual. He wanted to help."

Like he had here in Red Rock over the last few days. "No wonder he and Gavin became friends."

"They're not so different when you get down to it. Gavin might realize that, but I don't think Adam does."

"No." The way he spoke of Gavin made that abundantly clear, as if Adam felt a wide chasm existed between the good his friend did and the reality of his own existence. "I'll talk to him, okay?"

Sam used her knife to push a pile of chopped onion to the side. "It would settle my nerves a little if you did."

She wasn't sure what bothered Sam more—that this was *Adam* they were talking about, or that Cindy herself rarely acted without having all the information she could gather. It must have seemed terribly out of character, even frighteningly so. "What is it you're afraid of, Sam?"

For several long moments the only noise was the sound of Sam slicing up the other half of the onion, her movements quick and rhythmic. "I've always thought people had a right to heal at their own rate," she said finally. "Werewolves have time. It took me two decades to accept some of the things I did the first year after my change. Others I'm still struggling with."

A chill swept through Cindy, leaving her cold except for one hard, burning knot in the pit of her stomach. "This has nothing to do with Preston, if that's what you think."

"Since we've never talked about Preston, I don't really have anything *to* think about. It's yours to share—or not—as you see fit. Thus far you haven't seen fit, and that's your business. All I can do is hope it's not eating you up from the inside."

She'd never talked about the alpha who'd turned her, then kept her caged for so many months she'd lost count. She *couldn't*, for reasons Sam would never understand. Joe suspected and maybe Keith did too, but only because they'd been there. They'd pulled her out of that cage, kicking and screaming.

Kicking and screaming.

Cindy shook herself and turned away from Sam. "We all have things that change us. I'm never going to be the person I was before it happened, but I'd like to think I've moved on. Made something of my life."

"The mistake is thinking one implies the other. I was making something of my life long before I moved on."

"Then maybe I'll never really move on." The second she spoke the words, Cindy didn't know whether to be horrified or relieved.

She heard the soft *click* as Sam set down her knife, then the whisper of footsteps across hardwood floor. The older woman sat next to her, close but not touching, and warm, comforting power curled around Cindy. "You're young, Cindy. I haven't pushed because seven years is nothing. Gavin and I had been married a decade before I told him some of the things I'd done. And I think...he'd known them all along. And he'd loved me anyway. I worried for nothing."

Because Alan Matthews hadn't broken her. Sam might have, in her weakest moments, almost given up, but she'd never betrayed herself. "I said I'd talk to Adam."

Maybe getting the truth out there would be a relief for him, and she could give him that. It might derail their headlong rush toward consummating their attraction, but Cindy wouldn't blame him for that either. Baring your soul was risky, sometimes embarrassing business.

Sometimes it left you with no option but to walk away.

By the time she'd retrieved a pan of lasagna from the deep

freezer, tried on three different shirts and laid out a crackling fire in the sitting room hearth, Cindy had to admit it was a date.

She burned her thumb checking the lasagna and cursed roundly. She had a date with a *vampire*, and nervous didn't begin to cover it.

"Wine," she said aloud. Something red to go with the lasagna, obviously, but she had no idea what Adam liked. She'd wait and let him choose.

She'd just finished chopping tomatoes for the salad when a knock on the door startled her. After wiping her hands carefully, Cindy walked down the hall and opened the door.

Adam stood on the other side, in beat-up jeans and flannel shirt. He seemed oblivious to the bite of the air, even though the breeze that lifted his hair was cold enough to send a shiver through her. "Sorry I'm late," he said by way of greeting. "Keith and Abby stopped by to talk to Sam and Gavin about their plan. They asked me to listen."

She stepped aside and waved him in. "What did they decide?"

"They're evacuating Red Rock, pretty much. Taking the refugees and those who can't fight to another sanctuary town."

It was a good move, one that would protect the weakest among them and afford them more time, but it wasn't a solution. "Gavin and Sam have to go, obviously, and Joe and Brynn."

Adam followed her back toward the kitchen. "I don't think Joe is happy about not being in the fight, but they need someone strong with them in case things go bad."

And Brynn was still far too shaky for a fight of this magnitude. "We'll all do what we have to do, I guess." She gestured toward the kitchen table. "Sit. I made lasagna. Well, I didn't *make* it. I took it out of the freezer. People feed me all the time so I don't cook for myself much, but you're probably used to that. Or used to be used to it. The country-doctor thing, I mean."

He looked like he was trying not to smile as he dropped into a chair. "Don't have much need for a doctor. I'm pretty hardy. Did get some help though when I accidentally cut off one of my fingers five years back."

"Let me guess. You'd taped it back on and hoped that would work."

"No, I know how to use a needle." His smile widened. "However, the angle was awkward and the results...a bit crooked."

Cindy laughed and pulled two bottles from the cupboard, one merlot and one cabernet, and held them out for his perusal. "Good news is, you got it done. The bad news is, if that healed at all, then yeah. You may as well have just taped it on."

"So the pack doctor told me. After the fact." He was running his hand along the edge of her table again, the gesture almost absent-minded. "Next time I slice off part of my hand, I'll do my best to keep that in mind."

Cindy watched him as he kept touching the table, almost as if testing its grain. "Dylan said you make furniture."

"Mmm. Or it's what I do these days, anyway." He rapped his knuckles against the top of the table. "Not bad quality."

"It came with the house." Cindy opened the merlot and poured two glasses. "What did you do when you were human?"

"Pretty much the same thing I do now. Hide in the woods with an ax. I remember it being a lot less comfortable in the lumber camp, though."

"Of course." Only he could take the phrase "vampire lumberjack" from humor to straight-faced reality. "How did you transition from a logging camp to fangs?"

"How do all stories start?" The corner of his mouth twisted up in wry amusement. "A woman. And you could find a few dozen men my age who would give you the same answer to the same damn question. Anna-Mae was partial to loggers."

"Was she looking for the perfect companion or just inordinately sloppy?"

"If she had motivation beyond her own amusement, she never shared it with me. She single-handedly made Bangor the epicenter for vampire activity for most of the nineteenth century. By the time I made my first trip to the brothels in the Devil's Half Acre I should have known better, but I was young and not very bright."

It seemed so ordinary, a horny young man's quest for sexual satisfaction, and yet it had changed the entire course of his life. "So she...turned you? What do you call it?"

"Shitty luck?"

"I mean the process," she told him gently. "How does it work? It's got to be more involved than drinking, or else I owe you one hell of a beating now."

"Magic." He spread his fingers out on the table and stared at his hand, his gaze slightly unfocused. "Intent. Every vampire develops their own ritual, if they do it enough for it to matter. Or they adopt the ritual of the one who made them, because it's what they know. We're no different than wolves, really. Magic taking root where it doesn't quite belong and never really fitting right. Only difference is the kind of magic. Life and death."

"Magic isn't destiny." She'd seen too many wolves deal in death, and with the kind of swift, efficient brutality she doubted Adam even had in him.

"You're being too literal. Everything lives and everything dies. The difference is the magic itself, not the people who use it."

Maybe the difference mattered to him, or to others. "The magic doesn't exist in a void. It's still channeled through people, good and bad. That's what *I* see."

Adam reached out his hand. "Come here."

"The lasagna's almost ready." She went anyway and slid her hand against his, just to feel the spark of awareness that passed between them.

"The lasagna will be all right." He lifted her fingers and brushed a feather-soft kiss against her knuckles. "Don't misunderstand me, Cindy. I don't think death magic is all bad any more than I think life magic is all good. I'm too old to be that idealistic."

Suddenly, she realized why she'd been harping on the subject. "I don't want you to think that's how I look at you. Death."

"I should have known better than to try to convince a doctor that death is not the enemy." He kissed her hand again, then released it. "But I'm glad, honey. Glad you don't think I'm the enemy."

"Pain." She slid one of the wine glasses to him. "Pain is the enemy, not death."

"Pain," he echoed. "That is something we can agree on."

Cindy thought they probably agreed on a lot of things, which made their attraction even more dangerous. "Time to eat."

Surely they could enjoy dinner before they had to talk of serious matters, and certainly before she had to apologize again.

Eating dinner with her was a mistake.

Cindy was the sort of woman he'd always been stupid about. Smart women. Tough women who didn't need or even want his protection. They reminded him of Joan, the stubborn, fool-headed young alpha who'd led the wolves with him for such a brief time. But Joan had been a lady, a well-born society debutante who'd scolded him for his coarse language and rough manners. That the man she'd eventually fallen in love with had been coarser and rougher than Adam didn't matter—he'd never been partial to prissy ladies and no amount of power could have sparked attraction between them even if she'd been willing.

The woman sipping wine on the other side of the worn wooden table was anything but prissy. She was barefoot now, in jeans that hugged slender but strong legs and a shirt with a neckline low enough to make any man's mouth water. She wore no impractical shoes with heels high enough to break an ankle or expensive fabrics that cost a fortune. Her clothes were comfortable and well worn, and it made him harder than any satin or stiletto. She was *real*.

And Christ, he wanted her.

She wanted him too. Her gaze lingered on his mouth and his hands, and she absently rubbed her thumb against the bowl of her wine glass.

"Cindy." Her name rumbled out of him, sounding like a caress. An invitation. *Which it is.*

She smiled. "Adam."

The sound of her lips around his name was almost as hot as the thought of her lips around his cock, an image he hadn't been able to banish since she'd tried to get on her knees for him. "We going to get dumb over each other now?"

"This?" She glanced at the table and divided the last of the wine between their glasses. "This isn't dumb. It's just dinner."

"Oh, dinner is innocent. I bet what we're going to do before the end of the night isn't."

"Mmm." She pushed her plate back and rose. "Come to the living room and bring your wine. We're going to talk." Her hip brushed his shoulder as she walked past him.

He followed, but slowly. Slow enough to admire the curve of her waist and way her jeans clung to her ass. "And what should we talk about?"

She curled up on the sofa and tucked her feet under her. "I need to apologize for not letting you talk when you wanted to. It was rude and stupid."

It had been self-defense, and he was old enough to recognize it. "No law says you have to tell me your darkest secrets or listen to mine."

"No, but avoiding it hasn't been working so well for us."

He opened his mouth to protest again, but something about her stopped him. Her posture, or the look in her eyes—he wasn't sure *what* it was, but instinct told him to proceed carefully. "I suppose it hasn't."

Cindy smoothed her hair behind her ear and turned her face toward the crackling fire. "Tell me what happened."

It was easier this time. Maybe because he'd already told the story to Sasha and Dylan, so the edges weren't so raw, or maybe because Cindy didn't have the sharp eagerness of a historian confronted with a primary source.

Because it was easier, he found himself telling her more. About how it was Astrid who came to him first, and about Astrid's girlfriend, Maggie, a tired, terrified woman in danger of having her will beaten out of her. He even told her about Joan and the surprising strength she'd hidden so carefully beneath her polished society veneer, and for the first time the thought of his two accomplices brought a flicker of fondness instead of only pain and loss.

He told her everything about how it started, but nothing about how it had ended. And because he wasn't quite ready to, he sidestepped the matter entirely. "Joan's still alive, I think. She married a friend of Gavin's and they took over some tiny little island together. Turned it into the first sanctuary town."

"Breckenridge Island," Cindy murmured. "Gavin talks about it sometimes."

Which meant Joan had kept in contact with Gavin—or Seamus had. It had been easier for Seamus and Gavin, whose involvement in the tragedy had been as heroes come to save the day. In the aftermath, Adam and Joan had fought to meet each other's eyes, both struggling under the weight of their losses. So many lives broken, and four lost forever, including Astrid, who had died to keep Maggie safe.

Joan had retreated to her island with a new lover to shelter her in her grief, and Adam had returned to the only place he felt comfortable—the quiet expanse of the Great North Woods.

"I'm sorry." Cindy touched his hand, her eyes bright, reflecting his own sadness. "For what happened, and because you still hurt."

"It was a long time ago." He covered her hand with his own, smoothing his fingertips along her skin just to enjoy her soft warmth. "But yes. I'm not so full of pride that I can't admit it hurts sometimes."

She studied him in silence for a few moments. "Who told you what happened to me? Gavin?"

"Gavin." Her expression was hard to read, so he stroked her hand again. "He didn't tell me much, and I wouldn't have pried. People deserve privacy in their pasts."

"Wouldn't have done any good. He doesn't know everything." She pulled her hand from his and sat back against the other end of the couch. "When I was twenty-six, an alpha named Preston kidnapped me. He turned me himself. Beat me, caged me, you name it."

Anger would do her no good at this point, even if her too-careful recitation stirred long-banked rage to life inside him. Only decades of practice kept his voice steady. "He tried to break you. Your spirit."

"Yeah." She laughed, the sound high and brittle. "But I didn't break. I *shattered*...into about a million pieces. Then Preston put them back together, exactly the way he wanted them."

He knew he was in trouble when her vulnerable pain *hurt* so much. He'd never been good at words, not the clever, gentle kind required for diplomacy or comfort. But he could give her truth. "You're wrong. Maybe he broke your mind, or your resolve, but your spirit is there, Cindy. I've felt it."

She didn't respond or react, just stared into the fire, tears spiking her lashes. "He died almost three years later. One of his betas killed him and took over. Kendall. By then, Gavin and Sam had heard about me from some of the refugees. They sent Joe and Keith to rescue me." A shudder wracked her. "I didn't want to leave. They thought I was scared to, but I couldn't go. Not until I made Kendall pay, even though he was no worse than Preston."

Worse than her mind and resolve. The bastard had broken

her heart, had turned her own emotions against her. Adam had seen all too closely how enough abuse could inure a person to the pain, until the absence of pain felt like kindness. Few of the rabid alphas he'd met in his day had had the patience for such an endeavor, fewer still the control, but those who did...

He didn't know what words to offer her, what he could say that might give her some comfort. "And did you? Make him pay, I mean."

"I killed him. For Preston." She wiped her cheeks. "Your mind plays tricks on you after a while. You get to this point where you're so starved, for *everything*, that simple decency feels like something magical. And—and I—" She broke off with a sob. "It's stupid. It's a fucking survival instinct, and I know that. I *know it.*"

His heart ached for her, and his words weren't enough. So he whispered her name and opened his arms. She climbed into his lap, buried her face against his shoulder and cried.

It was a level of trust he hadn't expected from her, and it brought warmth and terror in equal measure. He was bad enough with words, but the responsibility of someone's emotions, of her heart and protection...

He'd once failed so spectacularly that he'd never again allowed the risk. No one came to him for comfort. The young alphas in Bedagi Creek had come to him for friendship, or out of curiosity. Women from the pack had come to him for the pleasure of his bed, but never anything that extended beyond one afternoon or one night. Never anything important.

Holding Cindy was easy. So was smoothing his fingers through her hair. He concentrated on the feel of soft blonde strands beneath his fingertips and tried to ignore the fear that built as tears soaked his shirt. Almost eighty years had passed, but he might be back where he'd started—unable to be enough.

Eventually, the tears stopped, and she went lax in his arms. Her breathing slowed, evened into the rhythms of sleep.

Frantic, dirty sex on every surface in her house would have been less dangerous than the quiet, trusting way she curled against him. Perhaps he shouldn't have laughed at Gavin's prediction that Cindy would break him.

There was only scant comfort in the knowledge that no one had predicted how much he'd like it.

Chapter Five

Cindy woke to the sun peeking through the curtains and a hard male body warm against her back. *Adam.*

She snuggled deeper into his arms and froze when she realized they were both clothed. Memories of the night before rushed to the forefront—confessions, secrets and her own mortifying tears.

The arm draped over her body tightened, keeping her tucked against Adam's chest. "Go back to sleep. I hate dawn."

"For obvious reasons?" She hated the huskiness of her voice, the slightly breathless note.

"The sun won't kill me, but I don't like it. Didn't like it when I was alive, either." His breath tickled the nape of her neck. "Always wished I could laze about in bed, like I imagined rich people did."

He probably came from a time when being wealthy meant gentlemanly pursuits that didn't involve work at all. "No sleeping in for me, either. I would have been solidly middle-class. My father was a doctor."

"Oh yes?" His low, sexy chuckle elicited a shiver. "My father was a carpenter, but he had a poor head for business. We were lucky to have food to put on the table most nights."

The conversation somehow managed to be more intimate than the fact that they'd slept together, even innocently and fully clothed. Cindy rolled to her back and tried not to think about how close his face was to hers. "You're never cold. I thought vampires were supposed to be. More Hollywood bullshit?"

"Are you going to change into a monstrous half-human, half-beast creature and rampage through the streets?"

"Only if I don't get my coffee." The retort was automatic and embarrassingly defensive. He always rendered her silly, tongue-tied, and it made her sound like an idiot.

Adam just laughed. "A detail left out of the legends, then."

Cindy sat up. "You turn me into a moron."

"No, I make you blunt and cranky." He tucked one hand behind his head and grinned at her. "Lucky for me, I find cranky women very appealing."

"You're awful chipper for someone who hates mornings."

"Pretty women ease the pain."

Was she this annoying, giving flip answers to everything? "I'm sorry I unloaded on you last night." She smoothed a wrinkle from the quilt. "Thanks for staying, but I'm okay now."

"Didn't just stay for you, sweetheart." His hand slid over hers, fingers curling tight. "You listened to me too."

Cindy's chest tightened. She'd found Adam attractive from the moment she'd seen him, but that was vastly different from the tenderness he evoked now. "This is—" She couldn't even choke out the words. He *knew* it was crazy, had said as much the night before. *We going to get dumb over each other now?*

She'd told herself over and over that it was a bad idea. It was a *terrible* idea, but that didn't matter. It didn't change the way she felt.

"You know the worst things there are to know about me," she whispered. "Don't you want to go?"

"You don't know the worst thing there is to know about me." His fingers tightened around her hand, and his eyes held a haunted look, full of guilt and self-blame. "I let them go. I cut the bonds. They were my people, and they were being hurt, tortured. To wear us down, to take the power and make us weak. I had to choose, and I chose to let them go."

"What were your other options?"

"To let the magic drain the people with me, the wolves who were still free. I made a choice, but no choice would have been good. And that's because I set myself so high. I had no business having that sort of power with no thought of how to use it."

You didn't have to put yourself in that sort of position to be faced with impossible choices. For the first time, Cindy allowed herself to think of her relationship with Preston like that— simply a way to survive a no-win situation, to stay alive long enough to live.

"There are things I know," she said slowly. "If I'd kept fighting him, Preston would have killed me. Same thing if I'd pretended to be happy with his...affections. So I know that my mind did what it had to do. What I'm still working on is understanding that I didn't do the right thing. I did the *only* thing, and sometimes that's all there is."

"Sometimes that's all there is," he agreed, his voice rough. "But he didn't break your spirit. You've come farther in seven years than I have in over seventy. That's spirit. That's strength."

"Yes, and maybe it'd be easier if I were as broken as I should be. I wouldn't have to worry that I could have done more, that all my rationalizations are bullshit." Suppressed tears burned her throat. "I wouldn't have to consider the possibility that I gave that bastard the one thing he was never supposed to be able to touch, and for no damn good reason at all."

"*That's* bullshit." Adam sat up smoothly, bringing his face close to hers. "It's not a competition to see who can suffer the longest. The fact that I hid in the woods for eight decades doesn't make my pain real. It makes me a tired, bad-tempered fool."

"You're like a *mule*." Even as she rasped out the words, she lifted her hands to frame his cheeks. "When I start calling you stubborn, you know you have a real problem."

"I'm old enough to be set in my ways. I earned every damn scrap of stubborn I have." He turned his head and kissed her thumb. "All of it, honey."

He was fascinating, and he scared the hell out of her. "Last chance, Adam," she whispered. "Don't you want to go?"

"Fuck, no."

Fighting the inevitable was exhausting, so Cindy let go and touched her mouth to his. She meant it to be a slow exploration, but her hands shook as she rested them on his shoulders. Arousal coursed through her, hotter and faster than anything she could have expected, and she quickly deepened the kiss.

His fingers thrust into her hair, holding her head still as his tongue stroked over hers. She had to get closer, so she angled her leg over his and slid into his lap.

He stared up at her from glazed, hungry eyes. "We doing

this for the right reasons?"

She'd already lost track. "What are the right reasons?"

"Because we're so hot for each other that we can't stop ourselves."

"I didn't think there was ever a question about that." Cindy shifted in his lap, easing her hips against his. He was hard between her legs, solid and hot, and he groaned as she rocked down against him.

His hands fisted in her hair, tilted her head back until his lips brushed her throat. "Best reason in the world, then."

The simple touch streaked hot pleasure through her. "Does lazing about in bed like rich people include torrid sexual encounters?"

"Even if it didn't, I don't mind a little revisionist history." His tongue dragged across the skin over her pounding pulse, and dark, hot magic twisted tight between them. "The past isn't as pretty as people like to pretend these days."

"Nostalgia's easier." Certainly easier than trying to maintain a conversation while he licked her throat. "Adam."

"Cindy." Another lick, a little faster. Rougher.

"You're a tease." She turned her head and bit his earlobe, almost hard enough to hurt.

"Am I?" He braced his hands on her shoulders and pushed her back against the rumpled blankets. "Seems to me I'm plenty willing to follow through."

"So the unresolved sexual tension is my fault?" Playing around felt good, almost as good as having him lean over her with the promise of such heat in his eyes.

"Or we're just both responsible adults in the middle of a crisis." His fingers trailed down her body, teasing at her breasts through the fabric of her shirt. "Mostly responsible, anyway."

Cindy moaned, feeling less responsible by the second. She needed his hands on her bare skin, so she dragged the thin cotton up and over her head. The fabric had barely cleared her hands when he rewarded her, cupping her flesh with warm, work-roughened hands.

There was no stifling the cry that rose in her throat. She wanted him too much, and denial had driven her almost to the point of pain. "Don't stop touching me this time. *Please.*"

"We don't have time for me to take you like I want." His

voice was as harsh as his fingers were gentle, a delicious contrast. "But I'm not leaving this bed until I see you come."

Cindy trapped his hands against her skin. "Don't jinx us like that. We have time, plenty of it."

"Shh." He lifted his hands, moving hers easily enough. They ended up trapped against the bed as he leaned down and let his breath feather over one tight nipple. "Stop thinking so much."

She strained toward his mouth, caught between another whimper and a laugh. "It's what I do."

"Not anymore," he whispered, then closed his lips around her.

Everything in her zeroed in on that single touch, focused on the hot pull of his mouth and the way he slicked his tongue, rough and wet, over her nipple. She forgot to think, forgot *everything* except how to moan his name.

He groaned and lifted his head, eyes blazing. "My name sounds good on your lips."

She yanked her hands free and pulled his mouth to hers. There was no finesse in it, no careful caresses specifically crafted to make him want her more. All she could manage was need, and she poured it into every second of the kiss.

What she got back was passion, pure and simple. He tilted his head and pressed closer, his deliberation fading. Pain lanced through the pleasure as her tongue snagged on the tip of a fang, and Adam stiffened at the hint of coppery blood.

He lifted his head, breathing ragged. "Sorry, that wasn't—not on purpose."

"I know." Cindy rubbed her tongue against the roof of her mouth until she felt the tiny wound close.

"I'm not in control. I'm not—" He laughed and shook his head before leaning down to kiss the corner of her mouth. "I know you don't want blood and sex to get confused. I'll try harder."

"It doesn't matter." She gripped the front of his shirt and kissed him firmly. "As long as you want the sex more, I mean. Of course you want my—my blood." It felt odd to say, and even odder to be fine with it.

"No." Adam caught her hands again, this time pressing them to the bed on either side of her head. "I want you. The blood is a means to an end, Cindy. Sometimes it's to give me strength, and sometimes..."

He nipped her lower lip and she felt the tiniest prick before his tongue slid over the spot. Magic roared to life and heat crashed into her as he kissed her again, and this time she felt each hard thrust of his tongue as a hot, tugging pull deep inside her.

Cindy had already come to associate it with him, the dizzying combination of too much and not enough, and she bucked under him. His grip on her wrists held, somehow soothing the most primitive, animal part of her. Adam was strong, commanding, and she wanted him.

She relaxed without thinking then, pulled her mouth from his and bared her throat.

A wolf might have taken that invitation and bitten her, leaving a very human mark that served an instinctive purpose. Instead Adam licked her pulse and settled his body over hers, his hips cradled between her thighs so his first rocking grind let her feel the hard length of his erection through their jeans.

The sensation wrenched a cry and a shudder from her. "*Adam.*" She needed him closer, his skin against hers. Him inside her.

"Don't move your hands," he whispered, then slipped away, leaving a blazing trail of hot, wet kisses along her body as he went. Down, down until his breath blew hot against the skin just above her jeans and his fingers tugged at the button.

Anticipation sang in her veins, and she lifted her hips before he even got her pants unzipped. He just chuckled and eased her pants and underwear down. The fabric hit the floor and his hands returned, on the inside of her knees this time and urging her legs apart. "You're gorgeous."

Her hands shook, but she left them on the bed. "Take off your shirt."

A slow, wicked smile quirked his lips as he jerked the flannel shirt up. A tight, white undershirt twisted with it, riding up to give her a glimpse of a well-muscled abdomen before he wrestled both over his head with a frustrated snarl.

He tossed the discarded shirts into the growing pile next to the bed and grasped her legs again. "Better?"

"Beautiful." He was both rugged and elegant, lean and strong. Smooth and rough.

Teasing and determined. His hands slid slowly up the insides of her thighs, and his gaze never left her face as his thumbs drew swooping half-circles on her skin. When they finally grazed her aching flesh, he groaned and ran one up to brush the slightest touch against her clit.

Cindy wanted to close her eyes, tilt back her head and drink in every touch until her body fell apart. But what she wanted more was to watch him as her pleasure grew, see the way his own stare heated as he pushed her over the edge.

She held his gaze and moved, just a little, chasing his thumb with her hips. He made a quiet, satisfied noise and shifted his other hand down, one finger teasing just inside her. "You're hot. Wet. So damn ready."

"Yeah, I am." Fire streaked through her, and she panted his name. "Take off the rest of your clothes."

"No." The bed shifted under her as he moved lower, wedging his shoulders between her knees. When his breath fell against her skin again, it tickled her inner thigh. "You can move your hands, if you want. I don't mind a woman yanking my hair while I've got my tongue inside her."

Cindy's breath caught. "Fuck." She'd pay him back for this sensual torment, for every single second of—

His tongue stroked over her clit, and her breath escaped on a relieved sob. She'd never been so close to orgasm—so painfully close—with barely a touch, but denial was starting to take its toll. They'd been making out like teenagers, stealing kisses and grinding against each other.

Even now, he moved so slowly she wanted to scream. "You're killing me."

He pushed her legs wider, the soft licks deepening into something demanding. Pleasure flooded her, so intense she saw stars, and she couldn't stop her hips from thrusting up against his mouth.

Cindy clutched Adam's shoulders and tried to watch him as he worked her with his lips and tongue. He needed to make her come; she could feel the hunger in the fine tremor of his hands on her thighs.

"I should make you wait," she whispered, but it was no use. She couldn't tease him when she was flying apart, shaking as he drew her to the edge and beyond in a desperate explosion of tension and longing.

His fingers stroked inside her again, one first, then another, thrusting deep as he flattened his tongue against her clit. His groan vibrated against her, making the world spin.

"It'll never be enough," he murmured against her, twisting his fingers. "You could come a hundred times and it wouldn't be enough."

Another wave of pleasure thundered through her. Cindy screamed his name, her ears ringing with the force of her orgasm, and drove her fingers into his hair.

He lifted his head and swore, and she realized the ringing noise was unmistakably coming from the extension telephone by her bed.

She scrambled to answer it, her limbs still shaky. "Hello?"

"Cindy?" It was Sam's voice. "Are you okay?"

"Yeah." The word came out breathless and froggy, so Cindy cleared her throat. "I'm fine. Is something wrong?"

"I wanted to make sure you hadn't forgotten the meeting this morning." A brief pause. "Not that I usually find you particularly forgetful, but Gavin will be awake soon and might notice that Adam never came back."

"Right." She chanced a glance at Adam, who had rolled to his back and covered his face with his arm. "Adam's coming. With me. To the meeting."

Adam choked on a noise that sounded half laugh, half groan.

"Well. In that case, I suppose I'll see you two shortly." Cindy couldn't tell if Sam was worried or fighting laughter.

"Uh-huh." She dropped the receiver back in the cradle and checked the clock before kneeling over Adam's legs. "We've got ten minutes. Are you going to slap my hands again if I try to take off your pants?"

His laughter cut off, and this time there was no mistaking the noise he made for anything but a groan. "Christ, no."

His cock strained against the fly of his jeans, and the buttons gave way with only a little coaxing. Cindy lingered, her hand barely grazing his erection through his boxers.

A snarl tore free of him. "My turn to get teased?"

He deserved it, and she'd sworn she'd do it too—taunt him with the promise of pleasure until he was as desperate as she was. Only he already looked desperate, and she found herself wanting only to ease that need.

She touched his face as she kissed him softly. "No teasing."

His lips seized hers as he arched up, grinding his cock against her hand. Cindy kissed him hard, then dropped her mouth to his jaw and chest. She trailed her tongue down his stomach and tugged gently at the waistband of his boxers.

"Cindy." His fingernails scraped teasingly along her scalp as he buried his fingers in her hair. "God, woman, you will be the death of me."

"Really?" His erection was long and thick, hard under her hand when she gripped him. "I'd rather be the life of you." She licked him once, from base to tip, and looked up to meet his eyes as she closed her mouth around him.

This time he gasped her name, or at least the first part of it. His hips popped up off the bed, just an inch or so before he stilled, but the lack of control was enough to send a throb of heat through her.

Slow wouldn't do. She sucked him hard and deep, as hungry for his pleasure as he had been for hers. He grasped at her hair and moaned, just noises at first, then words. Her name, and encouragement, jumbled together with whispered promises of the things he'd do to her when they had time, the ways he'd take her, work at her, claim her.

He came with flattering speed and a low, throaty noise that rasped out of his chest and tugged at her body *and* heart.

If life were perfect, she could curl against his chest and kiss him until their ardor rose again. Instead, she rested her forehead on his denim-clad thigh. "I hate this meeting already."

A rusty chuckle answered her as he relaxed his hand and stroked her hair. "Me too. There aren't enough showers in the world to save us from Gavin's angry glares. Maybe Sam will convince him to stay in bed."

"I don't care." She'd intended to make him feel better about risking his friend's wrath, but she surprised herself by finding she meant the words. "I don't care what anyone thinks about this but *us*."

Warmth kindled in his eyes as he moved his stroking fingers from her hair to her cheek. "Me either."

Cindy climbed in his lap and kissed him, careful to avoid pressing her body to his. "We have to go."

"I know." His tongue snuck out. Traced her lip. "Now."

"Fuck." She shuddered and climbed off the bed. Digging through her dresser for fresh clothes provided a distraction, but she didn't dare look back at him, sated and debauched on her bed. "Getting dressed now."

The bed creaked, and she heard his feet hit the floor on the other side of the bed. "I'm going into the bathroom to clean up. Meet you downstairs in five minutes?"

"Sounds good."

When he'd gone, she dropped her face to her hands. She'd known the night before that she was in danger of losing her heart to Adam. What she hadn't known was how imminent that danger was.

Fifty percent of men in the room were glaring at Adam like they'd gladly kill him.

Granted, in this case fifty percent amounted to two, but Gavin and Joe had more than enough ire between them to make up an army's worth of disapproval. Dylan looked more unsettled than upset, though he seemed to be splitting his worry between Sasha and Brynn, who Sam had seated at the opposite end of the table, as if Adam were in danger of lunging at any moment.

He should have been. A week ago the power surging through Brynn had made his mouth water. It hadn't settled in that time; if anything, the chaos and upset of recent weeks had whipped the feral energy inside her to a frenzy of magic. Tempting, to be sure. But easily resisted.

Too easily resisted, and that spelled trouble.

Keith, at least, had more important things on his mind. "Did you find anything that will do what I need?"

Sasha toyed with the aged volume in front of her, then slid the book toward Keith. "I'll need Adam's help, and Cindy's, but I think it'll work."

Keith squinted at the book for a few moments, then shook his head. "It's gibberish to me. Translate?"

"It's not that complicated," Dylan said, leaning forward with all the eagerness of an excited puppy. "It's a spell that combines bits of magic from all three—"

Keith held up a hand. "I don't need to know how it works, just that it will. You're sure this will convince Recco and the vampire that the refugees are still in town?"

She nodded. "I'll be able to...sort of broadcast their auras.

To anyone who knows what one is like, it should feel like a vampire's blood bond. Like *Adam's* bond."

Adam stirred himself to ask a question, even with Joe's stare burning a hole in the side of his head. "What do you need from me?"

The witch lifted a slightly nervous gaze to his. "I need to feel what a blood bond is like from a vampire's perspective. Dylan's offered to let you feed and form the bond so I can familiarize myself with it."

Not an intimacy he particularly wanted to share with Dylan, but if the town and its people were at stake...

Adam glanced at Cindy, who hesitated before asking, "Would you rather I do it instead?"

He bit back the immediate negative because it would require too much explanation. A bond with Cindy would certainly be preferable—until Sasha started probing at it with her magic. There was no telling what she would learn about the complicated tangle of affection and lust twisting inside him.

Of course, he couldn't admit it out loud.

Dylan saved him by shaking his head. "No, Sasha needs to pull the bond into herself to learn how to duplicate the feeling, which will link her to whoever shares the bond. She's familiar with me, and I'd rather be the one connected to her. Adam, you won't have to hold the bond with me for more than a few minutes at most."

For the first time, Adam felt sincere gratitude to Dylan. "I can do that."

"What about me?" Cindy asked.

Sasha closed the spell book. "I need you to gather blood from the refugees, as well as anyone else who's leaving. A drop from each should do it."

"Dylan, you can help her," Keith said from the end of the table. "The refugees could use a friendly face."

Gavin spoke. "Most of us are going to spend the day getting ready to go, or helping others do the same. We'll center everything at the bar. That should make your task easier, Cindy."

"It should," she admitted. "Having everybody in the same place."

And by nightfall the town would be all but empty, most of

the weaker inhabitants gone, along with Joe and Brynn. Neither looked particularly happy about that as Keith and Gavin discussed the evacuation route, but neither argued, either. Red Rock was a town where people trusted their leaders, a town where responsibility and honor lived side-by-side.

For the first time in years, Adam wondered what sort of town Joan and Seamus had built with the remnants of his people. Maybe it was something like this. Something safe. Something *good*.

"Adam?"

He started and realized Keith was looking at him, his expression expectant. "Yes?"

"Are you okay staying with them at the bar in case Sasha and Cindy have questions?"

"Of course."

Gavin pushed back his chair and rose. "If it's all right, Keith, I need Adam's help with something."

Keith nodded, clearly distracted, and Adam spared a smile for Cindy before rising to follow Gavin out into the backyard.

He was braced for an angry accusation, but Gavin only pulled a cigarette from his pocket and stared at it. "I've already asked too much of you, but I—" He groaned. "This is hell. My pack's going into a fight, and I have to tuck tail and run in the other direction."

Reminding him that the pack belonged to Keith now would only make it worse. Besides, once upon a time, Gavin had helped him save his own pack, his own life. Honor demanded he repay the wolf for the assistance. "You can ask whatever you want. I owe you too much."

"Help them." The entreaty was hoarse. "They're strong. They can handle this, but...in some ways they're so *young*, Adam. I don't know if we were ever that young."

"We weren't young in the same ways they are," Adam agreed. "It's a different time. A different damn world. They've been through hell, but none of them were born into it. Doesn't mean much when push comes to shove though, does it? Joan was a wide-eyed kid and she's the one who went out and made something of her life. Sometimes us broken old bastards need to let the people who aren't so damn tired take the lead."

Gavin looked through the window set in the door. "Time for me to let go, is that what you mean?"

"Time for you to step back." Adam rubbed at the back of his neck and closed his eyes. "Me, on the other hand... It's time for me to step up."

"You're here now. That's what matters."

"Is it?"

Gavin knew exactly what he meant. He tensed and avoided Adam's eyes. "I tried to warn you about Cindy."

The phrasing annoyed Adam for no reason he could figure. "Maybe you should have warned her about me."

Gavin snorted. "Cindy's stronger than she knows. If you two become involved and it goes bad, she'll be fine. Hurt, but fine. You?" Worry creased his face. "I'm afraid of what would happen if you fell in love with her and then lost her."

His pride rebelled at that, but he was too old to let it sting him for long. "She reminds me of Astrid, a little."

"Oh, Jesus Christ." Gavin's hands closed into fists.

Adam realized how it sounded too late. "Oh, shit Gavin, not like that. I'm not... Christ, don't be an idiot."

"What the hell am I supposed to think, Adam? You mourned Astrid for years, longer than anyone else you lost in that whole mess. I figured it out a long time ago."

"Then you figured out the wrong thing." Adam scuffed his boot on the ground and shook his head. "Astrid didn't want me, and I failed her. I spent forty years trying to convince myself those two facts weren't related."

"What did you figure out?"

"That I'm not that kind of bastard. That I did every God damned thing I could to save them." He closed his eyes. "And that's the terrifying part, isn't it? I'm back where I started, with a woman I've got complicated feelings for, only this time my brain's all muddled and it'll hurt a thousand times more if I fuck it all up."

"There's a world of difference between this and Boston, Adam. You're not saving these people. You're helping them save themselves."

It all felt the same now—crushing responsibility. "I promise I'll do better by your people than I did by my own."

Gavin's expression turned bleak. "If that's how you see this, you need to go. Today, when everyone else leaves. You can head back east."

"Damn it, Gavin, what do you want me to *say*?"

The door swung open, and Cindy stepped out on the back porch, her arms crossed over her chest. "Is everything all right?"

Adam snapped his mouth shut and drew in a sharp breath before letting himself reply. "Fine, Cindy. Gavin and I were just having a spirited little chat."

She hesitated. "Gavin? Are you being an ass?"

"It's my resting state, love." His tone fell just short of teasing. "Ask anyone."

Cindy wasn't buying it. "Sam wanted to see you."

"Guess that's my cue, then." He looked at Adam. "We can talk more before Sammie and I leave."

He didn't doubt Gavin would find time, even if there wasn't any to be readily had. "I look forward to it."

Gavin brushed a hand over Cindy's shoulder as they passed each other on the porch steps. She gave him a strained smile in return and gave Adam a questioning look as the door closed.

The wind tugged at a strand of her hair, pulling it across her neck. Adam reached out and smoothed it back into place with a smile. "History. Ancient history."

"He wasn't giving you a hard time over staying at my place last night?"

"Maybe a little of that too." It didn't seem prudent to tell Cindy that Gavin was concerned over the state of Adam's heart instead of hers.

"Ignore it," she urged quietly. "We don't deal with change very well around here, but once we get used to things..." Her words trailed off, and her cheeks reddened.

It was his fault she thought he was taking off for Maine as soon as the dust cleared, and he didn't know what to say. Promising that he wouldn't might put too much pressure on them both, but a reassuring lie was still a lie. He settled for a middle ground. "At least Gavin will have other things to think about. I'll stick around long enough once he gets back to yell at me until it's out of his system."

She nodded silently and looked away. "I have to get set up at the bar. I'll see you later."

The last thing he wanted to do was spend another hour

listening to werewolves bicker over evacuation and battle plans. "I'll come with you. They'll be fine without me."

"Okay." Cindy held out her hand. "I'm glad you're here, Adam, and it has nothing to do with this fight."

"Me too." Her hand was small for being so strong, but he liked the feel of it curled in his. "Let's go before they drag us back in there."

Her smile widened, and she pulled him down and kissed him, soft and slow and warm. It wasn't the easy kiss of a convenient lover or a casual sex partner. Her lips under his made his heart race and his blood heat, and signaled danger. Too much danger.

He supposed with the world falling in around them a bit more danger wouldn't matter, which made it easy to kiss her again.

Chapter Six

Cindy laid the last of the folded shirts into Gavin's suitcase and held up the small white paper bag she'd brought from her office. "Everything is clearly labeled with instructions. Some are only in case of emergency. Call me if you can. Otherwise, ask Joe."

"We'll be fine, Cindy." Sam didn't look up from her desk, the scratch of pen on paper almost as loud as her voice. "I need to talk to you about some worst-case scenarios before I leave."

They couldn't afford pretense. All it did was stave off the inevitable. "All right."

"I keep contacts in Helena, and some in Minneapolis. This town wouldn't have survived cut off from everything, not even with my money." She signed the bottom of the page, her signature a mess of loops and swirls, then pushed the paper away. "When Keith left a few years ago, I made some changes in my estate. Everyone knows I inherited money from my father, but most people don't know how much."

Sam had never denied her a request for a necessary piece of equipment or technology, regardless of the expense. "I always assumed you had plenty."

"And I do. I've always kept my investment risks conservative. Red Rock's needs are supported entirely by the interest, and during the years we don't lend assistance to other packs, I tend to reinvest the extra." Sam folded the paper carefully and slipped it into an envelope. "If something happens to us, the bulk of the money goes to Keith first, then Joe, then you."

The unspoken line of succession. Cindy cleared her throat. "What do you need me to do?"

"You just need to know. Keith knows, and he's telling Joe. I've also set up accounts for all three of you. Emergency funds. If the transfer of the estate doesn't go smoothly, you'll have enough to keep the town running for a year or so." Sam held up the envelope. "Debit cards and checks are in here, as well as some cash. I keep an emergency stash in the darkroom Gavin built me. The bottom box in my stack of chemicals."

The extent of Sam's planning scared the hell out of her. "Are you taking extra pains to be prepared, or do you have some reason to think you won't make it back?"

The older woman's smile was exhausted but real. "I think we're going to drive to St. Anthony, and Albert and Sally's great-grandchildren are going to crawl all over Gavin until he never wants to leave. And you lot will do us proud. But if things go badly, I want to know everyone will be taken care of."

Sam was so *tired*, even more so than Gavin. Cindy closed the suitcase. "We had the best mentors, didn't we? You two have taught us everything."

"You of all people know how badly we wanted children. And now we have them."

Tears threatened, and Cindy blinked them back. "I'd be dead if it weren't for you and Gavin."

"Oh, honey." The chair scraped across the floor. "Come here."

She wanted to fall into Sam's arms, to let the woman who was usually her friend be her mother. Instead, she folded her into a hug. "You take care of Gavin and of yourself. Don't worry about anything else."

"I'll always worry about you." Sam was tall, tall enough to kiss the top of Cindy's head. "I don't know what you're doing with Adam, but all I need to know is one thing. Is it making you happier than you were?"

"That's a reasonable question." Cindy laughed and wiped her cheeks. "I like him. I don't know what we're doing either, but he makes me happy."

Sam smiled and released her. "Good. Sometimes all we need is a little joy. I'm going to tuck the envelope in my desk drawer. It's got contact numbers in it too. Not just for Idaho, but for Seamus and Joan in Maine."

"Joan." Maybe, after everything had settled, Adam would take her number and get in touch with her. Pick up the frayed threads of friendship, maybe even visit.

The pain that lanced through her at the thought of him leaving was so sudden and shocking that Cindy almost gasped. Only one hand braced on the back of a chair kept her from swaying.

Sam's eyebrows came together. "Adam and Joan were never... I mean, if that's what you're thinking, it's foolish. Joan's been happily married longer than I've been alive."

"What? No, that's not—" She took a step back. "I know how things were between them."

"Then I don't understand."

As if the puzzled expression on Sam's face hadn't told Cindy as much. "Just occurred to me, that's all. That Adam probably won't be staying."

"Oh." Sam moved to the bed and hoisted the suitcase. Her next words were slow, too casual...and a clearer sign of worry than the hugs and tears had been. "It's just occurred to you? Or it just matters more now?"

"Both, I guess." It was easy to be rational, to recognize and accept the harshest realities when your heart wasn't in danger. She'd known he would leave—he lived across the country, for Christ's sake—but she hadn't *felt* it until now.

Sam nodded but didn't reply until she'd set the suitcase on the floor and turned to face Cindy again. "It'll work out, but don't forget what I said about Adam being more like Gavin than he knows. You can see what this is doing to Gavin, not being able to protect his people. Adam takes things even harder." Sam smiled and clasped Cindy's hand. "But that means he's worth it. All the men who care hard are worth it, whether they know it or not."

Adam was something beyond oblivious, and far more damaging. Events almost a century past had convinced him of his lack of worth. Of his weakness. "Adam and I have more in common than he realizes, I think."

"Maybe you do." Sam didn't sound particularly surprised. But then, she wouldn't be.

"Work on Gavin while you're gone." Cindy smiled. "He still thinks Adam is taking advantage of me."

"All Gavin wants is to see both of you happy, be that together or apart." Sam nudged the suitcase with her foot. "You put his medication in here, didn't you?"

"Along with the instructions." She hugged Sam again. "Tell Sally and Al that I said hi."

Sam held her a little longer than usual, but when she let go her eyes and expression were clear. "You better run on. Tell Keith and Abby where the money is. I'll make sure Joe knows too."

"Come back," Cindy found herself saying. "There's more to this sanctuary thing than money. We need you."

"You don't need us." Confidence filled Sam's voice, along with warmth and pride. "But I sure as hell am coming back."

"The best of both worlds, then. You can come back to a relaxing, fulfilling retirement."

"That's the plan, anyway. Take care, Cindy."

Stepping back took a conscious effort, and Cindy crossed her arms over her chest. They both had more to do, and not much time left. "I have to check on a few of the refugees before you guys head out. I'll see you when I see you, Sam."

She ducked out of the room and hurried down the stairs before the tears choking her could find their way free. They'd planned all they could, and the rest was up to chance. They'd make it or they wouldn't.

Only time would tell.

Sasha opened the apartment door before Adam managed to knock. "We're ready."

It would be uncharitable to accuse them of being excited. "Of course you are. Let's get this over with."

She'd set out books and herbs on the coffee table in the living room. Folded beside the spell components lay a white cotton cloth dotted with dozens of spots blood. Adam paused to examine it, brushing his fingers along the edge of the fabric. "The Helena wolves?"

"Yes. Well—" She flushed. "Most of them. Cindy thought it would be more believable if it seemed like not everyone survived."

Adam considered it, weighing the possibility against what he'd felt from the other vampire. "He knows I stole the bonds. He can't know I released them. It's not an easy thing to do, so he might not even know it's a possibility. Yeah, if I'd kept taking power from the weak and injured, they'd be dead now."

Sasha knelt and flipped through one of the books. "Cindy's smart about those things."

It seemed like an offhand statement, but at the base it was anything but innocent. "About the horrible things people do to each other?"

"No, not just that." She looked up at him thoughtfully. "Eventualities. Looking at the big picture. I would have made sure I didn't miss anyone when I collected the blood, and that would have been wrong. It's too neat. Suspicious."

"I suppose so." Adam straightened and surveyed the cluttered room. "Where's Dylan?"

"Talking to Bobby. He'll be here soon." Sasha closed the book carefully. "We should talk about what I plan to do. It can be jarring, and I'd rather warn you now than have you angry or embarrassed."

"All right." He lowered himself to the couch more to put himself on eye level than out of any real desire to sit. "Tell me, then."

"It's more intimate than you know, my process," she confessed. "I've grown accustomed to ignoring the baser aspects of my magic, but I'll still be privy to your knowledge—and your thoughts—for a short time. Most people find that uncomfortable."

Adam had to tell himself not to show his amusement. "Sasha, sweetheart, I was bound to a witch and a werewolf for nearly four years. Most of the bonds weren't intimate, but Joan and Astrid and I had to learn how to stay out of each other's heads."

"Don't be condescending, Adam," she said mildly. "This isn't as simple as a bond. Your experience will help you keep Dylan out of your thoughts, but you can't hide from this magic. If you could, the spell wouldn't work."

He was showing his usual talent for communication. "I didn't mean I could keep you out. I was saying I'm used to it." He smiled a little. "You don't know invasive until you've had a prissy teetotaler debutante getting judgmental with you over every inappropriate thought. Just promise not to faint, and I'll be fine."

A gentle smile answered his. "I'll try to be strong."

The staircase outside rattled, the uneven footsteps giving the impression of someone taking the stairs two at a time, and the door popped open. Dylan bustled in, slightly out of breath, his red hair disheveled. "Am I late?"

"Not at all." Sasha's face lit at the sight of him. "We were just talking about the spell."

Dylan's grin was all for Sasha as he kicked the door shut behind him. "Oh good, I'm not too late for the biting."

It was impossible not to poke at him a little. "Unless you want me to skip the middle man and just bite her. She looks tasty enough."

"Behave," she admonished.

"I'm sorry, did I give you two the impression I was prone to good behavior at some point?"

"No, but a girl can hope."

"Let me know how the hoping works for you, sweetheart."

Dylan groaned. "Christ, Adam, you've got some sort of uncanny valley of inappropriate humor. I don't know if I want to laugh or stab you."

The words made sense on their own, but Adam couldn't figure out how in hell they fit together. "An uncanny what?"

"You know. The uncanny valley?" Dylan made a vague gesture. "When robots get so real they're almost..." He trailed off, looking a little uncertain.

Adam stared at him.

Dylan cleared his throat. "Don't you ever watch movies?"

"I don't have a television, Dylan."

"Yeah. Right." The young werewolf considered that for a moment, then grinned. "Your jokes are only funny when nothing's going wrong or everything's going wrong. Hold off a few days before telling any more, huh?"

It made him smile in spite of himself. "I'll take that under advisement."

Sasha held up a book. "You two finished?"

Adam arched an eyebrow at Dylan, who had the grace to look mildly contrite as he answered. "Yeah. We're finished."

"Then we have a spell to prepare."

Dylan nodded. "Should Adam just bite me? Or do we need to do something first?"

She scribbled something on a notepad and shook her head. "I need to know some things. Can I ask you a few questions, Adam?" She looked up, her eyes dark and guarded. "Tough questions."

It took effort to keep his expression placid as he nodded. "If they're necessary."

"I wouldn't ask if they weren't."

"Then go ahead."

She laid down her pen. "The reason we need to do it this way, with you biting Dylan, is so I can truly feel what it's like. But there are aspects of the experience that will be missing. I need to know what emotions you might experience if there's nothing holding you back. If your plan is to take and take."

Uneasiness stirred. "If I wanted to be like him."

Her lips pressed into a thin line. "If we wanted to make him believe you're just as greedy as he is and just as determined to make us all yours."

It wasn't something Adam had ever wanted to consider closely, but he supposed he didn't have to. He'd felt the other vampire, had endured the slimy touch of grasping magic and hungry power with every bond he'd broken. "I have the feel of him in my head. Do you have any way to take that?"

Sasha nodded slowly. "If you'll let me see that, I can work with it."

Adam held out his hand silently, and Sasha laid her palm against his and wove their fingers together. Energy thrummed, charging the room until it felt like the moments before an electrical storm, dry but somehow heavy. Oppressive.

Then magic flared in an almost tangible wave, and Sasha sucked in a sharp breath as the air around him tightened.

The sensation of having someone drift through his thoughts hadn't gotten any less uncomfortable in the intervening decades. It was easy to remember how Joan had looked after the occasional accidental intrusion, her pale face tight with the disapproval she clung to as her only defense. He'd given her plenty to disapprove of in that time, maybe more than he should have, but she'd needed that fire and confidence to fight.

It might have been another lifetime, but he hadn't forgotten how to order his mind and push only the thoughts he wanted to share to the forefront. He delivered the memory of the rival vampire, his hatred and bloodlust and all the greedy entitlement that festered until nausea roiled inside Adam.

He gave the witch what she needed with most of his

attention, but the rest he focused on keeping one thing safe. The memories of Cindy he bundled up tight, layering them in every protective trick he knew. Sasha might be discreet, but Adam couldn't suppress an odd sort of jealousy at the idea of anyone seeing Cindy the way he had. Absurd, when she'd clearly enjoyed her share of lovers, but there was something powerful about remembering her blond hair spread over the pillow in a tousled cloud while she stared up at him and smiled...

No, those memories he held safe. Tight. They warmed him from the inside as Sasha explored his more readily accessible memories. Then she pulled away, though it took another minute for the magic in the room to settle.

Sasha's usually gentle eyes blazed, and she breathed heavily. "I think I have what I need."

Dylan cleared his throat. "So...time for the biting?"

She reached for him and kissed his mouth lightly. It would have looked like a casual caress, if not for the rise of magic that accompanied it. "Ready, darling?"

"Always." Dylan's voice had dropped a little, taken on a husky quality Adam felt better not thinking too closely about. The two of them exuded self-satisfied infatuation with a steadiness that might make it love. Puppy love, granted, but love just the same.

He hated being a little jealous, and it made him curt. "Please tell me I don't have to feed while you two are necking."

"Don't be rude." Sasha looked flustered, and almost glared at him as she pulled away and grasped Dylan's hand.

Guilt stirred, and he hated that too, especially when Dylan shot him a coolly disapproving look that shouldn't have carried much punch. Of course, he shouldn't have liked the damn kid so much either.

Too late for should-haves. Adam held out his hand. "Your arm is easy enough. I don't need much."

Dylan extended his arm in silence, his fingers still curled around Sasha's. Adam shifted closer and fought another cascade of memories, these painted with remembered fear and frustration. He'd fed from Seamus like this once, a moment of desperation when power had been the only thing that could save the people in his care.

Seamus had been willing, but his wolf had struggled. Had

fought the rush of magic until straight-laced, prissy little Joan had knelt in front of Seamus and distracted him with the clumsy kiss that had started their eighty-year relationship.

Eight fucking decades, and he was back where he'd started. Sasha stared up at Dylan like no one else existed, and Adam waited for the loneliness that had gripped him when he'd watched Joan do the same thing.

He waited...and it didn't come.

Dylan's fingers curled into a fist, and he turned to slant an expectant look at Adam. "Am I doing something wrong, or do I look really unappetizing?"

No loneliness, just exasperation laced with an odd affection. "Just thinking. I know that fad went out before you were born, but it's good for the soul."

"Huh." Dylan turned back to Sasha, a tiny smile playing around his lips. "Guess vampires have souls."

"Quit teasing him. He's doing his best." Sasha held tight to Dylan's hand but took a small step back. "It's time. I need to cast the spell so Recco and his vampire will think the refugees are still here. That they can come, stomp us into the ground and get them back."

"It's time," Adam agreed. He took a deep breath and pushed everything from his mind. Joan and Seamus were easy—memories of them were like ghosts fading a little more with each passing year. Dylan and Sasha were harder, but it was Cindy who haunted his thoughts as he closed his eyes and gathered the power slumbering inside.

He would do this because he had to, because he owed Gavin and liked Sasha and Dylan and believed in the dream of this place. He'd do it for them, and wouldn't wonder how much of his determination and stubborn will had solidified into the need for action when Cindy had turned those big, tired eyes on him and smiled through her nerves and fear.

It was a comfortable sort of denial, and he clung to it as he lowered his mouth to Dylan's arm. Better for them all if he was simply doing a good deed. Maybe no one would ever find out just how far he might go to earn one of Cindy's smiles.

Chapter Seven

By the time dusk fell and shadows lengthened in the streets, the town had emptied. Cindy drew her jacket more tightly around her as she walked back to her house alone.

She passed the deserted bar on her way. She didn't have to be told where everyone was. They faced certain attack in the next few days, and were bound to be outnumbered when that attack came. Keith and Abby would be holed up at their house, Dylan and Sasha at the apartment she'd claimed above the bar. The others would be home, as well, completely absorbed in spending what could be their last few hours with their loved ones.

It reminded Cindy that she didn't have any left.

Her route brought her to her back door, the one she used most often. *Only strangers come through the front door, Cynthia.* Her mother's words. Her mother, who'd never given up hope that she'd find her little Cindy, her only daughter, even after she'd been missing for years.

She'd been lucky. She'd been able to see her mom again, to tell her she was all right and set her mind at ease. It had been difficult at first, trying to explain where she'd been and why she couldn't go to the police or simply resume her old life. Finally, she'd told her mother just enough of the truth to make her understand that something fundamentally life-altering had happened to her, and there was no going back.

Only forward.

Cindy had lost her mother to cancer only a few years after escaping from her ordeal at the hands of the Dayton alphas, and one of the last things her mother had made her promise at the end of her very long fight was that she would continue to do what she had to. To survive.

To keep moving forward.

Light spilled out of the window above the sink, and Cindy could see Adam moving around in the kitchen. His propensity for drinking blood and advanced age aside, her mother would have loved him. He had exactly the combination of blunt honesty and humor she'd always appreciated. "And he's easy on the eyes, Mom," she whispered. "Nothing not to like."

His dark hair glinted gold as he bent his head over his task. Then he froze, looked up through the window and smiled at her, wide and relaxed enough to show a hint of fang.

Cindy laughed helplessly and reached for the door. She didn't have a mate or a husband, but she *did* have a fascinating vampire in her kitchen, and that suited her just fine.

The gentle warmth of the kitchen enveloped her as she peeled off her jacket in the entryway. "Smells good. What is it?"

"Whichever casserole dish was closest to the top. Barely figured out your oven though." He jerked his thumb in the direction of the stovetop. "It's got as many buttons as Emily and Ethan's, and that thing scares me half to death."

"Unless the middle is still frozen, it looks like it worked out okay." She laid her hand over his and relished the surge of desire that rose. "You didn't have to do this. I would have."

"Used to feeding myself." His voice deepened, taking on a warm, deep timbre. "Been doing it a while now."

"I meant..." She trailed off, because it didn't matter. "I'm scared, Adam."

Adam turned and hooked an arm around her shoulders. "I know, honey."

"Do you? Because it's not about how dangerous everything is, or what we're going to face. I'm scared of *me*."

"Then maybe I don't know." His other arm snaked around her waist and urged her close. "So tell me."

It was hard to articulate because she barely understood it herself. "I'm not afraid to die. I mean, I wasn't...until I realized that nobody knows me, not really." She swallowed hard. "I've probably opened up to you these last few days more than anybody else, ever."

"Hey, now." Warm fingers brushed against her chin and tilted her head back. "You think that means anything? That people only know you if you tell them what to know?"

"Probably not. Feels that way though." She closed her fingers around his forearms and held on, letting his strength flow into her. "Maybe your mind just plays tricks on you on a night like this."

He stroked her cheek, rough fingertips gentle as they slid against her skin. "Maybe. Don't fool yourself, Cindy. The people here know you, and they love you. Doesn't take a genius to notice."

"Yeah." She turned her head and closed her eyes when her lips brushed his hand.

"Tell me," he whispered, voice rough as sandpaper. His thumb brushed over her lips. "Tell me the things you want someone to know."

In the end, there was only one thing that mattered. "I've never wanted anything the way I want you."

"You can have me, sweetheart. I'm all yours."

She had to kiss him, if only to quiet the yearning. Cindy drew him closer and rubbed her cheek against his before skating her lips across the corner of his mouth. "All mine." The words sparked a different kind of need, the need to confirm his admission.

To mark him.

Her mouth trailed over his jaw and down to his neck. She growled and licked him gently, then bit him, hard.

His breath hissed out in a desperate curse. The hand at her back clenched tight, closing around her shirt and pressing her hard against the bulk of his body. "I like it when you bite."

"Shh." She kissed him, and her last defense broke apart inside her, the final wall she'd held between them. There was no telling how long it would last—a night or a month or a lifetime—but she had him now.

She had him, and not just his body. Even the wildest of his kisses had been carefully controlled, but now he showed no such restraint. His mouth slanted over hers, hard and so hungry he didn't seem capable of holding back.

One fang pierced her lip, and the hint of blood forced a hard groan from him. Hot hands clutched at her ass and dragged her up his body until her toes barely touched the floor.

Cindy pulled her mouth from his with a ragged breath.

"Take me here, no more waiting."

Adam backed her up two steps and hoisted her onto the table, then froze. "Fuck. Condoms."

She answered absently, her attention already on the buttons lining the front of the worn flannel shirt he wore. "The drawer closest to the entryway."

He caught her hands and coaxed them away. "Take off your shirt. I'll be right back."

She watched him cross the room as she stripped the cotton over her head. "Most people come to the clinic during office hours, but sometimes..."

Adam turned back to her, an economy size box of condoms in his hand, and a smile played about his lips. "You should have told me you had high expectations. Flatter my enormous ego."

A laugh bubbled up. "You're beautiful, and your ego doesn't need my help."

"You sure?" He tossed the box on the table and stopped in front of her, his large hands falling to her knees. "Because I'm fighting quite the battle here. Part of me wants to take you upstairs and love you right, slow and patient. The rest of me..."

The heat sparking in his eyes stole her breath, and Cindy cradled his face between her hands. "Why can't we do both?"

"Cindy, I was born in the nineteenth century. I should be too damn *old* to do both." Gentle pressure eased her legs apart as he wedged his hips between her thighs. "You make me forget I'm old and broken."

Because he wasn't. Damaged like she was, maybe, but not broken. "I think you're perfect...for me."

"Good." His fingers curled in her hair and urged her head back. Adam brushed a hot kiss to the spot where her pulse throbbed just under the skin, then teased it with his tongue. "You wolves and your marks. I'm not going to bite you. Not yet. Not until the second time."

She clutched his shoulders and wiggled to the edge of the table, where her hips could press tight against his. "I like it when you bite too."

"Soon." His mouth moved lower, pausing at the hollow of her throat so his tongue could trace slow, wicked patterns. He kept at it, tormenting her with the barest press of teeth, never enough to give more than a hint before his tongue was there, ravenous as he explored the curve of her breast.

What he seemed to want more than anything was her pleasure. His lips grazed her nipple through the thin fabric of her bra, followed by the wet rasp of his tongue. Cindy hissed in a breath and arched to his mouth, determined to give him what he desired.

His fingers fumbled with her bra strap and a groan left him, as he lifted his head and snapped it without warning. Glazed, eager eyes found hers as he stripped the fabric away. "I'm impatient tonight."

The mental image of the two of them entwined on her bed, naked and wild with hunger, drove a moan from her throat. "I approve."

"I hope so." He returned his mouth to her breast, encasing her nipple before his tongue flicked out.

A new wave of dizzy pleasure washed through her as he unbuttoned her jeans. She lifted her hips and helped him push the denim down her legs.

Adam raised his head and claimed her lips with a hoarse moan, and his hands returned to her body. He stroked and caressed, explored with fingers that grew clumsy every time she gasped or moaned. Every time she tensed and jerked into his touch.

Cindy braced her hands on the table behind her as she kicked off her shoes and pants. "Your clothes."

He shed his shirt and reached for his belt, hands shaking. "Tell me you want this like I do. Fast, on the damn table, because I swear to *Christ*, Cindy, I'll take you right here."

She'd go crazy if he didn't. Her gaze traced the lines of his body, from his broad shoulders down to his stomach and the dark line of hair that disappeared beneath his jeans. "I need you." She met his eyes. "It's been too long already."

"Too damn long," he agreed, the words nothing more than a rasping whisper. His belt came free and he jerked his pants open, gaze still fixed to hers. "Hand me a condom."

Cindy felt for the box and ripped it open. Strings of packets tumbled out, and she snatched one before it could fall. "Can I do it?"

He answered with a rough laugh as his fingers skated up her thigh. "You can wrap your hand around my cock just about any damn time you want."

The foil tore easily, and Cindy gripped his shaft for a moment before smoothing the latex down its hard length. She'd had him in her mouth, but nothing came close to feeling as good as the way he thrust into her touch, like he was desperate to be buried in her body.

He didn't even get his pants off, not all the way. The rough denim chafed the insides of her thighs as he hooked his fingers under her legs and dragged her closer, until she was precariously balanced on the edge of the table and his cock slipped against her as he ground his hips against hers. "You ready?"

"I already told you yes." Shaking with anticipation, she wound her arms around his neck and licked his throat where she'd bitten him. "Don't ask now. Take."

"I don't take." He ground the words between clenched teeth as he adjusted her hips with his hands. "Not metaphorically—" A tiny thrust, just enough to push the head of his cock inside her, and Cindy had to bite her lip to keep from crying out. He rocked again and groaned. "And not actually. I give. I'll give you all of me. Can you take it?"

The effort it took to form a reply was almost too much. "You don't take, but I'm supposed to?"

"Isn't that what you're doing?" His hand slapped the table behind her as he leaned her back a little, the sudden movement driving him deeper. "Taking every damn inch of me?"

"But I'm giving you *my* body—" The word broke into a moan she couldn't hold back. "Giving and taking, Adam. It has to be both to be enough."

He wrapped his free arm around her back and held her tight to him. "Giving and taking," he agreed in a hoarse whisper, then surged forward until his hips bumped hers, seating him so deep inside her that thinking became an impossibility.

She could only *feel*, and what she felt was fire. Every tiny movement shocked her with sensation, drawing her closer to the edge. "*Adam.*"

The steel of his arm around her body tightened as he lifted her from the table completely and sank into the nearby chair without releasing her. "Just like this." He helped her move, kept her so close that the coarse hair on his chest abraded her nipples as he pulled her down hard. "Show me. How fast, how hard, how deep. How you want me to take you."

There was no way she *didn't* want him, but her tongue wouldn't cooperate when she tried to tell him that. So she grasped the arched back of the chair and rocked over him, pushing her toes off the hardwood floor.

He panted and watched her through lidded, glazed eyes, his hands resting lightly on her hips until he caught the rhythm. Then he helped, lifting her just a little higher and pulling her down harder, driving into her with a choked noise of pleasure.

Cindy cried out and caught his mouth again as heat streaked through her. Kissing him helped her focus on something besides falling apart in his arms, and she needed that, to imprint this moment in her memory the way Adam had already branded himself on her heart.

He tore his mouth from hers and pressed his lips to her ear, the gravelly tones of his voice rough and low. "Better than I imagined. Better than the dirty dreams. You're better than everything, riding me."

Sheer force of will drove her to meet his sensual torment with her own. She rocked down, tilted her hips tight against his, and froze. "Tell me what *you* want."

His fingers spasmed on her hips, trying to move her, but she was strong. A frustrated growl worked its way up out of his throat. "I want to watch you come when it's just me, just my body and my cock inside you. No magic but us."

How long had it been since he'd connected with someone without magic? Without blood? "No feeding." Cindy kissed him softly and held his gaze as she leaned back and began to move again. "Watch me."

No one had ever stared at her like her eyes held the only pleasure anyone could want. His hands kept her moving, kept guiding her up and down, but his gaze stayed locked on hers. "You're so damn wet, so damn *hot.*"

The words washed over her along with the sweet weight of his stare, driving her wild. Nothing had ever been as important as release—taking his and giving him hers.

She rocked harder, moaning his name when the friction sent her spinning, need racing through her. Her toes slipped on the floor, and she clutched his shoulders. "More. Adam, please—"

Muscle bunched under her fingers, and the world spun.

Adam lowered her gently to the floor, then braced his hands next to her shoulders and levered his body up. He kept up the rhythm she liked, thrusting quick and deep before withdrawing just slowly enough to let her feel every inch of him.

She drew her legs up to grasp his hips as everything clenched, tense and tight. His next thrust set off the first hot pulses of orgasm inside her, and they quickly gathered into a cascade of pleasure that curled her toes. She heard her own voice, far away and pleading, begging him not to stop.

He didn't, sinking into her over and over, his raspy words of encouragement fading into hard, panting snarls. "Come again."

It was impossible not to. Cindy bit her lip and tried not to scream as another wave mounted over the first. Adam threw back his head, exposing the strong column of his throat and the mark she'd left on it. "Fuck, *fuck—*"

His thrusts lost their steady pace, and his hips snapped against hers. Once, twice more, then grinding down as a moan of relief tore free of him, riding on a rush of power that flooded the kitchen with pleasure.

Cindy trembled under him, panting, torn between satiation and a need that wouldn't be fulfilled until she'd had him time and again. "Thank you."

Adam groaned and rolled over, dragging her with him. He hissed when his back hit the floor, then swore roughly. "Next time I swear I'll make it upstairs. The floor's too damn cold."

"I didn't notice." It was too late for the truth of the words to scare her. She nestled closer with a soft sigh. "Are you hungry?"

"Mmm." His hands traced a long, lazy path from her shoulders to her hips. "Just for you."

She smiled. "Then why did you heat dinner?"

"Can't live on sex alone. Figured we'd need it before the night's out."

It would be hours before her need for food outweighed her desire for him. "Thinking ahead, huh?"

"Trying to think at all." His thumbs swept along her sides. "It's not a night for thinking. It's a night for clinging to everything good."

"Like this?" She didn't need an answer, so she kissed him one more time, slowly. His mouth parted and he let her take her fill before his fingers curled in her hair and his tongue thrust between her lips, proving him still every bit as hungry as he'd been.

"If she didn't stop kissing him, they'd stay on the floor." "Not so fast." Cindy pulled away carefully, climbed to her feet and held out her hand. "Floor's cold, remember? My bed, on the other hand..."

She might not have forever, but she had tonight. She'd make the most of it, and deal with the rest as it came.

Knowing they probably weren't the only people fucking themselves into exhaustion didn't make Adam feel any less reckless for fighting back sleep. The night passed in a blur of skin and moans, interrupted only by a trip to the kitchen to reheat the forgotten casserole. He'd indulged Cindy shamelessly, mindlessly, unable to deny her every time she reached for him.

He was drunk on her even now as she dozed in his arms under blankets tangled beyond hope. His preternaturally enhanced stamina felt strained, though there was a simple solution to that too.

Blood.

He hadn't taken it. Not when she'd offered the second time, not when her pulse had throbbed beneath his tongue. He'd taken her mouth and her body, had buried his face between her thighs and reveled in her taste and her screams...and he hadn't once twisted magic up inside her. Every panting whimper, every whisper of his name had been her need for him. A man.

Drunk indeed.

"I can feel you thinking," she murmured finally.

"I do it sometimes." He stroked his thumb over the soft skin of her hip and kissed the back of her neck. "Usually try not to get caught. Ruins my ax-wielding psychopath image."

She wouldn't be distracted. "What are you thinking about?"

"I'm thinking I'll need power soon, and I should want it more. But it's...nice like this."

Cindy turned in his arms and rubbed her cheek against his chest. "Does feeding have to be about sex?"

It didn't seem like the time to remind her that he'd been intending to feed off of Dylan. "No. It has to be about *something* to be effective, but that doesn't mean sex all the time."

"No, I meant—" Her cheek heated. "Will it be about sex if it's about *me*, or can we have something different?"

He'd fed from women without sex. Only a few weeks ago he'd taken power from Emily and given it to Ethan, fueled by nothing but asexual affection and desperation. But Cindy...

Oh, it could be good. It could be amazing.

It could reveal too damn much.

She deserved to know that. Adam stroked her hair and tried to find the right words. "It's...intimate. With sex it's about the pleasure, and everything's lost in that. But without it, it's harder to hide. Not that I want to hide from you, but you may not want me rolling around in your most personal feelings."

Cindy looked up at him, her eyes bright even in the darkness. "You have a right. They're all about you."

The knowledge roused something primitive inside him. "Doesn't give me the right. Does give me a powerful curiosity, though."

"Then feed," she whispered huskily. "I want you to, Adam."

He could only resist temptation so far. "Roll over again. On your side, with your back to me."

She did, nestling back against him, her head tilted to expose her neck and throat. He smoothed her hair back, then pressed a soft kiss to her shoulder. "Can I use magic to make sure it doesn't hurt?"

"Nothing but us, remember? It won't hurt for long."

He didn't want it to hurt at all, but when he slid his arm around her waist her fingers found his and twined around them with such sweet trust that his chest ached. The skin of her neck was warm against his lips as he lowered his mouth and bit her.

She gasped, and that trust bloomed inside him, stronger than the pain of his fangs cutting through her skin. Stronger than anything. Her hand tightened around his, and the trust gave way to affection and *need*, so much need...

He'd never realized that being needed could feel so good. Or maybe he'd just never been needed for what he was instead of what he could be.

Cindy moaned his name softly, and the need magnified until it became something almost like a plea. Power rose, a thousand times more potent than fear or lust or desperation, because it was *her*, and all the wildness inside her whirling around and around until he was lost in an ocean of life.

In the end, he didn't take much. He didn't need much, because a tiny bit of blood went a long way when it packed such a punch. He turned his face to her hair and panted for breath as the magic settled, shaken by the depth of their connection. No magical bonds, no binding spells or blood connections...the power had revealed the depth of their growing feelings but it hadn't created that intimacy.

No, they'd done that themselves, somehow. Which meant he was a thousand miles past screwed.

She reached up and touched his cheek. "Do you think, when this is over...that you might stay for a while?"

The part of him that had lain bruised and broken for so many years urged caution. Permanence was a short step from failure, and more than anything, more than *living*, he didn't want to fail Cindy.

If you fail Cindy, it won't matter. There won't be a later. Adam tightened his arms around Cindy as the unhelpful thought drifted up, morbid and unwelcome. Agreeing because he had nothing to lose felt like a betrayal of the quiet warmth kindled between them.

Cindy deserved more than that.

Adam turned his head and kissed her palm softly. "I think Maine'll be just fine without me for a while."

She smiled. "Maybe someday soon, Montana can live without me for a few weeks at a time too."

It wasn't quite a commitment, but it also wasn't a cowardly retreat. Adam brushed a kiss to the top of her head this time and closed his eyes. "Might make my cabin a little less lonely."

"A little louder, anyway."

"You should know I've only had electricity out there for five years. The girl who sells my furniture for me whined until I let her boyfriend have it set up. She tried to give me a computer too, but there are limits."

"No technological advances past the first half of the twentieth century?" Cindy teased.

"Nothing that might be smarter than I am."

She laughed. "Like my oven."

That laughter melted a tiny bit of his heart. "Like your

oven. Don't know how I feel about microwaves, either. Something unnatural about that."

"Don't worry, it won't boil your insides if you stand too close." Her words had slowed. "Trust me. I'm a doctor."

"A tired doctor." The blankets were a hopeless mess, but by dawn it would be chilly. He untangled them and covered them both, then relaxed with her body tucked close to his. "Get some rest, sweetheart. God knows we won't be getting much tomorrow."

"Mmm." Her breathing deepened. "Rest."

Adam needed to rest too, but not even the quiet sounds of the night could ease his restless tension. The woman in his arms trusted him—too much, maybe. Now there was no choice. He had to find a way to defeat their enemy, because failing again, failing *her*—

The first time had broken his will. Failing now might break what was left of his heart.

Chapter Eight

Two days of nothing but waiting, and Cindy was ready to scream.

She glared at Keith across the kitchen. "How are you not freaking out as badly as I am?"

Keith jabbed a fork into the hunk of meat in the skillet in front of him and flipped it over without looking up. "I'm older and wiser."

"Older, yes. Wiser? Keep dreaming."

"Maybe I'm just better at hiding it." He turned and leaned back against the counter. "So here we are again. Me, cooking steak for a double date. Should I go make scary protective noises at the vampire?"

"God, no. Not you too." Cindy dropped her head back against the wall with a thud. "Things are too dangerous right now for anyone to worry about something as mundane as my love life."

"Love life, huh?"

She cursed the blush that rose in her cheeks. "Sex life, whatever. You know what I meant."

Keith's insufferable grin didn't waver. "Pretty sure you meant love life. But what do I know? You guys just keep me around to burn meat."

Cindy refused to shy away from the conversation. Keith had always been there for her, and that hadn't changed just because he was now her alpha. "I like him. A lot. Gavin thinks it's a bad idea, but I don't care."

"I don't know if Gavin thinks it's a *bad* idea." He nodded to a chair. "Sit. I want to talk serious for a second."

She took her coffee cup with her. "What's wrong?"

Keith hesitated just long enough for her to know she wouldn't like what was coming. "Sam told me she talked to you about what happened when Joe and I went to get you. And knowing Sam, she skated around it in dizzy circles without *saying* anything, because the woman's a God damned hypocrite when it comes to who gets to have secrets."

She had to look away. "You don't talk this much unless you have a point."

"My point is, I knew. Most of us knew. But Dylan didn't, and Adam doesn't. And the only way I think this is a bad idea is if you're just picking men who won't ever have to—"

"I told Adam what happened with Preston. Everything." Cindy clutched her mug and stared at the table.

Keith didn't speak. A fork clicked against the edge of the pan, then a sharp sizzle rose, proof he'd flipped the steak again. Another *clink* and soft footsteps, then Keith's lips brushed the top of her head in an affectionate, almost paternal kiss. "No growly protective noises. I'm glad you found someone to tell."

"Thank you, Keith." She hadn't wanted to argue or defend her involvement with Adam, and relief left her weak. "It's not that I didn't trust you or Sam or anyone else. It was about *me*, about being ready to understand. What happened with Preston helped make me who I am, but it isn't who I am."

"I know." Keith slid a finger under her chin and tilted her head up. "Listen to me. I love Sam like I loved my own mother, but she's not any more infallible than the rest of us. You figured out something she's still working on, and you don't need to worry about taking your time getting there."

"I do need to worry about hiding from myself, though. I'm tired of it, Keith."

"Then I'm glad you stopped. But only because *you're* tired of it. Not because someone else thinks you needed to."

She offered him a small smile. "I didn't plan on this, but I care about him. He cares about me. What we need now is time to figure out what that means."

"Time." Keith let out a bitter laugh as he turned back toward the stove. "What the fuck is up with time, anyway? We should have been fighting two days ago. I can't figure out what in hell they're waiting for."

"Maybe Recco is battling more dissent. Maybe he's trying to

fool us into thinking an attack won't come so we'll let down our guard." Cindy shrugged. "Or maybe he's just messing with us."

"Or maybe Sasha and Adam are right, and the vampire's the one pulling the strings."

Unthinkable, except that Sasha would know better than anyone. She and Dylan were the only ones who had come close to meeting the vampire, albeit through magic, and the witch seemed certain the vampire was dominant. "I suppose so."

Keith stabbed his fork into one of the steaks hard enough to show his frustration. "They don't understand. Dylan doesn't, either. They don't understand why it's *wrong*."

"For the new leader in Helena to hand over power to a vampire?" Cindy could barely fathom it herself. "More proof he doesn't deserve to be anyone's alpha, if you ask me."

"Gavin's been preparing to hand this town to me for forty years, and it still tore him up, even halfway to death's door. It's Alan Matthews all over again. It's crazy, and you can't plan for crazy."

The words—and the lack of control they indicated—should have scared her even worse. Instead, a curious peace stole through her. "Yes, you can. You prepare yourself to the best of your ability, but acknowledge that you have to deal with things as they come."

Keith dumped both steaks onto a nearby plate and dropped the still-sizzling skillet into the sink. "You're right. I know you're right. Hell, a few months ago I was telling Gavin the same thing. Now I understand how much harder it is to see when you can feel every single life on your shoulders."

Cindy abandoned her coffee and pulled two beers from the refrigerator. "I'm intimately acquainted with the feeling."

"I suppose you would be." He accepted one of the beers with a smile. "Should we go save your new friend from Abby? She had a lot of questions to ask him."

Abby was one of the few people who wouldn't use the opportunity to truly interrogate Adam. "Is she ready for this? To be your mate, an alpha in her own right?"

"In the ways that matter." Keith drained half of the beer, then closed his eyes. "She doesn't understand our traditions, our culture. But she understands protecting the people in her care. The rest will come."

Abby was strong, and Cindy had no doubt that she could

handle whatever happened, as long as she had Keith's help. "What did she want to talk to Adam about?"

"No idea. She wouldn't say."

Knowing Abby, she'd wanted an excuse to show Adam that not everyone in Red Rock was bothered by his presence in town—or in Cindy's life. "You have a sneaky, matchmaking woman, Winston."

Keith's smile made him look more like a man in love than a badass warrior. "And I like her just fine that way."

"As always, your talent for understatement amazes me."

"Decades of practice, sweetheart."

"How does Abby *deal* with you?"

"You really want to know all the details?"

"No, she doesn't." Abby stood in the doorway, looking amused. "Are you two done teasing each other? Or were you having a serious conversation?"

"Too many serious conversations." Cindy grimaced. "I think I'll stick with teasing."

Keith drifted across the kitchen, a seemingly absent-minded movement that nonetheless put him within arm's reach of Abby. He made it look natural—instinctive, even—to toss his arm around her shoulders and drag her tight against his side. "Where'd you dump the vampire?"

Adam was right behind her, and Keith knew it. Cindy pushed back her chair and beckoned. "Want a beer?"

"Sure." Adam sidestepped the embracing couple and offered Cindy a small, quiet smile. "It's surreal, isn't it?"

"Which part? Dinner, or that we might have to cut this scene of domestic bliss short because our watch shift starts in an hour?"

"The latter. If this is what being under siege feels like, I'm glad I was a lumberjack instead of a soldier."

Keith made a rude noise. "If being under siege was this cushy, I would have stayed a soldier."

"It's the waiting." Cindy remembered it well from her emergency rotations in school. "The waiting is a killer. Too much time to think."

Adam lifted a hand and touched her cheek. "At least it gives us time to talk."

They'd done nothing but talk for the last two days, but

there was still so much to say. "There is that."
The wicked glint in his eyes was a reminder that they had taken a few breaks from talking. "And now that I've jinxed it, maybe we should eat."

"Or maybe—" A distant howl split the night, and Cindy jumped to her feet so quickly she overturned her bottle, spilling beer across the table. "That's Mac."

Keith had already started for the door, but he pulled up sharply and pointed at Adam. "You watch her damn back. Cindy forgets everything when people are hurt."

"We'll take care of our part, Winston. Go."

Cindy snatched up the bag she'd brought with her. "You can join the fight, Adam. They need everyone they can get. I'll call if I need you."

Abby and Keith's footsteps sounded loud on the front porch as Adam shook his head. "Keith's with Abby. Dylan's with Sasha. I'm with you. Keith's no fool, Cindy. He understands instinct."

No point in arguing, even if she wanted to. Cindy hurried out the door as more howls rose in the night. "Sounds like it's coming from the main road into town."

Adam paused outside the door to snatch up his weapons, matching hatchets with wickedly keen edges that had been polished until they gleamed. "Not what we'd expected, but it'll make 'em easier to kill."

Unless they didn't fear making a full frontal assault because they vastly outnumbered the Red Rock wolves and knew it, or because they had more fighters slipping quietly through the woods for a flank attack. Cindy drew a deep, sharp breath. "We have to hurry."

The end of the main street already looked like a battlefield, with wolves fighting on four legs *and* two, with weapons as well as claws and fists. Guns fired, knives gleamed, jaws snapped—and Cindy almost stumbled under the oppressive weight of sick power that filled the air.

"Something's wrong," she whispered, the words eclipsed by shouts and screams.

"The magic." Adam's voice sounded strained. His eyes followed the path of one of the wolves, who charged recklessly down the main road toward them, every stride jerky and uneven. Adam's fingers tightened on his weapons, but he didn't move. "They're fighting it."

"You mean they're being controlled somehow?"

"I don't know. It doesn't..." He bit off a snarl. "We need to find Dylan and Sasha."

"We need—" Cindy cursed. "Mac. They would have gotten to him first, and I don't see him."

The staggering wolf lunged toward Adam, who met the movement with a strong swing and broadsided the werewolf's head with the side of his hatchet. He went down in a crumpled pile of fur, and Adam shook his head. "It's wrong. The magic feels wrong, but I don't know why."

She gripped her bag so tightly her knuckles ached. "I *know*. Come on."

"Stay behind me," Adam replied shortly, then took off toward the bar. The attacking wolves charged him, but he knocked them back with singular ease, making it clear he was used to using the blades on more than trees.

Two familiar wolves, Julie and Hans, met them in the street, Mac sagging between them. "He fell not far from his post," Julie said with a grimace. They stumbled under Mac's weight and lowered him to the ground.

The ashen hue of his skin scared the hell out of Cindy. "Hey, Mac," she said soothingly. "I was looking for you."

One arm was a ruined mess, and his abdomen had been torn open. "Found me."

"Smartass." There wasn't much she could do. His healing was sluggish at best, too slow to outpace injuries this severe. "Julie, Hans, you two go. I'll stabilize him here, and Adam can help me get him to the bar."

"Tell my wife—" Mac's words caught on a cough, deep and racking. "Love her. Kids too."

Pretty words were a waste of time. "All I need is ten minutes. If you can hold on that long..."

A snarl sounded from their left, followed by a grunt, a pained yelp and a thud as a body hit the dirt. Adam's shout cut through the air. "Gennaro!"

Mac shuddered and groaned. Cindy looked up from her bag and caught his eyes as she gathered gauze in both hands. "I mean it, Mac. Just a few minutes more. I'll catch up to this, give you a fighting chance."

A grunt, which might have been assent. "Stubborn bitch."

"You don't know the half of it, sweetie."

Sasha came running, bounding down an alley with Dylan on all fours at her side. "He knows them. Dylan says—" She clutched her side and panted. "Dylan says these wolves wouldn't be fighting."

"He knows them from where?" Adam snapped, tension clear in his voice.

Dylan yipped and butted his head against Sasha's hip. She closed her eyes, almost as if listening. "The towns Alan took over. The ones he kept around for the money."

"What the hell did they do? Fill them up with magic and send them out here?"

The witch went pale. "I think that's exactly what they did."

Cindy secured the last roll of gauze around Mac. "Help me get him to the bar, and you can talk to Keith. There's got to be something we can do."

The bar wasn't far, but the trip was chaotic. Keith met them halfway, his eyes worried. "One of you better know what the fuck is going on, because none of this makes sense. I swear to God, half of them are trying to run away now, but every time they hit the town limits something turns them back."

"Magic," Adam gritted out as an unfamiliar man arrived at his side. Keith gestured and the man eased Mac from Adam's grip and helped Cindy move him into the bar. "Dylan thinks these wolves are from the towns Alan took over. Cannon fodder."

Keith looked at the witch. "Do we need to try to restrain them? Other than Mac, most of the damage they're doing is accidental. As soon as they started meeting resistance, whatever was keeping them focused broke, I guess."

Sasha looked grave. "I can dispel the magic binding them, but to do that I have to dispel *all* the magic, even the spell we cast to make Recco and the vampire think the refugees were still here."

"Adam? Thoughts?"

"They're full of power," Adam watched as one of Keith's men took down a crazy-eyed attacker. "External power. Wild, probably power the vampire harvested from the pack and forced on them. They'll make Brynn look subdued, and they'll suffer without an outlet."

"And they'll die if they keep fighting us." Keith didn't hesitate. "Free them, Sasha. I'll spread the word to restrain them if possible."

She hesitated, her gaze flickering to Adam. "What he said about an outlet..."

He knew where she was going and cut her off with a sharp gesture. "We'll deal with it afterwards. There's got to be a temporary alpha out there, or a leader. One wolf he's feeding the power through. We need to find him."

"And kill him?" It was Keith, quiet and practical.

Adam just wished he had an answer. "If it comes to that."

Keith nodded and shot off, leaving Adam with Sasha, who stared at him. "Before I separate them, I need to know. Will you help those wolves?"

"Take that magic into myself, you mean?" He tried to fill his words with derision, but underneath some tiny part of him rejoiced. The power was wild, untamed—but he was an expert. A vampire who'd played with blood bonds in a way few could dream of. In the darkest depths of his soul he was hungry for it—hungrier than he'd ever been in his life, and that dark otherself whispered promises of what they could do with that power. *Anything.*

Sasha spoke. "If you can't, it might be more merciful to kill them than to break the bonds."

Adam turned to look down the street again, at the ragged, disjointed fighting. Some of the wolves had already died, and more lay injured or unconscious, disabled by wolves who had instinctively recognized that the fight wasn't quite right. Keith had already begun to gather up the stragglers, some of whom fought him wildly. Others seemed almost relieved, throwing themselves to the ground at his feet and begging in disjointed words that weren't audible from so far away, though the tone was clear: relief.

They were innocents, twisted inside and fighting the power the same way Brynn did. For Brynn, the power was always there. These wolves just needed relief once.

With their power, you can keep Cindy safe.

The thought triggered an instinctive reaction, intense and so overwhelming the words escaped from his numb lips without thought. "I'll do it."

The witch nodded and sank to her knees. Her hands dug into the earth, almost as if she was trying to root herself in it. She began to murmur, slow words that increased in speed until they became a feverish, rhythmic chant.

Magic snapped through the air, leaving a pulse that rolled out from Sasha in ever-growing waves, something that brushed against magic and swept it away. The night fell still, silent, even the spell-sick wolves who'd attacked them.

Then the first one screamed.

Adam closed his eyes and reached for the energy around them, invoking that ghostly echo so that when he opened them again he could trace the eddies of power.

Sasha burned the brightest, lit up like a rainbow of magic—life and death, earth and spirit. A shimmering green cord connected her to Dylan, whose subdued aura held sharp, protective edges as he hovered close to his witch. As Adam watched, the bond between them flared and snapped, leaving a mere echo in its place.

Turning gave Adam a clear view down the street. The wolves of Red Rock burned brightly too, but the light around them was eclipsed by the angry power roiling in the invading wolves. Sickly green edged with red and black, the power of the wild that had been twisted with death.

After that, it should have been easy. Every wolf had a thin bond trailing away, magic running inexorably back to its anchor. It had been the same way among his wolves, a secret he'd never told Joan because he delighted in her consternation when he never had any trouble finding her. Every wolf in their pack had been bound to her with chains of magic, visible only to someone who knew how to look.

Adam knew how to look—but as he did, the first bond snapped, succumbing to the lingering power of Sasha's magic.

With every pulse, more bonds disappeared. Adam set off at a run, following the tug as more and more of the flickering bonds tangled together, all flowing toward the same source.

At the center of the quickly vanishing web he found Abby and a young man who couldn't have been older than twenty. The werewolf huddled on his hands and knees, bleeding and shaking. "What happened?"

Abby clutched one bruised hand. "I don't understand. We

were fighting, and then he started trying to herd everyone back the way they came."

So their leader, at least, had been strong enough to fight the madness. "These aren't Helena wolves. Dylan said they're from nearby towns that paid tithes." Adam sank to his knees and laid a soothing hand on the boy's back. "They've got more power shoved in them than Brynn does right now, and it's making them crazy."

"Jesus."

The boy tried to scramble away, but Adam cursed and caught his shoulders, holding him steady. "Son, listen to me. The bonds between you and the other wolves are snapping, and every time one does all that power snaps right back to you. Let me take it, so it won't hurt anymore."

"Take." His terrified voice cracked. "That's all anyone ever does. Even when they give back, it's nothing but pain."

"No more pain," Adam promised, gentling his voice. "Just one drop of blood, that's all I need. One drop freely given, and any pain will skip right on past you and come to me."

He nodded. "I don't care if you kill me. Just make it stop."

The pain in those tired, hopeless words shredded Adam's nerves as he reached for the boy's wrist. It didn't take much, a tiny prick of teeth and the first taste of blood, and magic roiled up, hungry and eager.

Forging the connection hurt, but it was a pain Adam could master. He let the connection fall into place and braced himself against the onslaught of power, but even that wasn't enough. It roared over him, *through* him, flooded him in life and death and pain and grief and sorrow, so much sorrow he wanted to *weep*—

It didn't stop. More bonds broke, still failing under the press of Sasha's spell, but the bond between him and the boy stayed strong. Adam siphoned off a tiny bit of the power to strengthen it, using it to reinforce the connection until not even Sasha's magic could break it. With each shattered binding, more power slammed into him, until he was full of it, floating on it.

Madness beckoned, but Adam closed his eyes and forced it away with one thought. One face. One need. "Cindy. I have to get back to Cindy."

Abby was already kneeling by the boy, who'd gone limp in

her arms. Her face was calm, but her eyes saw too much. "She'll be at the bar. Hurry."

If the run from the bar had been chaotic, the walk back was eerie. The intruders had dropped where they stood as their bonds failed, and perplexed-looking defenders milled about as Keith organized them to start gathering the fallen.

Inside, Cindy stood by the raised stagelike dais, cleaning up. She grinned as she gathered discarded plastic and paper, along with opened packages of medical paraphernalia and bloodied gauze.

She looked up when he walked in, her smile widening. "Hey, Mac's going to be—" The words cut off in a harsh intake of breath, and she dropped the half-full trash bag she held. "What's wrong, Adam?"

Every instinct focused on her, but he was afraid to take another step. "I had to take their power."

"The wolves?" She reached for him. "How do you get rid of it?"

"I don't know. There are rituals...spells, maybe." The darkest part of his soul protested, and he crushed the rebellion ruthlessly. "Getting rid of power isn't exactly a common goal, sweetheart."

"There has to be a way. We'll find one."

Sasha walked in and leaned against the open door, one hand tangled in Dylan's fur. "I only know of one way. Adam...is familiar with it."

A shudder worked through him, and he was helpless to stop it. "Those were weak wolves, Sasha. Subordinates. Submissives. The only one with serious power was Joan."

"We have to do something, don't we?"

Cindy laid a hand on his cheek. "Christ, Adam, you're burning up."

"I know." He closed his eyes and clutched at her shoulders, using her presence to ground him. "It has to be Winston. Someone needs to get him."

"I'm already here." A strong hand locked around Adam's elbow. "Cindy, help me get him to a chair."

It was all Adam could do to keep from driving his elbow into Keith's chest. "I'm not an invalid, Winston." It came out as a snarl.

Keith had no problem snarling right back. "Park your ego at the door and sit your ass down. If you don't care about yourself, think about Cindy."

"Yes, think about Cindy," she interjected. "Is someone going to tell me what's going on?"

Chapter Nine

Cindy had thought she couldn't get more terrified than when Mac had been brought to her, torn and bleeding, and she'd had to confront the possibility that it could have been her, or any of them.

It could have been Adam.

But that fear paled next to this, next to him looking half-dead and half-crazy in turn, and Sasha talking about doing something that sounded suspiciously like—

"No." She knelt in front of him, gripping his hand as tightly as she could. "You don't have to forge these bonds. You can give it to me."

His hand came up to cup her cheek, and he managed a weak smile. "No. At least I have practice with this."

All that wouldn't matter if it broke him. "Are you sure?"

"No." His thumb swept over her lips, a gentle, tender touch. "What I have to ask of you is far worse. I only hope you won't hate me for it."

She had only one answer, and she meant it with everything in her. "Anything."

Adam closed his eyes. "With this much power, I can protect the town. If I bind your wolves to me, the way I did it before, they'll heal a hundred times faster. They'll be stronger. And with their strength at my disposal, their *willing* strength, this vampire doesn't stand a chance."

A curious numbness unfurled inside her, and she shook her head. "You said you had no business having that sort of power with no thought of how to use it. Does that mean you—you've figured it out?"

"No, sweet Cindy. It means I can save your town and your

wolves, but I might become a monster."

The numbness splintered into horror. "Adam—"

"Shh." He looked up to where Keith still hovered, then shifted his gaze to Sasha and Dylan, who watched in silence. "Can we get a few moments?"

Sasha backed away. "We'll check on things outside."

Cindy heard them file out, but she couldn't tear her gaze away from Adam's face. His lips and cheeks were red with fever, his eyes glassy. "You can't sacrifice yourself for us. It isn't right."

His other hand came up, both cradling her face. "It's too late, Cindy. I already took the power, and I can't contain it all. Forgive me. I need you to forgive me, for not waiting—"

She cut off his frantic words with a quick, hard kiss. "Nothing to forgive, Adam. Just...tell me what you need me to do."

"Stay with me." He smoothed his thumbs over her cheeks, his voice dropping to a whisper. "I'll fight with everything in me, darling. For you, for your friends...but they're not just words. Power corrupts. No vampire I've heard of has taken this much power before. You'll need to bring me back. And if you can't..."

Her eyes burned, and she couldn't breathe. Adam would rather die than live that way—out of control, mad with power. A danger to others. She knew that.

She knew it.

It didn't help. Cindy realized she was holding her breath, and she released it on a ragged sob. Her first instinct was to argue, and her second was to demand that he ask someone—anyone—else to bear this responsibility. To shoulder the burden of killing him.

But she couldn't. There was no one else with a fighting chance of breaking through his madness, if it came to that. She had the best chance of holding him there, of keeping him anchored and sane.

She blinked until the tears clouding her vision fell, tracing hot lines down her cheeks. "Tell me how to do it quickly. I don't—don't want it to hurt."

Adam pressed his lips to her forehead. "Sever the spinal cord. But I swear to God, Cindy, I'm going to try."

"Please." She held his wrists and closed her eyes. "Does

this mean I have to stay outside the spell?"

"Yes. I don't want you in it." He kissed her forehead again, then each eyelid. "I can bring the vampire here. Once I have the power, I'll find him. Challenge him. He'll know I took what was his, and he'll come."

And then, one way or another, it would end. "We'll be ready."

"I know." His mouth covered hers and he kissed her, hard and hungry, so desperate it felt like he was trying to condense a lifetime of kisses into one moment.

But it couldn't last forever. Cindy heard footsteps, and Abby murmured their names. "No more time. The kid—the leader? He said everyone else was an hour behind them at most, and they're bound to be in a hurry now. We need to do this."

Adam released her and lifted his head. "Keith and Sasha."

"I'll get them." Cindy wiped her face as she rose. She had to have a moment to compose herself, to strengthen her resolve.

Outside, Keith was standing with Dylan, who'd shifted and found a pair of sweatpants somewhere. "The kid might have been the strongest one they had," Dylan murmured as Cindy stopped next to them. "Matthews only let a pack stay in a nearby town if they tithed heavily, and he went in once a year to stamp out anyone strong enough to present a challenge. They're going to be as helpless as the Helena subordinates would have been."

Keith shook his head. "You of all people know better than to underestimate a wolf with nothing to lose, Gennaro. You took down Alan Matthews with a handgun after all of us had failed. Maybe we can give them a little hope worth fighting for."

"Adam's ready for you and Sasha." Cindy marveled at how steady and calm the words sounded.

Keith nodded to Dylan. "Go talk to the ones you know."

"Yes, sir."

Keith turned to Cindy next and grasped her arms. "You okay, sweetheart?"

"No." She laughed helplessly. "I won't be part of it, Keith. The pack bonding. I'm the safety switch, I guess. If things go wrong."

For one second, he stared. Then he swore viciously as his

fingers tightened. "I'm going to kill that son of a bitch."

"There's no one else, just me." It was a truth she could barely fathom. "He trusts *me*."

"Cindy, you don't—" He cut off and cursed again. "Damn it all to hell, we don't even have time to fight about it. Sasha! With me, and explain what the hell's going on."

The witch was there in an instant. "We need to redistribute all the power Adam took from the wolves. He's going to use me and you to do it."

"Is this like that spell he used in the thirties?"

"Pretty much exactly." She frowned apologetically. "I don't have time to find another way."

"Fine." Keith's hand slid down to curl around Cindy's hand, squeezing. "Let's do this. And Cindy, I want to leave someone else with you, so if something has to happen..."

It might be easier to let someone else be the one to end Adam's life, but it could haunt her for the rest of hers. "I can do this, Keith. I will, for him."

There was a moment of silence as they pushed through the door, and Keith nodded. "Sasha? What do we do?"

When she answered, she addressed Adam. "Bind Keith. After that, I'll draw the bond into myself and thread it out to the rest of the pack."

It wasn't showy, though energy gathered in the room until it felt like every molecule was electrified. Sizzling. Keith held out his arm without waiting to be asked, and Adam grasped his wrist in silence. A muscle in Keith's cheek twitched when Adam bit him, but the vampire's throat worked only once before he pulled back, eyes squeezed shut and jaw clenched.

The first proof that anything had happened was Keith's sharp inhalation. Magic wound through the room, but it tasted like Keith, not Adam. It built until Cindy's ears buzzed, as if all this power was a living, noisy thing, whispering its demands of them all.

Sasha stepped forward, and the buzzing grew louder. She held out one hand, her fingers hovering just shy of Keith's skin. The electric atmosphere intensified, and magic began to lash through the air.

Cindy closed her eyes as energy zipped around her, questing. Searching. She waited for it to envelop her...

But it never did. When Sasha finally dropped her hand and opened her eyes, Cindy stood alone. The magic had solidified, webbed around her, but she was untouched. She shivered. "Is it done?"

Keith's voice seemed to echo. "It's done. Christ. If this is what Brynn feels like half the time, no wonder she starts so many damn fights."

"Power can make you reckless." Adam came to his feet. There was something graceful and almost predatory about the way his gaze drifted across the room and fixed on her. "You should gather the wolves. If I challenge the vampire, it should be one-on-one, but I doubt he'll hold to the rules once he realizes I have what he wants."

He was watching her, so Cindy blinked. "You—you want me to do it?"

Keith had already started for the door. "Stay with him. Sasha, you too." His voice brooked no argument.

The door slammed behind him, but Adam still watched her. Darkness stirred in his gaze, and he held out a hand. "Cindy."

She couldn't look away. "Adam." His hand was hot under hers, but steady.

He seemed oblivious to Sasha's presence as he pulled Cindy forward until her body stretched out against his. "Tell me you're not afraid of me. Tell me you'll still want me if we make it through this."

Perhaps he could feel her fear—not completely, but enough to misunderstand it. "I'm terrified, but I want you, Adam, always. If we make it through this..." She lifted her hands to his face. "Even if we don't."

He shuddered under her touch. "I'm too damn old to fall in love, and too damn smart to fall this fast. But hell, Cindy, if we don't... I would have—"

Her chest ached, and she had to press her fingers over his mouth to stop the words. "Tell me in a while?" Outside, she heard distant, threatening howls. "Just a little while now."

Adam jerked her hand away and claimed her lips in a kiss so hard his fangs scratched her lips. Cindy met it eagerly, glad for the tiny wounds she knew his teeth would leave. It was a little more of him she could have for a bit longer, even if things went badly.

When the howls rose again, he tore himself away and spun,

striding for the door with jerky, abrupt steps, as if he had to force himself to walk away. And walk away he did, out the door and into the street, where his voice rose along with the borrowed power in a challenge that must have echoed off the hills. *"I challenge you for blood rights to the state of Montana and every wolf within its borders. Show yourself or forfeit."*

Adam didn't even know the enemy's name.

It was a trivial detail to be concerned about when the mountains around them vibrated with the roars of challenging wolves. Magic thrummed in his veins, magic he'd stolen mixed with power freely given, and the world lay crisp and sharp around him, connected to him in a way he'd never imagined.

He could number the pine needles on distant trees and count the grains of sand in the rocky gravel stretched out before him. Somewhere on the edge of town a furious force gathered, the vampire marshaling death and life as he screamed a wordless response to Adam's challenge. Too far gone to remember the rituals, or too lost to madness to care.

Recco's wolves streamed down the street, healthy and hungry for a fight. The real warriors, the ones Red Rock would have to defeat in order to live free. Safe.

A small gray wolf shot past him and stood in front of him, snarling, legs stiff and trembling. He could feel the others, but not her. Not Cindy.

She launched herself at the first attacker to head his way, jaws snapping in ferocious, protective rage. The wolf yelped and went down, and Adam shuddered and fought the need to draw more power, to take it from Red Rock's defenders and channel it into a weapon to protect Cindy.

Cindy didn't need his protection. She fought like she'd been trained, which she had been, knowing Keith and Joe. Another wolf fell before her and still the vampire didn't appear, though his presence weighted the air, left it heavy.

So much magic, so many bonds, but no bridge between them. Without a link, there was no way to force his enemy to show himself. Not before the situation was dire and lives had been lost. No way except—

A wolf got past Cindy and lunged for Adam's throat, and he twisted fast and wrapped both arms around its body. Sharp teeth snapped shut an inch away from his face, and arrogance grew inside Adam, reckless and unchecked.

Ignoring the battle around them, he lifted his arm and shoved it into the wolf's mouth. Those deadly teeth tore into his skin, shredding his arm as the startled beast bit down. Hard, almost hard enough to snap bone, and pain ripped through Adam like shattering glass, burning away everything but his goal. "Drink, you flea-ridden fucker."

Crazed though the wolf might be, it clearly recognized danger. As it should—over time Adam's blood would poison the wolf, death magic festering until it consumed the creature from the inside. It tried to pull back, but wrenching its head only carved deeper paths in Adam's arm, and the blood ran freely.

Too freely. It wasn't the easiest way to forge a connection. There was no gift here, no willing participant. Adam used the excess magic thrumming inside him to force the bond into place with brutal strength before releasing the wolf, letting the creature fall to the ground in a whimpering, confused sprawl. Adam ignored the hot slick of blood running down his arm and closed his eyes, tracing that tentative bond back to the wolf.

Without the power surging inside him it would have been impossible, but it was so easy to reach out and draw in a little from Red Rock's defenders. Savage, willing magic rose at his slightest thought, and with it he seized energy from the wolf at his feet, wrapping himself in its aura as he found the second bond and followed it back to its source.

The vampire sat at the center like a bloated spider, huddling in the protective web he'd made from the wolves' life force. Magic didn't carry thoughts easily, but intentions were clear enough. The coward meant to use his wolves, use them up if he had to, anything to drain the reserves of the defenders.

Fear permeated the connections, the fear of the attackers, whose opponents healed faster than any wolf should, and fear from the vampire himself, who couldn't understand why Adam's circle of power shone strong and controlled where his was a chaotic mess.

It was such a mess that the vampire didn't even notice when Adam stole the first wolf from him. He snatched the bond as easy as breathing, and added it to the endless reservoir of strength building inside him. The second came to him just as easily, but with the third a roar split the air, and the attacking wolves went wild as the vampire lost his grip on sanity and charged.

Adam opened his eyes to find Cindy hovering, her fur streaked with blood, and none of it hers. She'd obviously heard the roar, the *challenge*, and she lunged only to draw up short. She wouldn't leave him, but she didn't have to.

The vampire would come to them.

Then he did, a pale specter who charged down the street, knocking people and skirmishing wolves out of his path. He was past his prime, the evidence of too much magic twisting his frame, leaving him physically weak.

The power inside him was another story. At any other time, Adam would have been wary of it. Now, he welcomed the chance to extinguish it, like a licked fingertip on a lit match head.

"You can't have them." Even his voice was unholy, an echo of itself rasping free of his throat. "They're *mine!*"

Adam laughed, let the sound ring out and echo off the surrounding buildings. Words came, stiffly formal and dripping with disdainful challenge that felt more real than he intended. "You're a mewling, pathetic boy trying to play a man's game. I invented the rules, you fool. You think to best me?"

"I know about you." The vampire smiled viciously. "You spent the last century hiding from this power like a little girl. You don't deserve it."

The words should have hurt more, but what could possibly hurt him now? He was fucking invincible. "I may not deserve it, but I'm the one who's got it. You couldn't quite pull it off, could you, you sorry bastard."

"Your way is weak. You give them too much power."

"And your way is working out for you?" Adam spit on the ground. "Let them go, or I'll take them from you. Every last one."

Cindy snarled, and the vampire looked at her. "Or I'll take yours from you," he murmured.

Faces flashed before his eyes. Women and girls, young wolves who had been taken from him, tortured and killed to teach him his place in the world. They'd been his to protect, his to hold safe for all that they'd given their loyalty to Joan. They'd been *his*—

—and not one of them had touched him as deeply as Cindy.

For the first time in his too-long existence, someone had

stirred the embers of affection until love simmered just beneath the surface, ready to burst into flames. Cindy was life. Cindy was everything.

Adam dragged power from God-knew-where and flung it at his foe as he lunged, sense and reason gone. No one would touch Cindy, not while he lived. Not if he had to kill every last one of them to keep her safe.

Magic shattered through the night. Cindy's first instinct was to tuck her tail and run, to get out of the way of such ravenous, uncontrolled power. Then Adam charged past her and she realized it was coming from *him*.

Her back legs almost gave out as the two vampires clashed. Adam had the clear advantage in strength and sheer physical brawn, but the invader had command of the attacking wolves, who abandoned their battles and converged on the center of town, more than ready to tear Adam apart.

Cindy howled a protest and hit the nearest one. He held his ground, paws scrabbling on the asphalt, and snapped at her. But Keith had taught her to fight, and she ducked those jaws and countered by raking sharp nails across the wolf's eyes.

Her adversary rolled away with a pained yelp. A familiar wolf pounced on him—Keith, who snapped his jaws shut on the back of his enemy's neck. More wolves from Red Rock appeared, and some werewolves in human form holding weapons that had become all but useless in the writhing throng of fighting bodies.

There was nothing to do but keep fighting, so she did, until Keith stumbled and fell under a sloppy attack he should have been able to fend off with ease. He bounded immediately to his paws, but his fatigue was plain.

The wolves were beginning to falter, allies *and* enemies, and it took Cindy several seconds to realize that Adam and the other vampire were still fighting, going strong when others were beginning to succumb to exhaustion.

They were draining the wolves.

Cindy fought free of the melee and panted for breath. She remained outside the bond; she'd be fine, but she didn't know how long that would be true of the other Red Rock wolves. If Adam didn't kill the vampire soon, they might all fall.

Or she could do it herself.

The thought sent a shiver racing through her. *Well, why*

not? Adam had told her how—*sever the spinal cord*—and the vampire was distracted, fully focused on defeating his most dangerous enemy.

Adam had left his hatchets leaning against the outside wall of the bar, not far from the door. Cindy shifted back to her human form when she reached them, shivering a little in the night air. Her hand trembled, and she steadied it by closing her fingers tightly around the handle of one hatchet.

With most of the attack centered around Adam, she had a clear path to the other vampire. *One swing, Cindy. End this.*

No one blocked her or moved to protect the vampire. Perhaps they could only do his bidding, and his own hubris wouldn't allow him to believe anyone but Adam posed a threat to him.

Maybe they wanted to be free of him.

She caught the vampire on the side of the neck. Blood spurted, but he didn't fall. Instead he roared in pain and spun, lashing out blindly. The blow landed, snapping her head to one side, and pain exploded through her cheek and jaw.

"Cindy!" Her name tore free of Adam's throat, rage and terror shredding it into a pained cry as the invading vampire lunged for her, fingers grasping for her hair. His mouth opened, baring gruesomely sharp fangs.

He almost bit her. His teeth scraped her neck in a rough, glancing blow, fangs slicing across skin instead of piercing. The pain helped her focus, driving her determination as she hit him in the side of the head, knocking him away.

He grabbed at her arm, the one holding the blade. It drew her attention, and she didn't see his fist coming at her again until connected, knocking her back in a wild stumble.

As Cindy recovered, she caught sight of Adam, practically walking over combatants to get to her, a terrible fury twisting his features. If he engaged the vampire while in the grip of such blinding rage...

The vampire reached for her. She sidestepped his grasp and swung again, this time burying the hatchet in the pale skin at the back of his neck. The blade wasn't big enough to take off his head, but it didn't have to. As soon as she felt it bite through his spine, she let go and fell back.

The vampire started to fall, but Adam snarled and finished the job she'd started, grabbing his enemy's head and separating it from his body with brute strength and wrath alone.

Magic crackled in the air like electricity, the shock nearly audible in the sudden hush. The attacking wolves began to drop one by one, sprawling to the ground in eerie silence.

Cindy almost fell to her knees. Adam looked wild, his eyes wide with almost berserker rage, and it was only then that she remembered the fallen vampire could well be the least of her worries.

She held out her hand. "Adam."

He flung the head aside and reached for her, fingers slicking over her blood-soaked skin with an urgency that betrayed his terror. "They hurt you. They *hurt you*."

The side of her face throbbed, but nothing else pained her. "No, I'm fine. It's not mine. Not my blood."

His hands tightened on her arms, bearing down until she knew she'd have bruises that wouldn't heal overnight. "I'll protect you. Forever."

The words should have sounded like heaven, but the wild power surging through him perverted the sentiment. He'd protect her with stolen magic, with the bonds he'd never wanted to keep. "Adam, you have to let go."

"I'm not strong enough without them." A desperate, shamed admission that he whispered with closed eyes. "I can't do it again. I can't fail this time. Last time I let them go and I wasn't strong enough."

More of the ghosts haunting him, and this time they could kill him. "Adam, please."

"They killed them one by one, to keep me in line. I let them go to save them, and I only killed them faster."

Damn it. "You tried. Just like you have to try now."

His fingers tightened. "I will try. I won't let them hurt you."

"This isn't the way to do that," she argued desperately. "You can't keep everyone bound to you. Not like this."

Dylan appeared, smeared with blood and tense. "Sasha can't break herself free. Not herself and not the wolves. He's holding them too damn tight and people are starting to hurt."

Cindy nodded but kept her attention on Adam. She slid her hands up to his face and whispered to him, desperate to make him hear her. "You don't want me hurt. I understand that, but you need to know that you *will* hurt me if you do this. I can't let you put my friends in danger."

The first glimmer of sense returned to his eyes, and his hands came up to cover hers. "I don't—I don't know if I can—" But he closed his eyes and shuddered, and with her skin pressed tight to his she felt the stir of magic.

It looked agonizing. His body shook as that tenuous power grew, gathering inside him, and her wolf wanted to shy away.

She stood firm. Tighter and tighter it wound, until Adam whispered a curse and it snapped, flying out in a thousand directions.

Dylan staggered and groaned. Keith hit the ground on his knees, and Abby followed, one arm thrown protectively over him despite her own shakiness.

Terror threatened to choke Cindy, and she shook Adam, just enough to make him look at her. "Are you all right? Talk to me."

His glazed eyes took forever to focus on her face. He smiled, tired and tentative, and touched her cheek. "I would have loved you with everything I had."

He collapsed without warning and Cindy followed him, pain splintering through her. She remembered what it had cost him to break the bonds over the refugees, and these had been far more numerous, and stronger. Tighter.

He needed to feed, and there was only one way she could think of to get him to do it. "No magic but us," she whispered, and kissed him hard. As his teeth cut into her lower lip, she silently begged him to take what she offered.

Beneath her, Adam stirred. His tongue slid against her lip, wet and hot, and when he plunged past her teeth to taste her, the coppery tang of her blood flavored his kiss. Energy burned inside her, still riled from the fight and her own fear, but the longer they kissed the softer it became, soaking into him through the magic they'd made together.

Breaking the kiss was unfathomable, and Cindy held on even when he rolled her onto her back and covered her with his body.

An eternity passed before he pulled away and planted his hands on either side of her head, levering the bulk of his weight off of her. "You pack a hell of a punch in a tiny bit of blood, lover."

She was floating, giddy with relief. "Do you feel okay?"

"I'll make it." He sounded hoarse, ragged around the edges. He rolled again and brought her on top of him. "Too damn cold for you to be sprawled naked on the ground."

Keith's dry voice cut through their moment. "It's too damn cold for *anyone* to be out here naked. You two feel like getting your asses inside? I think it's time to clean up and call our people home."

Home. "What about the alpha? Recco, I mean."

"Dead." Keith's darkly amused laugh rumbled through the night. "Abby ate his head, which might just make her the new alpha of Helena."

"Fantastic." Cindy swallowed hard. "Unless you literally mean she ate his head, in which case I might be sick."

"Purely figurative. Either way, someone's going to have to clean house in Helena. Gavin may have to come out of retirement yet."

With the support of a nearby sanctuary city, Gavin could handle things in Red Rock, at least for a few more years. "He'll be thrilled to hear it."

"Less thrilled if he's mourning the death of his favorite doctor, who froze her fool ass off." Keith's voice was filled with fond exasperation, cut with the buzz of victory.

They'd won. Helena had been defeated, and their way of life was safe. Cindy looked down at Adam. "I don't give a damn if we're lying in the street and I'm naked and everyone I know is watching. I love you."

Adam's fingers drifted up to smooth her hair back from her forehead, and his quiet smile was all for her. "Love you too, Dr. Shepherd."

Words she never thought she'd hear, not from someone like Adam. Happy tears stung her eyes, and she sank down to his chest. "Take me home."

Chapter Ten

With all the changes in his life over the past six months, it had taken Adam a while to notice a subtle but profound one: having male friends.

He'd spent decades in the woods with the occasional female playmate as his only real company. Even in recent years, it had been Emily who had cut a path to his door, towing her reluctant mate behind her. During the time he'd spent on the farm with his witch and his wolves, he'd been surrounded by women, and then the token men had regarded him with more suspicion than friendship.

In Red Rock, friends were everywhere. He had Keith's steady respect, Gavin's long-standing friendship and Dylan's nervous but endearing curiosity. Even Joe had come around...somewhat. Enough to join Keith and Dylan more often than not as the four of them chopped and sawed and leveled and hammered.

Building a house was more complicated now than it had been in the thirties, when he'd hidden himself away in the northern part of Maine. Dylan had shown an unexpected flair for the eccentricities of modern plumbing—something he self-deprecatingly credited to his former landlord's ineptitude, and Keith had droned on about wiring and voltages until Adam's eyes had glazed over. Without them, the project might have stalled before it got started.

With them, though, Adam had built a house.

It wasn't grand or fancy, but it had something more valuable. Every corner, every room, every bit of it bore Cindy's touch, details they'd worked out together during the long winter months when Red Rock had seemed like a snowy dream, cut off from the world and locked in the post-battle revelry of people who hadn't expected to win.

Of course, they weren't building it very fast. Dylan had other duties to deal with most of the week, and Joe and Keith could only help on the weekends, when they needed a break from the hard work of rebuilding the Helena pack. But they still showed up, almost every weekend, and it meant more to Adam than he'd realized at first.

They finished the inside paneling on the morning of Gavin's birthday, and Adam celebrated by pulling three chilled beers from a nearby cooler. "I was expecting Dylan by now. I imagine he's gotten distracted, though."

Joe accepted his beer. "That's one way to put it. He's probably still over at Cindy's with Sasha."

"Boy moves fast," Keith drawled as he twisted the cap off his beer. "I hear Sam keeps butting her ass in, trying to 'loan' him money for an engagement ring. Subtle like a grenade."

Adam couldn't help but laugh. "Samantha's a little old-fashioned, and Gavin's not exactly from a time where babies are supposed to come before marriage. But Dylan's fine. He lowers his eyes and yes ma'ams Sam until she backs off, then ignores her."

"Eh, he'll get Sasha down the aisle soon." Joe sat against the wall and stretched out his legs, mindless of the plaster dust. Keith used one hand to hoist himself up onto a sawhorse, balancing precariously.

They both looked relaxed. At home. Adam drained half his beer and shrugged. "Don't think either of them cares. They're happy. That's what matters."

"Cindy's happy too," Keith murmured. "Which is good. Now we don't have to bring it, *Rise of the Lycans* style."

A long winter in front of Cindy's television hadn't made the younger generation's idea of humor much easier to understand, but Adam had learned to shrug it off. "If that means you're going to stop plotting my death, I'm relieved."

Joe grinned. "If Cindy were in the throes of some hormonally induced bad judgment, it would have faded by now. Which means she really does love you, and we're duty-bound to at least *try* to like you."

"I bet I'm not hard to like from Helena."

"Nah, you're all right."

Keith lifted his beer. "To Red Rock's own vampire lumberjack." His eyes glinted with a humor that made him look more like a mischievous young buck than a man nearing his fifth decade. "So your house is pretty damn close to done. You owe us. Tell us how the hell Gavin has a dark secret that involves a madam with a pet monkey."

Gavin would murder him, and Adam didn't care. He settled back against the table and took another sip of his beer. "Well, old Gavin wasn't always the most law-abiding of men. He ran with a pretty wild crowd of bootleggers, and one of their favorite stomping grounds was owned by the infamous Black Magic Betty, a madam who might've been a witch to boot, and she'd trained her little pet monkey to pick men's pockets while the girls had them distracted..."

Both men laughed as Adam played up the tale, spinning out the story of Gavin's legendary run through the brothel, stark naked and determined to bring the thieving monkey to justice. Reminiscing didn't hurt anymore; his lingering ghosts had been more than exorcised over the months, as Cindy had coaxed tales of the past from him. Slowly at first, as if she knew how much it still hurt sometimes, but always there. Always caring.

Joe and Keith's laughter reminded him how nice it was to have friends, but it was eclipsed by how very nice it was to have Cindy.

That warmth carried him through two more beers and a dozen stories that would surely have Gavin running him out of Red Rock. By the time Adam made the short walk back toward Cindy's house, the sun had dipped toward the edge of the trees and people had already filled the streets, their laughter echoing through town as they converged on the bar to begin preparations for Gavin's birthday party.

More laughter drifted from the living room as he pushed open the back door, but the voice was too high to belong to the young refugee doctor who'd been spending most of his time learning the ropes of Cindy's day-to-day job.

Cindy ducked into the kitchen, a pleased smile playing at the corners of her mouth. "I was wondering where you were."

"Telling Keith and Joe stories about criminal life in the nineteen twenties." Her eyes held a hint of mischievousness that probably meant trouble. "We have company?"

"*You* have company." She stretched out her hand. "Come into the living room."

Still perplexed, he slid his fingers into hers and followed willingly enough—until she tugged him over the threshold into the living room and he found himself face to face with the past.

Joan.

So many years had passed, but there was no mistaking her. She had aged gracefully, her dark hair swept with silver but her face still smooth, and only a few wrinkles to mark the decades she'd lived. Smile lines, they looked like, and it mended something he hadn't known was broken to realize in that instant that Joan had lived a happy life.

She smiled at him from her spot on the couch, tentative but friendly, as if her husband wasn't wrapped half around her and watching Adam with a wariness that said more than a thousand verbal threats. In spite of her smiles, Joan was nervous enough to have Seamus's back up. The werewolf might be even older than Gavin, but Adam could see the past in him, the dangerous criminal who'd crashed into their lives in the midst of chaos and swept prim and proper Joan off her feet.

The air was redolent with protective magic, and it took Adam a moment to realize it wasn't just coming from Seamus. Cindy all but shook with it, a dominant wolf ready to keep her mate safe by any means necessary, and Adam tensed, recognizing the potential for unpleasantness hovering in the air.

Joan noticed it as well. Her lips pursed, as if laughter might erupt at any moment. "Oh, Adam. Say something, before one of them explodes. It would be a depressingly short fight, since Seamus is too old fashioned to hit a girl."

"Chauvinism has its advantages," Cindy interjected. "Advantages I'd be unashamed to press."

The old wolf eyed her. "I think she really *would* kick my ass."

Cindy relaxed a little. "And it would serve you right for underestimating me."

Some of the tension dissolved as Seamus laughed. "A pretty lady? Never."

"Behave," Joan murmured, and the slightly exasperated tone sent Adam spinning back to the past. Not to the painful memories of when it had all gone wrong, but to the good times. Long nights around a family-sized table he'd put together himself, with Joan presiding at the head, wreathed more often than not in blushes and stern disapproval every time the conversation had grown ribald.

He doubted she was a prim little innocent now, not after nearly a century of marriage to a barely-reformed blackguard like Seamus Whelan, but she could still make a man feel like a misbehaving schoolboy with a stern look. She held the look for a moment, then dissolved into laughter. "I don't get nearly as much practice as I used to. Now that I'm a great-grandmother, people have started guarding their tongue around me. I hope you'll all be amazingly inappropriate."

Adam felt his own smile form, wide and easy and free of lingering sadness as he hooked an arm around Cindy's waist and pulled her close. "What do you think? Is anyone likely to say anything remotely appropriate to her the entire time she's here?"

"Only if Seamus and Gavin glower at them." Cindy softened the words with a wink.

"Trouble," Joan's husband declared, laughing. "Sure you can handle her?"

"Nope," Adam replied easily. "But who wants a woman they can handle?"

"No man worth having." Joan found Adam's gaze, and he saw his own relief mirrored in her dark brown eyes. They softened, and she tilted her head, her voice dropping to barely above a whisper. "A long time ago you told me to let Seamus love me."

The memory came easily enough. Numb with pain, magically drained. Seamus and Joan had come to the rescue, covered in blood and radiating the sort of power that only came when two strong people became one mind, one heart.

He'd felt so alone, so damn tired. So confident in his own unworthiness. "I remember. And I remember you asking me a question too."

"If you'd ever let anyone love you."

"That's the one." He'd lied. At the time he'd told himself he'd done it well, and she'd believed him. Maybe they'd both been fools. "I told you I would. Someday."

Joan nodded. "Someday was worth the wait, I think."

"I hope so." Cindy leaned up and kissed his cheek. "Catch up. I'm going to make coffee, and Seamus is going to help me."

The man mock-groaned. "But I'm old."

"And I'm a doctor," she shot back. "Buck up and come on. You'll be fine."

He followed her through the doorway into the kitchen, leaving Adam and Joan alone. "So," he said as he sank into a chair. "I suppose we have a lot to catch up on."

"We certainly do. Where do you want to start?"

Gavin's quiet birthday celebration had turned into an out-and-out shindig. Werewolves and humans filled the bar and spilled out into the warm spring night. The tired old jukebox had been retired for the evening, replaced with a half-dozen strategically placed speakers and an MP3 player, which Adam had declared damnably small and more like magic than any spell Sasha had ever woven.

Sasha herself was enthroned on the dais next to Samantha and Gavin. Dylan had finally been persuaded to leave her side for a laughing dance with Abby, whose smile lit up the room.

Everyone was happy and jovial. Wolves and humans, a witch and one vampire. Red Rock had never seen a celebration like this, but hopefully it would see many, many more.

"I think Seamus is scandalizing Brynn," Adam murmured from behind Cindy, sliding one arm around her waist. "I bet she didn't know she could be scandalized."

It would take some uncouth comments, indeed. Cindy watched as Seamus said something and then chuckled as Brynn blushed redder than Sasha's hair. "I bet he has some wild stories to tell."

"I'm guessing so. He and Joan make an odd match. A bootlegger and a teetotaler debutante." Adam's lips brushed her ear. "Almost as odd as a vampire lumberjack and a werewolf doctor."

A thrill of awareness and arousal raced through her. "Around here, odd matches are the rule rather than the exception. No one bats an eye, you know."

"Think they'd bat an eye if we slipped out of the festivities early?"

Even if they did, Cindy didn't give a damn, and she told him as much. "Let's get out of here."

The music was loud enough to spill out into the still, clear night. Adam held her hand and led her past couples who'd drifted out into the street to dance under the stars. Cindy threw a wave to Mac, who'd fully recovered from his injuries and was enjoying a dance with his wife.

Life is good. It was written in the smiles and laughter of the revelers outside, and it echoed in Cindy's heart.

Adam pulled her down the street, away from her house, so she dug in her heels and asked, "Where are we going?"

"Not telling." He grinned and tugged at her hand. "Walk, or do you want to go there over my shoulder?"

"These are my options?"

"Or we can stand in the street arguing about it until someone drags us back to the party."

"Good point." She affected a sigh and let him drag her along. "Be gentle with me."

Adam steered her toward the long path that led up to their new property. "You're smart. You can figure it out."

"The house?" Even though Adam had devoted every spare moment to construction, it was still far from done. "What are you plotting?"

"You'll see" was the only reply.

The woods opened up into a clearing near the top of the hill, where Adam had built their home. Under the silvered light from the moon, the cabin looked like a postcard come to life, an idyllic log cabin set alone in the forest. He guided her up the front steps and inside, then nodded to the hallway that led to the master bedroom in the back.

She held on to his hand, pulling him behind her as she walked down the hall. "Do I need to close my eyes or—oh. Oh God." She looked around the bedroom in awe. "It's finished."

"Just the bedroom...but everyone helped." He smiled, a little bit rueful. "Mostly so we'd have a place to stay now that your protégé has all but moved in to your old house."

"He'll make a good country doctor, once he settles in." She couldn't take her eyes from the wide bed that dominated the room, the walls, even the polished hardwood floor.

The walls had been painted dark blue and tan, colors echoed in the curtains and a coverlet that had to be Abby's handiwork. Framed photos hung around the room, candid shots of Adam and Cindy, proof that Gavin and Sam had helped too. The frames were recognizable as Gavin's solid, impeccable work, and only Sam could have captured the moments in the photographs.

"I don't know what to say." She gave immediate lie to the words by whispering, "I love you."

"I love you too, sweetheart." He wrapped his arms around her waist and pressed a kiss to the top of her head. "Joan was right. You're worth the wait. Worth everything."

"So are you." She'd tried to hide from him, to shut him out of her heart, but her struggle had been short-lived and futile. He'd dashed past every defense and taken her heart in his hands, and she realized now that it didn't matter. He would always protect her, always love her.

That brought a smile to her face as she pushed him toward the bed. "Is there anywhere you need to be anytime soon?"

"No." He tumbled onto the bed and brought her with him, leaving her sprawled against his chest. "I intend to be right here. With you. Pretty much forever."

It was a sentiment that was all too easy to return. Easy as breathing, the most satisfying thing she'd ever done. "Forever."

About the Author

How do you make a Moira Rogers? Take a former forensic science and nursing student obsessed with paranormal romance and add a computer programmer with a passion for gritty urban fantasy. To learn more about this romance-writing, crime-fighting duo, visit their webpage at www.moirarogers.com, or drop them an email at moira@moirarogers.com. (Disclaimer: crime-fighting abilities may appear only in the aforementioned fevered imaginations.)

She's ready to fight at his side.
He's fighting for the strength to let her go.

Sanctuary Lost
© 2009 Moira Rogers
Red Rock Pass, Book 2.

If there's one thing that Brynn Adler hates, it's feeling helpless and vulnerable in unfamiliar territory. Three weeks ago, life tossed her into just such a world. A world of werewolves she never knew existed—until she found out her sister was one of them.

The pack seems determined to hurry her back to the normal world of humans. But after everything she's witnessed, she's not sure she wants to go—especially if it means leaving not only her sister behind, but the one man who makes her forget her life is falling apart.

Now all she has to do is convince him to agree to a plan to force the pack to let her stay.

Joe Mitchell has been battling his protective instincts since he rescued Brynn from her kidnapper. Getting involved with her is a bad idea for a lot of reasons. She's on shaky emotional ground, and a supernatural war is no place for a human woman. He's not about to let her make a hasty decision, one that will only bring her pain and regret.

Now all he has to do is let her go.

Warning: This book contains violence, a war between werewolf packs, hot, primal sex and sexual power games with a badass ex-Special Forces alpha who will do anything to keep his lover safe.

Available now in ebook from Samhain Publishing.
Available in the print collection Sanctuary from Samhain Publishing.

GREAT CHEAP FUN

Discover eBooks!

THE FASTEST WAY TO GET THE HOTTEST NAMES

Get your favorite authors on your favorite reader, long before they're out in print! Ebooks from Samhain go wherever you go, and work with whatever you carry—Palm, PDF, Mobi, Kindle, nook, and more.

WWW.SAMHAINPUBLISHING.COM

CPSIA information can be obtained at www.ICGtesting.com
226269LV00003B/1/P